Bella... A French Life

Marilyn Z. Tomlins

Raven Crest Books

Copyright © 2013 Marilyn Z. Tomlins

ISBN-13: 978-0-9926700-3-0
ISBN-10: 0-99-267003-9

AUTHOR'S NOTE

Thank you Dave Lyons of Raven Crest Books for publishing this novel.

I also say thank you to: Louise McDermott (for always listening); Charmaine Olinsky Howard (for always encouraging); Deidre Vogtmannsberger (for that charming verdict regarding the ending which brings a smile to my face); Lynda Desgris (for telling me about the *trou normand* and how one eats oysters in Normandy).

I also offer a special thank you to Paula Rae Gibson who offered me the photograph of model Allison Willow for the cover of this novel

CHAPTER ONE

The holidaymakers have returned home. And yesterday the wind rose. The holidaymakers going home and the wind rising mean it is the end of summer.

I do not know what I will do to pass the time this winter.

God, I hate winter.

The family to the right set off first. She's a teacher; he is a doctor. I did not tell them that I too am a physician. At least, I used to be. I would have had to tell them something about myself. Of course, this I would not have wanted to do. They would have asked, "Gave it up?" Whatever I would have replied, would have led to another question. Even to several questions. That dreadful thing that had happened to the Brissard twin would have come back to me. Not that it has ever left me. No, it is with me like an ugly mole on one's back; you can cover it with a frilly blouse, but sure to God, one knows it is still there.

Du Pont is the family's surname.

"Easy to remember," he said.

I am bound to see them again next summer because they have bought the house next door.

"Paid two hundred thousand francs for it," she boasted.

My parents had bought this house of mine for fifteen thousand francs. The old man from whom they bought it wanted to go into an old-age home. That was in 1947. It is 1986 now.

1

I was four. Marius, my brother, still had to be born.

Oh dear! I have now revealed my age, and I planned not to mention anyone's age.

My name is Bella Wolff.

I should have had a name like Françoise du Pont. This is the name of the woman who stayed next door. Her husband's name is Martin. Martin du Pont. Nice uncomplicated names. Martin du Pont; Françoise du Pont. No one need to ask, "Where are you from?"

My father's name was Rodolph Wolff. He was German. A German soldier. A *Wehrmacht* soldier.

My mother's name was Henriette Desmarais. She was French. She fell in love with my father the moment she set eyes on him. He was one of the victors. She - one of the defeated.

Hardly ever did my mother speak of what had happened to her during those years of the Second World War. Of *l'occupation allemande*. What I know about it I heard from others, some of them having meant well, others having enlightened me in order to harm my mother. Harm my mother more.

As I heard, on the day the war ended, my mother's brothers fetched her from the café where she was a waitress and dragged her to the barbershop where one of their cousins worked. They wanted the cousin to shave their sister's head. That was what was done to French women who had slept with German soldiers. My uncles thought that by having their sister's head shaved themselves they would save her the humiliation of having angry villagers do so. When she had not a hair left on her head, they handed her over to the angry villagers, who marched her with the other women, who had had German lovers - the *horizontal collaborators* - through the streets. My father had by then left - fled France with the other German soldiers. I have often wondered what went through my mother's mind on that day, her lover gone and not there to protect her. To defend her.

2

My father was an honourable German soldier. This was what he always said to me and my brother. He said that he fought his country's enemy justly and decently; he had nothing to do with concentration camps.

He was also an honourable man. This is what I say, because after the Germans had signed the official capitulation with the Allies and the war was over, he returned to the village and went straight to my grandfather's house to ask for my mother's hand. "Yes, marry the whore and afterwards you can both get out of my sight," my grandfather told him. He marched my mother and father to the priest and the priest made them confess their sin of having indulged in sexual intercourse out of wedlock and to have produced a bastard child. I was two years old. The priest told them to go down on their knees to ask, to *beg* the Good Lord for His forgiveness. "To beg it will have to be because you have indeed sinned."

The following Saturday afternoon the priest married my mother and my father.

My grandfather forced my mother to wear a black dress and cover her head in a black mourning veil. He himself wore a black tie. My grandmother was also dressed in black and also wore a black mourning veil. My uncles insisted that I should be present at the wedding: I, the bastard, fruit of my parents' whoring. My Uncle Georges carried me to the church and put me down in the front pew and there I sat all alone; no one wanted to sit beside me. "She is contaminated," Uncle Georges told the priest. I carried German germs. The germs were in my blood, in my veins and arteries, in my intestines, and in my heart and soul. I was doomed.

After the wedding my parents and I left immediately for Germany. We were welcomed by my father's family. I cannot remember this, but my mother told me about it when the Brissard twin died. "If you think this is the end of the world, let me tell you that my people - your grandparents, uncles and aunts - spat at me on the day I married your father. That is what can be called *the end of the world.*"

We did not remain living in Germany. We came back to France. We did not go back to the village, but we came here to Normandy, here to Sainte-Marie-sur-Brecque, and to this house, Le Presbytère, which, as planned, my parents had turned into a guest house and of which I am the owner today.

Here, no one knew anything about us.

"Wolff," the locals said on hearing our surname. "You are Jewish and German and you survived Hitler. Bravo!"

My father did not reply and neither did my mother and when my brother was born, they baptized him in the old Catholic church, Notre Dame Sainte-Marie, which stands on the village square, and no one ever called us Jews again.

-0-

CHAPTER TWO

One of the Brissard twins name was Antony.

He would not breathe.

"Oh, one is enough," groaned Mrs Brissard.

She made a lot of noise during the birth of her two sons: André and Antony.

"Can't we shut her up, Doc?" Nurse Bonnec, twenty-two and only recently graduated from nursing college, whispered.

Mr Brissard, a farmer, was sitting unconcernedly in the corridor, smoking a *Gauloises* and blowing grey rings into the air. If I had not known that he was the one who put this woman in the family way, I would have thought that he had wandered into the hospital by mistake.

Antony was tiny. He was red from head to toe, and yes, all babies on birth are red from head to toe, but the redness would fade, but this had not happened as far as Antony was concerned.

"As long as his hair's not going to remain red," said Mr Brissard, in from the corridor.

He slapped his thick thighs with his fat hands.

I wondered how Mrs Brissard could have lain down with him; I know that if he had come anywhere near me, I would have run.

André, the first-born, took to his mother's teat like a puppy to that of a bitch. Antony closing his tiny little mouth and when we forced his mother's large, red, drooling nipple between his pale lips, he would not swallow.

"Do with him what we do with lambs," advised Mr Brissard.

"And Mr Brissard, what exactly do you do with lambs?" I asked.

"Doc, we let the little bugger starve, and mark my words, when he's hungry, he'll take the teat."

I struggled for two hours to feed Antony, first by holding him to his mother's breast and next by trying to get him to drink milk from a bottle, but to no avail. He died in my arms.

"Jesus Christ, get a priest! My child can't die a heathen!" shouted Mr Brissard, running around his wife's bed.

He was suddenly concerned.

"Get a priest!" I passed the demand on to Nurse Bonnec.

"How do I do that and whatever for?"

"Because my child can't die a heathen!" shouted Mr Brissard.

Saliva ran down his chin - his two chins.

"But he's dead already," replied Nurse Bonnec, her pretty face as grey as that of the dead twin.

"For God's sake, Bonnec, keep your voice down, and go get a priest," I whispered.

"Where? How?"

"Ask reception and if they do not know where to get one from, tell them, I tell them to go and find out."

Mrs Brissard, who had earlier been so adamant that one baby was enough, lay flat on her back, her legs up in the air and spread wide as if ready to receive her husband's sperm in order to make a replacement for the dead Antony.

"Mrs Brissard," I said, "let us cover you."

Nurse Bonnec, blonde curls falling over her grey face, returned.

"They do not know where to find a priest, and they ask whether we do not know that our country's law on secularity also applies to hospitals."

"But there's still a chapel at the hospital. I pass it every day on my way up from the parking bay. There must be a priest in there."

"The chapel is closed for renovation. Has been for two years."

"And I suppose the priests are sunning themselves on the Riviera," came from Mr Brissard.

"Don't worry, sir, I will find you a priest," I told him, complacently.

At the front desk I told the receptionist I needed a priest and I needed him fast.

A priest came. He was young, looked as if it had not yet been necessary for him to shave. I have no idea where the receptionist found him. He held a crucifix on a long string of wooden beads over the dead baby, said a prayer, made the sign of the cross and offered his condolences to Mr and Mrs Brissard, both of them crying.

"What I want to know, Father, is what kind of hospital is this? My wife gives birth to two healthy boys, and what do you know, one kicks the bucket," asked - stated - Mr Brissard.

"I am sure, *monsieur*, your son is with our Heavenly Father," replied the priest.

"*Merde*! Heavenly Father! My arse! He should be here and nowhere else! There is going to come a day when I'm going to need help on the farm ..."

"Now, *monsieur* ... I ..."

Anxiously the priest brushed sweat from his unlined forehead.

I felt sorry for him. I touched his nervously twitching arm.

"Thank you, Father. You may go now."

"This is most unfortunate," Mr Raisse, the hospital director, kept on saying to me.

He and I were in the morgue, standing beside each other at the autopsy table, an overpowering odour of disinfectant rising from it. The Brissard twin's tiny, lifeless, naked body lay on the table, ready to be cut open.

The autopsy surgeon pulled at his white surgical gloves and a powdery dust rose up in the air.

"If the parents insist. But why do this to the poor little blighter."

I closed my eyes. I had attended autopsies before, but none had been on a newborn.

The autopsy surgeon shot me a worried glance.

"No need for you to stay, Doc."

I ran up the stairs, ignoring the elevator, back to the third floor and the maternity section. Mr Brissard was showing André off to admiring relatives. Mrs Brissard, sitting with her legs hanging over the side of her bed, was drinking coffee from a goblet on which was the hospital's name: *CHU Hôpital des Chartreux*. She was swallowing noisily. André was no longer naked but in a yellow suit with white buttons. Blue lambs danced on the buttons. He was asleep and I wondered how he was managing to do so because his father kept pulling his tiny bent baby legs.

A week passed and Mrs Brissard and André had already returned to the farm, and Mr Raisse called me to his office.

The Brissards were accusing me of negligence.

"I tried to keep this unfortunate incident within the hospital walls."

He moved his thick-lens glasses down over his nose and stared at me with his short-sighted brown eyes.

The autopsy had shown that the baby died of asphyxiation.

"Asphyxiation?"

My head whirled: could I have been so stupid?

"Yes, there was a lump of phlegm in his windpipe. Of course, you could not have known. It was something which had happened during the process of birth. But the parents are going to go to the papers. Most unfortunate. Never has Chartreux Hospital had something like this happen."

"Mr Raisse, he died more than two hours after he was born, so it could not have been phlegm which killed him. There must have been a heart or lung anomaly."

I held onto his desk so that I would not topple over.

"All the same. Unfortunate. Unfortunate. What can I say?"

There were rumours that President Giscard d'Estaing was going to offer him the position of minister of health in Prime Minister Jacques Chirac's government.

"What would you like me to do, sir?"

"What would you like to do?"

"I am a doctor ..."

"And a very good one too."

"Are you blaming me for the child's death?"

My lips had started to twitch uncontrollably.

"The parents are upset. They want heads to fall. Mind you, they are not after money, so Chartreux Hospital would not have to pay them any compensation. But to use the word blame, well, blame's a strong word."

The Paris daily *France-Soir* ran the story on their front page the following morning and that evening at eight o'clock *Antenne 2* news led with the story. Anchor Léon Zitrone said that the parents wanted a police enquiry.

Two uniformed coppers, one a captain, came to the hospital.

The captain, a tall dark man in his forties, looked ill at ease with this task he had been given.

"I beg your pardon, Madame … Sir…"

Mr Raisse offered the captain his hand.

"Let's get this unpleasantness over with, Captain."

For eight months I waited for the police to complete their investigation. Mr Raisse, who had not been offered the job of Minister of Health after all, had become more and more agitated as the weeks passed, and on the day of the court hearing he, dressed in his best suit, ignored me, had not even shot a brief glance in my direction, not even once. My brother and Marion, his girlfriend, accompanied me to the courtroom in the *Palais de Justice* building. On our arrival there were half a dozen journalists on the avenue in front of the building. They shouted questions at me. Two press photographers snapped me when I left the court after the hearing. I was cleared of the charge of negligence, but as Mrs Brissard said, holding eight-month-old André to her generous bosom which was covered in black mourning, "His little brother is in our thoughts all the time. We can't stop thinking of him, of our little Antony. Oh well, he's with *le Bon Dieu* now at least, and should one not be thankful for small mercies?"

Mr Raisse had not wanted me to resign while the case was still pending, but once the verdict was given, he made it clear that I would be much happier working at another hospital.

"Not that I would request your resignation."

"If you really want to come and help me, who am I to turn you down," said my mother.

I had told her I was finished with doctoring and I was heading for the guest house to work with her.

"Bella, you are such a good doctor. You should not throw in the towel. Believe me, I understand how you feel, but give the matter time, think about it," advised Marius.

He too is a doctor.

I told him I have done my thinking.

I left Paris.

-0-

CHAPTER THREE

It is Thursday.

I enjoy breakfast in the kitchen these days and have done so since I have started closing the guest house for the winter and do not reopen it until Easter. Breakfast though is too sophisticated a word for what I have: a croissant and a bowl of black coffee. No butter. No jam. Several bowls of coffee. *I must cut down on the coffee, but what the hell.*

This morning, I am driving down to the village. I always go there on a Thursday - market day. The first time I did so, in 1976, the year of the Brissard twin's death and the trial, everyone looked at me. I cried driving back to Le Presbytère. The problem that morning, which is ten years ago, was Miss Bernadette Jambenoire, village spinster, school principal and grapevine, but also World War Two Resistance heroine and concentration camp internee, and, accordingly, untouchable.

Miss Jambenoire had always hated my parents: my father, because he was a German, and my mother for having betrayed her people by marrying him. She hated me too. To her I was venom from the loins of *un sale Boche*. A filthy German. She first called me this when I was just six years old. It was my first day at school and she walked into my classroom, her grey hair pulled into two buns which clung to the back of her ears like large warts, and when she and Miss Matigot, my teacher, stopped at my desk, that was what I heard her call me.

"What's *un sale Boche* and what are loins?" I asked my

11

mother.

"Watch your language, Bella, or I will rinse your mouth with soap?" she warned.

As my mother threatened me with a soap mouthwash only when I had said something really bad, like *merde*, I knew what Miss Jambenoire called me must be very bad. I therefore decided I had to know what it meant and I asked one of those uncles of mine who had dragged my mother to the barbershop to have her head shaved, and, smiling mockingly, he enlightened me, and the next day at school I stuck my tongue out at Miss Jambenoire. Behind her back though, so there was no reprisal, but … Jesus, did it make me feel good.

But that morning, ten years ago, at the market, it was Miss Jambenoire who had the upper hand.

I was buying quail eggs from a farmer's wife.

Miss Jambenoire walked up.

"I heard you were back."

No salutation.

"Good morning, Miss Jambenoire. Yes, I'm back. I'm going to help my mother with the guest house for a while."

I tried to smile.

She cracked the knuckles of her left hand against the palm of her right hand.

"*Ooh la la!* In that case you must watch it with those tiny eggs. We wouldn't want anyone choking to death at Le Presbytère, do we? And those eggs. So small. They can so easily get caught in the windpipe, *non?*"

She had lifted her voice and every eye focused on me.

I have tried since to ignore this woman, not always, I admit, successfully.

-0-

It is half past nine.

I wash the bowl and the cutlery and leaving it to dry on the drying rack, I throw a cardigan around my shoulders, and I head for the parking bay; Le Presbytère's kitchen opens onto an inner courtyard and the underground parking bay is at the other end of it.

A change I brought to the guest house on joining my mother was, that I, inspired by Frida Kahlo, had a tile maker from the nearby region of Morbihan, transform what was a bare, cemented courtyard into that of a Mexican *hacienda*. My mother, I must say, never took to the look of the new courtyard - to the clusters of exotic plants with their colourful flowers, to the mango tree which rapidly grew tall - obviously in search of light and hot air - but which has to this day not offered me its fruit, to the palm tree of which the branches droop in the rain, to the hanging baskets of dark-green ferns, to the red terracotta walls, the blue-tiled floor, and to the yellow-tiled sundial which is draped in a climbing rose, which just does not flower and of which the buds wither each time the palm's branches begin to droop, as if in commiseration.

The parking bay is large and looks even larger this morning, because, with no guests in residence, there are only three vehicles parked here. One is the guest house's yellow Volkswagen *Combi* in which Fred, my porter, gardener and overall handyman takes guests on excursions, most of these to Saint Michael's Mount, the mount being just a few kilometres away and this area of Normandy's main attraction. The second is my mother's grey Citroën *Deux Chevaux*, old and dented and rusting, which stands on blocks these days. I should sell the car, or give it away, but I don't have it in me to do so. I have already stuck 'for sale' notices in the display window of several of the village's shops, but I never go through with a sale because to do so will be like discarding with part of my mother. The third car is my new Mercedes. It is the appetising dark green of a Mediterranean olive.

It is just a ten-minute drive from Le Presbytère down to Sainte-Marie-sur-Brecque, and often have I jogged the distance, even walked it despite it is uphill on my return, but I will be buying a few things at the open-air market this morning, so I will take the car.

I run the wipers over the Merc's windscreen. Because of the mist that rises from the sea down below all the windows up here need a regular wipe.

While the wipers swirl, I turn the ignition key.

My father taught me to drive when I was still at 'uni'. I planned to open a practice somewhere around here and as a country GP I would have needed to be mobile. I remained living in Paris: I loved going to museums and one day I met a man and loved him too, and, all plans of leaving the capital, vanished. Jean-Louis was the man's name.

Will I ever get him out of my head?

I park on narrow, cobbled Rue Charlemagne which runs from Le Square, Sainte-Marie-sur-Brecque's only square. It is here that the farmers and second-hand dealers set up their stalls.

This morning, some of the stalls are already under winter canvassing. Thanks to Alphonse Pares, our energetic socialist mayor, strings of coloured lights twining between the stalls throw a rainbow over the carcasses, cauliflowers, camembert cheeses, clothes and bric-a-brac to be sold here today.

On the eastern side of the square stands our Notre Dame Sainte-Marie church, there where my parents baptised Marius. Tourists always say that the design of the church is most unusual. Built with the grey granite of our surrounding hills, it is circular like the crown of a bowler hat, a triangular wooden bell-tower perching on the top. A red-tiled porch shelters the church's double wooden doorway, there where our village priest, old Father Pierre, stands on Sundays after early morning mass holding a dented empty *petit pois* tin which he expects the worshippers to fill, but not with peas, but with shiny five-franc coins. The porch has been here for as long as I can remember, its sole purpose, as far as I can tell, to offer the

14

suppliant priest protection from wind and rain, and the occasional snow.

A tin sculpture of the Holy Virgin stands in the middle of the square. Everything about Jesus' mother is peculiarly long and thin: face, torso, limbs, fingers, feet. She was a gift from the children of a late Swedish sculptor who used to holiday in the village each summer, and, as Mayor Pares is forever telling us, one should not look a gift horse in the mouth.

Jesus' mother stands on a piece of granite which matches that of the church, and she looks east towards God's House. Although Father Pierre denies that this is so, we all think that he had a hand in which way she was to face, because her back is turned on the Vaybee; La Viérge-sur-Brecque bar and restaurant. Le Vaybee belongs to the portly Frascot, Fred's brother, best cook in the whole world of veal *à la normande*. Father Pierre though is not averse to a free *ballon de vin rouge* at the counter each noon before Mrs Celeste, his housekeeper, serves him lunch.

I start my visit to the market at the Vaybee with my third or fourth black coffee of the day: I purposely do not keep track of how many I drink.

"Quiet up at your place, Miss?" asks Frascot.

"I've already closed, Frascot."

"So Fred tells me. Mind you, Miss, it's gonna be a cold winter 'cause the trawler guys are a-bring'en in a lot of skate, squid and scallops and if that ain't a sign of one, I am a yokel and I've no business being in the resto business."

Every autumn, at the start of the skate, squid and scallop season, which is now, Frascot predicts a cold winter.

Stalls line the square.

As always, I walk over to the stall of farmer LeGros first. It is one of those already under canvas.

"Going to be a cold winter, Miss," greets Mrs LeGros.

She is wearing a hand-knitted jersey over the red,

cotton frock she has worn each summer for at least half a dozen years.

"I would like to buy some chicken this morning, Mrs LeGros."

She points to hens hanging by their long, thin necks to which tuffs of bloodied feathers cling.

"Must I do the necessary 'cause you still don't want the feet and the head, do you, Miss?"

"Certainly no feet or head, Mrs LeGros."

"You don't know what's nice."

She shifts her weight from one of her legs, covered up to her knee in flesh-coloured stockings, and poles the nearest hen. I watch her sling it down onto a bloodied wooden plank. As always happens during this ritual, I am reminded of the autopsy on the Brissard twin. I close my eyes, and hearing the thump that means that the hen's head and feet are lying on top of a heap of heads, feet, hairy tails and hairy paws, I open them again. At the end of the day, she will give these bloody and hairy bits to the beggars from the bigger towns, who each Thursday hitch lifts to the village on the farmers' trucks, with the sole purpose of receiving such alms.

As it is also the season for pheasant and hare I buy one of each and again I close my eyes while Mrs LeGros chops off the unwanted bits. It is also cauliflower, courgette squash and beet season, and I stop at the stall beside that of the LeGros - that of farmer Janvier - and I hand Mrs Janvier my wicker basket to fill.

"Frascot tells me you've already closed for winter, Miss."

"So I did."

"Any big plans for the winter?"

"Neither big nor small."

"*Ooh la la*, you should put something big in your life, if you ask me. You like it big, don't you, my darling?"

A large woman, she winks, and her diminutive husband, his waist narrower than one of her upper arms, shakes his head at his wife's brazenness in referring to my nun-like celibacy.

My shopping done, I am tempted to return to the Vaybee for another cup of coffee, but through its open door I see the tall, thin, grey figure of Miss Jambenoire at the bar. She has *Le Monde* open on the zinc-top in front of her. She's eighty years old, and each Thursday she's here in the market, to, as she says, stock up with genuine French food and not the foreign rubbish of supermarkets. She never talks to me, just as she had never addressed a word to my father; she did speak to my mother, but always about the weather, and always did she call her, *you poor thing*.

I walk around the square. The three and four-storey half-timbered buildings that line it are seemingly on fire, but as I know, it is the noon sun reflecting in the windows. Red, pink and white geraniums and begonias, in window boxes, are in their final flowering before winter's hiatus. Leaves of a bay tree growing in a white cube container on a balcony are turning yellow. A sure sign that winter is approaching.

I set off for home.

-0-

CHAPTER FOUR

The road from Sainte-Marie-sur-Brecque to Le Presbytère is a modest one.

Leaving Le Square and continuing down Rue Charlemagne, I drive past timbered cottages which have been transformed into bed-and-breakfasts by English expatriates. I pass the primary school where I was a pupil until I went to high school in the town of Nantes. I turn right into wide, tree-lined, tarred Route Avranches which was once the only road to the inland town of Avranches, and after about two hundred metres, there where the council has erected a board to indicate the way to the guest house, but only after my father had given them a bribe of a few thousand francs, I turn right again.

The road I am on now is narrow but tarred like Route Avranches and winds through cliffs, but after a while, it straightens out. Alongside the car is dark-green pasture land which is this morning, like almost every morning of the year, dotted with ewes, rams and lambs, most of these destined to become our local speciality - *agneaux pré-salé*. Roasted leg of salt marsh lamb. Our guests loved my mother's *agneaux pré-salé* which, in my child mind, was excellent only because I had helped her with the cooking when in reality my only contribution had been that I inserted cloves of garlic into incisions she had already made in the meat. Since her death six years ago, it is Gertrude who does all the cooking at Le Presbytère. Gertrude - Gertrude Duc - Fred and Frascot's cousin. Like Fred and Le Presbytère's housemaids, Honorine and Martine, she is off until my Easter re-opening.

Once through the pastureland, the road starts to climb and becomes somewhat potholed. I look back towards the coast, towards the Bay of Saint-Michel, down below. I open the window on my side by a chink, and a little wind caresses the back of my neck. Some evenings, after Gertrude had finished her shift, I'll drive her back to her home in the village, and whenever I open a window, she warns me about the dangers of a draught.

"Bad if you have your menses or if you're in the other way."

The other way: *pregnant*.

"Gertrude, I am not pregnant," I will say.

In my side mirror, a Brittany Ferries boat is sailing towards Saint-Malo. Its passengers will be gathering together heavy luggage and boisterous children, ready to start another sojourn at the expatriates' B&Bs. On days when the wind blows hard this way, we, here on land, hear the warnings over the ship's loudspeakers asking the passengers not to block the doorways. The tourists will be bringing whole nut chocolate bars, lemon cream biscuits and pots of *Marmite* to their ex-pat hosts. "Allow me to pay you for these," Mrs Ex-Pat will say, and the holidaymaker will reply: "Not on your nelly, love. Just enjoy the stuff. You must so miss England."

The holidaymakers will go to Saint Michael's Mount, pantingly climb up to the abbey, browse the souvenir shops for fridge magnets and embroidered tea doilies, eat a *Mère Poulard* omelette and a *crêpe*, complain about the fucking French overcharging as always, and complain even more when they pay a franc to spend a penny. But, back in England, they will show relatives and friends the photographs they took. "God, but France is beautiful," they will say.

Behind me, the sun, high in the sky, turns the golden

statue of Archangel Michael atop the spire of the mount's abbey into a ball of golden flames. I am reminded of how Joan of Arc had described him to her English judges in 1431.

Was he naked?

Do you think that Our Lord had nothing in which to clothe him?

Did he have hair?

And why would they have cut it …? But no, I do not know if he has hair. He had wings on his shoulders, but no crown on his head. I saw him with the eyes of my body, just as I see you… I saw him with my corporal eyes.

How do you know it was him?

He told me, "I am Michael, the protector of France".

Here, on the spire, he stands with those wings stretched to the sky. But not only his wings, so too his sword, perhaps yet again ready to protect France, perhaps from those English tourists on the ferry.

The bay's tide is not yet in and cars and coaches are driving along the causeway linking the mount to the mainland. When I first returned after the Brissard twin's death, the speed with which the tide rose at the equinoxes used to fascinate me; *à la vitesse d'un cheval du gallop* - at the speed of a galloping horse - according to Victor Hugo. There are always tourists who try to beat the tide to the mount.

Jean-Louis and I too once tried to do so.

It was in a month of June, and it was in the year before the Brissard twin's death. Jean-Louis and I had been lovers for just a month and he had not yet met my widowed mother and I suggested he should come with me to Le Presbytère for the weekend. We drove down in his metallic silver Porsche which he had bought just the month before. It was his first major purchase since he and Colette, his wife, split, and his colleagues at his legal firm teased him about it, about how girls love blokes with fast cars.

"*Et puis alors,*" he said when I too teased him about the

Porsche.

How many times have I not heard Jean-Louis say *et puis alors*? So what then?

On that June weekend, on that walk, he spoke of how he missed his two little girls who were living with their mother.

"They would have loved being here today."

"Have they seen the mount?"

"Col - their mother - and I brought them here once, yes, but they were small still ..."

"So, they would not remember anything of it," I interrupted.

"You can be very abrupt if you so wish, you know Bella," he said.

He was angry.

"What would you have wanted me to say, Jean-Louis? You miss your girls, and I feel bad about that."

"Mother, I did not break up his marriage," I had told my mother when I first told her about Jean-Louis.

"But, Bella, a man with a past. How unfortunate."

"We all have pasts, Mother."

I had hers in mind, hers and that of my father, and she realised what I meant because we never again spoke of 'pasts'. Not even when I also had a past; an ex-lover and a child in its grave because of me.

The walk took us just under two hours. We set off from the beach at the town of Genêts some six kilometres from the mount. Ahead of us Frascot's teenage boy, Didier, was acting as guide to a group of noisy middle-aged German *frauen* who wore flowery sleeveless tops and khaki shorts, their hairy arms and legs splattered with sludge. As I knew, they would tip him when they reached the mount and, as I also knew, he would not spend the money but give it to his father to bank for him for the day he would be going to Paris to study medicine at the Sorbonne.

On the mount, Jean-Louis and I, the two of us, like the German women, dressed in shorts and tops, and our laced sandals dangling from around our necks, went for a coffee at one of the cafés on cobbled, twisting, climbing Grande Rue, the mount's only street.

Again, he spoke of his girls.

"Carmen has done well at school, but Charissa has received a bad report. Col - their mother - and I are really worried about her."

Never could he say his wife's name. One of my colleagues at Chartreux Hospital even thought that his wife's name was Col. "What an odd name," she had said.

"Have you been to speak to the girl's teacher?" I asked Jean-Louis.

"We will do so in September when schools reopen after the summer holiday."

Not Col, but *we*.

But on that day he and she were no longer a *we*. He and I were the *we*.

"Bella, my dear child, what did you expect?" my mother asked when Jean-Louis and I were no longer a couple.

"I don't know what you mean, Mother."

"The way you get them is the way you lose them, Bella."

"Mother, I did not break up his marriage. Anyway, he is back with her, so no harm done," I replied.

After the coffee, Jean-Louis and I hitched a ride on a tourist coach back to Genêts where the Porsche was parked. He allowed me to drive back to Le Presbytère, and, on this road, and about where I am now, I stepped on the accelerator and he grabbed the dashboard as if fearing we were going to plunge off the road, yet, he did not tell me to slow down. His face was flushed with excitement.

At the end of the day we drove back to Paris and he was behind the wheel.

Dropping me off at my apartment in the Latin Quarter he did not get out of the car but leaned over me to open the door on my side for me.

"Bella, why does your mother think you broke up my marriage?" he asked.

"She also thinks you will drop me for another woman."

"*Et puis alors,*" he said.

-0-

CHAPTER FIVE

Getting back from the village, a moment ago, I parked the Mercedes between the *Deux Chevaux* and the *Combi*, and here I stand in the kitchen.

I ought to unpack my market purchases. The pheasant and the hare need to go into the freezer. The chicken I will roast today; it will be food for me for at least three meals.

Oh, I will do it in a moment!

I walk to the window to feel the soil of a Peace Lily in a terracotta pot placed on the sill. The plant, already potted, was a gift from Fred this past summer.

"Not too much water, Miss, but don't let the soil dry out either," he cautioned.

One of its white lilies has started to turn green at the edges as Fred said it would at the end of the current flowering cycle.

I touch the flower's spadix. Its yellow powder sticks to my fingers. I wonder whether the powder is poisonous; Fred did not say and usually he points out what is poisonous.

The plant's long, curly, pointed leaves are covered in a thin layer of dust. I spray them with tap water and they are shiny again.

I remain at the window; it looks out onto my Frida Kahlo courtyard. My mother asked me who Frida Kahlo was. My father would have known. In those first years after the war, he, dabbling with Communism, was an admirer of Frida's husband, Diego Rivera.

"First a Hitlerite, now a Stalinist. What will he become next? A Jehova Witness?" my uncles commented among themselves.

-0-

My parents kept the guest house open all year round. Even my mother, after my father's death twelve years ago, did so. When I joined her here and suggested that we close for the cold months, she fervidly refused.

"No, Bella, no. Guests must know that they are always welcome here."

The first time I did a winter closing was in 1980, six years ago and after the Paris specialists told me my mother's lung cancer was incurable. When she and I got back here from Paris where she had been hospitalised and I told her we would be closing for the winter, she did not protest; had not said a word. I presumed she understood that I, as a doctor, knew her death was not far in the future and I would want time to spend with her; time to care for her.

One evening, death very near, she kind of acknowledged that she understood.

She took my hand.

"Bella, dear child, couples do not have children so that they are there to care for them when they are old and ill, but thank you, thank you so much."

Her eyes glistened.

After she passed on, I made my decision to close each winter final. I sent a picture postcard showing the mount's abbey to all our regular guests to let them know Le Presbytère would be closed each year from the third week of September to the following Easter. Some had heard of my mother's illness and passing and replied with black-bordered sympathy cards on which were printed or scribbled sentimental words about her being in heaven. Gertrude, without checking with me whether it would be alright, arranged the cards on the ledge above the fireplace in the drawing room and when there was no space left there, on the sideboard in the dining room, exactly as my mother used to do with our Christmas cards. Deep into one sleepless night I, the cards' sentimental messages irritating me, chucked the cards into a plastic bin liner and dropped it into one of the guest house's large green dustbins and before Gertrude even realised the cards had been taken down, dustmen had already carted the bins off.

The first winter with Le Presbytère closed I did not feel alone here. Neither did I feel lonely. I had time to travel. I flew to America. I flew first class and on an open ticket so I could stay there for as long as I wished; the 'long' happened to be short because snow storms chased me back home. The following winter, I went to Paris, taking the train from the town of Nantes. In Paris, I caught up with friends. I took nostalgic strolls through the Latin Quarter where I had lived. I went to Chartreux Hospital to look around. The visit provoked such painful memories of the Brissard twin's death that I ran from the place. The following winter I took the ferry to England and I played tourist in London. I took a coach trip to Bath with what seemed a hundred Japanese tourists, and another coach trip to Dover to see whether the surrounding cliffs were really white. That winter I also took a ferry to the Channel Isles and I returned home with duty free perfume and the telephone numbers of people I had met but who I would never call.

I also had time to read during these past winters. On my trips to Paris I bought books at *FNAC* in Montparnasse and in the American bookshop *Brentano's* on Avenue de l'Opera, and back here I made an index card for each book and filed the cards in shoe boxes the girl from the village's *André* shoe shop kindly gave me. I transformed my mother's sewing room which used to be my father's workroom where he made decorative candles as a hobby, into a library room, and in perfect alphabetical order I arranged the books on shelves Fred made for me.

"You look like a bored woman," Marius's wife said, walking into the library room one day.

"I love books, Marion."

Marius married Marion soon after my trial and they are the parents of four beautiful children; two girls and two boys whose names I have a problem remembering. Or rather, I know the names but I get mixed up with whose is which.

Marius agreed with Marion.

"All these books, Bella, hell. One of these days there won't be any space left in this house for guests."

Ignoring the two's remarks, I kept on going to Paris to buy books, but one day, walking into my library room and tripping over a pile of them for which I had no shelf space, I wondered whether my book buying was not out of control. Was it not that I was taking refuge in books? I could crawl in between the words, yes; lose all sense of time and place and the terrible reality of the loneliness of my life.

When Le Presbytère is open I do not have much time to spend in the library room, but over the past few days, I have been sitting in there every evening, not really reading, just flipping through the books like someone searching for a certain phrase or quotation. Of course, I was only passing time. But I do love the room, love its dark look and the smell of its air which I recognise is the subtle scent of wood and of candle wax, the latter still present from the days of my father's candle making.

When the guest house is open, I keep the library room locked because I do not want 'strangers' to walk in there and probably leave with a book: guests do so like to explore every nook and corner of the house.

"How can I dust in there if the door's locked, Miss?" asks Honorine always.

"I'll dust, Honorine," I always tell her.

The only thing about the room is that it is silent.

28

But, so is the house when there are no guests here.

And do you know that silence makes the loudest noise?

It is only two weeks since Le Presbytère has been closed, but already the house's silence is barking in my ears like a pack of mad dogs.

-0-

There are times when Marion - she, the redhead with the large drop earrings and the mini skirts - looks at me with such pity in her mascara-lined, brown eyes. She must think that I, in my comfortable shoes, flesh-coloured tights, skirts of a modest length and unprovocative tightness, is a dried-out old hag.

"Do you know how beautiful you are, Bella Wolff?" asked Jean-Louis one day.

It was our first date.

"One of my neighbours thinks her bulldog is beautiful," I brushed the compliment into oblivion.

-0-

Jean-Louis and I met when he came to Chartreux Hospital to see the baby his sister had just given birth to.

He stood beside her bed, to me, at first glance, an ordinary man. His hair, brown; his eyes, brown. Of medium height like our compatriots, and slim like them too. It being spring, he wore a yellow T-shirt, jeans and white trainers.

"My bruv," said my patient.

"Hello," he said.

He was smiling and something happened to his eyes, they brightened like a child's when eating ice cream.

"Hello," I replied.

It was as if we were longtime pals.

"How did my sis do, Doctor?"

Bruv. Sis. A happy family. Unlike mine; my brother and

I never use pet names.

My shift ended. I was walking down the stairs and I saw him walking along the corridor and towards the staircase. He lifted a hand in greeting.

"Doctor Wolff - thank you. My sister said you were just great during the birth. She was nervous. First baby."

"Women usually are but they do all tend to settle into the process and when it's their fourth time, they're sipping tea during the birth."

"I'll tell you what."

He lightly touched my arm.

"What?"

"I do not know whether hospitals are like schools - where teachers and students are not allowed to ... uh ... mix ... but could I offer you a coffee?"

"At varsity we are taught not to get personal with patients, not to become involved in a patient's life."

"What a pity, because the coffee in the cafeteria is quite good. I thought it would be atrocious like that of other public places, like railway stations, but no, I was pleasantly surprised."

His hand was again on my arm.

"A coffee would be great, thank you," I said. "And you're not a patient, are you?"

The pretty waitress, her full, round breasts bursting out of her grey frock with her name on its breast pocket - Claire - filled two polystyrene goblets with black coffee.

"Grab us a table and I will bring these over," said my patient's brother.

Claire handed me two plastic spatula-like white spoons.

"Sugar's on the table, Doc."

At the table, my patient's brother took two paper-wrapped lumps of sugar from a metal container. He handed one lump to me.

"Not for me, thanks."

"In that case, I'll take your lump home. Will save on buying sugar."

He winked.

"Really?"

"I have a friend who actually does do that."

"Perhaps he is poor."

My patient's brother shook his head.

"He is a lawyer. I am a lawyer too."

"Do you plead for the life of serial killers?" I asked.

Again, he shook his head.

"I am a contract lawyer. I work exclusively for the big conglomerates."

"So you need not nick sugar lumps."

"Neither would you, being a doctor and all that. But tell me, why did you choose to become a paediatrician?"

Why? I thought it would be pleasant working with babies.

"I played mummies when I was little."

I had thought of that for an answer just at that moment.

"Only mummies? Or mummies and daddies?"

"No daddies, no. I was ahead of time. My mummies were all single."

"So, if you are a mummy, do I take it that there is no daddy?"

"I'm not a mummy."

"Neither am I."

I laughed at his witticisms and so did he.

"But I am a father," he said, no trace of a smile on his face anymore. "I have two daughters. I'm ... uh ... their mother and I have split. I live on my own."

"I live on my own too. I'm single. A spinster. That hideous word. *Spinster*. What do I spin?"

He nodded.

"I see what you mean."

He offered me another coffee but I declined it and I told him I ought to be going and I left and he remained sitting at the table and at the door I turned round and I saw he was standing at the bar talking to the busty Claire. I had not asked his name, and neither had he asked mine. My first name, that is.

The following afternoon, signing in for my shift, I saw that his sister and the baby were discharged that morning.

I put the guy out of my mind.

A week later he called 'Maternity' and left a message for me to call Jean-Louis.

That evening, I dialled the number.

"Now, I know your name, Jean-Louis," I said.

He asked me to have dinner with him.

-0-

CHAPTER SIX

It is Sunday. I could have slept in this morning, but I woke at six, and knowing I would not be able to fall asleep again, I got up.

These September mornings are cool and misty and as I was shivering in my cotton nightdress I put on my black 'house' jersey, the one I bought ages ago at the *Prisunic* shop which is next to *Le Drug Store Publicis* on Place Saint Germain-des-Prés in Paris. I am ashamed to admit I never wash this jersey because each time I wear it, I decide it is in such a dreadful state that I am going to chuck it out with the domestic waste, just as I chucked out the sympathy cards I received on my mother's passing.

I am standing at one of the two bay windows of Le Presbytère's drawing room. I am sipping my first coffee of the morning. I warm my cold hands against the bowl. I always fill a bowl to the top. This is where I always come to stand when I have guests but want a moment for myself.

The villagers say this house is haunted.

In the time when my father was still alive some guests spoke of an owl having hooted outside their bedroom window all through the night.

"What the hell do they expect?" my father always asked my mother.

"Exactly! They are out in the country here and there is nothing abnormal about an owl hooting. Or a toad croaking. Or a dog barking."

Those guests never returned.

According to my mother, long before the guests' complaints about abnormal activity in and around the house, I already behaved as if I were communicating with someone only I could see. She told me that I used to stand in my cot looking to the corner of my bedroom, my eyes wide open with fear, but also with interest, and on some nights I just could not fall asleep. She said I tried to climb from my cot and each time they tried to get me to stay in the cot, I pointed to the corner of the room as if I wanted to tell them I wanted to go there. Marius, as my mother told me, had no such problems with his room.

"It's the bloody nuns," said my father.

"It's the bloody Huns," retorted my uncles.

The 'Huns' was reference to my father's Nazi past.

The 'nuns' was reference to the house's past.

Once, as the name Le Presbytère implies, this house had a religious connection. It used to be a rest home for nuns.

Not always did my parents tell our guests about the nuns, and now neither do I, but here, in the wall above the bay window, is a small round recessed niche. It is empty. Not always was it so. If I pull over a chair and stand on it so my eyes are parallel to the niche, I will see a series of minuscule holes, holes as if dry rot is attacking the house, but as I know, the holes form a crucifix.

"There was a cross here in the niche. Gave me the creeps," said the old man before he had sold the house to my parents.

"What did he do with the cross?" I asked my mother.

"He burnt it."

Always, my mother, who said she believed in nothing, crossed herself.

-0-

I have drunk my coffee.

34

I would like to refill the bowl, but I am going to resist the temptation. Gertrude always says, quoting Father Pierre: remove the temptation and you remove the sin.

Behind the house the sun is rising. I can tell because the house is warming up, and in the distance, down below on the mount, a beam of sunlight is again reflecting off Archangel Michael's outstretched wings.

As I can see there are as yet no cars or tourist coaches on the causeway linking the coast to the mount. I know, soon the tourists will start driving up.

Maybe a car with someone looking for a place to stay will come driving up here, hoot when they drive through the gate - all do this and I still have to figure out why - and drive slowly up my gravelled driveway which is lined with tall trellises from which droop pale jasmine, clematis, honeysuckle and climbing roses. As I always do, I will apologise for their unnecessary drive up the hill, and I will invite them in and offer them something to drink, a coffee if they are Americans, a cup of tea should they be English. And when they drive off, I will wonder whether I am doing right, closing for winter.

"Le Presbytère is yours, do with it as you wish," Marius had said.

My mother had just died and she, someone who believed in fair play, and, considering it fair and correct to do so, had left the house to both Marius and I, but he, saying he did not want to become a charlady, told me he would register the guest house in my name and if I so wished I could get rid of it - sell it, go on a cruise with the money and see the world, or I could live in warm and sunny California or Florida for a while. I did not wish to sell the house; having no desire to continue doctoring, what else was there for me to do but be a charlady.

On joining my mother and looking over the accounts, I was surprised at how well the guest house was doing.

She dismissed my compliments. It was, she said, the beauty of the house which was drawing guests.

One can see the house from afar, even from the sea beyond the mount, as I know from when I took the ferries to the Channel Isles.

The house is half-timbered, two-and-a-half storeys high, a ten-metre high Leyland Cyprus hedge, Fred's pride and joy and which I suspect he may love more than Paula his wife and the five children she brought into the world for him, encircling the property and separating it from the Du Ponts' house on one side, and on the other, the somewhat worse for wear cottage of a Dutch couple named Amster, who, when they are in residence in the summer, shoot whatever is in flight over our rooftops - robin red breasts, larks, wagtails, finches and even pigeons - with a slingshot, despite that I beg them not to.

Apart from the holes in the niche, there is more evidence here of the house's religious past. I am thinking of the rose window in one of the house's four dormer windows. The rose window depicts a golden-haired, red-robed Christ as a shepherd, a praying angel, in white, floating on each side of his head, and the Magdala in a white and light-green robe, and also in prayer, kneeling at his feet, white lambs and black calves grazing around the two of them.

This last summer an American guest asked me whether I have ever had the rose window valued.

"No."

"No?"

"No."

"Wow, lady! It must be worth a dollar or two!"

"Miss, before he leaves tomorrow, make sure the rose window is still here," had warned Martine.

Jean-Louis loved the rose window too.

"Is that a guest room?" he asked.

It was on that first visit of his to Le Presbytère when he and I walked across the bay with the German *frauen*.

"It's a single room, Jean-Louis."

"Can we sleep there?"

"It has a single bed."

"You won't hear me complaining."

Neither did I complain.

But I must not think of him yet again.

-0-

The grandfather clock in the drawing room begins to chime.

I listen to Handel's *I know that my redeemer liveth.*

The clock came with us from Germany. My father was always the one who did the winding. After his death, it had become my mother's task, and now, after her death, mine.

My father had a good singing voice and some days he sang quietly to the chime.

He lives to silence all my fears ... He lives to wipe away my tears ... He lives to calm my troubled heart ... He lives all blessings to impart ...

When I was a child he taught me the words. Not yet have I found solace in them.

When guests are here, I silence the clock so they are not disturbed, but alone now, I silence it only at night so it does not wake me from the little sleep my insomnia allows me.

The chiming stops and four short strikes follow. It means it is a quarter past something; past eight, or perhaps only still a quarter past seven.

Or maybe, it is already a quarter past nine and there is less left of this day than I thought.

-0-

CHAPTER SEVEN

Someone, I cannot recall who, said, pray that your loneliness may spur you into finding something to live for, great enough to die for.

It is the second week of October now and Le Presbytère has been closed for a month.

Last weekend Marius, Marion and the four children came to visit.

"Bella, are you not lonely in this big old house?" asked Marion.

"Come down to Paris," suggested Marius.

I lied.

"I'm going to have the house painted, so I must be here."

"You had it painted last year," Marion chipped in.

"Two years ago."

"So for God's sake, why do you have to have it painted again?" asked Marius.

"Because ... you know ..."

"Oh rubbish, Bella!"

When he and I were children we used to play a game my parents called *because- because*: because it is for me to know and for you to find out.

-0-

Happy, fulfilled Marion, yes, I am lonely, dear sister-in-law, but I will not admit it. I will not admit it to anyone, not even to myself.

39

When I go to the market on Thursdays just so I will be able to have a chat — a chat with Frascot and Mrs LeGros and Mrs Janvier - I tell myself I have to go to the market because I need to buy food, although I well know my freezer is full and so too my fridge. When I walk from room to room here at Le Presbytère, or rather, when my mind is chasing me from room to room because if I stand or sit down, the walls move in on me, I tell myself I am checking there are no intruders here.

But, no, no, no, damn it no.

I will not admit that I am lonely.

Alone, yes. Sure.

But only when Le Presbytère is closed, because this is a large house, and in the middle of the night, it seems even larger.

"Henriette's *Boche* must have been helping himself to the fleeing Yids' money," said those uncles of mine.

My parents had just then returned to France and had bought the property.

What my parents did not tell my uncles was that they bought the house with a loan my Grandfather Desmarais helped them procure from the bank. My grandfather, probably regretting he had been so hard on them when they wanted to get married, threatened the bank manager that, unless he gave the couple the fifteen thousand francs they needed for the house, he would reveal that nasty little secret of his, which he was hiding from the entire world. The nasty little secret was that in 1944 Mr Director had denounced his own wife to the Gestapo for hiding a Special Air Service paratrooper on her father's farm.

My mother told me what her father had said to the bank manager.

"If you want everyone to know that the poor Marguerite was gassed in Auschwitz because you squealed on her, so your strumpet, Rose the Whore, the best cock sucker this side of the Atlantic, could become your wife, you refuse my daughter and son-in-law the loan."

Guests describe the house as beautiful. The vast garden is beautiful; the *Louis XV* furniture in the drawing room is beautiful; the marble floors are beautiful; the stone staircase is beautiful; the wrought-iron balustrade is beautiful; the heavy chintz curtains in the bedrooms are beautiful; the dove-grey tiles in the bathrooms are beautiful.

Beautiful. Beautiful. Beautiful.

After I had transformed the courtyard, I still wanted to put more of my own stamp on the house, but I waited until my mother's passing to decide to replace the house's *Louis XV* furniture; I had always found the furniture sombre. So I discussed with Georges, Sainte-Marie-sur-Brecque's auctioneer, that I may ask him to sell the furniture for me, and I made a trip to Paris and looked at modern furniture in *Bazar Hotel de Ville* department store. I returned with the store's catalogue but without having made any purchases. "Miss Bella, what horrible furniture!" exclaimed Fred when he paged through the catalogue. Therefore, I kept the *Louis XV*, yet at night when the old settees and *chaises longues* creak as if ghosts are holding a tea party in the drawing room, I regret I did not buy the *Bazar Hotel de Ville* furniture. Or, for that matter that, when I had come to live here, I had not brought some of the furniture from my Paris apartment with me. Like the black and white bedroom suite with the king size bed with the white damask headboard and the side storage drawers.

Jean-Louis liked the bedroom suite. He did not though see it on our first date.

When I called him back as he requested in the message he left for me at Chartreux Hospital, he invited me for dinner.

"Doc, if you say you will be washing your hair, I will understand."

"I will not be washing my hair. And please not *doc* or I might just bring my forceps along."

He waited for me on the terrace of a bistro on the Latin Quarter's Place Saint Michel. Having agreed that we would dine informally, he was without a jacket, and I wore a floral summer dress although a cool breeze had risen. He saw me walk up and got to his feet.

"What was your day like?" he asked.

"No emergencies. And yours?"

"One emergency."

"Was it solved?"

"Solved."

He grinned with obvious satisfaction.

A few minutes later, we walked along the narrow, pedestrian Rue Saint Séverin, Greek restaurants lining the street. An overhead loudspeaker bombarded our eardrums with Mikis Theodarikis's *Syrtaki* and the Greek expatriates standing outside their restaurants tried to persuade us with Zorba-like leaps and bounds to step inside. We passed a girl in a long white cotton frock, her yellow hair flowing to her waist, her feet in slip-on sandals and her toenails varnished turquoise. Over and above *Syrtaki*, she was succeeding in singing Joan Baez' *Ballad of Sacco and Vanzetti* to her own guitar accompaniment.

Here's to you Nicola and Bart ... Rest forever here in our hearts ... The last and final moment is yours ... That agony is your triumph! ...

A waiter in a navy and white striped sailor's T-shirt and Maurice Chevalier boater stepped from one of the restaurants and clapped his encouragement. It was to the *Syrtaki* though.

We chose a restaurant which Jean-Louis had been to before although the maitre d' and his staff manifested no recognition.

"May I be racist?" whispered Jean-Louis.

"Be racist."

"We French all look alike to Greeks."

A platter of lobsters on crushed ice which I saw in the restaurant's window on coming in, looked inviting, but Jean-Louis suggested we have the *plat du jour*.

"I hate the waiting in restaurants, Bella."

"The *plat du jour* will be great."

Plastic ivy and geraniums hung from a beamed ceiling which was too shiny to be of natural wood, and dusty bottles of *Retsina* stood at one end of the bar. The maitre d' pulled a table away from a wall and motioned we were to sit there. A Boxwood Ball plant, as real as the ivy and geraniums, stood on each side of the table.

"Privacy," said the maitre d'. He winked.

The *plat du jour* was spinach and feta pie.

"What was the emergency, may I know?" I asked.

"My wife - ex-wife - no wife, as we are not divorced - not yet anyway - suffers from chronic colitis so she wants me to have the girls for a week so she can go to a health farm."

"Colitis? I thought colitis went out of fashion when the *Belle Époque* ended. One doesn't even hear of it anymore."

"Well, Doctor Wolff," he said, "now, you have heard of a case."

"I thought the emergency was at work. Had I known it was something so personal, I would not have asked," I apologised.

"My marriage was work. Hard work."

'Joan Baez' appeared at the door and asked the maitre d' if she could come inside. He said yes. She went to stand at the bar, one sandaled foot on the foot railing and her guitar resting on her raised knee. She began to tune the guitar, turning the tuner clockwise and listening to the sound of the string under her right middle finger, she turned the tuner anti-clockwise, and nodding satisfaction, she tapped a rhythm out on the body of the guitar with the flat of her left hand.

Jean-Louis refilled our glasses from a carafe filled with *Retsina*.

'Joan Baez' began to sing.

In restless dreams I walked alone Narrow streets of cobblestone ... 'Neath the halo of a street lamp I turned my collar to the cold and damp ...When my eyes were stabbed by the flash of a neon light ...That split the night ... And touched the sound of silence ...

The sounds of silence: Simon and Garfunkel.

Jean-Louis and I listened in a silence of our own.

Her song sung, 'Joan Baez' called out whether there was anyone who would buy her a *Coca* – a Coca Cola. Jean-Louis signalled to the maitre d' that he could serve the girl the soft drink. She drank up, flicked her head as a thank you, and left, her guitar banging against her flat bottom.

"Simon and Garfunkel. I like them," said Jean-Louis.

"I like Joan Baez."

"I knew a girl like that long ago. Not like Joan Baez of course, but this young singer here. It was in my student days. She was a busker in the Métro."

"Not all that long ago surely."

"Sufficiently long enough so that I can no longer recall her touch on my body."

He leaned over towards me.

"Was she pretty?" I asked.

"Not particularly. Not like you."

"Pretty? Me?"

I hoped I was not going to blush.

"I thought all pretty girls knew they were pretty."

I was blushing. I could feel heat sweep over my face.

"Do you know how beautiful you are, Bella Wolff?"

Again, he touched my arm the way he had done at Chartreux Hospital.

"One of my neighbours thinks her bulldog is beautiful," I told him.

Our waiter brought us the bill and two wrapped peppermint sweets.

"Allow me to pay half of this," I suggested.

"No question of it, but I can see you are going to be stubbornly independent."

He pulled his gold credit card from his wallet.

Back on the street he asked whether I would like something else to drink.

"I will be totally dependent and allow you to decide," I replied, demurely.

"Ok. Close your eyes and take my hand."

His wedding band on the ring finger of his left hand was cold against my skin.

"I can't see a thing, Jean-Louis," I told him.

He moved my hand to his arm.

"People are looking at us with such pity. The beautiful young woman and her guide dog."

I giggled.

"Now, you are confusing them."

He led me, stumbling beside him on my sling-backs, to a small, dark bar on the river bank beside Notre Dame Cathedral. A black musician in a white silk suit and red tie had just finished at an upright piano and was acknowledging the patrons' applause.

"That's Harry. He's from New Orleans."

"I can see you retraced an old route tonight."

Jean-Louis pondered for a moment.

"But ... I've found you at long last."

My apartment was close to where we were.

"I'm walking home, but how will you get home, Jean-Louis?" I asked.

"Métro."

"I'll walk with you to the station."

Some hippies, the young men in fraying multi-coloured Bermuda shorts and dreadlocks, and the young girls, their unwashed hair in side ponytails, their lips purple and their skirts flowing to their bare feet, were chanting *Hare Krishna Hare Krishna Krishna Krishna Hare Hare Hare Rama Hare Rama Rama Rama Hare Hare* outside Saint-Michel Métro Station.

"I'm sorry," said Jean-Louis.

We were standing at the steps leading down to the station.

"For what?" I asked.

"For not being able to say I have never done this before."

I folded my hands in mock prayer and began to chant

to the hippies' *Hare Krishna.*

Bless me, Holy Father, for I, Jean-Louis, Paris lawyer, have sinned, have sinned … sinned.

Jean-Louis planted a kiss of goodbye on my cheek, and I on his.

"*Ciao!*" he said.

"*Ciao!*" I said.

I walked back to my apartment.

-0-

CHAPTER EIGHT

The blustery autumn wind is turning the sea choppy and dark this morning.

I am standing in the drawing room again, at the bay window beneath the empty niche. I am already on my third bowl of black coffee.

A silver-grey motorcycle is on the road down below and it turns onto Le Presbytère's driveway. Marius has a motorcycle. I wonder if it could be him paying me a surprise visit. But no, the motorcycle has a sidecar which Marius's does not have; when Marion goes riding with him, which is not that often because she says the crash helmet which the law obliges her to wear, flattens her hundred and fifty-franc blow waves, she is a pillion passenger. The sidecar is loaded high and whatever is being transported up here to the house, is covered in a sheet of canvas; one end of the canvas is flapping in the wind. I fear the wind might rip it off altogether in which case it could become entangled in the motorcycle's wheels.

Samy, the lad who looks after my wood-fired boiler which supplies the house not only with hot water but also central heating, is due this morning at eleven for his annual one-hundred-franc overhaul. It could be him on the motorcycle, but, he has a small white van, so why would he be on a motorcycle?

I go into the kitchen; I reheat the kettle for yet another bowl of coffee.

The soil under Fred's Peace Lily is damp. Fred - dear

Fred - will also be coming to Le Presbytère any day now to clean up in the garden. He will sweep up the fallen leaves and make a bonfire and he will ask whether I would like him to grill me a piece of meat seeing the fire's burning so nicely. He will cover some of our delicate plants with sheets of plastic for the winter and bring the most delicate indoors until the warmer weather returns. And he will tell me how exhausted he is, and because I did not accept his offer of a grilled piece of meat, he will ask whether I am cooking anything nice for dinner.

"The usual fare of pizza or quiche, Fred."

"No problem with that, Miss."

He will stay for dinner.

Perhaps it is Fred on the motorcycle; maybe he has bought himself one. We all have dreams, do we not? His is to win the national *loto* one Saturday evening when he will buy himself a Harley Davidson. Until now the nearest he has got to a Harley Davidson was three correct numbers out of the *lotos'* five, and riding pillion down to Sainte-Marie-sur-Brecque on Marius's bike.

Le Presbytère's front door bell rings. Fred has a key and would not have to ring. Samy does not have a key and he will have to ring.

"The door is locked," says the stranger at the door.

The man is dressed in black and beige leather; trousers tucked into high boots, shirt and waistcoat under a windbreaker. Black leather gloves. Marius dresses like this too when he is on his bike.

"I saw you on the road riding this way, sir. Are you lost?"

The biker is also wearing a black crash helmet and he takes it off and puts it down on the crazy paving of the porch at the front door. His hair is greying; once it was black. The helmet rolls over with a clank. He picks it up and pushes it under his left arm. I see he is also wearing a thin leather tie. Marion who shops on Paris' chic and expensive Faubourg-Saint-Honoré will describe him as

48

nattily dressed.

"Did I come to the wrong place? I'm looking for Le Presbytère. My apologies if I am disturbing you."

I nod.

"This is Le Presbytère, yes, and please do not apologise. I am the one who has to apologise because I must appear very unwelcoming making you stand here."

He smiles.

He has a dimple in his chin. "How do you shave in there?" Audrey Hepburn had asked Cary Grant in *Charade*. Just a few nights ago one of our French television networks reran the 1960s-something film.

"Having established that this is Le Presbytère, may I come in?"

"I'm closed."

His motorcycle with the sidecar is parked under a copse of trees. In the summer I set tables and chairs out there and the students I employ as seasonal restaurant staff serve my guests snacks and drinks. Some nights the students get their friends to come and make music and the guests dance.

"Closed, for the moment, or, closed for good?" asks the biker.

"For the winter. I will reopen at Easter."

"They did not tell me down in the village - what's its name?"

"Sainte-Marie-sur-Brecque."

"Sainte-Marie-sur-Brecque, yes. I spent the night in Avranches and I would not want to have to ride all the way back there right away."

A gust of wind scatters leaves from the garden onto the tiled porch and somewhere in the house a door slams.

"You better come in," I say.

"Are you sure?"

He looks at his dusty boots and at the spotless marble floor behind me. When I took over the guest house on my mother's passing, I had the floorboards pulled up and replaced with marble flooring. I had this done for Honorine and Martine because they made such a palaver each Monday morning which was the day the wooden floor was always polished.

I nod.

"Don't worry about the floor."

"You're kind."

"Would you like a coffee or a cup of tea perhaps?"

"If it's not too much trouble, a cup of tea would be great."

"So come through to the kitchen."

I watch him looking around, his lips stretched to an inquisitive smile.

Coming in from the front garden one is in a small windowless room. What my parents never told guests, and which I also never tell them, is this small windowless room used to be the nuns' confessional. As the old man who sold the house to my parents told them, it was here, in this room, where, once a week, the nuns confessed their mortal sins to the priest who rode Jesus-style on the back of an ass, all the way from the village to the house. The only item of furniture in the room - the only item there is space for - is a French *secrétaire* desk on which lies the register guests are obliged by law to fill in and sign, and which tall, slim and dapper Captain Contepomi of the *gendarmerie* comes to check each Friday. Like all such desks mine too has a secret drawer concealed under its concertina lid. My father kept his will in the secret drawer, and so too did my mother, and, as I discovered on her death when I went to retrieve her will, she hid other papers - newspaper clippings - in the secret drawer too. She had, despite her apparent lack of interest in what the papers were reporting about the Brissard twin's death and my trial, bought the Paris tabloid, *Le Parisien libéré,* every day to read about it.

In the kitchen, the biker pays no attention to the pretty yellow tiles of the walls, the gleaming, spotlessly-clean steel of the stove and the oven, and to the large oak work table around which a dozen people can sit. It is the window which grabs his attention. Or rather, the courtyard behind it - my Frida Kahlo courtyard.

I point to one of the chairs around the work table.

"Do sit down."

"My name is Colin Lerwick."

Do I introduce myself too? Or is it enough that he should know this is the guest house, Le Presbytère?

"This is my guest house," I say.

"Are you Mrs Wolff? They told me down in the village - what's its name? - that the guest house belongs to Mrs Wolff."

"It's Sainte-Marie-sur-Brecque. The village. And I am Bella Wolff. And yes I am the owner of the guest house. Of the property. And there is no Mr. Wolff here because my father passed away a few years ago. My parents were the owners here before me."

"You will make an excellent journalist, Miss Wolff."

"How come?"

"You supplied enough information in one breath for an intro."

"Intro?"

"The start of an article."

"Are you a journalist?"

"Yes."

The kettle whistles.

"Thank you, Miss Wolff," he says pointing at the kettle, "a cuppa is just what I need."

Jean-Louis said *thank you Miss Wolff* to me once.

-0-

CHAPTER NINE

Forgetting is not easy. It takes a long time and it is a painful process. There is of course the possibility that one is not able to forget, that the pain goes on and on.

After our Greek dinner Jean-Louis gave no sign of life for a week. Then, to my surprise, he called to my apartment after work.

"I've been in Geneva. A client. Have you ever been there?"

"No."

I was truthful.

"It's a beautiful city. Small for a city, but to me that is its charm."

"It sounds as if the Swiss tourist office is one of your clients."

He laughed. It was a laugh which I could not interpret. I wondered what would Sigmund Freud's analyses have been? Would he have called the laugh a snicker or a chuckle or a cackle? Would he have said the laugh had been spontaneous, or that it manifested superiority because the one who laughed had been to Geneva and the listener not? Or would Freud have said that Jean-Louis had laughed to hide or disguise his embarrassment for a silence of a week and for having offered me a frivolous excuse.

I gave up on Freud.

"Jean-Louis, why did you phone?"

"I am calling to invite you for dinner. This time I will let you choose the restaurant. I am thinking of tomorrow evening."

"I am not a habitué of any Paris restaurant."

"In that case," he said, "will you allow me to choose the restaurant?"

"Yes."

"And I take this as a 'yes' we can have dinner tomorrow evening?"

"Yes."

He left a message on my answerphone that he has chosen a restaurant in Montmartre. He said he would meet me there at seven thirty unless I wanted him to pick me up at my apartment in which case I had to call him to give him the address. I did not call.

La Butte Montmartre on a warm night!

-0-

We were to meet on Place du Tertre.

I doubted the wisdom of meeting on the square because of its popularity with tourists, and I was right, there was something like a crowd mulling around.

I spotted Jean-Louis in conversation with two couples of the well-to-do tourist kind; the women had designer bags slung over their bony shoulders, and between the men's fat index and middle fingers hung burning cigars.

Seeing Jean-Louis I felt a flush of excitement rising from my chest: I'd forgotten how good-looking he was. He wore jeans, white shirt and a navy blazer and pointed black shoes. Marion would have described him as 'smart casual'. To me he was simply gorgeous.

He put both his hands on my shoulders and kissed me in greeting on both my cheeks.

"You look great, Bella."

I wore beige slacks, a black blouse and a black velvet poncho which I'd bought when at a medical conference in Milan, and yes, I had tried to look good - good for him.

The tourist menus of the restaurants that lined the

square offered things like an *assiette de charcuteries* or a *petit pâté chaud de lapin* which they suggested should be followed by a main course of *suprême de poulet* or a *rôti de veau forestière*. Starters, main course and dessert cost the meagre sum of twelve francs.

A waiter with a black bow tie which needed straightening directed Jean-Louis and me to one of Chez Eugène's red-checkered tables set out in a marquee on the square.

"I am not a habitué - I want you to know," said Jean-Louis.

Shards of coloured light from overhead decorations illuminated the façades of the three- or four-storey buildings which bordered the square. A bearded artist in a navy-blue artist's blouse came to our table and offered to do a sketch of me for fifty francs. I said no and he approached another table where, having received the solicited agreement, he sat down on a folding stool which had been slung over his shoulder. He opened an easel which had been flung over his other shoulder. His model sat in solemn pose while he produced with nimble strokes a perfect duplication of her heavy-jawed, double-chinned, middle-aged face with a stick of charcoal on a white sheet of paper.

A woman in a long white dress, her hair under a black turban, walked up to our table. She slapped a deck of tarot cards down in front of me and asked me to draw a card so she could tell me what the future held for me. She wore a death-head silver ring; the eyes were red stones.

It was strange but before the woman walked up to us, sitting there opposite Jean-Louis at Chez Eugène, I wondered what the future held for him and me, indeed whether we had one - as a couple.

When I was at the high school in Nantes I had dabbled with mysticism. My mother nearly fainted when I started to speak of guardian angels, spirit guides and the *beyond*. I was doing that because there was this girl in my class whose mother was a medium and one weekend when I stayed over at their house her mother had held a séance. My classmate, her mother, I and some neighbours of theirs sat at a table holding hands and suddenly a man's voice came from what sounded like underneath the table. The man spoke in a drowsy, heavily-accented voice. He said he was Bella's grandfather. He said his name was Johann Wolff. He wanted me to listen to what he had to tell me. It was that Adolf Hitler was a good man. My grandfather had been a Brown Shirt during - no - before World War Two had broken out even, but as it was something which was never mentioned at home, there was no way my classmate's mother could have known that or anything else about my grandfather. I had told my mother what my Grandfather Wolff had told me and she had very nearly fainted again. "Bella, all I need in my life is for you to go believe in such crap!" she shouted. I do not know whether she had told my father what his deceased father was seemingly up to.

My classmate's name was Flora and she was as dainty as her name implied and she telephones me occasionally to offer me guidance because she claims to possess the power to speak to the deceased as her mother had done. I, however, no longer believe in such things. Not after I had kept my eyes closed for hours on end trying to get my guardian angel to speak to me, to tell me which questions I would be asked in my *baccalaureat* school-leaving examination, and to give me the answers into the bargain so I would not have to do any revision, but no one had replied.

I smiled at the tarot reader.

"No thank you."

"Pity," she said, "because my spirit guide tells me you will very soon be very happy."

"I hope you do not believe in nonsense like this, Bella," said Jean-Louis.

He motioned to the woman to leave me alone, and she,

her black turban having slipped over her eyes and temporarily blinded, stumbled as she walked away.

I felt sorry for her.

-0-

"Why are you single, Bella?"

We'd finished our first course of avocado and were cutting our way around the leg of the duck of our main course - a *confit de canard* - and at a nearby table, the tarot reader, having pushed the turban away from her face, was telling the future of the lady who had had her portrait painted earlier.

"Of course you reply only if you want to," said Jean-Louis.

I put my knife and fork down.

"I've never loved a man enough to marry him."

"How much must you love a man for that?"

"I must believe that without him the sun will never shine again."

I had replied without hesitation.

He swivelled the wine in his glass.

"Could you love a man like that?"

He'd been looking down at his wine glass, but he looked up and straight into my eyes.

Quickly, I looked down, swivelled the wine in my glass and suddenly the wine looked as red as freshly spilled blood. The thought of spilled blood, so much part of my life, made me shiver slightly.

"I do not know if I could, Jean-Louis."

"Come on, look at me," he urged.

He took the glass from me and put it down on the table.

I looked up.

"Jean-Louis, I do know my mother loved my father like that. He was a *Wehrmacht* soldier. She had become a horizontal collaborator for her love of him."

57

He put his glass down beside mine. The wine in it also looked as red as freshly spilled blood.

Again, I shivered.

He sighed.

"Bella, love is not ideal," he said. "It is a road covered in potholes."

What to say?

A woman in platform heels and lacquered *chignon,* her eyebrows thin black arches, walked over and stopping at our table she began to belt out Edith Piaf's *Non, Je ne regrette rien* to the accompaniment of an accordion played by a man in baggy grey flannels, black hair greased back and greying sideburns.

Non, rien de rien ... Non, je ne regrette rien ... Ni le bien qu'on m'a fait ... Ni le mal; tout ça m'est bien égal ... Non, rien de rien ... Non, je ne regrette rien ... Car ma vie, car mes joies ... Aujourd'hui, ça commence avec toi ...

She had the pronounced guttural *r* of Provence just as Piaf used to have.

"Beautiful," said Jean-Louis. "I adore the late Piaf."

The waiter with the crooked bow tie rushed up and appeared to enjoy the performance as well but after the woman's final *aujourd'hui, ça commence avec toi*, which had drowned all conversation at the tables, he whispered something to her and she and the accordionist walked away, her platforms noisy on the cobblestones.

"Too much disturbance here tonight. I apologise," said the waiter to no one in particular.

"We enjoyed that," Jean-Louis told him.

"Sorry ...," said the waiter, "but the boss does not want the guests to be disturbed."

Some new arrivals sat down at the table next to ours and a red-faced man took a packet of still sealed *Gitanes* from his pocket. He ripped open the blue packet and lit up, and turning to face our table, he blew white rings of smoke into our faces.

"Now, this *is* disturbance," I said.

Jean-Louis asked the waiter for the bill.

"And no halving, Bella."

It was close to midnight and Place du Tertre's artists had already packed up their easels and had wandered off, and the tourists had also begun to leave and the waiters were clearing the tables and chatting and laughing at whatever they were talking about.

Jean-Louis pointed in the direction of Sacré-Coeur Basilica. Only the spire of its tallest bulbous white dome could be seen over the rooftops.

"Let's walk that way, Bella."

Overhead clouds had gathered and at the foot of the Montmartre hill Paris was shrouded in a dark veil like a woman, her religion obliging her to cover herself from the world.

The funicular from the hill down to the cobbled streets of the *Butte* had already stopped running for the night and Jean-Louis and I descended by the steps to red-light Pigalle where the *p'tites femmes* were still plying their trade, their mascara-lined eyes red with too many *pastis* or perhaps only with exhaustion after having had to satisfy too many men for one night.

"I'll go home now," I told Jean-Louis.

"So will I."

I still did not know where he lived.

"Where is your apartment?"

"Eiffel Tower. Bordering the Seine."

It was a long Métro ride from Pigalle and a noisy drunk made conversation impossible. We reached Concorde station where both of us were to change to different lines but Jean-Louis said he will escort me to Saint-Michel station, there where I had bid him goodnight a week earlier. At the station we both descended.

"Shall we do this again?" Jean-Louis asked.

We were standing on the same spot where we had stood the week before.

"That would be nice," I replied.

"If this were a Claude Lelouch film this is where we kiss, Bella."

Above our heads the moon had crept from behind a white cloud.

"But life is not a Claude Lelouch film, Jean-Louis."

"I know, dear Bella, I know," he murmured.

Like the week before, he planted a kiss of goodbye on each of my cheeks, and I, on his, and he ran down the steps back into the station, but he halted and turned around.

"Thank you, Miss Wolff."

He waved.

And I waved too.

I quickly turned and set off for my apartment.

-0-

CHAPTER TEN

"What is it with the French and black coffee?" asks Colin Lerwick.

"I don't know but I do know I should be cutting down."

"Did your doctor tell you that, because, I believe, one should not take too much notice of what doctors say?"

"I am a doctor."

"Oh Lord," he says, "I will have to apologise for having said that."

"I am not now working as a doctor."

We are sitting facing one another at the work table in my kitchen. He's drunk a first cup of tea and has accepted a second. I put a plate of *sablé* biscuits dotted with tiny morsels of chocolate on the table and he has already eaten several and has just helped himself to another.

He has a fine forehead; my mother would have said that such a forehead portrayed intelligence. He is looking at me as if waiting for the right moment to make a statement or ask for a favour; his eyes are brown like those of Jean-Louis, and like his, they are most extraordinarily penetrating.

"This is a most beautiful house," he says.

"Thank you. It is my home and not an investment."

"Do you need a large staff here?"

"At the height of summer, yes."

"They did not tell me down in the village - what's its name? - that you were closed."

He has told me this already.

"They should have."

"I am looking for a place to stay for a couple of months. Perhaps longer. I have to finish a book. I write. I am a writer."

"You said you were a journalist."

His cheeks are clean shaven and shiny as if he had shaved just a moment earlier.

"Writer. I write. Articles. Books. I am writing a book about Boris Pasternak. The Russian poet."

"I know who Pasternak was."

"I'm sorry. I did not mean to imply that you did not."

"That's ok."

"My agent and publisher are waiting for the manuscript. I need total peace and quiet. I can't write with people around me."

"So a guest house would not be suitable."

"A guest house which is closed, yes, that would be."

"I sing when I put the machine over the floors in the morning."

"Will you allow me to stay, Miss Wolff? I will pay the bill in advance, of course."

"And you will not be a nuisance. You will make your own bed, clean your room, bathroom and toilet yourself, and - cross your heart and hope you die."

He smiles.

"You will not even know I am here, Miss Wolff."

"My supper is the same every night, Mr Lerwick."

"I can boil an egg. And I learnt how to make a bed when I did my military service in the R.A.F."

"We French have a soft spot for the Royal Air Force because of how its young men came to help us during the war, but I'm sorry, I still have to insist that I can't allow you to stay. I do really close each winter and if I have to make an exception to that rule this winter, next winter more people will arrive wanting to stay."

The door bell rings again. It will be Samy. I did not

hear his van drive up.

"Excuse me. I'll be right back."

"Let myself in, Miss. Hope you do not mind," says Samy.

He is already halfway across the drawing room.

Always impatient, always in a hurry, he says he will go straight down to the boiler room and come and see me afterwards. The pungent odour of a blocked drain clings to him; it always does which might explain why, at twenty, despite that he is good-looking with his curly black hair and blue eyes he does not yet have a girlfriend.

"I will be in the kitchen, Samy," I tell him.

I find Colin Lerwick in the courtyard.

"I hope you do not mind. I stepped out to admire this splendid corner."

"It is lovely, is it not?"

"Reminds me of Spain. I lived in Madrid for a couple of years. Was based there for the news agency I was with."

"I was inspired by Frida Kahlo."

"Frida Kahlo! Strange. Before I decided on the Pasternak book I was toiling with the idea to write about her. The Trotsky connection - you know. Or to write about Trotsky for that matter."

"I think you made the right decision to have settled on Pasternak."

"I was in Peredelkino this past summer - research - and I went to Pasternak's grave. I will show you the photos I took of the grave - but of course I will not be staying ..."

"I would like to go to Peredelkino one day."

"You should go by train from Moscow. Pasternak had always taken the train there. I have photos of his *dacha* too."

How pleasant to be talking to someone with the same interests.

"How far are you with your book?" I ask.

"I ought to be able to write 'the end' by the end of the year. Well … if this is to happen, I ought to be on my way or ..."

Overhead the sky has darkened to the colour of chocolate ice cream.

"Look up," I interrupt him, "look how dark the sky's become. It is going to rain."

Now what made me tell him that?

He groans.

"I do not relish the thought of being on my bike in the rain."

Should I let him stay?

-0-

"Miss, your friend ... one will say he is an English lord," says Samy.

We are standing beside Samy's van. I left Colin Lerwick sitting in the kitchen with another cup of tea.

"Thank your boss for me, Samy."

He is in the blue cotton overalls and blue cap of a French worker.

"The boss will bill you, Miss, and I will come to check that all's working well just before Christmas."

He lifts his working man's blue cap in greeting. Curls fall over his forehead.

He gets into his van and holds the door open with his foot.

"That's a man you can trust, Miss, if you will allow me to say so."

He is flipping his head towards the house behind us.

Trust. I wondered whether I could trust Jean-Louis. Trust him, that should I love him, he would not throw that love back into my face.

-0-

CHAPTER ELEVEN

Jean-Louis left another message for me on my answerphone.

He said he had a meeting scheduled in Geneva and he wondered whether I would not like to join him there. *Seeing it would give you an opportunity to visit Geneva.* He would have to leave Paris the following morning - Wednesday - but he would be free from the Thursday evening. We would have the weekend in Switzerland. *Let me know. Call.* He left his office number and I called and his secretary gave me the name of the Geneva hotel where he would be staying as well as the hotel's phone number.

"He's had to leave today already, but I could call him for you and pass on a message if you wish, Dr Wolff," said the secretary.

"Tell Jean-Louis I will see him in Geneva. I will make my own accommodation arrangement. I will arrive on Friday around noon," I told her.

I was not a child; I knew what would be happening in Geneva. And I wanted it to happen.

I arrived on the noon high-speed train. I had booked a room in one of the hotels overlooking Cornavin railway station. Jean-Louis was staying in a five-star on the lake front.

I stood for a long time at the window of my room. Long blue trams pulled up at shelters on the square between the grey-stone station building and my modern glass-fronted hotel. People poured from the trams, some,

65

wearily pulling suitcases, disappeared into the station building; others shot across the tram lines, and rushed off, away from the station. The Swiss flag – white cross in a red square - which I had seen till then only on photographs, fluttered from the roof of the station and from the roofs of the other hotels on the square. I took a small bottle of mineral water from the mini bar and drank it down in one gulp. In the bathroom I cleaned my teeth and next I went to ask the *concierge* which way the lake was.

Lac Léman was still like a spatter of blue paint on an artist's frock. *Genfersee*. My father often spoke of the lake and he always called it Genfersee; before the war he studied the humanities at the city's university. "Humanities. My arse! Fucking *Boche!*" one of my uncles, misunderstanding what was meant by 'humanities', once said and loud enough for all of our guests to hear.

Still in the black trouser suit and flat-heeled black shoes in which I had travelled, I walked along the lake for about half an hour, admired the magnificent glass-fronted hotels, one of them where Jean-Louis was staying, and I admired the blue-rinses of the old Swiss ladies walking their small fluffy dogs along the promenade, and I returned to the hotel and called Jean-Louis.

"What's your hotel like?" he asked.

"Without doubt, not like yours."

"Is it bad?"

There was concern in his voice.

"It's very nice, Jean-Louis. I have a huge window and I can see all of Switzerland from it."

"I've hired a car. I will come pick you up. We will go for tea in Montreux."

I again cleaned my teeth and I combed my hair and I waited on the pavement.

He drove up and descended from the car - a hired metallic-silver Porsche.

"Glad I am to see you. Thank you for coming," he said.

We shook hands like two people who did not know each other well.

"Hello, Jean-Louis," I said. "How are you?"

He gave a little laugh.

"Better, now you are here, thank you."

He pulled me towards him and his lips rested on my forehead, and it was for more than a fleeting moment. I felt like throwing my arms around him and holding him, but I did not even lift my arms.

"Are you moving on, sir?" asked the hotel's doorman, dressed theatrically, in a navy blue uniform with red tassels dangling from the tunic's padded shoulders.

"We're moving on, yes," replied Jean-Louis, not a trace of a smile on his face.

We took a narrow side road away from the station and after a few minutes we were on a highway. The Porsche was comfortable; the seats deep and soft, and the engine silent. Jean-Louis said a Porsche was his favourite car.

"Do you need the air con?" he asked.

"I'm ok."

He was again in jeans and white shirt, but he wore a white blazer, and black leather shoes. He must have felt my eyes on him because he turned towards me and his lips smiled. I could not see his eyes because they were hidden behind square-framed, brown tortoiseshell sunglasses. I looked at his hands on the steering wheel. I have always had something about a man's hands. *The hand has twenty-seven bones of which fourteen are the phalanges of the fingers.* I am quoting from an anatomy text book from my first year at 'uni'. Jean-Louis' hands were smooth: there were no bulging veins or scars on the top and his nails were cut round and short and shone like those of a baby. They were not a working man's hands, the hands of a man who toils the soil or lays bricks, no, they were the hands of a surgeon; yes, possibly the hands of a surgeon. I fought the urge to lay one of my own on one of them.

On our right was the lake. Pleasure boats, moored in

small marinas, bobbed on the clear water, and a red motorboat pulled a water skier, a young girl - a child still - in a wet suit and crash helmet, behind it. On our left were sloping green pastures where cows, their udders hanging full and low, grazed between rolling green Alpine hills.

Jean-Louis was silent, so I tried to make conversation.

"Looks pleasant."

We passed a small chalet with a red-tiled roof and red geraniums in yellow window boxes. A woman was hanging wet white sheets on a line in the back garden. Two small blond boys kicked a football out in the front garden.

"Could you live here?" asked Jean-Louis.

"In this chalet?"

"No. Here. Just here."

"Yes, why not? I could keep a cow and make cheese. Each week I'll take my cheese to the open-air market. So, yes, I could live here. Happily."

We drove past a small timber-framed chapel. A bell clanged harshly over the tender hum of the Porsche's engine.

"Are you religious, Bella?"

"Meaning?"

"Do you believe in God? A God?"

"I believe in ... something ... some power ... some force ..."

"Same here. I have a cousin who is a priest. He is praying for my lost soul."

We reached Clarens, a village of luxury villas, all with colourful gardens, and within a few minutes, if a sign beside the road was to be believed, we were in the town of Montreux.

We pulled up in front of what could only have been the town's smartest and most expensive hotel with floors of windows behind wrought-iron balconies which were covered in more red geraniums shaded by reddish-pink tarpaulins.

"We will have tea here," said Jean-Louis.

A doorman in a red uniform with silver braids told us to leave the car, he would get the car jockey to park it in the car park. A maitre d' in a well-pressed dark-blue suit escorted us to a table for two on a terrace which overlooked the lake. About a dozen tables were laid for lunch: the table cloths were white, the napkins pink. There was a small glass vase with flowers on each table. The flowers were plastic: once they must have been red but they had faded to orange. The stems and leaves had darkened to brown.

The maitre d' called over a waiter who was laying tables and taking much care in the task of measuring the distance between a white porcelain plate on a table and the sterling silver cutlery to each side of it. The waiter was dressed in black trousers and long-sleeved white shirt and thin black tie. I noticed his tie clip matched his cufflinks: the hotel's logo of a small boat with mast and sails on what looked like gold but was probably not. He handed each of us a menu as large as a broadsheet.

I looked at Jean-Louis.

"Are you an habitué?"

"Never been here in my life."

"So, I can't allow you to decide what we should order."

He smacked his lips like a schoolboy on a day's outing with his class.

"All looks delicious, but shall we say: tea for two and the cake trolley?"

"I am supposed to be on a diet."

"From where I'm sitting you do not need it. You look ... divine."

The cakes were French and Swiss: small pastry gondolas filled with cranberries, chocolate *mousse* in small cups made of dark chocolate, meringues filled with frangipane, tiny croissants and vermicelli boats.

I poured the tea. Jean-Louis watched me closely. He said not a word. I picked up one of the meringues and he chose one of the vermicelli boats.

"Why don't you say something?" I asked.

"Why would you not accept my offer of a room in my hotel?"

"Because."

"Oh, come on, Bella. You would have had a room of your own."

He sounded angry.

"I'm comfortable where I am," I told him.

"Oh, I don't know! Hell, you are stubborn!"

He noisily threw his spoon down on the table.

A gull landed on the table beside ours and the waiter rushed over and slapped a white teacloth against the table to chase the bird. It flapped its long white wings as if to fly away but stayed where it was.

"*Woosh!Woosh!*" hissed the waiter.

The gull turned and fixed one tiny beady eye on Jean-Louis and me and, flapping its wings, flew off.

The waiter returned to his previous spot at the entrance to the terrace, the white teacloth folded and hanging over his left arm.

Jean-Louis stroked my hair.

"Bella ... let me tell you ... let me tell you ... I find you ... extremely exciting."

"Jean-Louis, I find you extremely exciting too," I confessed.

The hand which had stroked my hair was resting on my shoulder. His touch was light.

"For now, Bella, that will do for me."

We were no longer the only patrons on the terrace, but we might have been. We only had eyes for one another.

After tea we drove away from the town into the snow-topped peaks of the Alps behind the town. The clock on the dashboard showed it was close to five o'clock. It was getting cool in the car and shadows had started to fall over the lake behind us.

"I can drive like this forever," said Jean-Louis.

The road had narrowed and the Porsche's automatic

gearbox noiselessly switched to a higher gear. We passed a blue and white road sign. It showed we were driving towards a place named Rochers-de-Naye, which, as I read, was 2045 metres above sea level. I looked at Jean-Louis, asking with my eyes whether that was where we were heading, but he ignored my glance and stepped on the accelerator. Montreux grew tinier behind us and the lake grew larger until it was as huge as an ocean.

Lights had started to go on in Montreux and when we reached Rochers-de-Naye it turned out to be just one two-storey grey stone building. We reached it at the same time as a cogwheel train with no passengers, but which quickly began to fill as waiting backpackers scrambled on for the journey back down the mountain to Montreux.

Jean-Louis parked the car with others in front of the grey building where several people with tanned faces and necks were sitting on a terrace drinking frothy beer from patterned tankards. He asked whether I was thirsty and I said I was not and he suggested we should go for a walk.

"Before night comes."

He took me by the hand and we walked along a path which led us around the grey building and up a bare hillock of the same grey stone as the hotel and most of the buildings I had seen in Geneva. We walked in silence, his body close to mine and his breath warm and soft in my neck. Behind us the cogwheel train's engine clanked into motion and the train started its descent.

"Do you know something, Bella, right now I do not care a damn if we have been abandoned here on this barren hill," said Jean-Louis.

We stopped walking.

"What do you want me to say to that, Jean-Louis?" I asked.

"That you also do not care."

He did not give me time to reply; he put his arms around me and drew me to him, quite roughly, urgently. And yes, I also did not care if we, he and I, had been abandoned on that barren hill, because I felt an intense desire to remain there, there in his arms. Forever.

The two-storey grey building was a hotel. I was embarrassed we were booking in without luggage.

"For the night?" asked the receptionist, a confident young woman with a look of having-seen-it-before on her face.

Oh Jesus, the technicalities of sex. Had I blushed? I think I had.

We listened to the receptionist's directions to our room and the time breakfast would be served the following morning. She chose a key from a board behind her and held it up as if she was showing us a trophy. She had a smile from one ear-ringed ear to another. Jean-Louis lifted his right foot from the floor as if he wanted to burst into a sprint. To escape the amused young woman or to get to the room she has chosen for us? I tried to make myself as small as possible behind him.

"Second floor," said she.

"Thank you, Miss," said Jean-Louis.

"Leave the key with reception, should you go out, Sir."

"Thank you, Miss," he repeated.

He was smiling.

We started climbing the wooden twisting stairs: there was no lift.

Halfway up, Jean-Louis felt for my hand. He had begun to take two steps at a time. I could not keep up with his pace. He let go of my hand. I slipped. He looked back. He was no longer smiling. I, on the contrary, had started to giggle, giggle like a teenage virgin. I was of course neither a teenager nor a virgin. My giggling grew louder. Reaching the corridor, I tried not to giggle anymore. I did not want to alert those behind the closed doors which we were passing of our imminent activity. At our room, Jean-Louis, like an inexperienced and nervous teenager, fumbled with the key, struggling to fit it into the lock. Amused, I watched.

He succeeded in fitting the key into the lock and he pushed open the door. He stepped inside. I followed. The room was small, its double bed almost filling it. A bland smell of detergent filled our nostrils. I closed the door and locked it. A 'In Case of a Fire' notice hung behind the door. Also a 'Do Not Disturb' notice.

We had come to a halt a few paces towards the bed. I looked at Jean-Louis. He let his white blazer slip from his shoulders, grabbing it before it hit the bare floorboards which were creaking under our weight, to fling it onto an upright chair beside a small table on which stood a platter with an electric kettle and what would be needed for making coffee or tea.

I felt a little faint, faint with the excitement rising in me.

He turned to me.

"Bella ...?"

He took my head in his hands and rested his lips against my eyelids, gently, but quickly he dropped his head so that his mouth was parallel to mine and next he pressed his warm and wet lips against mine, pushing hard against my mouth as if he was about to eat me. He was hurting me. I groan of pain escaped me. He released his grip and so suddenly and violently did he do so I almost lost my balance, but quickly he pushed me onto the bed behind us.

"I need the bathroom," he said. "Just a moment."

He halted at the window, opened it and reached for the green shutter behind it, which he closed, removing from sight the bare grey hillock where we had a few minutes earlier walked.

"That's better," he said.

The room, thus darkened, its ambience was less harsh, more intimate. Even the bland smell of detergent seemed to have gone, or we had become accustomed to it.

I sat on the bed, motionless.

The man about to become my lover disappeared into the bathroom. A couple of minutes later he reappeared. He was naked, his right hand covering his slightly erect manhood. To keep it under control?

Oh no!

From the corridor came footsteps.

I took a sharp breath and held it. Was someone going to knock on the door to offer us a pre-dinner drink?

Jean-Louis too looked towards the door.

The only other light in the room came from underneath it. A shadow passed in the light. There was no knock. The footsteps ambled along the corridor.

Exhaling audibly, Jean-Louis walked over to me and pulled me to my feet by my hands.

"Let me undress you," he murmured.

He rolled my jacket off my shoulders and chucked it on top of his but it slipped to the floor. We did not pick it up. He rolled my trousers down over my buttocks, his hands lightly touching my skin. I wiggled for the trousers to fall to my ankles and stepped from them. His hands hot and trembling slightly, he turned me around and unhooked my bra.

I, too, had begun to tremble slightly.

"Let me help you, Bella."

He meant with my panty.

He slipped his hands over my hips and with a hurried movement he rolled my panty down over my legs. Suddenly embarrassed at my nakedness, I raised my arms to my breasts and covered them.

I was feeling breathless.

Jean-Louis knelt on the floor and took hold of my panty to slip it over my naked feet. He looked up at the dark half-moon of pubic hair which hid the only part of me left to be discovered.

"I like that," he whispered.

He pushed the fingers of one hand through the hair and, spreading his fingers, he moved his hand over my stomach to my belly button. At the same time he brought his head down to my stomach, pressed his lips against my skin, and eased me backwards onto the bed.

He lowered his body onto mine and slivers of light passing through the shutters made him look like some strange creature from outer space, or from the depth of the ocean, about to devour me.

I waited.

Using his legs and his right hand he forced my legs, still hanging over the edge of the bed, apart. With his left hand, pushed under my body, he lifted me, lining me up for the carnal embrace which was to follow. I could feel him inside me and I was surprised by the urgency with which he pumped my body. With his right hand he pulled at my hair, wet with perspiration, and clinging to my face.

Suddenly, he stopped moving.

"A moment please," he said.

I could feel him slipping from me and next his sperm spurted onto my stomach. His eyes were closed, the veins on his forehead pumped full of blood.

He rolled off me, his features relaxed, his eyes shiny with content.

"Your turn now," he said.

He began to stroke my legs, his fingers slowly moving to between my thighs. When my features too were relaxed, he playfully bit the tip of my nose.

Holding one another, Jean-Louis and I slept for a while, and on waking, he started to stroke my breasts. First tenderly, next, urgently, and we made love again, not just once but again and again and with less urgency than the first time. Each time he withdrew and spilled his life-giving seed over my thighs.

Neither needed any tricks to arouse or satisfy the other.

He was completely lost in this lady and this lady in him.

"Bella, sweetie, it is going on for nine," he said finally.

Nine in the morning; not nine at night. Breakfast was served until ten. We gathered up our clothes and tried to straighten out the creases. We were hungry.

After breakfast we drove back to Geneva and Jean-Louis dropped me at my hotel.

"Don't come in," I told him. "I need to brush up."

"If you are sure."

The rest of that weekend was bliss. Jean-Louis and I went for walks along the lake; we went on one of the lake steamers for a cruise. We dined in a quaint basement room of a restaurant in the old town where a man in green knickerbockers was yodelling as if his life depended on it, and on the Saturday night Jean-Louis came up to my room and he phoned down to Room Service for a bottle of *Krug* and I saw the bill the waiter handed him and I nearly fainted.

"This will feed a family of four for a week," I protested.

"Listen to me, Bella, I am a poor man's son and I paid for my studies myself working nights as a dishwasher in a restaurant, so you saying that does not make me feel ashamed," he replied.

Our lovemaking was a wonderful replay of that of the previous afternoon and night.

-0-

Back in Paris, I telephoned my mother.

"I am with someone, Mom."

"I hope he is nice, Bella."

Nice. From the Latin *nescius,* which originally meant ignorant, silly, foolish, incapable. Today's meaning: kind, agreeable, pleasant, and delightful.

All that and more. Jean-Louis was all that and more.

I was in love.

-0-

CHAPTER TWELVE

Colin Lerwick is still in the courtyard. He is sitting on one of the benches I have out here. He has put his leather windbreaker back on; it has clouded over and a cool wind has started up.

He gets up when he sees me.

"I'll be on my way."

"No! First let us see what the clouds are planning for you."

I sit down beside him. A blue canopy from which hang yellow tassels shelters us. I saw such a bench on one of Frida Kahlo's paintings and I searched throughout the region for one and finally found it in the *Bazar Hotel de Ville* catalogue.

"It rains often here in Normandy, does it not?"asks Colin Lerwick.

"Not more than anywhere else. It's a myth, really, that it always rains in Normandy and Brittany."

"What brought you here, if I may be so bold as to ask?"

"Someone had to run the guest house after my mother's death. My brother did not want to do so. He is a doctor."

"You too are a doctor, you said."

"Not a practising one. Not anymore."

"I see."

He wants an explanation. I can see it in his eyes.

"Would you like a drink? Something stronger than tea

perhaps?" I ask him quickly.

"I would love it. Thank you."

"Do you have a preference? I have just about anything and everything in the bar."

"I hate *pastis*, so if you can discard that one I will give you a free hand, though I ask you not to let it be a heavy hand. I have to get my bike down the hill and perhaps all the way to Avranches."

I return with two long-stemmed *coupes*.

"*Kir Royale*," I explain.

"I know *Kir*, but what is a *Kir Royale*?"

"One uses champagne instead of white wine."

"My, my, Dr. Wolff, what extravagance!"

"Please, not the doctor bit, I ask you."

"What - who - shall we drink to?" he asks.

"To Normandy where it hardly ever rains."

"This really is out of this world!" he says.

He had downed just one mouthful of the drink.

"I made it with *Bollinger*. It's best this way."

"I would have to ride up here tomorrow for another."

I laugh.

"I drink it - *Kir Royale* - when I'm happy and when I'm sad. Sometimes I drink it when I'm alone. When I have company I consider it obligatory. I trifle with it if I'm not hungry and I drink it when I am. Otherwise I never touch it, unless I'm thirsty."

"You do?"

I laugh yet again.

"Sir, I stole that from Mrs Bollinger. She of course said it of her champagne."

"I was wondering …"

Now, he is laughing too.

It starts to rain; tiny drops so light that the wind flings them in all directions. Above our heads the tassels begin to swing, next, to slap against the canopy. Soon, they are heavy with rainwater and drooping like tulips in a May downpour.

"Shall we run for it?" I ask, my face wet and my feet getting so because the rain has started to come down really hard and puddles have formed on the tiled surface of the courtyard.

"No, let us hold out …"

There is a clap of thunder from the direction of the bay which cannot be seen when one is in the courtyard. There is another, and, as if on cue from someone who is very angry up in heaven, the clouds above us begin to roll. Without a word, Colin Lerwick and I jump up and start running for cover. We almost collide dashing through the kitchen door, and he grabs me at the elbow to stop me from falling down.

We are both laughing. Laughing like two people who have known each other for years. Two friends who have known each other for years.

-0-

When Le Presbytère is closed, I treat myself by sleeping in the biggest of my seven guest bedrooms. The room is on the first floor and directly above the drawing room and it has two bay windows. Always, the last thing that Honorine and Martine do before they clock off until the following Easter is to help me move my things from my usual quarters - the small bedroom beside the 'Rose Window' room - and always, the first thing I do on this autumnal migration of mine is to air the en-suite bathroom to rid it of the smell of lavender from the *Bien Être* eau de cologne, its habitual August occupant, Mrs Mathews from Hull, buys duty-free on the ferry which brings her across the Channel.

"Why do you use this bedroom in particular, Miss, when you can use any of the others?" Honorine once wanted to know.

I do so because this was the bedroom which my mother always allowed Jean-Louis and me to have on our

79

weekends at Le Presbytère.

-0-

I am standing at one of the bay windows and I watch the wind and lashing rain bend the branches of the trees growing in my front garden. I love a storm, and this is a storm, and if I were alone here now I would be out there, standing with my feet pressed into the mud and my face lifted to the angry heaven to receive its caress. My father also loved storms. Once he said to me: "Bella, *kleine liebling*, for the man, sound in body and serene of mind, there is no such thing as bad weather; every day has its beauty, and storms, which whip the blood, do but make it pulse more vigorously." He quoted George Gissing as I learnt only later when he was already gone.

Despite that I love storms, could Colin Lerwick ride back to the village or to Avranches in such a raging gale, or would I have to let him stay here for the night? I make sure that Honorine and Martine clean the house up thoroughly before they go off for the winter, so the bedrooms are clean. All I would have to do would be to make a bed for him.

If I do not want him too near to my bedroom, I could put him up in one of the two ground floor bedrooms. They have direct access to the garden, so usually I let a physically handicapped guest, who uses a wheelchair, stay there. One such guest is Tony from Colorado, a former American Air Force fighter pilot who had lost his legs when his plane was shot down over Hanoi, and who, each summer when he comes to stay, tells me war stories. "*Mash*, the movie - Jesus, Ma'am! Vietnam was worse than that! Those Viets ... what cruel little bastards ..!"

What about food tonight? I would have to give him something to eat. Breakfast tomorrow morning would not be a problem because I always have a bag of croissants in the freezer, but supper tonight will be a problem.

I find him in the drawing room.

He is standing at one of the bay windows and watching the storm as I have been doing upstairs. He turns round when he hears me behind him.

"This is ... just so unfortunate," I say.

He nods.

"What do you suggest, Miss Wolff?"

I cannot let this man ride down the hill in such rain.

"I could let you have a room for tonight. I mean, you would get drenched riding down to the village now, Sir."

"I can! Oh, that's really kind of you, Miss Wolff. Do you have a ... a ... perhaps a small room - like a maid's room so I would not be putting you out? And please not the 'sir'; it makes me feel ... ancient."

"My staff do not live on the premises so I do not have a maid's room."

"Oh dear!"

"No, that's alright. I have two bedrooms on the ground floor. You would want to unload your bike and you would not have to carry everything up the stairs. I am though afraid both rooms are small."

"Good grief no, the smallest room in the world will be just fine. Excellent! Wonderful! Thank you!"

I lead the way to the room Tony always has and which I think of as the 'Tony from Colorado' room.

"I am not going to charge you for tonight. As I said - the room is small ..."

"I will pay you for tonight."

He is smiling mischievously like a schoolboy who is teasing one of the spotty, skinny or plump girls in his class.

It makes me smile too, but I am sure I am blushing because blushing has always been a problem for me. "Bella, you're blonde, my girl, so you will be prone to blushing," my mother used to say.

"I will get some sheets and blankets, Mr Lerwick, and if you would like to bring your stuff in."

"Will do, but please, if we are going to spend the night

together, also do not call me Mr Lerwick. Do please call me Colin."

He is still smiling that mischievous smile, and I know I am blushing because my face is suddenly hot, hot like it used to become when I was a child and was coming down with a cold and my mother made me bend over the washbasin which was filled with steaming-hot water into which she had infused dried oregano and thyme, a towel over my head.

"I'll get the sheets."

I rush from the room.

"Ok. Thanks."

He spoke to my disappearing back.

-0-

CHAPTER THIRTEEN

Gertrude is the only one who ever cooks here at Le Presbytère.

I wish she's here this evening because I would like to give Colin Lerwick - Colin - something really tasty to eat; when he's back in England he can tell his friends about the guest house and more holidaymakers will come my way.

Gertrude could have done one of her specialities: *saumon grillé au beurre d'anchois.* Grilled salmon with anchovy butter. I would have asked her to serve it with another of her specialities: *Pommes Anna.* Anna Potatoes, or as we call them here at the guest house, Gertrude Potatoes - thin slices of firm-fleshed potatoes, salted and peppered and doused with melted butter and baked in the oven until crispy and golden. And a cassis sorbet for dessert. She would have sent Fred to the Janviers' farm for the blackcurrants and I would have had to tell her to have a light hand with the *crème de cassis* because we were having an English gentleman for dinner and not a French stevedore.

Colin is back in the drawing room. The empty niche has caught his attention. He is standing in front of it and looking closely at it.

He turns: he must have heard me behind him.

"If you do not mind me asking, why is there nothing in here, Miss Wolff?"

"Look closer."

"May I call you Bella?"

"Of course."

"Well, Bella, I need not look closer because I've already done so and I've seen there are tiny holes here which form a crucifix. Did you perhaps have a devout woodworm?"

"Nuns. Not woodworm."

"Nuns?"

"Yes. Nuns. The house was once a nunnery. Or rather, it was part of a convent. Nuns came up here to rest and recuperate from illness. This was long before my parents' acquired the property."

"Interesting ..."

"Perhaps not, because I must warn you that the villagers believe the house is haunted."

"Because of the nuns?"

"Because of the nuns, yes. The villagers' story is that the pest had broken out here in the house among the nuns - I'm speaking of the 19th century now - and in order not to alarm the locals the padre had the victims buried secretly in the garden at the back of the house."

"And it's those nuns wandering around here?"

"You've got it."

"Do you believe in such things?"

"Ghosts?"

"Ghosts."

"I am not a believer - period."

"I thought doctors were. I would have thought the opposite should be true - who needs God when we have science and all that - but a doctor friend of mine has told me that doctors do believe in a higher power and that it guides their hand."

I must change the subject - quickly!

"I can't speak for doctors," I say, not looking at him. "I am a guest house keeper. As such I must apologise to you for the supper I am going to give you this evening. Or rather, for not going to give you a proper supper this evening. I am afraid I have never been into cooking. And Gertrude - Gertrude Duc - our chef, is such an excellent one that there is no need for me to cook. Mind you, Gertrude is adamant she is not another Paul Bocuse and ... but I am rambling on and will shut up now."

I look up and he is looking at me and his eyes are searching for mine.

"You are charming, Bella. Charming."

I only notice now that he has changed into jeans and a black sweater, and he is in trainers. A thin gold chain with a small oval medal like those one can buy at the mount's souvenir shops and which will very quickly turn black with rust in muggy weather, hangs around his neck.

"I am going to go into the kitchen now to see what I can give you to eat this evening," I say, ignoring what he has said to me and embarrassed he has said it.

"Please, do not go to any trouble, Bella."

"Even if I wish to do so I would not be able to because I do not have anything which will take more than ten minutes to prepare."

"I thought women were good at living on their own," he says.

He pouts his lips.

"That's sexist."

"So it is. I'm sorry. And oh, do excuse me my bad manners for saying something so personal. You do probably have someone living here with you. Someone who will be coming home from work."

"No one will be coming home from work."

He is fidgeting with the thin gold chain. I believe he is now the embarrassed one, and, because he has touched a raw nerve - my celibacy and my solitude - I think: *serves you right!*

-0-

Bless Noah for having given the hen shelter in his Arc in order for her to have survived the Great Flood and therefore enabling her to lay eggs for us. I will make us *oeufs pochés au curry* this evening. The English like curry, or so my English guests always tell me.

I have watched Gertrude going about the dish's preparation and cooking. She would always set out the ingredients on the work table: eggs, cup of wine vinegar, small bowl of béchamel sauce, curry powder and bowl of double cream - *crème fraiche*. And she always serves the dish on slices of fried bread which I will do too.

First, I add the vinegar to water and I bring the mixture to the boil. I hope I am not using too much vinegar. I break the eggs into the boiling vinegary mixture. The mixture starts to sizzle. I wait for the eggs to harden. First the whites do so and next, the yolks.

I hear Colin's footsteps on the marble floor. I hold my breath. I do not want him to come into the kitchen. My movements are clumsy, I know, and will become even more so, should I know that he is watching me. Silly I am, but I want him to think that I am perfect. I give a sigh of relief because the footsteps start to fade; he has returned to the 'Tony from Colorado' room.

The béchamel sauce is frozen - Gertrude made quite a lot of it and she has left it in the freezer - and I heat a generous portion in a saucepan. I add the curry powder to it. Bubbles begin to form on the surface of the sauce and I pop one of the bubbles with my pinkie. I lick the finger clean. The sauce is just right; not too spicy. The saucepan still on the stove, but the gas burner turned low, I work the fresh cream into the sauce, turning and turning until there are no bubbles left.

Finally, I begin to fry the slices of *pain de mie* in olive oil. The eggs and sauce I keep warm on a hot plate.

"Colin!"

He will hear me, I know, because the 'Tony from Colorado' room is not far from the kitchen.

"Yes, Bella?"

"Supper is served!"

He walks in.

"You do not mind if I join you and if we eat in the kitchen?" I ask.

"I would have been insulted if you had not joined me and - I like your kitchen. I like your house. Very much."

He sits down at the work table where I have laid two settings; brown plastic cloth and brown paper napkins, but here is a touch of the elegant and expensive too because I have set out my Limoges porcelain with the name Le Presbytère in gilded lettering on each item, and my silver cutlery engraved with the name.

It was here in the kitchen where my parents, Marius and I always ate our meals, the staff always having joined us. Those meals were silent occasions; my mother did not tolerate conversation at table. "Interferes with the digestion," she stated. We could not even ask someone to pass the salt. Each had to look out for the other, which Honorine and Martine told me was what the nuns at their boarding school insisted upon too. *And in your godliness, brotherly kindness.* Did not one of the Apostles say so? Peter or John or James? Or Judas before he had made the opposite his legacy when he had denounced Jesus, as we had been taught at our Sunday morning Bible studies?

My truth is that when I am not alone at a table, I am no longer one for silence.

"Tell me, Colin, what do you think of French food?"

I have started eating.

"*Coq au vin*, to give you an example, is a bit rich for me. I love duck. *Canard à l'orange. Magret de canard.*"

"*Foie gras?*"

"Too rich for me too, I am afraid. And I do not like the force feeding bit."

"Like Brigitte Bardot."

"Good heavens who force fed her?"

His voice was full of childlike mischief and I giggle at his wisecrack and so does he.

He mops up the last of the egg on his plate with a square of fried bread and dips his head to pop it into his

87

mouth, obviously not wanting the egg to drip onto his shirt. It is somehow a very homely gesture and my heart sings because he is a guest and I want my guests to feel at home.

"Coffee?" I offer.

Alone here, I drink instant coffee, but when Gertrude is here Le Presbytère's *petit noir* is a delight. She grinds the coffee beans herself using a mortar and pestle, both of grey stone, the pestle standing on three short, tubby legs like a dwarfed headless monster. "This is how my gran did it on the farm," she always tells the admiring guests, they, admiring not only the end product but also the jive of the muscles in her huge upper arms as she crushes and grinds the dark-brown Arabica beans with the cork-shaped mortar.

"Coffee will be wonderful," Colin replies.

"Cognac with it?"

"Good heavens no! That will keep me awake all night."

I have not yet made his bed and while he drinks his coffee, remaining sitting at the work table, I go to do so.

I look around the room while I make the bed.

A small open leather suitcase is on the luggage rack. A book lies on top of the clothes in the case. It is Italo Calvino's *Difficult Loves* in Italian. A blue-grey portable Olivetti typewriter is on the dressing table in front of the bay window. A hundred-sheet pack of A4 white writing paper lies beside the typewriter. A *Hugo* pocket English-Russian/Russian-English dictionary and a copy of *The Statesman's Year-Book 1984-85* lie on the bedside table. I should not, but I pick up the year-book - *a quarter of a million facts on the world today* is written on the red cover. On the inside cover of the dictionary it says it will be *a most serviceable pocket reference-book.*

He must know Italian and maybe Russian too. A polyglot. I suppose he knows French too: we have been speaking in English. My mother knew English and always spoke English to our guests from across the Channel and from the States, and my father always spoke in German to our German guests. "Guests feel so much more welcome when one welcomes them in their own language," my mother always said, ignoring the fact the only foreign languages she knew were English and German, of the latter only a scattering she had learnt from my father.

Colin appears in the doorway.

"Could I help?"

"Thank you, but the bed's made now."

He says he will have an early night and I bid him a good one.

At the door, I turn round.

"The surname - Wolff. My father was German."

"Your mother?"

"French."

"My mother was foreign. Not English like my father."

"That's interesting!"

The storm has not abated and a clap of thunder right above the house drowns his reply but the look of discontent on his face tells me his mother, having been foreign and not English, is not something that pleases him. *Every family bears a cross,* my mother always said.

"The night is going to be cold," I tell him.

I will have to set the central heating's thermostat higher in the morning, I decide.

I go to silence the grandfather clock.

-0-

CHAPTER FOURTEEN

It is the hour of sunrise, always a time when the sky is tinged with yellow, and birdsong drifts from the garden, but this morning, the sky is murky and the birds are silent.

Through my bedroom window I can see Colin's motorcycle. The sheet of canvas over the sidecar is drenched and water runs from the handlebars and seat.

Would I have to allow him to keep the 'Tony from Colorado' room for another night? In such a case I will have to let him sign the register because Captain Contepomi, nice man as he is, will not be beyond suspecting I am trying to cheat the Receiver of Revenue by letting rooms without having the guests sign in.

I am surprised to see Colin is already up and sitting at the work table when I walk into the kitchen. Fortunately, I have changed from my nightdress and I am wearing a pretty jersey and not the house one. I have put some make-up on.

"Bella! Good morning. I hope I am not intruding," he greets me, jovially.

"You should have made yourself a cup of coffee or tea. And good morning to you too. Or rather, the morning does not look so good. The weather - I mean."

He tells me he listened to the weather forecast on *France Info* on his transistor earlier, and rain is on the menu for the day.

"For a few days, in fact."

I ask him what he would like to drink - tea or coffee.

"A cup of tea would be just the thing. Thank you, Bella."

I tell him I am going to have a cup of tea too, that I always start the day with a cup of tea.

"At the hospital the nurses always had a cup of tea waiting for the doctors, but as soon as we'd finished our first round of the wards, it was coffee, coffee, coffee. The strongest black coffee possible."

Oh God, have I said too much?

Chacun garde du fond du coeur un souvenir que ne veut pas mourir as Guy de Maupassant said, and now, because of what I have said, I might have to tell Colin of the souvenir at the bottom of my heart which also does not want to die: the death of the Brissard twin. Fortunately, he seems not to have heard what I have said.

"When do you think the rain will stop?" he asks, shooting a glance out the window.

"I would not want to guess, but the weather bureau is usually quite accurate. Hopefully the wind will drop."

My mother was buried on a day when the weather was like this. Marius and Marion and the children came from Paris. I thought a funeral was no place for a child, but Marius said children must know what death was and Marion seconded that. Many villagers attended the funeral and when it was over and the gravediggers started to fill the grave where she lay with my father, the only man she ever loved, the villagers offered us - Marius, Marion and me - their condolences. Two of my uncles - her brothers - were still alive and one of them had been overcome with coughing spasms in the church which I interpreted a result of trying to suppress sobs. I thought, "Good! Choke to death, you bastard!" Then, I remembered the Brissard twin having choked to death because I had not realised he had phlegm lodged in his windpipe, and I collapsed sobbing in a heap on the floor of the church.

Colin is saying something about Avranches and I have to ask him to repeat what he has said.

"If I could stay until the storm has passed. That was, what I was saying. That it would really be so kind of you to allow me to stay."

"It is such a pity you should see Normandy in this kind of weather."

I am trying to dodge the issue.

"If I could stay ...?"

"Let's see what the weather will do."

The grandfather clock begins to chime. *I know that my redeemer liveth* ...

Colin lifts up a hand for me not to speak; he is listening to the chiming.

"Beautiful!"

I nod my agreement.

"I did not hear that during the night."

"I silence the clock during the night."

"That was Handel."

"Yes. Handel. The clock ... my father brought the clock from Germany. It stood in his childhood home. It had miraculously survived the bombing of Berlin in World War Two when nothing else in the house had."

"My mother had a small watercolour which hung in her childhood home. The picture had survived several pogroms when just about everything else in the house was smashed or burnt. Tsarist pogroms. My mother was Russian. Polish Russian from the Polish-Russian Union, in fact."

"So like me, you are not all of one thing?" I ask after a short but heavy silence.

"Quite. My brother - I have just one ... the one sibling - and I did not even know our mother was not ... born in England. I mean she was so *very* English - to us in any case. We discovered this only on her death in 1970 when a brother of hers appeared from nowhere and enlightened us. My brother is a businessman. Manufactures garden gnomes. Of all things - garden gnomes."

"That's interesting."

He says nothing and the look of distress on his face warns me that, as I do, he also has a *raw nerve.*

"I've always disliked garden gnomes. When I was a child they scared me because I thought they were real and they were so very peculiar looking," I quickly say to change the subject.

"I also dislike garden gnomes, but, alas, for another reason."

He searches for my eyes with his.

I turn from his gaze and hastily I pop three frozen croissants into the oven, and I plug in the kettle to reheat it.

He points at the three croissants browning behind the oven's glass window.

"Three? I do not think I could manage three."

"One is for me. I have a croissant each morning. What will you have now, more tea or some coffee."

He asks for a cup of coffee.

"It is so peaceful here," he muses. He walks over to the Peace Lily and brushes a finger over the soil. "What a beautiful flower. I can see you have green thumbs."

"The garden is Fred's job. Fred is Le Presbytère's gardener - the handyman without whom I would not be able to get by."

"Was that Fred who came to work on the boiler yesterday?"

"No, that was Samy. He's a plumber down in the village."

"I am not good with remembering the names of flowers, so what is this one here?"

"It's a Peace Lily."

"Appropriate."

He starts to walk over to where I am standing in front of the stove. He is wearing his motorcycle leather again. He has shaved but he has missed a spot on his left cheek, the cheek nearest to me. An aroma of mint clings to him. Eau de toilet, or aftershave, or toothpaste? Jean-Louis used

Hermes's *Equipage Cologne,* the masculine scent of leather, tobacco and a forest on a frosty morning always clinging to his skin, his hair and his clothes. I adored the smell of him; I had even stupidly bought a flacon of it to spray the bed on those nights which he did not spend with me.

Suddenly, my head begins to spin and I have to lean against the stove to steady myself. *I must stop remembering.* Or is it Colin's closeness that has upset me? Is unnerving me?

"Sit down," I tell him, quickly and abruptly. "The croissants are warm now."

He does not sit down but stays beside me.

"Bella, would you allow me to stay? Until the weather has cleared - of course?"

One will say he is an English lord.

"Yes," I say. "You can stay till the wind dies down."

Those words slipped out.

-0-

When Geneva was over and Jean-Louis and I were driving into Paris from the Porte d'Italie on the southern border of the capital, he asked whether I would allow him to stay at my apartment for the night.

"I'll go straight to the office from there tomorrow morning," he explained, a hand briefly leaving the steering wheel to touch my face.

I had prepared for such an eventuality and had hurriedly tidied up before I set off for Gare de Lyon to catch the Geneva express.

On that first visit to my apartment, he stood for a long time in front of the photo of my father and mother on the mantelpiece in the sitting room.

"Your father was a handsome man. And look how beautiful your mother is," he said.

The photo was taken about four years after my birth. I can remember the morning the photographer came to Le

Presbytère. I watched him set up his big, black, box-shaped camera in the drawing room. He moved the settee, huffing as he pulled and pushed it to stand between the two bay windows, and explained to us about angles and light and aperture and shutter speed, all of which I, and I'm sure my parents too, understood not a word. He told my parents how they were to sit. "Not to cross the legs," he told my mother, tapping her lightly on her stockinged knee, and he asked my father to fold his arms in front of him, *like great men have the habit of doing for official portraits.* I watched, wide-eyed with interest and hoping he would also be taking my picture. He crawled underneath a piece of black cloth which was hanging over the camera and he pulled a string which set off a very bright flash of blue light. He did not take my picture; my parents had, as they explained to a tearful me, hired him only to take one photo - theirs.

"You should come to Normandy. Come to see my mother. She's still pretty," I told Jean-Louis.

The words had hardly been spoken and he had his engagement diary out of his briefcase and checking whether he would be free the following weekend.

"Superb!" he said, his face smiling. "I have nothing scheduled. I can fit in Normandy."

Fit in Normandy!

-0-

CHAPTER FIFTEEN

This morning the sky is the molten orange of an amber stone hundreds of years old.

I stand at my bedroom window, and I know the sun will rise today. The wind has already calmed to a soft caress, the leaves hardly moving, and the sea in the distance is an immobile grey cloth.

I dress quickly; I want to make Colin's breakfast because he would be eager to set off, to go and find a guest house. In the high season, a guest house keeper, whose place is fully booked, will refer a guest to another guest house or hotel, but I will not be able to recommend another Sainte-Marie-sur-Brecque guest house to Colin this morning because I know none will accept a guest who wants to stay for several months.

He is again already in the kitchen. He is sitting at the work table, looking towards the window, seemingly in deep thought, but a paperback lies open in front of him. I am wearing soft shoes so he has not heard me walk in and for a moment I stand still and silent and I watch him. His face, in profile, is extremely masculine - firm jaw, raised cheekbones, his forehead wide - and I had thought he was ordinary looking. Had I not also thought Jean-Louis was ordinary looking when I first set eyes on him? And look how I fell for him!

"Morning!" I greet Colin.

I tried to sound casual.

"Oh, good morning. I did not hear you walk in."

"I'm sorry. Did I give you a fright?"

He had looked startled for a moment.

"No, it's just that - that I thought you were - but no, you did not give me a fright. How did you sleep? Well, I hope?"

"How did *you* sleep? Strange room. Strange bed. I never sleep on a first night in a strange room."

"I slept well, thank you. I did not wake up at all during the night. Went off the moment my head hit the pillow."

He is not in his motorcycle leather, but in jeans and a short-sleeved white T-shirt and my heart misses a beat.

Hell, I am being stupid!

"You would have seen the weather has cleared," I rapidly say, hoping to steady my unsteady heartbeat.

"Bella, I would like not to have to leave today."

He is looking me straight in the eye. I think he is holding his breath awaiting my reply. My agreement.

"If you would like to spend another night here, it will not be a problem."

"No, not just this night. I would like you to reconsider me staying here longer. Like until Christmas - just before Christmas as I take it that you would be joining your family for Christmas, or some of them would probably be coming here."

"As yet I've no plans for Christmas, but let me heat the kettle and get your breakfast."

"Oh Bella, please ... do not go to any trouble. I do not eat in the mornings."

I sigh with relief: I thought he was going to beg me to stay.

"A cup of tea and a croissant ... is what it will be. Like yesterday morning."

"And it will be terrific. Thank you, Bella."

-0-

I will wait until I have some strong coffee in me before I

decide about having Colin Lerwick stay. I wonder what the legalities are about having a guest when the guest house is officially closed - registered as such at our town hall and at the regional tourist office. I would certainly have to telephone the *gendarmerie* and let Captain Contepomi know that he would have to come check my guest registry next Friday and the Friday after that and each Friday until Christmas. Or until Colin Lerwick leaves.

But have I decided to allow this man to stay?

My father always said decisions were made for us. I said this to Jean-Louis once. "Rubbish!" he snapped. "That is saying that you are not - that I am not - that we are not masters of our life. If I bugger up it is because of a decision I've made and not one which has been made for me by some invisible being, some spirit - or spook more likely."

So what is my decision?

Le Presbytère has ten rooms and one winter I calculated that if I walk through each of them, walk slowly, perhaps pause at a window or in front of a favourite ornament on a shelf or a favourite picture on a wall, I will get rid of between thirty and forty-five minutes of each lonely day. Oh Jesus, do I want another winter of walking through these ten silent rooms pleased that I am killing time?

So come on Bella Wolff, there is no spook to make the decision for you; make it yourself!

Colin is spreading Gertrude's strawberry jam - jam which won her the first prize of a video recorder at Avranche's food fair last summer - over one of his heated croissants.

"It's nice, is it not - the jam?" I ask.

"Delicious. I'm going to eat all of it - the jam - I'm afraid."

He spreads yet another spoonful of it over his second heated croissant.

"You would not be able to eat it all, not even in two

months here, because I have ten large jars of the stuff. Le Presbytère had a bumper strawberry crop this year - thanks to Fred's green thumbs - and Gertrude was cooking jam almost every day. The entire house had a sweet sticky smell and all the wasps of Normandy came to visit."

"Two months?" His cup is halfway to his lips. "Do I take it that you are allowing me to stay?"

Am I?

"I would have to let you have a nicer room - a bigger room. You would have to sign the register and ..."

"Pay in advance?"

There is teasing laughter in his voice.

"Pay in advance? Of course not! Don't be silly!"

Do not be silly. I said this to him yet I am the silly one. The stupid one. I have a rule - I close in winter - and now I have taken a guest, and this guest is a man I am finding very attractive. Yet, I do not want him to go. Not just yet.

Silly. Silly. Stupid. Stupid.

I have not thought it over. I have not balanced what would not be good about it against what would be.

Would there be anything good about it?

-0-

"I think I am falling in love with you, Bella," Jean-Louis said after we had been seeing each other for six weeks, and were spending a second weekend at Le Presbytère.

"Fair enough, Jean-Louis, you're not on your knees pledging undying love to me to only change your mind the moment we are on the highway driving back to the reality which is Paris," I replied.

"And what is the reality which is Paris?"

"The Paris air is polluted," I replied flatly, deliberately not wanting to admit to him -and to me - he is not a free man, free to go down on his knees to ask me to marry him.

"Come on, Bella, be serious. Do you at least fancy

100

me?" he asked.

"A little."

I had tried to sound casual about it.

"Fair enough," he said, echoing my words of a moment earlier.

"I'm being silly, Jean-Louis, don't take notice of what I say," I apologised.

"I love it when you are being silly, Bella. There is so much promise in your silliness. So, you fancy me a little, as you say. Perhaps it is a fancy which will deepen, deepen to *really like* and then to *crazy about* and then to ..."

"Ok! That's enough!" I interrupted him.

"Now you are angry!"

"Nope."

"Bella, my dear Bella," he said, "I know I am not free - not for the going on my knees stuff."

"So let us change the subject," I snapped.

I threw my hands, palms facing him, up in the air and he shook his head.

"Bella, changing the subject will be dodging the subject. What I want to say is this: I do plan to get a divorce but - but there is the future of the girls I must think of. I can't imagine ... losing them, not that I will, I suppose, but they may just hate me should their mother and I finalise our separation, if you follow what I am trying to say. Bella, I do sincerely wish us to have a future, to be committed to one another. This - you and me - is not just a fling as far as I am concerned. I do not know: is it just a fling for you? I do not know."

"I suggested we change the subject, Jean-Louis," I snapped yet again.

"So this *is* just a fling?"

I shook my head.

"I do not indulge in flings."

He was then the one who threw his arms up in the air.

"Oh forget this! I am going to walk down to the village. Are you coming with me?"

I did not go with him. He stayed in the village for several hours and when he returned my mother pointed out to me that she could smell wine on his breath.

"A man who drinks at the least little differences, Bella, is a man you give the boot to."

"What difference are you talking of, Mother?" I asked her.

"Differences. Plural. His wife. His children. He might have removed his wedding band - I know he was wearing one until quite recently because the mark is still on his finger - but, as sure as the fact that I am standing in front of you here now, is the fact that he is still bound to them. The wedding band's gone, yes, but it has been replaced with a mental shackle. This is always what happens when marriages break up."

"Bella, was that our first argument?" asked Jean-Louis.

Our weekend over, we had driven back to Paris and to my apartment.

"I do not know what you are talking about," I replied.

"Oh, sure you do," he said, his face flushed with anger.

He did not stay with me that night, and he slammed the door on leaving, and I was angry with myself.

Hell, I am a silly cow, I said to myself.

-0-

CHAPTER SIXTEEN

I choose the White Room for Colin. It is two rooms from mine and like mine it has a bay window overlooking the front garden.

"You ought to be comfortable in here."

He stands in the doorway, his briefcase on the floor behind him.

"I would have been equally comfortable in the 'Tony from Colorado' room, but thank you, Bella."

The White Room is, as its name implies, all in white; walls, bedspread, sheets, pillowcases, cushions, curtains. The other bedrooms have other colour schemes - pink, yellow, lilac - but I cannot picture this man in a room with pink, lilac or yellow walls and bedspread. And sleeping between pink sheets. Sometimes, I give this room to a young couple, and always to a honeymoon couple, but it is not a bridal room, because the elderly and old like it as much as the young ones.

I start making the queen-sized bed. I have silk sheets for the bed, but these I always reserve for the honeymooners. Knowing a man often cuts his face when shaving and wishing to protect my white towels, I hang navy-blue ones in the en-suite bathroom. I set out a range of Yves Rocher men's toiletries on the bathroom shelf: *Aztec* after-shave balm, anti-perspirant deodorant and eau de toilet. I accidentally press the spray dispenser on the eau de toilet container and a mist of the scent of cedar and ginseng envelopes me.

Through the window I can see Colin has started to unload the sidecar. I have been curious about the sidecar's contents and now I see he is carrying *Tesco* plastic shopping bags, all filled with books and cassettes, into the house. He takes a cassette player and a recorder from the sidecar. It would be interesting to know what music he likes, presuming these are music cassettes. Jean-Louis liked - I suppose he still does - women singers: Tina Turner, Whitney Houston, Madonna. "How can you possibly like James Brown?" he used to ask me when I always asked him to put James Brown's *Sex Machine* on the player when driving back to Paris from a weekend in Normandy.

I hear Colin come upstairs; light, rhythmic footsteps.

"Here!"

He stops at the door.

"I am giving you *so* much trouble, Bella." He walks towards the bathroom and looks into it. "I could not have asked for a nicer set-up. Mind you I like the 'Tony from Colorado' room downstairs too."

"You will be better off here."

"Thank you, dear Bella!"

He walks over to me as if he wants to touch me, but he abruptly comes to a halt as if he is on his motorcycle and has run into a red light.

I step back and out of his reach should he change his mind.

"When you have moved all your things up here, come down and sign the registry please."

He says he will.

-0-

It is Thursday and therefore market day.

I leave Colin to allow him to settle into the White Room and I go and change because I will be driving down to Sainte-Marie-sur-Brecque to shop. I have made a mental list of what I will be buying for his - our - meals. I may even call in on Gertrude to ask her if she could not perhaps one evening come up to Le Presbytère to cook something really nice, something special, for him - for us.

I slip into one of my sleeveless cotton summer frocks: the rain, gone, and the wind, calmed, the air has warmed up somewhat. For a change I wear heels, a pair of open-toed sandals I had bought when I was still at Chartreux Hospital but have not worn for a while.

What about some jewellery? I would not want to look like a Christmas tree, no, but a bracelet would not be out of place, and I ought also wear something around my neck because the frock is rather low-cut and I wish to cover the cleavage. For the first time in a while I search through my jewellery box. Lifting the lid *When the Saints Come Marching In* starts to play. I hope Colin will not hear the music because he may wonder what I am up to. I choose a bracelet and necklace set of large pink plastic beads made by hand by some unprivileged women somewhere in Mexico and which I bought in Paris on the Butte Montmartre. The full-length mirror in my wardrobe tells me the necklace indeed covers a large section of the bare skin of my throat and the cleavage and this pleases me.

On my way out, I stop outside the White Room.

"Colin, I'm driving down to the village for some provisions."

He is standing at the dressing table in front of the bay window, his back to the door.

He turns round.

"I will guard the fort in your absence, General."

He raises his right hand, his fingers together, his thumb tugged against the hollow of his hand, his forearm straight and horizontal to the floor, and with the tip of his forefinger he touches the outer edge of his right eyebrow. He is saluting me.

He has again put his typewriter on the dressing table. When I get back I will suggest we put a writing desk in the room. There is one in the packing room down in the basement which we can carry upstairs.

My Frida Kahlo courtyard is wet after the rain and I make sure not to step into a puddle of water or to let water from the hanging baskets of ferns drip onto me. I do though walk right into one of the palm trees and I become entangled in its dripping wet drooping branches.

"Bugger!" I swear out loud.

Feeling ridiculous and fearing I also look it, I swing round to see whether Colin is at the window and watching. Indeed, he is still standing at the window, a smile across his face. Or rather, he is suppressing laughter. He salutes me yet again; the same gesture as before.

He must have looked gorgeous in the dark-blue uniform of the R.A.F.

I wonder if he piloted planes. Bombers? Would he have agreed to bomb Hiroshima?

Oh shit Bella Wolff, pull yourself together.

-0-

It is a fine morning. It seems the storm, like a laxative, one of those chocolate-flavoured ones we gave patients at Chartreux Hospital to clear their stomachs, has cleared the air. The *pré-salé* pasture land is vividly green, the sky and the sea both sapphire blue in the brilliant sunshine. Having neither my period nor am I pregnant, I dismiss Gertrude's warning about the dangers of a draught and I turn the Merc's front windows down. I wonder if Colin is watching the road from the White Room's window. I know guests do always find the view from Le Presbytère irresistible and spend long minutes just standing by a window looking out. Should he be doing so, he will see the Merc, so I stick my left hand out the window and I wave like someone waving the checkered flag at the start of a Formula One race. Should he be watching and mentions the waving, I can always say I had seen a farmer and waved to him.

As always, I park on Rue Charlemagne. As my

shopping list is long, I have brought along my shopping trolley, which is on wheels. Whenever I go out shopping with my trolley I always feel good. I feel good again now. I feel good because I take the trolley only when I have to buy several things because Le Presbytère is open and I have a full house. In other words, I am not eating alone.

And, as always, I start my shopping excursion at the Vaybee.

Father Pierre is standing at the bar. He is dressed in black flannels and a black shirt with white buttons, the top two unbuttoned, and revealing dry, bushy grey hair.

He greets me with a smile.

"Miss Wolff, we do not see you half as often as we wish to."

The royal 'we'. Indeed he always says 'we' and I always wonder who is included in the 'we'. God? Or maybe just a couple of Jesus' Apostles?

He puts the glass of red wine from which he is sipping down on the zinc-top of the bar and holds a hand out to me.

"Father!"

I shake the offered hand of which the nails are too long and cut into my skin. It is far from noon so I wonder what he is doing at the Vaybee already.

"Mrs Celeste is on holiday. Gone to her son in Lille. Frascot is kindly allowing me to lunch here each day," he says as if mind-reading is his forte.

Frascot, his white plastic apron spotted with grease, steps through the door leading from the kitchen.

"Miss! Marketing, are you?"

"Marketing, Frascot."

"A long list?"

He points to my trolley.

"A long list. I've a guest staying."

"… nice …"

That was neither a statement nor a question.

I finish the black coffee in the small black cup Frascot

has placed in front of me without me having had to ask for it and I bid both him and Father Pierre, who has finished his wine and has just motioned to Frascot to fill up the glass, a good day. I wonder if the priest is paying for the wine and whether he will be paying for the lunches he will be having while Mrs Celeste is on holiday. I make a mental note to ask Fred when he comes round to Le Presbytère to do the gardening. He ought to be coming over the weekend because he says he cannot trust me with 'his' garden.

I stop at the Janviers' stall first. I hand Mrs Janvier my list of the fruit and vegetables I need and leaving my trolley with her for my purchases, I move on to the Legros' stall. This morning Mrs Legros is not wearing her red dress but a brown woollen skirt and red blouse.

"What it's to be on this glorious day, Miss?"

I hand her my list. She reads it out loud like a small child still learning to read. I have chicken, guinea fowl, duck, rabbit, sirloin steak and lamb cutlets listed. Mr Legros, slicing thin steaks from a block of bloody meat so large it could only have been cut from a horse's flank - yes, the Legros also sell horse meat - looks up.

"I say! I say! Your brother and family come to stay?"

I ignore the question.

"*Ooh la la*, Miss! Healthy appetite you have there!" he says.

"She's got her family over, do you not Miss," Mrs Legros tries again.

"No, Mrs Legros, there is a guest at Le Presbytère."

"I thought you close in winter, Miss," says her husband, still carving up the large carcass.

"I do, but an English writer needs a couple of months to finish a book, and so friends of his asked me if he could stay at Le Presbytère."

"A man! A couple of months! Well, I say! *Ooh la la!* Is he nice, Doc?" asks Mrs Legros.

"Mrs Legros," I say, "the man is a paying guest

therefore whether he is nice or not is neither here nor there."

"All the same, Miss, a nice man is even nicer than the nicest *steak tartare. Ooh la la!*"

Her *ooh la la* echoing in my ears, I walk back to the Janviers' stall to get my trolley.

"You are indeed buying a lot today, Miss?" says Mrs Janvier.

She pushes my trolley, almost packed to the top, from behind a table on which their produce is set out in small, colourful pyramids.

"What do I owe you, Mrs Janvier?"

"Got guests?"

"Got a guest."

"Family? Or someone interesting."

"Mrs Janvier, *Le Presbytère* has a guest."

I repeat the lie, or rather the half-lie, I have just told the Legros couple.

"Nice you not on your own, Miss. What with all the robberies and them ending in murder, as I see on the box, I sure am happy to know you have company this winter. It's a man, is it, your guest?" she asks.

"*Le Presbytère's* guest. It is a paying guest, and yes, it is a man."

"*Ooh la la!*"

Quickly I pay her and I grab my trolley and I return to the Legros stall for Mrs Legros to load my purchases into the trolley too.

"Now, do watch out, Doc."

Her husband is nodding beside her.

I am 'miss' to those here in the village, but occasionally one of them will call me 'doc' and I always wonder what is the factor which settles them on doing so. To my staff I am always 'miss'.

"Watch out for what, Mrs Legros?" I ask.

"Strange man in the house. One never can tell."

I thank her for her concern and I pay her and I walk

back to the Vaybee.

Father Pierre is sitting at a table. He has a white paper napkin tied around his neck, the large silver crucifix with the fake ruby stone which always hangs around his neck, now hidden from sight. Frascot sees me, waves, and starts to fill another small black cup with coffee. The cup filled, he holds it out to me, a sliver of steam rising from it.

"I hear it's a man you've got staying, Miss."

News does travel fast.

"I have an English writer staying at Le Presbytère, yes, Frascot."

Again, I repeat the half-lie although I am sure there is no need to do so; he would have heard it by now.

"Nice, is he?"

"He seems a well-brought-up person, as, I must point out, all Le Presbytère's guest usually are. I've had the odd moron putting cigarettes out on the carpet, but all in all, I've not had real trouble with a guest."

"You know him?"

"Who?"

"The young man."

"Did I describe him as a young man? He is a man of a certain age, and no, Frascot I know only he is English and a writer. He is a friend of friends who asked me to allow him to stay."

"Will we be meeting him?"

"Frascot, I've no idea whether he will be riding down to the village, but all my guests come down here sooner or later so he will probably come to the village."

"Fred said not a word about him."

"Fred does not know about him."

"Not! *Ooh la la!* Must be careful, Miss. One never knows. You up there on your own with a foreigner."

"He is hardly a foreigner. He is English. If you stretch out your arm you can touch his country."

"Let me tell you, Miss, the *Rosbifs* can be very odd at times. Queer they are - the blokes. Go for their own gender. Mind you who can blame them 'cause English women all look like horses and hung in the chest like cows in the hour before milking, they are."

Father Pierre, sitting at a table and tucking into half a roasted chicken, looks across at me.

"All God's flock, Doctor Wolff. All God's flock. Praise the Lord."

He waves a reprimanding greasy finger in Frascot's direction.

I thank Frascot for his concern over my safety just as I thanked Mrs Legros for hers.

"We hope to see you at mass, Dr Wolff. We have not seen you at mass for a while. *Tut tut tut*!" says the priest.

He waves a meaty chicken wing into the air.

I pull the heavy trolley back towards Rue Charlemagne for the drive home, but first I step into the village's one-roomed post office on Impasse de l'Abbaye beside the church. I want to telephone the *gendarmerie* to speak to Captain Contepomi.

Solange Marchadier, the village's portly post mistress, who is always asking me about remedies to prevent menopause, steps from behind her counter and throws her arms around me and kisses me on both cheeks, a lock of her dyed-yellow hair, falling into my mouth.

"Miss, I hear you've got a young man."

"I beg your pardon?"

"You've got a young man!"

"Solange, Le Presbytère has a guest which is what you must surely be talking of."

I ask her for a chip for the telephone and I leave the door of the phone booth open and I lift my voice speaking to the captain, telling him there is someone at the guest house. I want Solange to hear.

"If you would want to check the register, Captain."

I am angry with myself. Damn it! Why am I behaving like a teenager who has a boyfriend for the first time and is shy about it?

-0-

CHAPTER SEVENTEEN

I can hear Colin typing. At first, I could not make out what the noise was which I was hearing. I thought there was something wrong with the grandfather clock; sometimes a moth is caught in the teeth of the pendulum and its timekeeping becomes erratic. I soon though recognised the dull thuds as a typewriter's keys hitting a sheet of paper. I wonder if he is going to type every day. I presume he will because this is the reason why he is here. I may find the noise irritating, just as I always find the screeching of the wheels of a child's toy car, for example, irritating. I hope he is not going to type too early in the morning or late at night.

On my return from Sainte-Marie-sur-Brecque he came down to the garage and carried my trolley to the kitchen. "Come. Seeing I am the cause of this, allow me to help you," he said and before I could get a word of protestation out, he was already pushing the trolley across the courtyard. He stood watching while I laid my purchases out on the work table. "What beautiful potatoes," he said and picked one of the Janviers' new potatoes, earth still clinging to it, up from the table. Driving home I decided what I would give him to eat tonight. Knowing my English guests do not all go for rabbit, which we French love, I decided on a *boeuf miroton* and fortunately I decided to serve boiled potatoes with it. The dessert is going to be white grapes. These are the last of the season and Mrs Janvier charged me quite a bit for them. "What I do not sell today, Miss, will go into bottles tomorrow," she said with a wink.

With Gertrude's steel knife, sharp enough to cut a man's throat, I cut two steaks into small cubes. Quickly, I fry them in olive oil. Setting these aside, I gather together the needed ingredients - chopped onions, capers, flour, vinegar, meat stock, butter, parsley, breadcrumbs, a *bouquet garni,* and a bottle of dry white wine - and set them out on the work table. I told Colin dinner would be ready at seven tonight. I will lay one of the small tables in the dining room for him. I will eat in the kitchen as I do when I am alone here, and as he and I did last night.

It is six o'clock now and I start the cooking. I heat the butter in a large frying pan, blackened by years of use, and I add the onions. When the onions are fried to the colour of a summer tan, I add the vinegar, the stock, the wine and I sprinkle the flour over the liquid to thicken it. All, sizzling, I transfer the pan's contents to an oven-proof dish, and I add the meat, some salt and pepper and the *bouquet garni*, and I sprinkle the breadcrumbs over it, and the dish I pop into the oven, which is already hot.

I have often watched Gertrude prepare this dish although I have never tried cooking it myself, so I hope I am going about it the correct way. But what the hell, guests must take it as it comes, and I am already doing this one a favour having him stay, so should my *boeuf miroton* be nowhere as delicious as Gertrude's - so be it.

-0-

I cooked for Jean-Louis just once.

It was a Friday evening and he was staying with me at my Latin Quarter apartment for the weekend.

"We're having headless birds," I told him.

"What birds?"

"Headless."

"I thought it goes without saying we always chop off

the heads before cooking birds."

We sat down at the table. Two tall red candles in a tall wrought-iron candleholder that stood beside the table threw a circle of light over us.

"I am intrigued, Bella, about the birds who do not have heads."

He laughed mockingly, but not unkindly, which was his way, as I had learnt.

I fetched the food from the kitchen.

"Here you are."

He looked at what I put down on the table.

"Where are the birds?"

"Here."

I pointed at the plate in front of him.

"I thought you said we were having birds. I presumed you were talking of chicken or quail, but I see not the one or the other here."

Headless Birds - another of Gertrude's specials, which my guests adore - which is a mixture of minced veal and ham rolled in a thick rasher of bacon and baked in the oven on a bed of sliced tomatoes, chopped onions, omelette and cream, and covered in port.

"What a misnomer!" complained Jean-Louis.

He poked his fork into the meat.

"These are ordinary *paupiettes*, for chrissakes, Bella! And here I was expecting something really extraordinary!"

We ate in silence: he, gobbling down the food despite what he had said.

"They were nice, no?" I asked, not a morsel left on his plate.

"For goodness sake, Bella, it was plain and simple *paupiettes!*"

"So, they were *paupiettes*, but *paupiette*, which I had cooked ... chrissakes!"

He nodded.

"Yes ... and so you did ... and thank you, my darling. It was delicious ... and I am an oaf and I beg your forgiveness."

He planted an oily kiss on my cheek and his right hand rested on my left breast.

"Wipe your mouth," I told him.

-0-

Seven slow clear strikes drift from the drawing room.

Colin walks into the kitchen. Again, he looks fresh as if he has brushed up - washed his hair even, because his hair is wet and clings to his face, which makes him look rather clownish.

"I've noticed the clock does not chime Handel on the hour. Just strikes the time," he says.

"Does the chiming disturb you because if it does, I can quiet it?"

"Oh heavens no! It's beautiful!"

"Should you change your mind, do say so please."

"Something smells nice."

He looks towards the stove.

"You can sit down."

He shoots a glance at the place laid on the work table.

"Am I eating alone tonight?"

I shake my head.

"You are eating in the dining room."

"Who is eating here? The ghost of one of the nuns?"

"I am."

He is the one now to shake his head.

"No, I am not going to eat alone in there. I will eat here with you."

"It is not so comfortable eating in here."

"So, we will both eat in the dining room, that is, if you do not object to eating with me."

Without waiting for me to reply, he starts carrying the things I have set out on the work table to the dining room.

-0-

A fool eats; only a wise man knows how to dine.

Who said this? I think it was Brillant-Savarin.

I know my mother always reminded the staff that what guests have seen here in Normandy they might forget in time but that she never wanted them to forget what they had eaten here at Le Presbytère.

In the dining room, Colin and I sit facing one another at one of my tables which can seat four. Immediately, on sitting down, he had pulled the white damask napkin from the silver napkin ring. Now, the napkin lies on his lap. "Damask is so difficult to iron," my mother protested when I ordered the napkins from a shop in Ireland. "But look, Mother, look how beautiful they are," I protested pointing out their silver rose design. I ordered a hundred and just the other day I counted them and there were just ninety-four in the linen cupboard; someone had stolen six as well as one of the matching tablecloths.

"What opulence, Bella!" says Colin.

He sweeps his arms over the table laid with my Limoges porcelain, the silverware and the crystal glasses.

"You can help yourself, Colin."

He has dropped his hands onto his lap.

"Could you …?" he asks.

I scoop up a generous helping of the meat and two large potatoes and put these down on his plate.

"Hmmm … delicious," he says.

He has had a few mouthfuls.

There is a speck of parsley on his upper lip: I do not point it out to him.

I chose a bottle of *Nuits-Saint-Georges Les Cailles* from the cellar. He swirls the cherry-red liquid in his glass.

"Let us drink to Le Presbytère," he proposes.

He has raised his glass.

"*Gesundheit,*" I say.

"*Santé!*"

"My father always said *gesundheit.*"

Colin points to the bottle of wine.

"Good. Excellent."

"I am glad you like it because I must admit I am not a wine expert, but this *Nuits-Saint-George* was my father's favourite."

"That makes two of us not being wine experts, and, in fact, what I know about wine is dangerous. I always admire colleagues who can so superbly describe wine. Fresh, they call it, or silky, or full and fruity with just a touch of liquorice and a hint of vanilla. I wonder where they get such descriptions from."

"People can be terrible wine snobs. Some who come here certainly are. They insist on a *Nuits-Saint-Georges*, or a *Saint-Émilion* or a *Château-Margaux* - only the *premiers grands crus classés* wines that is - and then they complain when they see the bill."

"That's usually the case with snobs."

He is smiling scornfully.

Discreetly, I watch him. I am, of course, doing so only because I want to know whether he is really enjoying the food.

His hands, like Jean-Louis', also bear no witness to a life of hard physical labour. They are pale, unblemished; his nails, shiny like those of a woman who has just had a one hundred-franc manicure on Paris' Rue du Faubourg-St-Honoré. Small, dark hairs creep from under the black crocodile-skin strap of his watch. A Swiss watch? Ought to be, yes, because the suitcases he had carried in on his arrival bear the logos of French and Italian designers, and his socks, as I saw earlier when he crossed his legs and his trousers pulled up, are of silk.

"Thank you, Bella, for all the trouble you've gone to this evening ... today ... for me. This is a delicious meal," he says.

He's eaten what I served him.

"Would you like another helping?"

"I would love it, yes, please."

"No need to be polite."

"I am not being polite."

"Help yourself," I encourage him.

I push the two dishes towards him.

"Your guests must love it here."

He is scooping more of everything onto his plate.

"We have regulars, which, yes, shows there is something they like about the place."

We fall silent, the only sound is the delicate noise of cutlery scraping over porcelain, and of the grandfather clock ticking away the seconds. I am reminded of Talleyrand's paradox which my father always quoted. *Language was invented in order to conceal our thoughts from one another.* If this is so, Colin must have no thoughts he wishes to hide. Unlike me.

"Grapes?" I ask, confirming to myself I do have thoughts I wish to conceal.

He has finished his second helping of the *boeuf miroton*.

"Would love some."

I push the silver basket with the grapes towards him. He plucks a few grapes from a bunch and puts them down on my plate.

"I was not going to have any myself."

"But now you will have to."

He takes his dessert knife and starts to cut away the semi-translucent peel of each grape. Never have I seen anyone peel grapes. Astonished, I watch. He cuts each peeled grape in half and removes the pips with the tip of the knife.

"We French eat grapes peel and all," I say.

"That's how one should eat grapes, I've been told. The skin and pips are full of antioxidants apparently, which our bodies need, but you, the physician, should know more about this than I do. Were you in private practice by the way?"

Dangerous ground.

"Hospital. I was with a hospital?"

"Locally?"

119

"Paris."

"Ah, which one? And why did you give it up? I think it is so rewarding - healing people."

"It is."

"Which hospital was it?" he asks again.

"You wouldn't have heard of it. A small one. Chartreux Hospital."

I have dropped my voice and my eyes.

"Don't know it."

He has eaten the grapes.

"Coffee? Would you like a coffee or a tisane perhaps, Colin?"

"Tisane?"

"We French drink a tisane after a meal. To assist the digestion, that is."

"Ah, the doctor speaking."

"Not at all. It's common knowledge that a tisane will ease the digestive processes."

"In that case, I think I will try it. Not - I must say - that this meal will in any way play havoc with my digestive system. You are a fine chef, Bella. And I thank you!"

He remains sitting at the table while I am preparing the tisane in the kitchen.

"I chose citronella. It not only assists digestion but also boosts the immune system. And it relieves morning sickness," I explain, returning to the dining room.

"Morning sickness. Heavens!"

I fill two glasses with the deep-yellow tea from which drifts the sweet, tartly aroma of fresh lemons.

"I am a paediatrician," I say. "Used to be a paediatrician."

Oh hell. Why did I tell him that? I only have myself to blame should he now ask about it.

"How interesting. I mean it must be an interesting branch of the medical profession."

"It is. Was. For me."

"Why did you give it up? I mean it is lovely here and I

can understand that this place must have been irresistible
..."

"My mother fell ill. Died. So I came here. What do you
think of the tisane?"

"It's nice. I like it. But what made you give up your
medical work?"

I will have to try again to change the subject.

"Would you be looking around the region? I mean -
Normandy is beautiful and merits a visit. The mount, for
example, you ought to go there. I mean you must go there.
You might also walk the bay. Have you seen the Bayeux
tapestry? It's a little bit of a drive - bit of a ride - but it
would be worth it. But you must have seen it. I presume.
And the mount too. Though the mount is so extraordinary
one can see it over and over again. I can. At least. But you
may have no time to spare."

*Language was invented in order to conceal our thoughts from one
another.* Oh yes, Talleyrand knew what he was talking
about. *Papa, dear Papa, Talleyrand knew what he was talking
about.*

Colin pushes his chair back and gets up.

"I'm going to call it a day, Bella."

"Sure."

"Can I help you with the washing up?"

"Oh no. No need to. Thanks."

He nods.

"Good then, I will wish you a good night. Please do
not go to trouble to give me breakfast tomorrow morning.
I will just grab a cup of tea myself. I am sure I will find my
way around your lovely kitchen."

"Sleep well, Colin."

Did he notice I had not replied to his questions about
why I was no longer working as a doctor?

At the door he turns round.

"I will have time to spare. I will certainly visit the
mount. Thank you for suggesting it. Maybe - I don't know
- but maybe you would like to come with me one day? But

- it is as you wish, of course. It will have to be by car though - that is, if you do not wish to have the wind upset your hair. Kind of. Sort of. Your hair looks so nice every day."

-0-

I stack the dish washer and I clean up in the kitchen. It has started to rain again. The tinkling of a cow bell drifts from somewhere in the night. A dog howls. Up in the bedroom I pull the curtain aside and I put my face against the cold windowpane. I see only the black of the night. Land, sky, sea. Black. Black like the soul in its darkest hour. And I know all about that.

I crawl into bed and I pull the blanket over my head.

What got into me to have agreed to a guest this winter?

-0-

CHAPTER EIGHTEEN

Pulling a blanket over my head is something I used to do when I was a child. "Bella, *meine liebling*, hiding from a problem is not how to solve it," my father always said. He used to come and sit on my bed and always he sang the Christmas carol, *Rudolph, the red-nosed Reindeer* to try to cheer me up. *Rudolph, das kleine Rentier, seine Nase war so schön, denn sie war leuchtend rot. Das war nicht zu übersehn.* He sang until my head would pop from underneath the blanket when he would kiss me on my forehead and say, "There you are. Life's not bad, you know, my child."

The first time he coaxed me from underneath the blanket in this way was when Miss Matigot, my teacher, decided we in her class should draw up a family tree. She gave each of us a stencilled copy of a drawing of an oak tree onto which she had pasted thirty-four blank squares of paper. On these we were to write the names and whatever details of date and place of birth and death we had of our ancestors, going into the past as far as our great-great-great grandparents. I was eleven years old and I already knew what Miss Jambenoire talked about when she spoke of loins and of *un sale Boche*. I therefore knew my family tree was going to be different from those of my classmates. Of that of Marie Dumay who sat next to me, of Anselme Mathiot who sat behind me, of Nestor Toussaint, who was best in spelling, of Vincent Lebar who walked with elbow canes because he had polio when he was little, and of Florence Dubois whose father shot himself dead because his lumber business had gone bankrupt.

I took the drawing home as Miss Matigot said we should for our parents to help us fill in those thirty-four blank squares. "Ah *merde!*" I thought I heard my father exclaim when he saw the drawing. Had I not so feared the soap mouthwash, I would have said so too. One consolation was, that I knew, that with my mother's side of the family, I would not encounter a problem. Her people - the Desmarais - were French to every little hair on their body. Natives of Normandy, they had been marsh dwellers from way back and hence their surname. The family even had a coat of arms. My mother had a small tapestry on which the coat of arms showing green acacia branches around a suit of armour was embroidered in fine cross stitch. Proudly, she hung it in the first floor corridor.

After my father's initial expletive he announced he was not ashamed of being German. "I just do not want Bella to feel awkward in front of her classmates," he said.

Did I feel awkward!

"What do we have here?" Miss Matigot, her black hair braided into what I thought looked like a Roman emperor's crown, muttered on first seeing my tree.

"Miss! Miss!" Vincent Lebar called to her.

He banged one of his canes against the floor to attract her attention, as was his habit.

"Not now, Vincent."

She waved her right hand, the many metal bracelets hanging from her wrist, jingling like the bells around a cow's neck.

She called me to her table. A pencil stuck from the Roman crown. At times she took hold of the pencil to scratch underneath the hair; my classmates and I used to giggle about it saying behind her back that she had lice. She always did the scratching when she was angry, but on that morning she did not do so, which told me my family tree was not angering her. It had caught her interest.

"Bella, dear Bella, I see that your father was a German." she said quietly as if she and I were sharing a great secret.

"My father is still a German, Miss. When my mother goes voting he walks with her to the polling booth, but it is only because he does not want her to go on her own, as he is not allowed to vote because he is German. One day my brother and I will be able to vote because we are French."

"I see, Bella."

How could she not have seen what the situation was with all those German names, which my father had, eventually, proudly written down for me so I could copy them out onto the squares of white paper, stuck like the steps of a staircase over the left side of the oak tree. Wolff. Brunner. Hille. Werner. And more Wolff. Wolff. Wolff. The right side of the oak was for my mother's ancestors.

I was told I could return to my desk.

"Children!" Miss Matigot called out. "Bella's father was born in Berlin. Any of you have a parent who was not born here in France? It will be interesting to know."

"Miss! Miss! My father says her father is a *Boche*!" shouted Anselme Mathiot from his desk.

He kicked against the back of my chair as if to establish a fact.

"Anselme, if you wish to speak - as you know - you have to put up your arm and wait for me to give you permission to say something," Miss Matigot reprimanded him.

Anselme put up his arm, which like his face, was covered in freckles as large as wedding confetti.

"Yes, Anselme?" Miss Matigot acknowledged the raised arm.

"Miss, my father says Bella's father is a *Boche*."

"And what is a *Boche*, Anselme?"

"It is what Bella's father is, Miss."

Again, he kicked the back of my chair.

"Thank you, Anselme, for the information. Now, do sit

down."

Miss Matigot gave me a smile.

We had to pin the family trees to the blackboard with tiny coloured pins she had handed out. I thought I was going to bring up the boiled egg I had had for breakfast, my stomach heaved that much. There were all those French surnames on the family trees. Du Pont. Du Toit. Lacoffe. Leconte. Leborgne. Allais. Renard. Bruel.

"Your dad was a murderer!"

Anselme stood beside me at the blackboard and had whispered that to me.

"Did you say something, Anselme?" Miss Matigot asked.

She had stepped over to stand beside us.

"No, Miss. Nothing, Miss," said Anselme.

Later that day, in the playground, when my classmates were playing *escargot* - hopscotch - I sat out with Vincent Lebar as if I, like him, also had a shrivelled leg.

Walking home, knowing that my classmates knew what I had known since my first day at school with the help of Miss Jambenoire, I just wanted to cry, and, getting home and seeing my father, the sweat pouring over his handsome face and his blond hair pasted to his face from the effort he was putting into chopping up logs for our fireplace so we, his children and his wife, would not be cold, I, overwhelmed by my love for him, burst into tears.

"Bella, *meine liebling, was ist loss?*" he asked.

He reached for me.

"It's you … you're a *Boche* … and …"

I was going to say *and I love you all the same*, but the pain on my father's face at that moment had shut me up. Oh heaven! The pain … the pain I had caused him, my dear wonderful father having called him a *Boche!* The smile he had on seeing me was swept away as if it had been snatched off his face. And his eyes, his beautiful blue eyes, had become glassy and grey like the eyes of the dead fish at one of our Thursday markets.

"Don't you of all people speak to your father like that!" shouted my mother from behind me.

She told me to apologise to my father.

"Leave her, Henriette, leave the child ... she's just a child," my father begged.

"I will do no such thing, Rody!" she shouted.

Rody.

My mother always called my father Rody, and on the love letter she wrote him after he passed away and which Marius and I slipped between his ice-cold, stiff fingers – fingers, which would never hold our hands again - that was also how she addressed him. *My dear dear darling Rody.*

Standing at my father's side, the axe and the logs he had chopped, at their feet, my mother grabbed me by both my ears, by the lobes, and twisted them with all her might, so that I cried out with pain.

"You little bitch! Go to your room!"

I ran to my room to sit in a corner, my knees pulled up and my hands over my aching ears and I cried tears of shame. Sorrow and shame. Sorrow, because I knew everything there was to know about what the Germans did in the Second World War from books I helped myself to - ok, to be honest, which I had stolen - on the Wednesday afternoons on which our class was taken to the lending library in Avranches.

And shame not only because I had hurt my wonderful father, but because I did not want anyone to know I was half German.

Only years later, I was already studying medicine at the Sorbonne in Paris, did my mother ask me what happened at school that day and when I told her she turned around and walked away without having said a word, but that night I noticed that the Desmarais coat of arms was no longer hanging on the wall in the first floor corridor. That it hung nowhere. What she had done with it, I never discovered.

That night, I again pulled the blanket over my head.

-0-

CHAPTER NINETEEN

It would probably need a Sigmund Freud to explain why on some mornings the smell of Chartreux Hospital fills this house. This is so again this Friday morning. My nostrils are filled with the smell - I can even call it stench - of a mixture of stale urine, bloody bandages, weeping wounds, sweat, bland hospital soup, ether, and the mouthwash which the nurses gave the patients to get rid of their malodorous morning breath.

I wonder if Colin could also smell it this morning. He has gone out now. After breakfast - this morning I skipped having a croissant - he came in search of me and found me here in my library room.

He stood at the door, not stepping in.

"I will be out for a while, Bella."

I told him he would not have to tell me when he was going to go out.

"I just thought ..."

He did not finish the sentence.

I heard him rev the motorcycle's engine. *Vroom vroom vroom*!

For a moment I thought the engine would not take because when Marius's bike has been standing in the rain as Colin's has done since his arrival last Wednesday, the engine sometimes stalls.

The phone rings. I pick up the library room connection. It is Marion.

"How'z it?"

She is always in a good mood.

"I've taken a guest for the winter, Marion."

"Who's it? Anyone interesting? Not an old geriatric dear in need of a doctor?"

"It's a young English writer. Well, not exactly young."

"Like how old? Is he in a bath chair and in need of care, because in that case I am going to call you stupid."

"Our age."

"Mmm. Is he nice?"

"What do you mean by nice, Marion?"

I do so hate the word *nice*.

"Like does he have body odour, Bella? That would definitely make him not nice."

"For goodness sake, Marion!"

"So he *is* nice."

"He's a guest, Marion!"

"Mmm. Sounds promising."

"Why did you call?" I ask.

I want to change the direction her remarks are steering us.

"To ask how you were, Bella."

"I'm feeling fine. Excellent."

"Good."

I want to end the call.

"Give Marius and the girls my love."

"We are going skiing this Christmas. Switzerland. Saint Moritz. Very chic. Never been there. So we won't be coming up north."

So this is why she is phoning me.

"I think that I will go away for Christmas myself this year, Marion," I lie.

"Where to?"

"I rather fancy - Italy. Rome. Venice."

"Rome's awful at Christmas. Too many pilgrims and all crying buckets over the Pope's Urbi and Orbi. Not for me! As for Venice, it's damp in winter. Didn't you know? Your hair will go all frizzy. You will hate it."

"Thanks for being so encouraging, Marion."

We say goodbye.

I put the phone down.

Sitting still, thinking of the call, the large - over one thousand five hundred pages - German-English dictionary on the shelf in front of me draws my attention. I fetch it. It is heavy and slips from my hands and falls onto my desk. I flip it open. My eye catches the word *Schicksal*. Its gender is neutral - *das Schicksal*; the noun capitalised as they are in the German language and which looks so odd to me.

With my German, elementary as it is, taught to me, not at school, but by my father, I know that *Schicksal* means fate. Fate. Destiny. Karma. *Karma*: what we put into the universe, the universe will hand back to us. The good as well as the bad. *For you reap whatever you sow*: Book of Galatians, as Father Pierre so often reminds Sainte-Marie-sur-Brecque's faithless when they pass him on the street and he blocks their path to reprimand them for not attending mass. Terrible thought, when you come to think of it: reaping whatever we are sowing. Even more terrible is what always goes with it - according to Father Pierre that is: not only would *we* have to pay for *our* sins but so would our children, grandchildren, great grandchildren - those who come after us. *Who sinned, this man or his parents that he was born blind?* asked John the Apostle on seeing a blind man. Vindictive, if you ask me. Like shaving a woman's head because she fell in love with a German. Punishment, the French called it. And always did my uncles speak of the punishment that awaited my father for him having been a *Wehrmacht* soldier, for having worn the field-grey uniform. Therefore, from the time I read those books about the Second World War, I feared my father would reap what he had sown. So, understanding death as being a punishment, I used to seek out my father every morning on waking to make sure he had not died during the night. "You silly little person," he always said when I threw my arms around him, happy I had found him alive, yet troubled because I would, in that case, have to be the one who would have to do the reaping. I, not Marius. Why I never thought that my brother, as much my father's child as I, would have to do the reaping, I did not know.

I read what the large dictionary further writes about *das Schicksal*. It can be merciful. *Gnädiges Schicksal*. It is good to know this. It can be hard, bitter, adverse, unkind, tragic, inexorable, sinister, sad. Cruel: *Grausames Schicksal*. It is good to know this too because it eliminates nasty surprises.

I close the dictionary with a laugh. So much for *das Schicksal*: my father died in his sleep, never having had a day's illness in his life. "His heart just stopped Dr Alphonse told me," said my mother. She had telephoned me to Chartreux Hospital.

Truth, be told, at the Brissard twin's death, I did for a moment wonder whether it was not *grausames Schicksal* having come to collect its dues.

"Tell me, did the baby die because I was negligent?" I asked Nurse Bonnec.

"Of course not, Doc," she replied. "It was the hand of God."

The hand of God. Karma. Fate. Destiny. There you have it!

I put the dictionary back on the shelf and I walk from the library room, closing the door behind me. I will have to remember I am not alone here anymore and I will have to keep the door closed as I do when I have a house full of guests.

-0-

The Legros chicken which I bought two Thursdays ago has defrosted and it is lying on the work table in a pool of murky water. It will be our supper.

I try hard to remember how Gertrude once told me to go about cooking *poulet bonne femme*. This is what we will have tonight.

Wash and dry the chicken. Quarter it. Dice some carrot and a celery branch. Prepare some peas and do open a can of peas if you do not have fresh ones. Tinned peas it will have to be. Peel and slice some onions. Peeling the onions, I hold a matchstick between my lips so my eyes will not water. They water all the same. *Wash and dry some fresh parsley.* I must not chop it up because it is for decorating the final dish. *Wash and dry some white button mushrooms and chop them up too.* Not too finely, mind. *Get some salt and pepper from the cupboard in the larder. Get some rashers of lard from the fridge.* Before closing the fridge, I take out the dish with the butter, and I fetch the olive oil can from the larder. *Heat the butter and the olive oil.* I do so in Gertrude's favourite flameproof pot, the one with the pictures of some very yellow celery and very orange carrots around the side. I make sure the gas flame is not too high. *Wait till the butter has melted and add the chicken. Brown the chicken on all sides. When it is brown, add the vegetables and the lard and fry all for about five minutes before adding the mushrooms.*

For a while, I stand at the bay window behind which dusk is falling and I listen to the sound of sizzling coming from the stove. I tell myself I am cooking *poulet bonne femme* for the first time in my life.

Back at the stove, I stir the ingredients with Gertrude's big wooden spoon which she is inclined to lick when she should not do so. Always, I reprimand her.

"The chef must taste, Miss."

The ingredients, nicely brown, I pour a glass of dry white wine, and half a glass of chicken broth, and a few tablespoons of white port wine over it, and I cover the flameproof pot with its lid which also has very yellow celery and very orange carrots all along the rim. Gertrude usually allows the chicken to cook like this for about forty minutes and every now and then she pours a small glass of water into the pot.

"Mustn't dry out, must it, Miss."

The chicken cooking, I peel some potatoes and start boiling them in another of Gertrude's pretty pots.

Hoping that neither the chicken nor the potatoes would cook dry, and therefore burn, I go upstairs to my bedroom to make myself look presentable.

I powder my nose, shiny from the heat of the stove, and I want to comb my hair. My hair looks awful. A mess. "My little Blondie," my father sometimes called me, brushing my rebel curls with my mother's large brush, strands of her dark hair caught between the steel teeth. Blondie: the cartoon character, wife of Dagwood. It was my father's favourite cartoon strip. Whenever we went to Avranches he went to the newsagents to buy the London papers especially so he could read the *Blondie and Dagwood* cartoon strip.

Ought I to go to Salon Larissa, Sainte-Marie-sur-Brecque's hair salon next week, get Larissa to cut the mess? I have always hated my curls. I wanted straight hair like my mother. I never minded having blond hair though. Why, I do not know, especially as I should have hated being a blonde, because the German women on the photos in those books about the Second World War all had blonde hair.

Having slipped into a clean blouse and pair of jeans, I sit down at the window, the bay and the mount in front of me in the distance, now dark.

I wonder what time Colin will be back.

Of course, I only want to know because I do not want the food to be overcooked.

-0-

CHAPTER TWENTY

I am in the courtyard. Because of the threshing of the rain, the trees and plants have shed some of their leaves, and I have come to clean up. Night having fallen and, as I have not switched the lights on here, I am working in semi-darkness, the only light coming from the kitchen.

Colin returned a few minutes ago. It was a noisy return. Coming up the driveway he revved the motorcycle's engine as if he were a stuntman and preparing to become airborne and fly over the house's roof for a scene in an action film. I have decided not to ask him what that was about, just as I will not ask him where he has spent the day, whether he has had a pleasant day. *Not my business.* This is what I am telling myself.

He appears in the doorway.

"I'm just going to brush up and then I will be down for supper."

Fine. Sure. I have cooked. Cooked for you, my winter guest.

Back inside and carrying the food to the dining room, I see Colin has switched all the lights in the room off, but not the chandelier, which hangs right above the table where we have been sitting these past nights, and where I have again tonight set two places.

He sees me.

"I did not ask - I hope you do not mind, but I have switched off some of your beautiful chandeliers."

"No problem."

I do not look at him because I am not all that pleased

he is making himself so at home at Le Presbytère.

We sit down.

"Shall we just help ourselves?" I ask.

"Thank you, yes, and this looks delicious."

"I hope it will taste delicious too."

"Sure it will."

"Why? Why are you sure it will?"

I can see he is unable to interpret the mood behind the question.

"You're French," he says, hesitatingly.

"And so?"

"French cuisine … In England we believe all French can cook."

"Which is of course a myth."

I nearly accused him of sexism again. And racism.

"I suppose so," he says.

"It is so."

"What did you do today?" he changes the subject.

"My library needs a thorough clean up. I started on that."

"May I have a look at your books one day, please? I could not help noticing you have a few thousand. Must have a few thousand."

"I've a few."

Four thousand eight hundred and forty two: arranged alphabetically starting with A.Abdel-Malek's *'Egypte; Société Militaire'* which my father bought and ending with Stefan Zweig's *'The Royal Game'*, which I bought from one of Paris' bouquinists.

"Which is the last book you've read?" he asks.

I shrug, not sure to tell him about the German dictionary.

"No, don't reply to that. It was a stupid question. A childish one. I apologise."

"My father's German dictionary," I reply all the same, and of course, in all honesty.

"Lord! I do not think I've ever heard of anyone reading

a dictionary. I had a landlady once in Rome who read recipe books though."

"The dictionary caught my eye and I felt an urge to flip through it. I was not reading it as such. My eye then fell on a word."

"It would be interesting to know which word it was."

"It was the word *schicksal*."

"... destiny? Am I right to think it means destiny?"

I nod. I wait for his reaction, my lips tightly closed.

"Interesting."

"Do you believe in destiny, Colin?"

"I was going to ask you whether you do."

"I do not know whether I do."

"Your compatriot Voltaire did."

"You are referring to his *Zadig ou la Destinée*."

"You've read it!"

"Had to. School, you know. But I've a copy in my library. I did not buy it though. The book was my father's. It's a collector's item. Must be worth a small fortune. "

"Well, Voltaire was not the only one to believe one's life has been predestined and its course is beyond our - beyond human - control. May I speak of Pasternak?"

"Of course. Please do."

"The Russian speaks of *sud'ba* which my Russian-English dictionary translates as *destiny*. Destiny or *fate*. Life deals us our cards but - and this is the interpretation - we alone play the cards. One cold October day, snow cascading down on Moscow, Pasternak walked into the *Novy Mir* office and someone said to him: *Boris Leonidovich, let me introduce one of your most ardent admirers.* The admirer was Olga Ivinskaya, and so began one of the world's greatest but saddest love stories. That is *sud'ba*. Nearer home - a man who hated shopping and therefore tried never to have to go into a shop - had to buy a young lady, whom he was taking out for dinner, a bouquet of flowers so he had no choice but to go to a florist shop. It was in the cards which he had been dealt that from behind the counter stepped a most beautiful girl. Six months later they were married. That man was my father and the girl in the florist shop was my mother. That too is *sud'ba*."

"That's beautiful," I say.

"That's romantic. What we all need," he says.

The grandfather clock starts to chime. *He lives to silence all my fears ... He lives to wipe away my tears ... He lives to calm my troubled heart ... He lives all blessings to impart ...*

I wait for the time to strike. It is a quarter past nine. Just as my father used to do, Colin sung quietly to the chime. His voice, like that of my father, is a baritone.

Is it my imagination or did I this time find solace in those words?

Not wanting to know, I drop my eyes and hurriedly I resume eating, my knife and fork scraping over the porcelain. There is no movement or sound from Colin. Is he looking at me? I feel that so he is, but I do not dare look up and at him. I continue eating. My *poulet bonne femme* has turned out quite tasty; not too salty, not tough, yet not overcooked either. I hear Colin clear his throat.

"I wonder - I wonder if your clock will fit onto my bike? I would just love to take it with me when I leave."

His voice was loud and jovial. Too jovial to be natural.

When I leave was what he said. *Of course he will leave.*

The clock is ticking the seconds away. The ticking is suddenly ear-splittingly loud. Tick tock! Tick tock! Time never stands still.

"You would have to dismantle the clock. Break it up into pieces," I say, looking up.

He nods. It is a nod which has a waiting quality to it.

He rests his elbows on the table and drops his chin into his cupped hands and looks straight at me, wordlessly.

He is playing with me. God Almighty, he is playing with me; the cat playing with the mouse, waiting for his moment to strike. The cat's eyes are asking: Are you frightened of me ... because if you are not, you ought to be, because I am capable of devouring you! I will devour you!

No, bloody hell, this mouse is not for devouring.

"I'll wash up," I say.

"I'll come and help you."

"No!"

The word was almost a shout.

"In that case, I will go see if I can write a couple of hundred words. I won't type - don't worry. Rest assured, I won't type at night and rob you of your sleep."

At the door, he turns.

"I almost forgot to say, I will be out all of tomorrow."

"So will I."

I lied.

"In that case, don't prepare anything for dinner. I will grab something when I'm out. I will be off first thing in the morning, so I won't be having breakfast either. And oh yes, at what time at night will you be locking the front door?"

"I won't lock the door, not tomorrow night. You can lock it once you're back in."

-0-

CHAPTER TWENTY-ONE

Larissa is a redhead today. When I last came to the salon - about three months ago - she was a champagne-blonde. I have always found her regal in the Catherine Deneuve way; friendly but not to the extent of hugging and kissing her clients addressing them as *ma chérie*.

"Good morning, Dr Wolff. What can we do for you this morning?"

Larissa shows me to a lilac chair in front of a heart-shaped mirror within a lilac frame.

"Oh Larissa, just the usual," I tell her.

"The usual no longer looks like the usual, Doctor Wolff."

"Tell it to me, Larissa!"

"You should come in more often, Doctor Wolff."

She's a name person: it will be Doctor Wolff this and Doctor Wolff that as long as I am in here. *Should not have come.*

The tap water is cold.

"How's this for temperature, Doctor Wolff?"

"Could be a little warmer, thanks."

Her assistant, a young gay with green spiked hair, puts a cup of black coffee down beside the wash basin. Larissa tells him to take it back to the kitchen and to keep it warm as I will still be under the tap for a while. She pours cold shampoo over my hair twice and after having rubbed it in thoroughly, her long, red nails, digging into my scalp, she applies a cream conditioner. It smells of coconut; coconut as she tells me will make my hair grow really fast.

"Just don't get it onto your face because you will become all hairy. Ghrr!"

Jonny - the assistant - laughs revealing beautifully white teeth; he must have had an adoring mother who took him to the dentist every six months as our Ministry of Health advises, his equally adoring papa not having minded settling the bill.

When I was a child, I hated going to the dentist. It was excruciatingly painful - emotionally painful. Dr Henri Brodard was the dentist's name. His son was Baudelaire Brodard; he was my first ever boyfriend. Recalling both of the Brodards is still excruciatingly emotionally painful for me, but as there was not another dentist in Sainte-Marie-sur-Brecque it was not as if my mother could have taken Marius and me elsewhere to have our cavities filled. And ... Baudelaire was at my school, a class ahead of me, and with his Californian surfing looks - curly blond hair, bulging biceps and sky-blue eyes - he was not easy to ignore.

Dr Brodard was a Second World War hero. When France capitulated to the Nazi Germans in 1940, he set sail in the family pleasure boat for Dover and joined General Charles de Gaulle's Free French in London. There are two kinds of French. There are those who resisted the Nazi Germans and those who joined them - the collaborators. But no, I need to correct myself here. There was still another kind; the women who, like my mother had slept with German soldiers, either for money or for love, the one kind having been, to their compatriots, as bad as the other. Dr Brodard having been with De Gaulle in London, a detail he never failed to remind his patients of, was therefore of the right stuff.

"Wolff?" he queried, the first time my mother walked into his surgery, her hand firmly clutching mine. "Sounds familiar."

"We live here. Not in the village itself, but my husband

Rodolph and I own and run Le Presbytère."

"*Ah bon!*"

It was a snort.

He asked my name.

"Bella," my mother replied on my behalf.

I stood behind her, holding onto her skirt in fear, but at that stage my fear was provoked by the big green apparatus in front of me from which a dangerously sharp drill protruded, and not by the man himself.

"Come, sit down here, Miss Bella."

He pulled me away from my mother and pushed me down onto the brown leather chair under the big green apparatus. I wiggled in order to sit comfortably and one of my plaits - my hair was combed into two plaits those days - brushed against one of his hands which he went to wash under a tap in the room. He did not close the tap properly and for the rest of our visit it dripped water loudly into the stained sink underneath it.

Not on that visit, but on the next, a week later, Dr Brodard asked my mother straight out at which death camp my father was based during the war.

"He was in France during the war," she replied.

I could see she was trying hard to smile. Not to get angry.

"So, he was one of those who stole our art works and our wine - and women."

He looked at my mother, sniffing at the air, as if he could smell a stinking rotten tooth.

At that time, I have not yet read those books about the Second World War, so I did not understand Dr Brodard's rancour and I thought he, like my mother's family, just did not like the German people, so his remark did not upset me and I therefore could not understand why my mother cried when she told my father about our day at the dentist. Later, after I have read up about the Second World War and the dishy Baudelaire and I were sharing the sandwiches in our lunch boxes, I was the one who cried after each visit to the dentist. I cried because I so fancied Baudelaire and I wanted to become his wife when I was grown-up but feared his father would never accept me as his daughter-in-law.

Baudelaire - Beau as all in the village called him because of his good looks - and I used to go to the beach. He could swim, but I could not.

"You live by the sea and you can't swim. Explain that one to me, Bella."

He said that more than once.

One day he offered to teach me how. Despite my protests, he dragged me into the sea and with a boy's clumsiness at wooing, he kicked my feet from underneath me, and when I did not surface, he dived down to find me, and pulled me back to the surface.

"*Merde*," he said.

He shook his head like a wet dog who wanted to get water out of its eyes and ears. Immediately, he apologized for having used such an expletive, and I, wanting to show him I might not be able to swim, but I was certainly grown-up, called him a bugger, and of course I had no idea what the word meant. As there was no reaction of shock from him, I think he also did not know. The two of us - I never called him Beau because I loved the name Baudelaire and I had already decided that one day we would call the son we were going to produce Baudelaire too - used to kiss, but never did we go further than that. As it is, the kisses were never passionate; they were short closed-mouth kisses, his hands always behind his back and mine hanging uncertainly at my sides.

When I set off for the lycée in Nantes, Baudelaire too left, but for one of the top schools of Paris.

"I will write," he promised.

It was a promise which he sealed with another kiss, one which was a little longer and with more feeling behind it than those previous ones.

"I will wait for your first letter," I told him.

He never wrote.

Our paths crossed again in Paris when we were both at the Sorbonne but in different faculties because he was studying politics for a career in the diplomatic service. He was with a girl who I thought was a little plump, which surprised me, because he was so athletic and always stopped me from eating sweets saying it would make me fat and *fat was ugly*.

The girl's name was Anne; her father was a surgeon. Baudelaire told her I was studying medicine.

"Do you think you will make it? It's awfully hard getting a medical degree, you know," she told me.

I shot a glance at him, but he failed to come to my defence.

The remark she made at our next meeting hurt me even more. No, hurt is not the correct word: it knocked me sideways.

"Beau tells me your father was a guard in Auschwitz or somewhere equally horrible."

She had lifted her voice and all those who sat around us - it was at a concert at the Olympia music hall - swung round to see who the remark had been aimed at.

"My father ... my dad ... was in France during the war and nowhere near a concentration camp," I muttered.

I did not look at her, and neither at Baudelaire. I looked towards the stage where the musicians were tuning their instruments.

"Drop it, my love," Baudelaire said to fat Anne looking with love deep into her black eyes.

"No, why should I, Beau? Her father was a goddamn Nazi."

What was I to reply to that, because, yes, my father was a Nazi; he was in the *Wehrmacht* fighting for Hitler, so he was a Nazi.

That was a night I again pulled the blanket over my head.

-0-

I take Larissa for lunch at the Vaybee because it is Saturday and I do not fancy eating alone in a restaurant on a weekend day. I also invite Jonny but he does not *do lunch;* he is watching his figure.

Frascot says he is glad to see me.

"You should come in every day, Miss."

"Do you want to drive me to drink, Frascot?"

"He's homo," whispers Larissa to me, her eyes looking up from the handwritten menu.

"Frascot?"

"Noooooooo! Jonny?"

Homo – homosexual.

"I've guessed as much, Larissa."

"And such a nice guy too."

"Sure. Why shouldn't he be?"

"His parents do not know."

"So, he ought to tell them."

"They wouldn't understand. Deeply religious. Has own pew next door and every Sunday they are there, kissing the Bible and what not."

Next door - Notre Dame Sainte-Marie church.

We order Frascot's rabbit with three mustard sauces and he serves it in a large copper pot we are to keep sizzling hot on an open flame.

The rabbit is delicious as always and next we order apple pie with whipped cream.

"I think I will go down to the beach now, Larissa," I say.

"Oh my goodness, Doctor Wolff. Your hair!"

She throws her ringed hands up in the air.

"I hope the shampoo and dyes won't damage those baubles of yours, Larissa."

I know the stones in the baubles are not really precious stones: she claims they are.

"Just glass," she admits for the first time and winks.

"Well, I never!"

"Not to tell anyone though, Doctor Wolff."

She winks yet again.

I drive a short distance along the coast and away from the mount to the cove where Baudelaire and I used to go. He used to dive from one of the jutting rocks while I played in the sand like a child, but with the very grown-up thoughts of the day he and I will be loving parents to our own little Baudelaire.

I pull up on a grassy knoll and walk down to the beach. The sand is warm between my toes. I sit down on the very rock from which Baudelaire used to dive. I stretch my legs out in front of me so I am able to dip my feet into the clear blue sea. The water is icy, and quickly, with a shiver, I pull my legs back up and hold my feet up towards the sun to dry. I know should I fall into the sea, I, unable to swim, will drown.

Someone told me Baudelaire did not marry Anne but a diplomatic corps interpreter. I wonder if they have a son named Baudelaire.

-0-

Back at Le Presbytère there is no sign of Colin, but I remember I did not give him a key to the front door, so had he decided to return before nightfall, he would not have been able to get in and might have set off again.

Ought I give him a key?

If I do, might I not be making him feel too much at home? *But is this not what I want?* Just to make sure it is not, that I did not let Larissa make me look good in order to please Colin, I pick up my hairbrush and I brush her blow wave right out.

At midnight, I go to bed.

Soon, I hear the drone of Colin's motorcycle.

I wait for the click which means he is in the house and he is locking the front door. He goes straight to his room. Steady were his footsteps: so, he has not been drinking. Here at Le Presbytère we always listen for the footsteps to know whether to expect a problem from a guest who has had too many.

I hear the click of another door.

Colin has closed his bedroom door.

I hope to fall asleep quickly.

-0-

CHAPTER TWENTY-TWO

It is Wednesday and Fred is here to do the gardening.

"Miss, it was a good rain that fell," he says.

"Good, yes, Fred."

We are in the kitchen.

"Fred, I've broken our rule this winter. Le Presbytère has a guest."

I wait for his reaction, his reply.

"So I've heard. Frascot told me. "

Curiosity is written all over his face.

"Make yourself a bowl of coffee, Fred."

Colin has been at Le Presbytère for ten days now. He appears in the kitchen's doorway and Fred gasps for breath. Why? I can only guess he is struck by the good looks of Le Presbytère's guest.

"Good morning, Mr Fred. I am Colin."

Fred is wearing green Wellingtons to which dried mud clings and a green plastic apron over white overalls, so obviously he is the gardener I told Colin about.

Fred asks Colin whether he would like a bowl of coffee.

Eagerly, Colin accepts.

"Not a bowl though, Mr Fred. Just a small cup, please."

The two go out into the Frida Kahlo courtyard and, sipping their coffee, they walk from one exotic plant to another, Fred telling Colin whatever he knows about each plant. Colin is listening with genuine interest and asking questions. The two men are from such different worlds, yet they appear to be getting on well. It did not escape me that Fred did not like Jean-Louis and that the sentiment was mutual.

Fred brings the two emptied coffee cups to the kitchen.

"Miss, Mr Colin is going to help with the gardening today."

"Really? He's a man from the city, Fred, so I would say what he knows about gardening is dangerous."

"He climbs mountains, Miss."

"Mountains?" I ask. "Are you sure?"

"He climbed the Eiger, Miss. Told me."

"The Eiger?"

"Yes, Miss. He said it is in Switzerland, Miss."

A moment ago I was astonished. Now, I am angry, but not at Fred, but at myself. I have not managed to pierce Colin's reserve, but my gardener, a man with little education, has done so within minutes of meeting him. What does this make me? A woman with no social skills? A tongue-tied moron?

"People do. Climb mountains. Climb the Eiger. So what, Fred!" I say.

I can see Colin through the window. He is yet again saluting me. This time he is doing so with a gleeful, playful, boyish smile. He must have guessed Fred was telling me about the Eiger and he must have seen the surprise on my face.

I turn my back to the window.

"I'll leave the two of you to it, Fred. I will drive down to the village. Buy a few things."

Walking across the courtyard to the parking bay, I return Colin's salute. My salute, unlike those he offered me, is clumsy, my forefinger almost in my right eye. The gesture spreads a smile right across his face, his eyes becoming tiny buttons within a few thin lines.

"Please do see to it that Mr Colin does not fall from a tree because Le Presbytère's insurance does not cover such an eventuality," I call out to Fred, looking back.

I run down the steps to the parking bay.
I do not look back.

-0-

So Colin climbs mountains. My father also climbed mountains. He was good at skiing too; he was an excellent skier. That this was so led to one of the most painful episodes of my childhood.

One winter, Miss Jambenoire decided the school would go skiing on the Christmas break. She needed an experienced skier to accompany the children as their instructor. No volunteers came forward: Normans are good at swimming and not at skiing.

My father was able to ski almost before he was able to walk steadily. His family - Berliners - had each winter taken the train the seven-hundred or so kilometres south to the Bavarian ski resort of Mittenwald. The family owned a house there on the town's main street - I still have a photo of the house, a white two-storey with a grey slate roof that slanted almost to the ground on one side. In 1941 when Hitler's *Gebirgsjäger* mountain infantry was formed, my grandfather Johann suggested to my father, then already in France, that, because he was such an excellent skier, he should request to be transferred to the troop, considered an elite one. By then my father had met my mother and not having wanted to leave her, he ignored his father's suggestion. Strangely, never did my father ski again. Miss Jambenoire having been in search of a skiing instructor, my mother asked my father whether he would not like to go with the children.

"Henriette, what gives you the idea I would want to?" he asked.

His eyes sparkled: he obviously had already thought of it.

"If you do it, Bella and Marius can go along. I wouldn't want them to go with just anyone," she told him.

That night when I went to the kitchen to fetch a glass of milk, I heard them discuss it when I passed their bedroom. They were speaking in whispers, but a child hears whispering more clearly than the loudest scream.

The following morning my father put on his best suit for calling in on Miss Jambenoire, the woman who had until then refused to speak to him. She did so again. She told her secretary to tell my father to wait outside on the corridor because she was busy. My father stood out in that corridor for forty-five minutes just like an errant schoolboy waiting to be whipped. It amused the children; walking along the corridor on their way to the playground for their mid-morning break, they mimed a whipping. I must however in all honesty say it was not a gesture of malice on their part, but one of empathy; it was something we all did when one of our mates was sent to the headmistress's office for punishment.

Miss Jambenoire did not break her vow of silence towards my father. After having made him wait, she sent her secretary out to the corridor to tell him she did not speak to Nazis. That night I again heard my parents whisper to each other; on that occasion I went to stand outside their bedroom, hoping they would discuss what had happened at the school. Not long was I standing there, trembling in fear they might open the door, when they started to whisper.

"I thought the war is over," I heard my father say.

"Rody, it is," my mother replied.

"Not here, not here in the village, it is not," he said, his voice trembling with emotion.

He suggested we ought consider leaving for Germany.

"And leave behind Le Presbytère for which we have worked so hard. No, Rody, we must stand and fight," was what I heard my mother tell him.

"Henriette, they will never allow me to forget."

"But *we* love you. I love you, and our Bella and Marius love you," she argued.

I ran back to my room because what started in that bedroom then was not for little ears to hear.

A few days later a letter arrived at Le Presbytère which was signed *Bernadette Jambenoire (Miss), Head, Sainte-Marie-sur-Brecque Primary School.*

The woman wrote that because of a most unfortunate incident she has been compelled to cancel the children's skiing trip in the Alps. She did not supply further details, but she and her secretary did not fail to spread the news around the village that the Nazi Rodolph Wolff through his actions had made it impossible for the trip to continue.

"Say, Bella, are you a Nazi too like your father?" Marie Dumay whispered to me from her side of the bench she and I shared.

By then there was not a soul in the village who had not heard the story and Vincent Lebar told me that although he would not have been able to ski because of the polio, he looked forward to the trip.

"The doctor told my mom the fresh mountain air will do my weak lungs a world of good. I may now die because my lungs will pack it in, and Bella, it will all be your father's fault!"

Vincent Lebar did not die because my father stopped him from going to the Alps that Christmas: he lives in Paris, a married man with four children. He comes to the village often to put flowers on his parents' grave; he used to greet me when we passed in the village - said, "Hello, and how are you, Bella?" - but he no longer does so.

-0-

In Sainte-Marie-sur-Brecque I call in at the bakery, suitably named *Amandine* after Amandine, wife of the baker, Olivier Richer, but also after the *amandine,* the French almond cake, one of Olivier's specialities. Knowing Fred is always hungry when he comes gardening and that he will be so again today, I am looking for something to buy for lunch.

I point to a quiche on a refrigerated shelf.

"This looks just what I am after."

"It's for six, Miss," warns Amandine.

"Thanks, Amandine. A quiche big enough for six is just what I want."

Yellow curls fall over her face, which is always red from the heat from the back room, where I can see Olivier and an assistant using long flat boards dusted with flour to scoop baked *baguettes* from a wood-burning oven. I buy all Le Presbytères' bread and pastries from the Richers because baking over wood and not over gas or electricity, as is the norm these days here in France, gives their bread a crispy yellowish crust and a light interior much appreciated by my guests.

I can see Amandine is waiting for an explanation why I would want such a big quiche. I do not enlighten her.

"If you are having lunch guests, what about an *amandine*, Miss?" asks Olivier.

He has stepped from the backroom, and looking like a ghost with his face, hair, hands and arms covered in flour.

"Yes, why not? It will be nice with coffee afterwards."

After what asks Amandine's face while she transforms a piece of cardboard into a pretty box for the *amandine* which she ties with a pink string.

"Hold it by the string. It won't snap," she tells me.

The quiche too she puts in a box, but not a pretty pink one, and I put both boxes on the Merc's rear seat for the drive back to Le Presbytère.

-0-

The two men are in the front garden. Colin is also now wearing a green plastic apron - must be one of the spare ones Fred keeps in his neat gardening shed at the bottom of my back garden. Both were down on all fours when I drove through the gate, but they rise to their feet as I drive by. Fred never wears a hat, but Colin is wearing a baseball cap with the words *Big Apple* across the front; must be his own because Fred would not even know a baseball cap exists. I am happy to see Colin is not wearing his back to front as the youths do these days.

I park the Mercedes, next I go tell the men I have something for their lunch.

Fred smacks his lips.

"Thank you very much, Miss, feeling a bit peckish I must admit."

Colin stands with his feet a little apart, looking at me. He looks so assured, so confident what he was doing, when I arrived, was done well. He has a heap of dead leaves at his feet. He is wearing Wellingtons like Fred. They must be his own because I know Fred has just the one pair.

"I will leave the two of you - Fred ... Colin."

"What time would you like us at the table?" asks Colin.

He transfers his weight from one foot to another, suddenly not as confident as a moment ago. I wonder why.

Overhead clouds have started to form. I point at them.

"As soon as these open up, or should they pass us by, you can come through to the kitchen in ... shall we say ... about an hour?"

"It won't rain, Miss, so Colin and I will be with you in an hour."

Colin and I. They are indeed getting on well.

-0-

As I said, Fred did not like Jean-Louis. None of the staff did. As for my mother, uncertain about whether he would become her son-in-law and therefore treading carefully, tried not to reveal she did not like him either. Marius and Marion liked him. Marius, because of his guilt at distancing himself from my parents' health problems and letting me deal with those, and using Le Presbytère as a place for free weekends for him, his wife and children when they wanted to be served hand and foot. Marion, because she is a romantic.

"He is so charming, so dishy, dear sister-in-law. You should fence him in."

Jean-Louis was not to be fenced in.

Charissa and Carmen, his two daughters, told me so.

Jean-Louis decided to have a few friends over to his apartment.

"Will this be a party?" I wanted to know.

If so, I wanted to know what I should wear because at that stage of our relationship I had not met any of his friends and I wanted to make a good impression.

"Sort of a party. Yes."

"Do I therefore not have to wear a dress, but just a sort of dress?"

"You will steal the show, no matter what you wear, and should you wear nothing at all, even more so."

His eyes were fixed lovingly on me.

Jean-Louis' apartment was marvellous. I am sure many of his girlfriends would have wanted to move in with him just for the view of the Eiffel Tower from his windows, to wake up at night, the tower's dark shape at the foot of the bed like a sentinel. The apartment itself was a marvel too and I am sure when he gave it up to return to the family's apartment in the Paris suburb of artificial, boring and dull Neuilly, the hearts of its wealthy residents beating to the tick tock of the clock on the trading floor at Paris' *Bourse,* he missed, what he always dismissed as, *three hundred and thirty metres of wrought iron:* the tower.

The apartment was a split-level penthouse.

Of course he would be able to afford a split-level penthouse, he's a lawyer, Marius had scoffed.

The first time I went to the apartment - a few days after our return from Geneva - I thought I had walked into a dream orchestrated by Salvador Dali. The living-cum-dining room on the lower floor was vast. In one corner stood a light-grey corner sofa, a large, bare window behind it. In another corner stood a black Chesterfield sofa and a scarlet-red dining table with white upright café chairs around it. In the middle of the room stood a silver-white love chair and scattered across the black-and-white tiled floor were plastic poufs in every conceivable colour, the light from metal bow lamps reflecting off the plastic. On the wall facing the window hung a huge star-shaped mirror; I could not help thinking of the giant holes Jean-Louis had to make in the wall to hold the mirror in place and wondering what his landlord would make of those. On the other walls hung huge seri- and -lithographs of abstract landscapes and also a huge reproduction of Andy Warhol's *Marilyn Monroe*. In the bedroom, over a super king-size oriental platform bed with a dark blue fusion mattress, flanked on both sides by a bonsai tree, hung another huge reproduction, a serigraph of Salvador Dali's blue and grey *Sacrament of the Last Supper*. I thought the Dali so unsuitable for a bedroom and always, in our most intimate moments, I wished I had covered Jesus' face with a sheet, and silently did I always thank the twelve apostles on the painting for hiding their faces. Much more acceptable did I find Andy Warhol's *Che Guevara* which hung in the kitchen. Che was so very manly: I am sure he would have loved our nocturnal activities in the bedroom.

On the night of the party, I stood on Quai Branly, the tower on my left, and I looked across the Seine and up at Jean-Louis' building on Avenue President Kennedy. His windows shimmered in the half-light of evening, and I realised every bow lamp in the apartment must be switched on. I wore a new grey dress I bought on the insistence of Marion who accompanied me to her favourite Rue du Faubourg-St-Honoré boutique, and I suspected I looked elegant, even stunning, yet when I walked across the river on Pont d'Iena, my lips started to quiver with nervousness. In the elevator going up to the apartment, I could hardly breathe. What was I so nervous about?

Meeting Jean-Louis' friends?

I had a key to his apartment, but I thought it highly inappropriate to let myself in, so I rang the doorbell. A total stranger opened the door and told me to step right in. Jean-Louis, standing at the scarlet-red dining table saw me and waved to me to come over. He was talking to a grey-haired man in a dark suit and scarlet red tie which matched the table. I found it so ridiculous, that a real smile immediately replaced the quivering one.

Jean-Louis kissed me on both cheeks.

"*Belle belle ma belle* Bella," he whispered into my ear.

He took my hand, led me around the room, introducing me to people as we passed them. Pierre, Albert, Annie, Victor. Mike, who was from New York - *Hi Doc! I've got piles*, was his drunken greeting - and Ilze, who was from Hamburg - *Jean-Louis told me you are half German, how nice!*

In the kitchen, I was introduced to a blonde dressed from head to toe in white leather, who, was she not mixing pink and purple cocktails, I would have been mistaken for a giant meringue. Her name escapes me, but she was a dancer at the *Crazy Horse Saloon.*

Jean-Louis left me in the kitchen to return to his guests, some of them who had started to dance to a *slow* sung in American English - *luv* sang the singer and not *love* - coming from Jean-Louis' large and expensive steel and glass hi-fi player. Not wanting to dance and not having anything say to the Meringue I made my way up the wooden staircase, the usual creak of the wood muted by the music, to go to the bedroom. I was hoping to be able to sit down there for a few moments of isolation and reflection, but a surprise awaited me: two dark-haired girls sat on the bed, trying to solve the mystery of a Rubik Cube. I presumed they were Charissa and Carmen and they had taken their father's Cube from downstairs where he, having been unable to align the colours, had turned it into an ornament, its colours perfectly matching those of the room.

One of the girls looked up from the Cube.

"Good evening."

"Good evening. Any luck?"

I pointed to the Cube.

"It's easy to do," she snapped.

She childishly hid the unsolved Cube in the folds of the duvet quilt on the bed.

"In that case, you should show your father how to do it," I said.

"Who are you?" she asked.

"Are you my dad's new girlfriend?" asked the other girl.

"My name's Bella."

"I'm Carmen," said the girl who had spoken to me first.

She held a small hand out to me.

"I'm Charissa," said the other one.

"Hello, you two!"

"Are you my dad's new girlfriend?" Carmen repeated her sister's question.

"We know he has a girlfriend again because we could smell her when we walked into the bathroom on our arrival."

"Huh?"

"Not like smell in *stink*. Like in *Dior*."

"That's a relief."

The three of us laughed.

"What do you do, Bella?" Carmen wanted to know.

"How do you mean? I've come to your father's party."

"No. For a living."

"I'm a doctor."

"Gosh! Do you cut people open?" asked Charissa.

She rubbed a hand over her flat tummy.

"Depends."

"Like who do you cut open?" asked Carmen.

"Like little girls who ask too many questions."

"I'm twelve," Carmen quickly told me.

She stood up and visibly pulled herself upwards to appear tall and grownup.

"And how old are you, Charissa?"

"Fourteen. I was a mistake."

She brushed a dark curl from her pretty face.

"How do you mean?"

I wondered whether she meant what I thought she did.

"My mom became pregnant when she and my dad had not yet been to the town hall," she whispered as if the three of us were sharing a big secret.

Been to the town hall. Been to the town hall for the mayor to marry them.

"I see."

"Are you shocked?" asked Carmen.

"I ... no ... good heavens, no!"

I was shocked, yes. In a way. I was even a little angry because that was a detail Jean-Louis had not told me.

"Is my father going to marry you?" asked Carmen.

"Of course he's not! He never marries his girlfriends because he is married to Mom, you stupid!" Charissa angrily told Carmen.

"Our mother's name is Colette. She makes the nicest fries in the world," said Carmen.

"Can you make fries?" Charissa wanted to know from me.

"Yes."

"I bet your fries aren't anywhere as nice as Mom's."

Just then, Jean-Louis walked into the bedroom.

"Oh, so the three of you have met."

"She's pretty," said Carmen.

"Not ugly like that other one," said Charissa.

"Come on you two, stop your nonsense," reprimanded Jean-Louis.

The two screamed with laugher.

"Wow, she was ugly!" said Carmen.

Jean-Louis had blushed.

"I told you to stop your nonsense, so do so. Come on

downstairs and sing *Waterloo* for us," he told the two.

We made our way down the stairs. The Meringue and a black Adonis in tight jeans and shimmering tank-top were entwined in a fervent embrace which needed a bed, or judging by the urgency in their movements, just the floor under our feet.

Someone put Abba's *Waterloo* on the player and we formed a circle around Charissa and Carmen. The two clumsily started to move their legs forward and back and to the side to the beat of the music.

My my ... At Waterloo Napoleon did surrender ... Oh yeah ...

Everyone sang along, the voices drowning those of Anni-Frid and Agnetha.

Jean-Louis clicked his fingers and motioned for us to click ours. I experienced a moment of panic in case we were all to join in the dancing. I have never been good at dancing and I certainly could not keep a tune, so I would not have wanted to commence my apprenticeship imitating Anni-Frid or Agnetha with all his chic friends watching.

Fortunately, I was saved.

Jean-Louis stopped clicking his fingers and one after the other we, his guests, also stopped clicking ours.

The girls' movements were no longer clumsy.

In perfect harmony they sang, *My my...I tried to hold you back, but you were stronger... Oh yeah ... I feel like I win when I lose ... Waterloo ... My my ...*

The music stopped and Jean-Louis grabbed each girl around the waist and lifted both off the floor.

We cheered, and I could see the pride in his eyes.

At a quarter to twelve the guests started to leave. They searched through a stack of designer jackets and anoraks which lay on the Chesterfield, said *ciao* to the host and filed out in a row like people going for a bus, when I knew this class would have come either by taxi or in their expensive German cars.

Half an hour later, Jean-Louis, his hair tousled and wet,

sat on the corner sofa, Charissa and Carmen to his left, sharing a red pouf, and once again trying to solve the Cube. He patted on the sofa for me to join him. The girls, having seen his gesture, jumped up to go to him too, but he stopped them with a pointed finger and a shake of his head.

"Bella, I hardly had a chance to speak to you tonight," he whispered to me.

"Your party was a great success, so it does not matter," I whispered back.

"Bah!"

"No really. I think everyone had a good time. The girls ..."

He leaned towards me.

"They're staying for the weekend, so - so I would have to ask you to go. It's Col ... their mother's birthday and she's gone up to Deauville with friends, so they are with me for the weekend. Sorry!"

I immediately got to my feet.

"I thought, with the girls visiting, you had an opportunity to meet them."

Was he apologising to me?

"We met," I said.

"And?"

The girls were looking at us as if they knew our whispering was about them.

"I had imagined them - I don't know - blonde-haired, I think. Or at least having brown hair like you."

"Col ... their mother is blond."

I did not know!

"Natural?" I asked cattily.

"With the assistance of some stuff - *et puis alors*? "

I let it go.

"What do you make of them - the two?" he asked not looking at them and still keeping his voice down.

"They are pretty. Bright."

"Thank you! They do give me a problem or two, but

162

they are good kids, yes."

Forthright they were too as I could have told him because through them I then knew that he did not marry his girlfriends.

-0-

The kitchen smells like the dining room of a London two-star hotel at eight in the morning - of bacon and eggs and coffee - stale coffee being kept hot on a hotplate.

Colin and Fred walk in.

"Smells interesting," says Colin.

"Quiche," Fred informs him.

"How do you know?"

"Am I right, Miss? Amandine?"

"Amandine," I confirm.

The two sit down at the work table. They have taken their green plastic aprons off which lie on the ground outside the backdoor. Colin's hair is wet and tousled and a vision of Jean-Louis sitting on his corner sofa at the end of his party, his hair wet and tousled, appears in front of my eyes.

"Is it true that here in France all bread is homemade?" asks Colin, addressing me.

He is buttering a chunk of *baguette*.

"Not anymore these days, Colin," replies Fred on my behalf.

Colin looks at me.

"I think the invention of sliced bread in plastic wrappers is the greatest disaster to have befallen us in England."

"We've got those too here in the supermarkets and in the Arab *superettes* which are open at all hours," comes from Fred.

"Open all hours. That makes me laugh," says Colin.

Fred looks puzzled.

"I am referring to one of our - the U.K's sitcoms -

called *Open All Hours* which is about a corner grocer who seems never to be closed. Marvellous actor in it - Ronnie Barker. It ran during the seventies," Colin explains.

"My wife and I watch *Dallas*," says Fred.

He pulls his face into a growl in imitation of J.R. Ewing.

Something in Colin's posture of ennui tells me this vein of conversation is about to end, and it does.

We continue to eat in silence. I have cut a large wedge from the quiche for each of the two, and a much smaller one for me. Fred is eating his as one eats pizza; with his hands. I can see Colin is watching him with an expectant smile, contemplating whether a forkful of egg is going to fall onto the floor.

The quiche eaten, I ask Fred to cut the *amandine*.

"Have the two of you finished in the garden?" I ask.

"*Ooh la la*, no," mumbles Fred.

His mouth is full of cake.

I fill three small cups with black coffee.

"So, what must you still do out there, Fred?"

"The yew and the hawthorn will have to be trimmed, Miss. As I said to Colin, it is a pity that it's got to be done when it's almost November but we can't wait for spring. He and I are going to do it as soon as we've finished here. I'll help you wash up first though."

Colin is nodding.

"No need to help with the washing up," I tell him thinking this is why he is nodding.

He shakes his head.

"No, I was going to say something about the hawthorn. I was telling Fred the tree is an emblem of hope."

"We say the opposite," I tell him.

"Fred has told me."

Now, Fred is the one who is nodding.

"I told him, Miss. I told him to uproot a hawthorn - even just to cut one single branch from it - brings ill-luck. I told him, Miss, how I heard this hawthorn cry once. It was

164

on a Good Friday, Miss, you may remember. I thought it was a kitten which got itself trapped in the tree and was mewing, but no, there was no kitten in the tree. It was the tree which was crying. Miss, I told your parents about it."

Yes, I remember. My mother telephoned me to Paris to tell me about it and from that day on whenever I came to Le Presbytère for a weekend, I never passed the tree without putting both my hands flat against the trunk and remaining in that position for a few minutes. *Ill-luck was the last thing I needed.*

"Hell, Bella!" Jean-Louis always said when he saw me holding the tree. "You are a scientist, for goodness sake!"

"Doctor. Just a doctor," I used to reply.

"I'll choose to believe the tree is an emblem of hope. It's more comforting," I tell Colin.

He smiles.

"Would you like to know why it's supposed to be that?"

"Yes, please. Why?"

"Jesus' crown of thorns was apparently from a hawthorn tree and because his death was not in vain - the Resurrection you know - the tree thus represents hope. And the staff of Joseph of Arithmathea in whose garden and family tomb Jesus was laid to rest - buried - was also from a hawthorn."

"Whichever it is, Colin, that tree has to be trimmed today," states Fred.

Ill-luck is still the last thing I need.

-0-

I watch Fred and Colin. I do not stand in front of a window to do so, but do so when I pass in front of a window. They are back wearing the green plastic aprons. Fred too is wearing a baseball cap; on his are the words *I hate NY*. It must belong to Colin. The matey habit of sharing clothes is not something we do in my family; what

165

we need, we buy, but never will we borrow clothes from relatives or friends. Marion, when she was still Marius's girlfriend, once tried to persuade me to wear one of her very high-heeled pumps to a farewell party for one of Chartreux Hospital's surgeons. The look of astonishment on Marius's face warned her she should not expect me to accept her offer. Now, she knows what the situation is and even should she need a warmer jersey on a weekend here at Le Presbytère, she will not ask if I could help her out, but she will walk around shivering, slapping her arms in an effort to warm herself up.

Fred is sitting in the Japanese *seiza* position - he always does so effortlessly when gardening - cleaning up flower beds. I watch him cutting back our geraniums, pelargoniums, carnations, daisies and bell flowers which had all summer looked like coloured ribbons which have fallen from the hair of a little girl.

Where is Colin? Ah, he is at the bottom of the garden, close to the gate, and he is pushing a wheelbarrow this way.

I stand a little back from my bedroom window so as not to be seen, and I watch him.

He is picking up faded flower petals, yellowed leaves, twigs and branches which Fred must have thrown down on the ground. The wheelbarrow looks heavy because he keeps on stopping to wipe his brow and to take his cap off to brush his fingers through his hair which is wet with perspiration.

He looks up and I am not quick enough to pull back, and he sees me. He mouths something which looks like the word *hello* and he again lifts his cap, this time in greeting, but not to miss the opportunity to yet again sweep a hand through his wet hair.

My telephone rings and I can see the two men have heard the ring because both look up at the house.

"Bella," says Marion, "how are you?"

The niceties having been said, she tells me they also will

not be spending the November 1, All Saints' Day, weekend with me.

"We're going down to Monte Carlo. One of your brother's colleagues is getting engaged and throwing a party down there. Sorry, Bella, I do hope you have not been hoping we will be at Le Presbytère that weekend."

"Not at all, Marion. Give Prince Rainier my love when you see him."

I tried not to sound sarcastic - or bitter.

Her reply is a snort. She is a keen reader of gossip magazines and the tabloids and she can tell you every shenanigan a celebrity has got up to.

While I was on the phone both Fred and Colin, as I can see, have left the front garden. They must be in the back garden because I can hear the lawnmower's grating drone which always scares the birds who start flying between the trees, their wings flapping fearfully, just as they do when my neighbour, the Dutch Mr Amster, starts aiming at them with his slingshot.

Looking through the window of one of the bedrooms which look over the back garden, I see Fred is instructing Colin on the technicalities of the lawnmower. I am sure Fred is making this uncomplicated instrument out to be nothing short of a *Mirage* fighter jet. Colin is listening with interest, but maybe he is just having Fred on. Not knowing Colin - not knowing him at all - I do not know whether he is the type who would mock a simple man: Jean-Louis would have. He would have said to Fred, "Now, this is miraculous! What an invention! Who invented it, by the way? Einstein? Darwin? Van Gogh? Marcel Dassault?" Fred, who had not heard of any of those men, would have picked whichever name he had managed to catch, and Jean-Louis would have slapped him on the back, calling him a good sort.

Colin is now mowing the lawn, and Fred, wearing a safety helmet, mufflers, gloves, all of these padded, and large protective glasses, looking as if he is set to step from a space craft into space, has put a ladder up against the hawthorn tree.

I am not superstitious, I murmur to myself.

I walk under ladders; I break mirrors; I open an umbrella indoors; I spill salt; I have had black cats cross my path; I have put a *baguette* down upside down, and it has happened that I have left a white tablecloth on a table overnight and no one had died.

Fred, holding our chainsaw with both hands, starts to climb up the ladder. Halfway up he stops and pulls the chainsaw's starting cord and the engine kicks and spouts into motion. Colin stops mowing the lawn and is watching Fred. Balancing himself by pushing his knees against the ladder, Fred tests the speed of the chainsaw's blade by making a couple of small incisions in the branch nearest to him; wood splinters fly into the air - and my heart starts to race in fear. Obviously satisfied that the blade's running at the right speed, Fred begins to carve into the branch, the chainsaw's engine sounding like that of a helicopter preparing for take off. The branch plunges to the ground and he looks down to see where it has fallen. Soon, several branches lie on the ground, and he cuts the chainsaw's engine and slowly descends the ladder. At the bottom, having taken off the gloves, he gives Colin the thumbs up sign.

The wood will be stored in Le Presbytère's wood shed to dry out and ought to be ready for burning when Samy comes back just before Christmas to check if the boiler is still in good working order.

I really am not superstitious. No ill-luck with befall me because Fred has cut branches from my hawthorn tree.

-0-

I wait in the courtyard with more coffee and what has been left over of the *amandine,* while Fred and Colin get cleaned up. Colin's doing so in his bathroom; Fred, as he always does, is doing so under the tap in the scullery off the kitchen. After a few minutes Fred steps out into the courtyard.

"Miss Bella, about Paula's birthday, which, as you know, is in a few days' time. Colin will be coming to our party. He's a great guy, Miss, not at all a snob despite he's so learnt and writes newspapers and books and such stuff."

"That's nice, Fred, him coming to your party."

"Will you come too, Miss? Paula and I talked about it this morning and we thought it would be nice to have you join us. It's not going to be anything posh. Just the usual, in fact. We're going to grill a few sausages, open a few bottles of wine, have some beer. A bit of music too. Just as we always do."

Colin joined us while Fred was talking.

My parents never socialised with the staff, only ever having gone to their homes when there was a death in their family. I have however broken this unwritten rule of theirs, having attended the christenings of their children and their anniversary celebrations, never having wanted to hurt their feelings. Of late, though, I have been declining all invitations politely, yet the invitations have not ceased.

"You wouldn't miss me, Fred," I say.

Colin looks from me to Fred.

"Come on, Miss," says Fred. "Come and join us. My boys will be coming from Le Havre and you've not seen them for a while, and believe me, they are big men now. Handsome too, like you would not believe it."

Trying to think of a noncommittal reply to offer Fred, I look at Colin but he holds both his hands up in the air to indicate his neutrality on the matter.

"I've whipped some cream to have with what's left of the *amandine*," I say. "Shall we sit down?"

I point to one of the courtyard's small mosaic tables where I had set out the coffee things.

Don't be such a wet, Bella, is what Marius will say about

the birthday party, but Marion's comment will be quite the opposite: *Not with the staff, no, Bella, you should not mix with the staff.* If I do not know what to say to Fred it is not because I am a snob like Marion, but because I am doubtful about the wisdom of attending the party with Colin. I will have to drive him to Fred's place and drive him back here again. And what about the dancing at the party? Unlike Jean-Louis' parties this one will not be for just watching the kids dance, but for dancing the waltz and the foxtrot and the sensual tango to Fred and Paula's record collection of accordion music. *Miss, if you should come across the latest Yvette Horner compilation, please get one for us. I will fix up with you on your return.* How many times have I not heard Fred say this before I set off on a trip to Paris?

"Marion may be coming up for a few days, but leave it with me and I will get back to you, Fred," I lie.

"Mrs Marion can come too."

"I will tell her."

Fred shakes his head.

"Come to think of it, Miss, Mrs Marion won't have a nice time. But you Miss, you will. I'll see to it that you will."

I offer Fred an apologetic smile. I touch his arm.

Colin is looking down into his coffee cup.

At the door, I offer Fred my hand.

"Thanks. I'll give you a ring. About the party."

As I close the front door, I hear Colin running up the stairs to his bedroom.

-0-

I wake up from a vivid dream in the middle of the night.

In the dream I was back at my Paris apartment. I was standing at the window of the living room, looking out, but holding the lace curtain in front of me because I did not want anyone passing by on the street to see I was back because the apartment no longer belonged to me and I was trespassing. Then, I heard the sound of marching feet. First, the sound was muffled, coming from a distance, but quickly it grew louder, and I waited anxiously for the marchers to appear. Next, a voice shouted out *Achtung!* and soldiers in their field-grey *Wehrmacht* uniforms stepped into view. They were marching ten abreast and doing the goosestep - I thought, *oh so many of them* - and my father, holding a huge Swastika banner, which was blowing in the wind, was marching ahead of them. He swung round, saw me at the window and waved the banner at me as if it were a starting flag at a race, and immediately I started to waltz across my living room floor, all the time thinking I should not make a noise because my neighbours should not know I was back. Just then a key turned in the front door's lock and Marius walked in and he said to me, "Oh Bella, you are such a wet! Why dance alone when you can dance with Colin Lerwick?"

Awake, my heart pounding, I lie very still: I can still hear music. Have I forgotten to silence the clock? But no: Colin either has a radio on or he is playing a CD. I have pins and needles in my right leg, but I do not want to move my legs in case the bed creaks and will reveal to him that I am awake. That his music, has woken me up.

He is listening to Dvorak's *New World Symphony*. Not very loud, but Le Presbytère's walls are not thick.

My father always said we do not have to make decisions; they will be made for us.

I want to get to know this man who listens to Dvorak in the middle of the night.

I will go to Paula's birthday party.

-0-

171

CHAPTER TWENTY-THREE

It is the hour of the evening when colour starts to disappear so that sea, sky and land are all a murky brown.

I am driving to Sainte-Marie-sur-Brecque to Paula's birthday party. Colin sits beside me. Fred was delighted when I told him on the telephone I will be honoured to be part of their party.

"Miss, Amandine's baked Paula a most beautiful birthday cake, but it's a secret, she's not to know."

He sounded as excited as a child.

Colin, when I told him that, as I will be attending the party, I could give him a lift, showed little interest in my offer, saying he would hate himself if I were to put myself out further on his behalf. He appeared more concerned about what gift he should buy Paula.

"Would it be in order if I take her some chocolate?"

"That's a wonderful idea," I replied.

I was going to give her perfume.

Colin is sitting with his arms folded over his chest, his eyes on the road ahead of us. He looks uncomfortable, even a little apprehensive. Could it be because he does not trust my driving skill or is it because of the party, having to be with people who would be speaking French all evening? I cannot tell.

We reach the village. It is dark, the world no longer brown, but black. After my years living in Paris, it took me a little time to get accustomed to how black a night is up here in Normandy - in the countryside this is; a Paris night

173

is never really dark and unless one's curtains are thick, it is necessary to close the shutters for real blackness.

Fred and Paula's house is on the northern edge of the village, on Rue Carolles, a short street of white-washed cottages with grey-slated roofs standing in the middle of immaculately-mowed lawns so green one doubts their authenticity. It is here on this street where the village's bourgeoisie live, and if ever I doubt my generosity as far as the wages of Le Presbytère's staff is concerned, I take comfort in the fact if my gardener can live here, I am paying him well. Shooting a glance at Colin I can see astonishment on his face, and he looks down at the box of chocolates he has bought for Paula at a confectionery in Avranches as if he is doubting its suitability.

"Are you sure we've come to the right house, Bella?"

He fingers the box on his lap as if he is contemplating leaving it in the car.

"Yes, this is Fred's house, and Paula will love those."

I point to the box.

Fred is at the front door.

"Miss!"

"Good evening, Fred."

"*Monsieur*," he greets Colin, the comradeship of the day of the gardening gone, but only for a moment, because suddenly, with a bellow of a laugh, he throws his arms around Colin.

"Mate," murmurs Colin, obviously embarrassed at the enthusiastic welcome. Maybe also fearing Fred's going to grab him round the shoulders and plant a kiss on each of his cheeks.

Paula is out in the back garden as her voice, always high-pitched and with amazing potency, reveals. Fred calls her and she runs into the house and her greeting of a kiss on each of my cheeks is respectfully subdued.

"Happy birthday, Paula. May you have many more with your family around you."

I always add this bit about having the family around

when I wish someone a happy birthday. Or rather, I have been doing so since my mother's death: her dying, in a way, having robbed me of a family, because Marius, married and a father, has his own family.

I push my gift of perfume into Paula's hands, calloused from years of working in the village's drycleaners.

Fred introduces her to Colin.

"How do you do, Mr Colin," she says.

She offers him a limp hand to shake: her handshake always in total contrast to her voice.

Clumsily, he hands her the box of chocolates.

"Oh my! Thank you! But a gift is not necessary."

Yet, again, she offers him a limp hand to shake.

Fred and Paula's house is surprisingly small for its appearance of luxury, the purpose of each room clearly defined by furniture and decoration. In the dining room prints of fruit and vegetable still lifes hang on the walls and on a sideboard - covered in a white crocheted cloth - stand a bowl of plastic fruit and two red glass vases in which pink plastic roses are arranged, the taller of these at the back, green plastic sprigs between them. The pictures on the living room walls are *Impressionist* reproductions painted in oil on canvas and which look very real. Monet's *Irises* hangs on one wall and, as if in competition, Van Gogh's hangs on the facing wall. A white Chinese paper ball lamp hangs from the ceiling in the middle of the room, throwing a circle of light over the shimmering, plum-coloured, polyester rug on the floor. I know the house's three bedrooms are all pink and yellow and fluffy, and the kitchen is a copy of that of Le Presbytère - Fred's handiwork - but on a much smaller and less expensive scale.

Fred and Paula lead the way to the back garden. Coals are smouldering in a stone and brick barbeque, also a copy of the one at Le Presbytère, and which I know is also Fred's handiwork, him having nearly set himself alight when he lit the fire for the first time.

All the members of my staff are out in the garden. All greet me with a wave of the hand. Gertrude does so by engulfing me in her muscled arms as if I am drowning and she has to pull me out of the water, and she plants not just one kiss on each of my cheeks, but two.

All study Colin with respectful interest. No doubt, Fred has told them about him; I would like to know what he said.

Plates of sausages, some of these short and fat, others long and thin, made of pork, beef, veal, rabbit or chicken and flavoured with basil, fennel, thyme and even lavender, grown by Fred in their back garden and dried by Paula on sheets of newspaper in an airing cupboard, as well as red spicy *Merguez* glistening in their intestine casings, are laid out in rows on grills which are to be put over the coals once all the guests have arrived; about forty are expected. When Fred first planted the lavender none of us gave it much chance of growing in the Normandy climate, so much cooler and wetter than lavender's natural habitat of southern France, but we did not reckon with Fred's green thumbs. Now, the lavender bush, almost as tall as Fred himself, stands out in the front garden and all who pass by admire it, and to Fred's chagrin, they often steal a sprig.

The conversation is of insignificant things; it flies over our heads like the aromatic smoke from the barbeque because the grills with the sausages have been put on the coals.

Accordion music and hand clapping start to drift from the drawing room and Colin, who has been keeping to my side like a frightened child, frowns.

"This is accordion country," I whisper.

"Oh lordie!"

Colour is creeping over his face.

"It's alright. The young people will be doing the dancing."

The young people. Did I really say this?

-0-

As the late October night is cool rather than cold, we can either eat outside or inside; the choice is ours. The look of persuasion both Fred and Frascot gives me - he is doing the grilling of the sausages - tells me the intention is that guests are to eat outside. I am wearing jeans and a thick sweater, so, protected against the cool evening air, I suggest to Colin we take our plates and we sit on Fred's small, but well-tended patch of lawn. Colin too is in jeans and sweater but he says he is going to need the windbreaker he has brought along. He asks whether my car is locked because he has left it on the rear seat.

Frascot walks over to me.

"Miss, you did not tell us what a good-looking devil your guest is." he reprimands me.

"So he is, Frascot, yes."

I would never have agreed with Frascot if Colin was not out of earshot, but, not to give Frascot food for thought, I did use a tone as if I were agreeing about something banal, like the timetable for the Nantes-Paris train.

"Bring him down to the Vaybee, Miss. Does he eat snails?" asks Frascot.

"I've no idea whether he eats snails or not, but here he comes, so you can ask him yourself."

Colin joins us.

"Do you eat snails, Mr Colin?" asks Frascot.

"Love them. Why?"

"Oh good! Excellent! Miss Bella must therefore bring you down to the Vaybee - that's my bar here in the village - and the two of you can have some."

"Great idea. Will do," agrees Colin.

Several open bottles of *Sylvaner* stand on ice in buckets the size of a dustbin and placed alongside a makeshift bar of planks on chairs. In charge of the bar is Frascot's current girlfriend, Alice, long dyed-yellow hair falling over her heavily-made up face. Frascot, unlike his brother Fred who cannot be more a part of his wife if she were his Siamese twin, is a lady's man. Having divorced when still in his twenties, and not having remarried, he says he is making the best of a bad hand he has been dealt.

"Shall I fetch us a glass each?" Colin asks.

He points towards the bar.

"Good idea."

He returns with two fat glasses with short green stems: I recognise them from the Vaybee. Pools of light from overhanging lanterns reflect in the light-yellow wine.

"This is the life, Bella," says Colin, sitting down on the lawn beside me.

He clinks his glass against mine.

"Colin, who shall we drink to? Or to what?"

"Le Presbytère?"

I nod.

"*Santé*, Bella!"

"My father always said *Gesundheit*."

"You said your father was from Germany?" he asks.

"He was German, yes."

"Did it ...?" He stops. "No, never mind ..."

The top of Colin's head and his shoulders are lit by a streak of bright white light from an uncovered ceiling light in the kitchen behind us, but his face is in darkness and this makes it impossible for me to see the expression in his eyes, but I detected a tone of empathy in his voice.

"What were you going to say?" I ask.

"I was ... I wanted to ask whether your father's nationality was a problem?"

He is nursing his glass in his hands, and, as he has turned his head, I can see his face and I can see his eyes are searching mine. Searching for something in mine. The coward I am, I quickly look down, but the desire to share this burden of my family background with someone, with this man in particular, is too great, and I look up.

"It was an insurmountable problem, yes. My father was not just German, he was a soldier, one of Hitler's soldiers.

He was a Third Reich soldier. My mother was a horizontal collaborator. This was what a woman who slept with a German soldier was called. At the Germans' surrender, the head of such a woman was shaved. It was what happened to my mother, but my uncles - her brothers - had had the sense, if one can call it this, to get their cousin, a barber, to shave her head in private at his salon. In private and gently. This did not happen here in the village, but the villagers all know about it. I must say that today ... that no one has thrown it in my face for some years, but it was something which did happen when I was a child. And a teenager. When I was a student in Paris too. It was always *there*. It was like a terrible facial deformity."

The words just spurted from my mouth, spurted like vomit: I wanted to stop talking, fall silent, but once I had begun I could not stop. While I was speaking visions of my classmates - Marie Dumay, Vincent Lebac, Anselme Mathiot, Nestor Toussant, Florence Dubois - appeared in the light behind Colin. They were laughing, laughing at me. Baudelaire joined them, and so did Miss Jambenoire. They too were laughing at me.

"Well ... so ... it's old news ... so why go on about it?" I say.

I said this almost apologetically as if I were trying to make light of my terrible confession to this stranger sitting on the lawn opposite me, his glass of wine, halfway to his lips.

"I know," he says, "I understand exactly what you went through. My brother and I - please don't think I am making light of your experience - went through something similar. There were uncles and aunts - my father's brothers and sisters - and cousins and friends, even our neighbours, who made remarks about the fact that Tim and I - my brother and I - did not go to church on Sundays, and that, in fact, there was no religion at our house. On Sundays, when all along the street put on their best clothes and climbed into their cars to drive to the church two blocks away, Tim and I had to remain indoors. We protested. We did not understand why we could not also go to church. And then there was the Christmas school play. Each year as the Festive Season was approaching my mother gave us a letter to hand to our teacher to request that Tim and I should not participate in the play. So the two of us, along with the Muslim and Jewish pupils, had to stand in the corridor outside the school hall while the others were in there practising for the play. We used to go home crying. That was when we were still small. Later, as teenagers, we just felt very awkward at being cast aside - at being outsiders. We did not know why we were because we were neither Muslim nor Jewish. And then my mother died and her brother turned up and we discovered what it was all about."

"What was it all about?"

"My mother was a Russian Jewess. Oh, I know that today ... today it's of little importance, but class, class and origin and accent, were important when Tim and I were children, and, considered 'wogs', the two of us were outcast. I did though learn on enrolling at public school we were not quite the heathens we were thought to be because our one hundred percent English nanny had taken us to the vicarage to be baptised. But ... its old news ... as you've just said."

"Unfortunately, old news keeps on hurting, Colin."

He nods.

"Quite right. Unlike old shoes, it never becomes comfortable."

"I think you're managing alright."

"And so are you, Bella."

He leans forward and his eyes are again on mine, searching for something in mine as they did a few minutes earlier. Quickly, as if by impulse, he takes my right hand in both his hands, but as quickly, as if he has scorched his skin, he pulls his hands away. He looks away too; he looks to where Fred and Frascot are standing beside the barbeque. He waves to them when they notice him.

My thoughts in turmoil, I am unable to do or say anything.

"Miss! Come dance!"

Honorine, in a knee-length yellow dress with ruffles around the hem, stands behind Colin. I have no idea how long she has been standing here and what she has overheard or seen.

"Go," says Colin, looking at me again, his voice hardly above a whisper.

"Will you be coming too?"

"In a moment. Give me a moment."

Honorine's dress flaps around her knees as she pulls me into the house, and once in the living room, the plum-coloured polyester rug nowhere in sight, she pulls me against her to waltz with her to the accordion music coming from the turntable. She is leading me anti-clockwise around the room, her left hand on my hip, her right gripping my left elbow. We are waltzing and we are not doing it correctly, but Honorine is left-handed. Disregarding the music's rhythm she navigates us through gaps between the dancing couples, and I stumble after her. Colin stands in the doorway; he's trying hard not to laugh at what I am sure must be a spectacle. To make matters worse, I lose my balance, trip and leave one of my shoes standing forlornly on the floor for it to be trampled by dancing feet. The music stops. Benefiting from the lull in the dancing, I hobble to where my shoe is lying and step into it.

"That looked like fun, Bella."

Colin has appeared beside me.

"It was. Great fun. Honorine and I will be competing in the next ballroom world championships."

"Wouldn't want to miss it!"

He is laughing now.

At least, the spectacle my chambermaid and I have just supplied has cheered him.

Our glasses refilled, we look around for a place to sit, but with a sweating, breathless guest recovering on each of the chairs and five of them squeezed onto a three-seat sofa, we have no choice but to sit down on the floor, our legs pulled up and our backs against the wall.

"I love Van Gogh," says Colin.

He points at the Van Gogh reproduction hanging on the facing wall.

"So do I. When I was a child I had a small reproduction of his *Sunflowers* hanging in my bedroom. It wasn't a reproduction as such; it was a picture I'd torn from a magazine. But it was precious to me. It was real to me."

"This may sound weird, but I used to carry a postcard of the *Sunflowers* around with me. I'd bought it on a trip to Paris when I was a student. Cost ten centimes and that included the stamp which had already been stuck on it, but you have no idea what pleasure it gave me looking at that postcard."

"So you no longer have it?"

"An overzealous customs' officer at the airport in Moscow confiscated it. Suspected it conveyed some coded message; thought I was a spy. The Cold War thing you know. Do you still have your picture?"

"No, I do not, but in my case it was an overzealous chambermaid who relieved me of it: she broke it. She was cleaning the glass and knocked the picture down and both the frame and the glass were in pieces, so my mother would not allow me to buy another frame to hang the picture back up. She said it was bound to fall down again and I, or the maid, might cut ourselves very badly. I kept the picture though - in a drawer - and it started to turn yellow, as newsprint does, and when I left for high school in Nantes, I left the picture lying on my bed and on my return it was gone. I told myself I will get another. And one day I *will* get another. I have sort of told myself that one day, when I am really happy, I will buy another

Sunflowers reproduction. A small one. Just for me. To again hang in my bedroom."

"I have also been meaning to look for another *Sunflowers* postcard. Oh, I have seen many of them, but never have I been in the right frame of mind to buy one. Be really happy. Really content. Maybe, in love."

"I hope you will be - one day."

"Ditto."

He clicks his glass against mine.

-0-

"Would you like to dance, Bella?"

I have been wondering whether I should invite him to dance.

"Would love to. Yes."

His shirt is damp and beads of perspiration, shiny like tiny diamonds, cling to his hairline. He again smells of mint. I like it. I hope my *First* of Van Cleef & Arpels is as agreeable.

Someone has replaced the accordion music with gentler ballads. A bass guitar pulsates soothingly and the timbre of the sax is mellow as Lionel Richie sings, *Hello! Is it me you're looking for? I can see it in your eyes ... I can see it in your smile ...*

Colin starts to sing: his singing confirms to me he has a good voice.

You're all I have ever wanted, and my arms are open wide ... 'Cause you know just what to say ... And you know just what to do ...

"Come ...Bella ... sing along with me."

I shake my head.

And I want to tell you so much, I love you ... I long to see the sunlight in your hair ... and tell you time and time again how much I care ... Sometimes I feel my heart will overflow ... Hello, I have just got to let you know ...

Colin and I are not really dancing. We are just moving slowly to the music. Step right. Step left. Turn. Step left.

183

Step right. Turn. He puts both his hands on my hips, the movement bringing his face close to mine. I lift my arms and join my hands at the back of his neck. In this position our bodies could easily touch, but I keep my arms stretched out to prevent this happening. Colin's breathing is now coming in brief gasps. I am not fooling myself to believe this is because of the closeness of our bodies. No. It is because the smell of cigarette smoke and sweat is heavy in the room.

The music stops.

We keep on moving, he, keeping his hands on my hips, but I drop mine to a spot between two of the buttons of his shirt.

The music recommences.

It's now or never ... Come hold me tight ... Kiss me my darling ... Be mine tonight. Elvis Presley. Baudelaire liked Elvis and with him I once danced this *slow*. It was at a school picnic on the beach, one Friday evening. Overhead, the moon shone in all of its full-moon magnificence and underneath our feet the sand was cool and damp.

Elvis's voice fades out and Honorine and Martine, giggling, rush over to the player, and after a few seconds of discussion with Paula, the accordion music starts up again. Immediately, the dance floor fills up. The frown on Colin's face tells me we have done our dancing. We seek out Paula and Fred to thank them for a lovely evening.

-0-

We reach the Mercedes. The wine has made me just woozy enough to warn me I ought not to be driving a car.

"You drive, do you, Colin?"

He nods.

"Do you want me to drive?"

"Could you?" I ask.

"Will you trust me with your life?"

"I'm offering you the wheel because I'm not sure you

184

can trust me with yours."

I pass him the set of car keys. He unlocks the door on the passenger side and waits until I am seated and I have folded my cardigan around me before he walks around the front of the car to the driver's side.

"You comfy?" he asks.

He adjusts the seat to his height.

Ours is the only car on the road to Le Presbytère.

Behind us a few of the village's lights are still switched on and flickering timidly. The mount is dark but two red lights bobbing on the water in the distance signal the presence of a vessel. I had left one of Le Presbytère's garden lights on and it too flickers, but ahead of us. Colin's hands are resting lightly on the steering wheel, his fingers fitting into the wheel's grooves. *A man's hands. Why do I have this fascination with a man's hands?* He begins to tap out a tune against the wheel with his right hand. It is a tune only he can hear because all I am hearing is the purr of the car's engine. His left hand is on the wheel. No doubt sensing my eyes on him, he turns his head and looks at me. He smiles. There is something in the smile which signals protection, safety, amity.

"Sleep," he says. "Put your head back and close your eyes."

Like an obedient child, I put my head back.

I close my eyes, but sleep escapes me.

-0-

"Home," says Colin.

Quickly, I open my eyes. I sit up. No, home we are - I am - not yet. Le Presbytère is exactly six-hundred metres away. I know this from walking down to Sainte-Marie-sur-Brecque, a pedometer around one of my ankles. I had an argument with Jean-Louis about my measuring driven distance with a pedometer. "Christ, Bella, a pedometer is for measuring the distance covered in walking, not when you are in a bloody car."

Must banish him from my mind.

"Another six-hundred metres ... four-hundred still to go. It was six-hundred back there when you spoke, but now it is four-hundred ... rather three-hundred now," I say.

"Two-hundred ... one-fifty... fifty ...," he counts down.

Ahead of us, Le Presbytère is black.

A poem comes to mind.

Out of the night that covers me... Black as the pit from pole to pole ... I thank whatever gods may be ... For my unconquerable soul ... I am the master of my fate ... I am the captain of my soul ....

Who is the poet? I take mental note of having to find out. Perhaps Colin will know. Should I ask him?

"Colin?"

"Yes, Bella?"

Do I ask him?

"You enjoyed the evening?" I ask instead.

"Very much. And you."

"Yes."

"Shall I leave the car here?"

He has pulled up beside his motorcycle.

"Yes."

I put my right hand on the knob to open the door on my side.

"Allow me, Bella."

He leans over and puts his left hand over my right and pushes down hard. His face is very close to mine. *Mint!* The car door flings open.

"The key," he says.

Walking to the door I dig into my bag for the set of house keys.

When last did a man unlock a front door for me?

The night sky is decorated with silver stars. A long blast of a ship's horn wakes birds which have been sitting sleeping in the trees behind us. They flutter their wings and fly over the trees. One emits a short, chipped call.

Colin has a problem inserting the key in the front door's lock. I pretend I do not notice.

In the small front room I switch on just one light, the lamp on the desk. It throws a warm, calm light like that of a winter sunset across the room.

"I will go to bed," I say.

He frowns.

"I think I will do some writing. I won't type, don't worry."

I am the master of my fate ... I am the captain of my soul ...

"I want to look up something in the library," I tell him.

"Can I help?"

"Who wrote the poem that starts ... *Out of the night that covers me, bl ...?*"

"*... black as the pit from pole to pole?*"

I nod.

"William Ernest Henley. *Invictus...* unconquered."

"Why was he unconquered?"

"He suffered from tuberculosis as a child and had lost a leg at the age of seventeen because of it."

"Tuberculosis of the bone."

"That's right."

"I think I will go to bed."

Now, he is the one who nods.

In the silence of the night our footsteps reverberate off the walls.

"I will say goodnight, Bella."

We have reached his bedroom door.

"Goodnight, Colin."

His hand is on the doorknob.

"See you in the morning, Bella."

It is already morning.

-0-

CHAPTER TWENTY-FOUR

Hastily, I dress. I have overslept. I fell asleep the moment I slipped under the duvet and my sleep was sound. A sleep with no nightmares. Alas, it was also a sleep without dreams.

The rich aroma of coffee fills the air.

Colin is in the kitchen drinking coffee, the colour of fudge, from one of my bowls. He sits at the work table, tapping the forefinger of his free hand against the wood to the rhythm of a tune only he can hear. Maybe it is one of last night's songs which are still circling in his head. Yesterday's *Le Monde* lies open on the work table. He's been reading about the Iran-Contra Affair. Seeing me, he gets up.

"I helped myself to some coffee. I hope you do not mind."

"In no way."

"What's the norm here, Bella? Does one send a bouquet of flowers to the hostess after a party?"

"You gave Paula that beautiful box of chocolates."

"If you think it was sufficient."

"Sufficient."

"I think I'm going to work all morning. Write. At lunch time I'll ride down to Frascot's place for those snails."

"Good idea."

"You want me out of the way?"

"Of course not."

"I do not want to impose on your life, your lifestyle,

your way of living. So, if you want me out of the way ..."

"No. No. No. You are not imposing on my life. My lifestyle."

"Sit down, Bella," he says.

He points to the work table. He is wearing a grey sweater over the jeans he wore last night. He is clean-shaven as on every morning. This morning the aroma of mint does not cling to him.

I sit down. My head aches. I do really have a hangover.

"I think I may have ... have had too many glasses of wine last night."

"Nonsense."

He is now holding the bowl in both his hands.

From the bay drifts a long blast. I recognise it as the coastguards' foghorn. The sky which can be seen through the window and beyond the courtyard is opaque. I push my chair back and I walk over to the window and open it. A cold wind sweeps in and blows a page from *Le Monde* to the floor. Quickly, I close the window.

"You were ... so ...you were very pleasant last night. I mean at the party. Of course at the party. I could see all the members of your staff like you. Adore you. It's ... quite clear why they do. You are charming. I like you ..."

Abruptly he stops. He lowers his head, putting the bowl down roughly on the work table at the same time. Coffee spills to the table and begins to run down and drips onto the floor.

"I mean to say ... hell, I am gauche. What I mean is you are a very likeable person. It is obvious why this place is ... I mean ... what I mean is you are a natural hostess ... hostess as in guest house and not as in a ..."

Again, he stops.

Has he blushed?

"Bar ... club or a brothel," I finish the sentence for him.

Now, he is without doubt, blushing.

In silence, I watch him.

He fetches a wet cloth from the sink and mops up the coffee, first from the table and next, from the floor.

"Colin, leave it. I will do it later."

"I was going to say ... going to ask you to come to the Vaybee ...that is what Frascot's place is called, is it not ... with me."

"For the snails?"

"And for a ... a chat."

"Ok," I say. "It will be nice. Thank you."

I intend to pay. Pay my share at least.

-0-

Jean-Louis did not like the Vaybee, or Frascot.

"Jean-Louis, let's go to the Vaybee for lunch," I said to him on his third visit to Le Presbytère.

It was the beginning of the month of July and every room at Le Presbytère was taken and my mother, her hair tousled and her ankles swollen, was running around seeing to the comfort of our guests, so I thought it would be a good idea for Jean-Louis and me to reduce her burden by lunching out.

Sainte-Marie-sur-Brecque too was packed with tourists, the women in sleeveless frocks, their fat arms red from the sun, the men, in T-shirts and shorts or Bermudas, their hairy legs as red as the women's fat arms.

Jean-Louis pulled the metallic silver Porsche up in front of the Vaybee.

"Park around the corner," I told him.

"What's wrong with here?"

In the Vaybee hands pulled the red-checkered curtains apart to be able to see out.

"Parking here is so obviously to show off," I said.

"So let us show off. This car cost me a fortune."

A couple with two small children stopped at the Porsche. The man gave Jean-Louis the thumbs up sign. The two children were crying for ice cream. The woman gave each a flat-hand slap on the behind. They hollered louder.

I had telephoned Frascot to say I would need a table for two for lunch and he had prepared and reserved one for us which was beside a tall lamp, the shade of it made of white and pink seashells. I knew it was the table considered the best one in the place; best because it was secluded.

All the other tables of the Vaybee were taken and on each stood a large copper bowl of steamed mussels. At the table nearest to us sat two fat women of a certain age. They were pulling the shells of the mussels apart, each holding the full shell with one hand and gouging loose the orange mussel with the other part of the shell, which they had broken off with a firm twist. The only time they did not use their fingers was when they used a large soupspoon for eating the wine broth heavy with chopped onion, garlic and cream in which the mussels were served, and had been cooked in. The emptied shell they dropped onto a soup plate, taking care not to let go of the half they were using for the carving. Every couple of minutes, they dipped pieces of *baguette*, placed on the table in a wicker basket, into the broth, or, using their fingers, picked up a French fry from another copper bowl on the table.

Having watched the two women as I had done, Jean-Louis announced what we were going to eat.

"Mussels for sure."

"We will have the *moules-frites* too," I told Frascot.

"Cooked in wine or cider, Miss?"

"Wine, for goodness sake!" snapped Jean-Louis.

Within seconds of Frascot having put our mussels and fries on our table, Jean-Louis began to complain that the mussels were too small and he needed to eat at least six to get the taste. He also could not stand the sight of the other patrons, especially the two fat women, eating theirs.

"Jean-Louis, we're doing just as they do," I told him.

"But with elegance, Bella."

A morsel of garlic stuck to the side of his mouth. I did not tell him.

Later, driving through the village he, pointing at tourists, mocked the clothes they wore.

"They are on holiday, Jean-Louis," I defended them.

"Is that an excuse to look like something the cat had carried in?"

He had also criticised Frascot.

"God, what a country bumpkin," he said. "I'm surprised he's not by now poisoned the whole lot of you."

He was referring to Frascot's calloused hands. Before Frascot had opened the Vaybee he had been a fisherman, owner of a small boat, and using both floating and hand nets. "Was murder on the hands," he so often said to his patrons.

"How was the meal?" my mother asked Jean-Louis and me on getting back to Le Presbytère.

"A nightmare," Jean-Louis replied.

"What a pity. I must say though I am not surprised," she replied.

"Next time, we will have Frascot's veal," I told Jean-Louis.

"No bloody fear! There won't be a next time!" he retorted.

There was not.

-0-

"That looks delicious," says Colin.

He points to a copper pot of mussels on the table beside ours.

I again telephoned Frascot and asked him to keep a table for us. This time he mercifully did not keep the secluded one where Jean-Louis and I had sat.

"Do you want to change and have mussels instead?" I ask Colin.

"Uh … no, let us have the snails …"

The red-checkered curtains of the day Jean-Louis and I lunched in the Vaybee still hang in front of the windows and the red-checkered tablecloths of that day still cover the tables. The napkins are however now of paper, and white, and no longer of red damask cloth.

Few tables are taken. Father Pierre sits at one. He has finished some pork chops as the bones on his plate bear witness. The white napkin around his neck is speckled with grease and something green: Frascot always serves peas with pork chops. Peas and mashed potatoes.

"What with the snails, Mr Colin? Steak perhaps?" asks Frascot.

Colin looks at me.

"Just the snails, Frascot, if this is alright with you, Bella?"

"As starters?" asks Frascot.

"Just the snails," I confirm.

Colin nods his agreement.

"Wine?" enquires Frascot.

I shake my head.

"Driving."

"And what about you, Mr Colin?"

"Could I have just a glass of red please, Frascot?"

Frascot brings a wicker basket filled with chunks of *baguette* to our table.

"The glass of wine, please, Frascot?" I ask.

Father Pierre looks up from his plate of food and acknowledges my presence with a wave of a greasy hand.

"Father," I greet him.

He looks at Colin.

"Mister ... good day."

"Father," Colin acknowledges the salutation.

Frascot puts a carafe of red wine on the table.

"Glass only," I tell him.

"Leave it, Bella ... please," Colin tells me.

He smiles at Frascot.

"Women!" sighs Frascot. "Never want a man to enjoy

himself."

Colin shudders having swallowed a mouthful of the wine.

"Bad?" I ask.

"Sour."

I tell him I will call Frascot back and tell him.

"Please do not. He is such a nice man."

The snails, sizzling in garlic butter, are served in two white oven-proof dishes. There are six snail-shaped indentations in each dish, a snail in each indentation.

"Be careful, the dish is hot," warns Frascot, a napkin over one arm, from across the room.

Too late: Colin is sucking on a burnt forefinger.

"Doctor! Doctor!" he calls out laughingly.

Never have I found it easy to manipulate the pliers and fork one is supposed to eat snails with. When I have snails at home, and I am eating alone, I just hold the shell in a napkin and dig out the snail with the end of my knife. Here, in the restaurant, I cannot obviously do so. Colin, as I can see, has no problem loosening the snails from their shells.

Before long the empty shells are piled up on the side plates which Frascot gave us for this purpose.

"Dessert?" asks Frascot, back at our table.

He hands each of us a large menu: ice cream in various colours and shapes are on the front of it.

Father Pierre is slurping up a chocolate mousse. Judging by the state of the napkin around his neck, as brown spots have joined the green ones, he has a problem with his hand to mouth coordination.

"Whatever I am going to have," says Colin, "it will not be what the priest is having."

"Father Pierre."

"Is that his name? Well, he's gone and put me off chocolate for the rest of my life."

We order vanilla ice cream.

"Three blobs or four?" asks Frascot.

"One," I reply.

"Two," replies Colin. "And do you have any wafers?"

"Russian tongues," I enlighten a puzzled Frascot.

"Oh, I see. Yes, I have Russian tongues. Any coffee afterwards?"

"Shall we do the tisane thing, Bella?" asks Colin.

I nod.

"Frascot, no coffee but two citronella tisane, please."

I turn to Colin.

"You learn fast."

"From what I've seen of France over these few days with you, I like the lifestyle, so I am eager to learn."

"Could you live here?" I ask.

"In France?"

I nod again.

"Sure I could," he says. "I've lived in quite a few places, but France has always attracted me."

I ask him in which countries he has lived?

"I've lived in eighteen altogether. For my work. In England of course. Spain. Belgium, Germany, Switzerland, Italy ... on the island of Malta, Indonesia, India ... I won't go on. Here in France too ...once. It was during my student days. I had met this girl ... Celine was her name ... "

He is smiling. Perhaps he is remembering Celine.

"A girl in every port, so to speak, was it?" I ask.

"But not one was Miss Right." He looks me straight in the eyes. "And you, Bella?"

"I've not travelled ... much."

"I meant - has there been no Mr Right?"

"No Mr Right."

"Do you regret this?"

"Do you regret there has been no Miss Right, Colin?"

"As is always said in films - *I asked you first*. But I will reply nonetheless. I have ... how do I say this? The Celines of this world are a dime a dozen. Pretty faces; empty heads. Nice legs; empty heads. Big bosoms; empty heads. I like a woman with intelligence."

"No matter what she looks like?"

"I wouldn't go that far, no, Bella, to say what a woman looks like is of no importance to me."

He laughs and rubs his nose and trying to look at me over his nose his eyes are squinting a little. Is he embarrassed? Does he think he has said too much?

Frascot walks up with a small tray. The aroma of lemon hangs over the porcelain teapot on the tray.

"It's ready for drinking, Miss ... Mr Colin."

He puts the tea pot and two glasses on the table and walks off - Alice has walked in and is sitting behind the till - the tray banging against the side of his right hip.

I pour the tisane.

Frascot returns. He puts a small saucer on the table. On it lies the handwritten bill. He is always quick about bringing the bill. Two unwrapped peppermints the size of an olive lie on top of the bill.

Colin pulls the saucer over to his side of the table, picks up the bill and looks at it. He takes a brown wallet from the inside pocket of his jacket. The wallet is of ostrich leather. It is fairly old because sections of the leather have become worn out due to handling.

"Bella," he says. "To return to what we were talking about before. I find you ... quite ... quite what a man would ... would want in a woman."

He takes some notes from his wallet and drops them down onto the saucer.

"I'm adding twenty francs for the tip, is this enough?" he asks.

"It's generous."

He is looking down.

"One never knows about tipping," he says.

He looks up and at me.

"I have said ... I have said ... I like you, Bella. You are charming. I like being in your company."

Frascot is walking over to our table again.

"May I offer you cognac?" he asks.

Colin and I say "No, thank you" simultaneously.

Frascot picks up the saucer with the money, counts the notes and say thank you to Colin for the tip.

"Generous," he says.

"I told you," I tell Colin.

"Shall we go?" he asks.

"Yes, let's," I reply.

-0-

We are driving along the coast, following the curve of a sandy bay.

The weather has turned raw, cold. Above us wispy clouds are gathering.

It is just after four o'clock.

Colin suggested we drive for a while before we return to Le Presbytère. He is sitting with his hands on his lap. They are pressed palm to palm as if he is in prayer. The *Praying Hands* of Albrecht Dürer and I hate them so much. Once, at Chartreux Hospital, there was a couple whose baby was born prematurely at eight months and was jaundiced and had to be put on a ventilator. I told them that their little one would be fine and grow up into a great big rugby forward, but they did not believe me. They brought their parish priest to the hospital. The priest, a tall thin man with little hair and no eyebrows (chemotherapy?) said prayers and sprayed holy water over the baby and over the ventilator as well. I had tried to stop him from spraying the holy water, unsterilized as it would have been, over the child and the machine, but the baby's mother had violently pushed me out of the way.

"Doc, shall I call security?" Nurse Bonnec wanted to know.

"Let's handle it ourselves," I told her.

As soon as the couple and the priest left, Nurse Bonnec washed down the baby and sprayed the ventilator with an anti-septic fluid.

The following morning when I came on duty I saw neither the mother nor the father, but someone - perhaps it was the priest - had, during the night pasted a large reproduction of Albrecht Dürer's *Praying Hands* on each of the room's walls.

"Doc, do I take these down?" Nurse Bonnec wanted to know.

I told her to leave them but each time I was in that room I felt that at any moment those hands with the bulging veins were going to point an accusing finger at me for no longer believing. Believing God is the anchor, the only anchor, in this world of ours, so full of falsehood and cruelty.

"Come to think of it," Nurse Bonnec said to me once the couple had taken their baby home, "the priest's drawing might have saved the baby's life."

"Dürer's drawing, Nurse Bonnec," I corrected her. "And what had saved the baby's life was man's science."

"Whoever," she replied.

I hated those hands long before that incident at Chartreux Hospital. I hated them - and I still do - because one of my mother's brothers had on one of my father's birthdays given him the gift of a small sculpture of those hands and stuck between them was a gun. On the card which accompanied the sculpture that uncle of mine had written: "Hitler's hands. Ha!" "Sick bastard!" my mother said, throwing the sculpture in the bin in the kitchen. My father had not said a word. In the afternoon, no one around, I went to retrieve the sculpture because I wanted to smash it to bits. Morsels of domestic waste clung to the hands and rubbed off on mine. I put a hammer to the sculpture. Bang! Bang! Bang!

"Dürer," I say to Colin.

He looks at me, surprised.

"Huh?"

"Your hands."

He laughs but drops his hands to the seat.

"You must think I am praying you don't turn over the car."

Overhead the clouds are breaking up and beside the road, on the shore, a gull, its wings flapping, is trying to land on the water.

"Shall we head home?" I ask.

Home. My home. Not his.

"Yes let's, Bella. We've had a lovely outing. A great lunch. And all."

-0-

Back at Le Presbytère Colin says he will not be able to eat a thing this evening.

It has started to rain.

"I feel like getting some writing done," he tells me.

"Sure. Why not."

"Don't worry. I won't be typing."

In my room, I stand at the window. Night has fallen. There are only a few lights lit on the mount. A yellow tourist coach drives along the causeway taking the last of the day's visitors back to the mainland.

I must go downstairs to silence the clock.

Passing Colin's room I hear his voice. He is reciting a poem.

It swept, it swept on all the earth ... At every turning ... A candle on the table flared... A candle, burning ... Snow-moulded arrows, rings and stars ... The pane adorning ...A candle on the table shone ... A candle, burning ...

I stand still. I listen. I love the sound of the English tongue ... when it is being spoken by a man. I stand stock-still, too frightened to move in case the floor boards under my feet should squeak and alert Colin that I am outside his room.

And drops of molten candle wax ... Like tears were rolling ... And all was lost in snowy mist ... Grey-white and blurring ... A candle on the table stood ... A candle, burning ...

I recognise the poem. It is Pasternak's *A Winter Night*. Once, as part of a poetry lesson, Miss Matigot had asked me and my classmates to each choose a poem which the class would discuss. Having no clue which poem to choose, my father had suggested Pasternak's *A Winter Night*. He knew it by heart and recited it to me and he suggested in order for to make a good impression on Miss Matigot I should learn the poem by heart myself. I did, but alas, it had made no impression on her because my classmates had learnt their so-called favourite poem by heart too.

All February the snow-storm swept ... Each time returning ... A candle on the table wept ... A candle, burning ...

Colin falls silent.

"Bella, is that you?"

I almost run to the staircase.

The door of Colin's bedroom flings open.

I turn round.

"Sorry, did I disturb you? I'm just going downstairs to silence the clock."

"I thought one of the nuns may have come to pay us a visit."

"That was Pasternak," I say. "The poem."

"Yes. *A Winter Night*. I'm sorry. Was I ... speaking too loudly?"

"Good heavens, no. Not at all. That was beautiful. The poem. Pasternak. It was a favourite of my fathers. He knew it by heart. I wasn't eavesdropping though. Please don't think I was eavesdropping. I was just passing ... "

I am sure I am blushing but fortunately the hallway is in semi-darkness.

"Of course I won't think that," says Colin. "This is your house, Bella, and you are free to do whatever you wish in it."

"Well ... goodnight, Colin," I say.

"Nice day it was, Bella. Thank you."

201

I run down the stairs.

-0-

CHAPTER TWENTY-FIVE

So La Presbytère's winter guest likes a woman to be intelligent.

Jean-Louis used to say he liked his women to be intelligent at the workplace and stupid in bed.

"What am I?" I asked him.

"You are well balanced, but I would like you to be much, much more of a bad girl in bed."

It was a Saturday and I was spending the night at his place. He should have had the girls to stay but his wife had made a last minute decision to take them to her widowed mother's place outside the town of Fontainebleau.

"Give me some guidelines, Jean-Louis?" I requested.

"I would, for example, like it very much if I were to find your undergarments lying all over the living room in the morning, because it would mean there was urgency in your desire."

"Who is conservative now?" I retorted. "Undergarments! I ask you!"

"You know what I mean."

We were lying on his large bed, our naked bodies two small white boats in the dark blue sea formed by his fusion mattress, and I, shooting glances at Dali's *Sacrement of the Last Supper* and thinking Jesus was staring at us with disapproval.

"Undergarments!" I repeated.

"Bof," he said with a titter in his voice.

I swung my legs off the bed and my sweat-streaked

body followed.

"This is called a panty, for chrissakes. And this, Jean-Louis, is a bra. B-r-a."

I had retrieved my panty and my bra, both of white lace, from the chair beside the bed where I had undressed earlier, and I stood beside the bed, holding up the two.

I dropped both onto the bed, but as quickly I grabbed both and ran from the bedroom.

Downstairs in the living room I draped the bra over the backrest of Jean-Louis' black Chesterfield sofa and the panty I put down on his scarlet-red dining table. I placed his salt container in the crotch.

Back in the bedroom Jean-Louis lay on his back, his head resting in his cupped hands.

"What you've gone to do?" he asked.

"For me to know and for you to find out," I replied just as I used to do when, as children, Marius and I played our *because-because* game.

"Oh hell, Bella," he groaned.

Slowly, he sat up, slipped from the bed, and naked, he walked from the room.

Standing beside the bed, I did not take my eyes off his body for a moment.

His legs were well-shaped, almost like those of a woman, and he had two dimples of Venus above the groove between his firm oblong buttocks. *Fossae lumbales laterales... created by fibrous tissue between the posterior superior iliac spine and the skin ... is genetic ... considered a sign of beauty* ... Also from that anatomy text book from my first year at 'uni'. His waist was slim, too slim perhaps for a man, although when he was dressed this was not the impression I had. His back upright, smooth, but for a small beauty spot just below his right shoulder. "You must watch this and if it grows or changes colour consult a dermatologist," I had told him in Geneva after our first night of sex. "I have a gorgeous doctor who will watch it for me," he had replied.

His neck was smooth. "How do you manage to shave at the back of your neck?" I had asked him in Geneva. "Don't be silly," he had replied.

His brown hair, cut short, was tousled from lying down and glistened with perspiration; his ears, small and a little protruding. My mother had once told me having such ears was a sign of kindness. "I hope he will be kind too, Bella. Kind to you," she had said.

I lay down on the bed and soon I heard Jean-Louis' bare footsteps coming up the stairs.

"Damn!" I heard him say.

He must have knocked a toe.

Good grief. He was wearing my bra and panty.

"How do I look, Bella?" he asked.

He looked awful; I told him. He had pushed an apple into each bra cup and in his crotch, his manhood, half erect, protruded from the panty.

"I did not take you for someone suffering from eonism," I said.

He walked over to the bed; voluptuously he swayed his hips. At the bed, he struck a seductive pose, one foot on the bed and both hands on his hips.

"What's that? Eonism?" he asked.

"The male perversion to dress as a woman."

"How disgusting!"

Immediately, he stepped out of the panty and ripped off the bra, the two apples falling to the floor.

I patted the bed.

"Lie down. And what was that in my panty?"

"What should be in there now again."

He fell down beside me.

"The Court is in session," he said.

The Court is in session!

Oh, how those words gave me a thrill.

"Come here, Bella," he said.

He fell on to me, his face, always so beautiful, but at that moment distorted with concentration, right above mine. His manhood was rigid and straight and in its fullness it was searching for the sanctuary it wanted from me.

"Jean-Louis, I'm ready, darling," I whispered.

We climaxed together.

Later, I watched Jean-Louis walk to the bathroom. I heard water running: he was having a shower. I pulled the top sheet over my naked body, wet with perspiration. The Eiffel Tower, dark and silent, stood behind the large window which faced the bed.

As I was working the late afternoon shift at Chartreux Hospital, I allowed myself to fall asleep.

When I woke, there was no sign of Jean-Louis, but I saw a note stuck to the mirror above the basin in the bathroom.

Bella, darling, here you are, do please take a taxi home. Kisses and love from your J-L.

From the note protruded a 200 franc note.

It was nine in the morning.

I got back into the famous 'undergarments' which I picked up from the floor in front of the bed where Jean-Louis had dropped them.

I telephoned the *Taxi Bleu* company.

-0-

But I must stop remembering.

Who said God gave us memory so that we might have roses in December?

Whoever it was, I can tell this person, that I always, even in December, have an abundance of roses.

-0-

CHAPTER TWENTY-SIX

Each evening over dinner Colin tells me whether he will be in for dinner the next evening.

"Tomorrow evening I won't be here for dinner, Bella," he said.

He said this last night.

He wanted to know how one reached Paris from here. I told him he will have to get a local train at Avranches to Rennes and there he will have to get a train to Paris.

"It will take about an hour from Avranches to Rennes and about two hours from there to Paris."

He did not say whether he wanted to know because he was planning to go to Paris and I did not ask. My parents never questioned guests and neither do I.

"Also don't do breakfast for me, Bella," he added.

This morning, my room still dark, I heard him move about the house and I heard the click of the front door closing. I did not hear the vroom of his motorcycle's engine springing to life, but later I saw the bike was gone. He must have pushed it to the road so as not to wake me.

So, Le Presbytère's guest was going to spend a day in Paris. Often guests do. "Being so close to Paris we might as well go there," is what they always say.

Colin is probably meeting up with friends in Paris. Or a friend. And why not a lady friend? He is attractive. He is not a poor man. So?

-0-

Overhead the clouds are breaking up.

It had rained during the night, and the smell of sodden earth drifts through the open window to my left. I have decided to spend the day, or part of the day, on the mount, and here I am on this road I know so well. I slip a tape into the Merc's recorder and Lionel Richie's voice fills the silence. *Say you, say me; say it for always… That's the way it should be… Say you, say me; say it together… Naturally…*

Despite that I have not inherited my father's good voice, I sing along at full voice.

I had a dream I had an awesome dream… People in the park playing games in the dark… And what they played was a masquerade… And from behind the walls of doubt a voice was crying out…

One thing about being alone in a car, of being alone, is one can sing as loudly as one wants. One can also scream and shout and cry as loudly as one wants.

A mounted gray mare trots across the pasture land on my right, the lean frame of its horseman moving rhythmically up and down. I wave to the horseman; it is a refined 'royal' wave, its politeness making it a waste of time. I do not expect him to return my wave, but he does with his left hand, holding the reins with his right hand only, his heels pushed down into the stirrups.

As we go down life's lonesome highway … Seems the hardest thing to do is to find a friend or two…A helping hand – Some one who understands … That when you feel you've lost your way… You've got some one there to say "I'll show you."…

Now, the mare is cantering. A narrow, shallow stream, blue because of the distance, is ahead. The horseman, sitting up and leaning forward, is one with the mare. Before reaching the stream, the mare quickens her pace with three short strides. Next, mare and man are airborne, flying like some giant prehistoric bird. Once, on the other side of the stream, the horseman starts to pull back gently on the reins.

I step on the Merc's accelerator.

Lionel Ritchie is still singing. *Say you, say me; say it for always...That's the way it should be... Say you, say me; say it together...Naturally...*

The horseman, again holding the reins with just one hand, waves goodbye to me with the other.

-0-

I pull up close to the mount's Porte du Roi, the main entrance.

There are few cars parked here on the causeway - the *digue* - in front of the fortified gateway. The night's rain has probably persuaded those who were going to come here to Saint Michael's Mount today that the mount will be wet and windy.

One side of the gateway is ajar as it always is when the mount is open to visitors and behind it I can see Grande Rue. Several tourists, overdressed in anoraks, woollen bonnets, scarves and boots, are studying menus already on display outside restaurants, while others are choosing postcards from stands outside souvenir shops.

A young monk, dressed in the long, loose, black tunic and the black apron of the Benedictines, his feet in brown open-toe sandals, comes walking towards me. I know his face, but not his name. He walks past me, his open-toed, open-heeled, sandaled feet wet, obviously from having stepped into puddles of rain water. He passed without having acknowledged the smile I offered him. I look back and see him walk fast along the causeway: I can see a wicker basket hangs from around the back of his neck. He must be on his way to a shop on the mainland and will be returning with the basket filled with provisions.

Gertrude's mother, Mrs Yvette, no longer with us, used to cook for the monks and Gertrude tells a story of what a healthy appetite they have. Each Easter, the forty days of fasting of Lent over, her mother had to cook them her special of bread-crumbed monkfish baked in the monk's outdoor wood-fired clay and stone oven. A monk always accompanied her to the fishmonger in the nearby town of Saint-Malo to ensure the specimens she was going to buy had large and strong teeth: the monks made necklaces with the teeth for the souvenir shops to sell. It was before I had come to settle here, so I can only repeat what Gertrude tells us, and she says the tourists loved those necklaces. Today, Mrs Yvette in her grave, the monks cook their own meals so those monkfish necklaces are no longer to be found here on the mount.

Le Presbytère's winter guest having gone to Paris for the day, I will lunch on the mount. It is still only eleven o'clock, so first I will climb the steps up to the abbey.

I know Grande Rue's shop keepers and restaurateurs.

Edwige, her wrinkled eighty-year-old face always smiling, is standing outside her souvenir shop.

"Miss!" she greets me. Never *doc* for which I am always thankful. She has been in my life from when my parents opened the guest house.

She greets me with two kisses on each of my cheeks.

"I'm going to call it a day," she says.

She is going to retire to an old-age home in Rennes.

"Will you not miss the mount, Edwige?" I ask.

"The mount, yes, but not the stupid tourists. These days they want everything for nothing."

Hortense and Joël, her mentally challenged son, wave to me from the inside of their souvenir shop. I can see Joël wants to come outside, obviously to talk to me, but his mother, who is unpacking painted plates from a large carton on which is printed the words *Fragile – China,* sternly shakes her head. She points to the carton and he retrieves a plate from it which he places on a shelf behind him. On the picture painted on the plate, the mount is surrounded with a very blue sea on which tiny boats with red sails bob. Below the mount, in gilded lettering are the words, *Le Mont Saint Michel.*

Waiters in black trousers, white shirts and shiny black

patent-leather shoes are laying the tables in the restaurants. Red is the favourite colour for table cloths in the cheaper restaurants. White linen is that of the expensive ones, their matching napkins folded into lilies and placed on the porcelain side plates. Where the cloths are red, the napkins are of white paper and folded into pockets which hold the knife, fork and a spoon. "Paper napkins save on the laundry bill," as Frascot always says.

Build here and build high had said Archangel Michael to Aubert, Bishop of Avranches, and Aubert had done as instructed, and, now, there are nine-hundred steps from Grande Rue to the abbey. Often, have I climbed these steps and today I will do so again. Once a monk, seeing me out of breath as I was climbing, told me to zigzag up the steps and I will not become out of breath and certainly the climb will not exhaust me. Today, this is what I do. Right. Left. Right and left again. Japanese tourists coming up from behind me start to zigzag too. Some of the women begin to giggle. Perhaps they think I am playing the fool, or worse, I am drunk. If they are capable of giggling, I think, they do not have to copy my zigzag technique. At around the six-hundredth step several of the Japanese stop climbing and begin to take photographs of the granite marvel ahead of us.

I continue zigzagging, going up and up.

I know a stone bench in one of the abbey's many vaulted chambers and this is where I will sit for a while before I descend for lunch. I will not be stopping to rest because the zigzag way really does not make one tired but for a few minutes of contemplation.

To my delight, the Japanese are nowhere in sight.

-0-

The chamber where I choose to sit is long and narrow and along one wall stand six stone benches. But for a woman, old as I can tell from her shrunken frame and bent

211

shoulders, because her face I cannot see it being hidden under a black mourning veil, I am the only one in here. Centuries ago, in the wall behind me an embrasure had been chiselled to hold cannon. Before sitting down, I had stood at the embrasure, the rough stone cutting into my elbows, and looked at the sea in the distance, at this sea between France and England, a dull grey, and motionless at this hour of the day.

Against the wall, to my right, under an arch, hangs an icon from two long iron chains which have been affixed to the high vaulted ceiling. On the icon Mary is cradling baby Jesus in her left arm. She is in blue, wearing the traditional kerchief of the Orthodox Jewish woman that she was. Baby Jesus, usually naked on an icon, is in a green long-sleeved dress and a brown cloak. On the haloed Mary and the haloed Jesus' left drifts Archangel Michael, wings and sword aloft as here on the mount, and on their right drifts Archangel Gabriel holding a three-bar cross. The two archangels are gilded as is the frame around the icon.

The old woman gets to her feet and shuffles past me. She does not look at me. She is wearing bedroom slippers: *in this weather?* She reaches the icon and kisses it and next disappears through an archway to her right.

From somewhere above the abbey drifts three bell strokes. Almost immediately another three short strokes ring out. It is twelve o'clock on my watch and a monk must be sounding the noon Angelus. I wait for the third and final triple ring for confirmation. At its first stroke, a dove flies through the embrasure and with wings fluttering circles around the icon and, as the old woman has just done, it disappears through the archway on the right, its wings dipped, ready to land.

I sit very still.

As I child I adored the sound of bells ringing, and once, Miss Matigot asked my classmates and I what we wanted to be when we were grown up, and my answer was, "Miss, I am going to be a monk and I will ring the bells on the mount." Her reply was a smile and nod.

Inside the main gateway of our Sainte-Marie-sur-Brecque cemetery there hangs a copper bell, green with rust, from an iron crossbar attached between two granite rocks. The bell, and no one in the village can remember a time when it was not there, is only ever rung to announce a burial: three times three tolls if a man is to be laid to rest, and three times two tolls for a woman.

Father Pierre had tolled that bell for both my mother and father, the clanks resonating over the tombs.

-0-

I get up and walk from the chamber.

The Japanese from earlier reappear and begin to descend the steps down to Grande Rue with me. No need to zigzag now. One of the Japanese men points at me and next at his camera. I point at his camera and next at myself and I nod. He points to where I must stand: he wants the sea as background. His 'thank you' to me is a slight bow, his right hand lifted in front of him. Oddly, Le Presbytère has never had a Japanese or Chinese guest.

The usual bustle reigns on Grande Rue so I decide to skip lunch. The sky, a glowing blue because the day is after all not windy and wet, I turn off into a narrow footpath which winds between bare rocks. Behind me, towers the abbey, and Archangel Michael is brandishing his sword. As always.

And there was war in heaven: Michael and his angels fought against the dragon: and the dragon fought and his angels; And prevailed not; neither was their place found any more in heaven ...

And the great dragon was cast out, that old serpent, called the Devil, and Satan, which deceiveth the whole world: he was cast out into the earth, and his angels were cast out with him ...

Revelation 12, verses seven to nine.

I sit down on one of the rocks, one I always come to sit on. Near me, perching on another of the rocks, a gull

213

emits a high-pitched screech. "Would it not be nice if we can be little birds so we can fly across the sea?" I one day said to my father. "Do we have to be just little birds, Bella?" he replied. "I want us to be seagulls. We will be seagulls. We will flap our powerful wings and fly off on a journey which will take us across all the oceans of our world to lands we do not even know exist."

"Don't fill the child's head with wishful thinking, Rody," my mother reprimanded him.

Bella must know that man is bound to earth, she added. Bound to the earth like goats and sheep and donkeys.

Indeed, Mother, and to the innards of the earth we return.

-0-

After my father's burial I came here to the mount, took this footpath here and came to sit on this rock, 'my' rock as I think of it.

Rodolph Wolff was a Protestant, but his post-war experience in France having robbed him of his childhood faith, he had told my mother on more than one occasion he did not want a religious funeral.

"You can just throw me away," he used to joke.

Having received my mother's telephone call that my father had passed away, I immediately set off for Sainte-Marie-sur-Brecque. On my arrival, my mother's brothers, their wives and children and even a couple of grand-children were already gathered at Le Presbytère, the guest house's paying guests doing their best to remain out of sight. Marius and Marion still to arrive - they had left the girls with a friend in Paris - I, not wanting to be obliged to make conversation with those uncles of mine, drove down to the mount. It was a mid-summer day, a Monday, and business on Grande Rue was brisk, but I was in search of silence, so I took the footpath to this rock. After my father's burial, I, again seeking silence, came to sit here once more.

My father's burial was dignified.

"We cannot bury Mr Wolff without even a prayer," Father Pierre told my mother.

The priest had just then learnt from her she wanted to respect my father's wish not to have a funeral service.

"My husband was a Protestant," she feebly offered the priest as reason for such a wish.

"What will the villagers think of us?" asked one of my uncles.

The pallbearers, provided by the undertakers, carried my father's coffin from the guest house to their hearse parked under the copse of trees out front. At the cemetery, Father Pierre, having tolled the bell at the gate three times three, we stood around the freshly-dug hole in the ground, the coffin resting on ropes and which would gently lower it into the grave. A little way behind us stood four burly gravediggers in blue overalls, impatiently tapping their cracked fingers with the earth-filled fingernails, against their spades: they were eager to get their day's work done because their wage was a mere pittance.

"We are gathered here today to return the body of Rodolph Wolff to its rightful master: God our Father," began Father Pierre.

At that time, twelve years ago, he was still a young man with black hair and firm skin.

Following those words of his, a sigh - perhaps it was from my mother because the priest was not honouring my father's wish of keeping religion out of his burial - rose in the air.

Next, one of the mourners coughed.

It was a dry, artificial cough, which might have come from Marius as his way of telling our mother not to be angry at Father Pierre.

As for the priest, he, unperturbed by the interruption, opened the small leather-bound Bible which he was holding, flipped through it, and, also coughing, but a genuine cough filled with mucus, a shiny drop of it landing on his lower lip, swept his eyes over us.

"First Letter of John, Chapter 3, Verse 1," he said.

He began to read. *See the great love the Father has bestowed on us that we would be called children of God, and that is what we are.*

Again, he coughed, but without leaving a mucus deposit on his lower lip, and neither on his upper.

"… children of God," he repeated.

He spoke slowly, emphasising every word and looked towards my uncles, all of them dressed in black suits and wearing black ties.

Yet again, Father Pierre flipped through his Bible. Who had given him that Bible, I wondered? A loving, proud mother at his First Communion? A sad mother at his ordainment as a priest, crying silent tears because he will never give her a grandson or granddaughter?

"The Acts of the Apostles, Chapter 10, Verse 34," he said. "I will read if any of you want to follow the reading in … huh … your own Bible."

No one held a Bible.

He began to read. *As Peter said to the people, 'In truth, I see that God shows no partiality. Rather, in every nation whoever fears him and acts uprightly is acceptable to him. You know the word that he sent to the Israelites as he proclaimed peace through Jesus Christ, who is Lord of all. He commissioned us to preach to the people and testify that he is the one appointed by God as judge of the living and the dead. To him all the prophets bear witness, that everyone who believes in him will receive forgiveness of sins through his name.*

A honey bee buzzed around his head and Marius stepped forward as if he wanted to chase it, but quickly the bee flew off: he might have decided he did not yet want to die so was not going to sting the priest or any one of us.

The bee's interference had however resulted in Father Pierre closing his Bible and holding a hand out to my mother. She went to stand beside him.

"So, we are all children of God, and if we remember

what Peter had said, God shows no partiality. God has no favourites. God does not say, 'Come, you who are French, come let me embrace you', just as God does not say, 'Away with you who are not French'," he said.

While saying that he had looked at my mother, but next he swept his eyes over us and finally rested them on one of my uncles, the oldest of my mother's siblings and considered the head of the Desmarais clan.

"Child of God," he said, speaking into that uncle's face. "God is our judge. He is judge of the living and of the dead. We, His children, will receive His forgiveness. And today, here, we are burying one of God's children: Rodolph Wolff. We are burying one of us. We are burying him as one of us. We are all the same before our God."

After a short pause, his eyes closed as if in a silent prayer which he did not wish to share with us, he opened his eyes and swept them over us - right, left, and right again - and, his face up to the sky and his eyes yet again closed, he began to pray out loud.

"O God, thou who hast commanded us to love our neighbour, we now ask you to receive, through Your mercy the soul of this man for it to rest in peace in the company of Christ who died and now lives. Unite us, the living, together as a family in Christ, to sing Your praise forever and ever. Amen."

His prayer said, with a brief movement of his hands, he motioned to the pallbearers they could lower the coffin into the gravediggers' new hole. The coffin in the hole, he took my mother by the hand and led her to the grave. Beside the grave stood a bucket filled with red roses. Using his hands, he motioned to my mother that she could take a rose to drop on her husband's coffin.

For the next few minutes, in silence, each of us - Marius, Marion and I, and the mourners - dropped a rose onto the coffin. Marion also dropped a white handkerchief onto the coffin. Whether it was deliberate or an accident I did not know, but by the stern look Marius shot in her direction, I think it was not deliberate. As the hanky fluttered down to the coffin, I saw it was stained with my sister-in-laws bright red lipstick.

Back at Le Presbytère, Gertrude having been excused from attending the burial, was making a fuss over the lamb stew sizzling on two large three-legged pots set out in the back garden. One of Frascot's waiters, on loan to the guest house for the day, was filling glasses with champagne.

That was life, I thought: my father was dead and we were drinking to his happiness. Wherever he was.

Plates of stew being handed out, I slipped away to the mount.

-0-

CHAPTER TWENTY-SEVEN

It is a week ago that I went to sit on 'my' rock on the mount.

Colin is not back yet from Paris, but should be here before nightfall. He left a message on Le Presbytère's answerphone. *Bella, Bonjour. This is Colin. Just calling to say I will be staying in Paris a little longer and won't be back with you until Friday week. Bye for now. Oh, the weather's lousy here. See you!*

Paris in mid-November. The Christmas decorations will be going up or may be hanging already. Avenue des Champs-Élysées will be all tinsel and light, and in the windows of *Galaries Lafayette* glittering pink fairies will descend from the ceiling to snow-covered forests where animated bears and reindeers will be waiting with transparent coaches to take them … take them where? To some magic world perhaps. And over loudspeakers will come the voice of the late Tino Rossi: *Petit papa noël, quand tu descendra du ciel…*

It has been just like old times at Le Presbytère this past week. By old times I do not mean my childhood when my parents were here, but the years since my mother's illness and death and I began to close the guest house for winter.

I have been reading.

I phoned Marius and Marion in the evenings.

I watched American sitcoms on television.

Finally, I got down to dusting the library room, and I went driving around. I drove away from the mount to places with names sounding strange to the ears of our foreign guests. Conches-en-Ouche. Ferté-Fresnel. Crévecoeur-en-Auge.

Fred came round. He thought, Colin being English, he would be a chess player, and they could play a game. Yes, Fred is good at chess. He frowned when he heard Colin has gone to Paris for the week.

"Paris? Why do people go to Paris, Miss, I ask you?"

"Museums, Fred."

"Why did *he* go to Paris, Miss?"

"Fred, you surely know here at Le Presbytère we do not question our guests," I told him.

"Miss, I thought ..."

He did not finish the sentence and I thought, *Fred don't think.*

Yesterday, Thursday, I drove down to the village. I contemplated asking Gertrude if she could come up to Le Presbytère to cook Colin something nice on Saturday evening, but as I turned into her street I changed my mind and made a U-turn. He will eat whatever I will concoct with what I have in the freezer. I did however drive on to the bakery and asked Amandine for some dry cookies.

"Why not apple tart, Miss?"

"I need something that will keep. We had your great *amandine* last time so I would like something else this time."

"Ahh! This time? I say. I say. Sounds promising."

Amandine grinned from ear to ear and just then Olivier stepped from the back. He too was grinning from ear to ear.

"What do you suggest?" I quickly asked Amandine.

"Let me see. Something that will keep..."

"*Palmiers*," said Olivier. "I've just taken some from the oven. *Palmiers* and ... why not *madeleines*?"

"Indeed," I said, "why not *madeleines*?"

"Would you need jam?" Amandine asked.

I told her I still have a lot of Gertrude's strawberry jam,

but asked what she could suggest.

"Apricot jam," she said. "It's homemade too."

She put half a dozen large glass pots, which had once held mustard or gherkins, on the counter. She unscrewed the top of one, invited me to stick a finger into the deep orange jam to taste it. I duly did. Next, she stuck a spoon into the jam and offered me the halved apricot she had retrieved.

"Well, Miss?" she wanted to know.

'Very sweet' I said to myself, and 'smooth and velvety' I said to Amandine and Olivier, he standing beside her, the anticipation on his face telling me he had made the jam.

"Miss, forget about carrots, it's apricots that will keep you from going blind," said he.

What could I do after such advice?

I bought four pots of the jam.

-0-

Back at Le Presbytère the red light on the answerphone is flickering.

Bonjour, Bella. It's Colin here, the by now familiar voice said.

Just to confirm, I will be back tomorrow at the end of the day. Will probably be dark already. By the way, I met someone who knows you. A lawyer. Charming man. So too his wife. Met them at a party. Will tell you all about it tomorrow. Bye for now.

I know just one Paris lawyer and just one Paris lawyer knows me.

Oh my God, what did Jean-Louis tell Colin about me?

-0-

Will we ever understand life's reasoning?

I sit, in my bedroom, a guest house keeper when I should be in Paris practising as a doctor. From the time when I was still no higher than three apples, as is said here,

I wanted to be a doctor. This is to say but for the short period when I wanted to become a monk in order to ring church bells. Passing my school-leaving *baccalauriat* examination was not hard; "She's a bright girl our Bella," my father told guests. Neither were my medical studies hard. Not all that hard.

Full of dreams was my head when after having done my internship at Chartreux Hospital they offered me the permanent position as head of their maternity clinic. I received a salary which allowed me to live comfortably, to buy whichever pair of shoes or handbag which caught my fancy and not to have to think whether I could afford it when I invited colleagues for dinner at an expensive restaurant. And here I am, this evening, waiting for La Presbytère's winter guest to return, he who had spent the week in Paris having done there probably all the magical things I had once done there. I would, if I could, put the clock back and back and back to when I was not a guest house keeper but a young girl with dreams.

I am sitting at the window, yes, quite comfortably, looking into the distance, to the mount at the end of this day, smothered in a grey mist.

Handel's *I know that my redeemer liveth* drifts from downstairs.

He lives to silence all my fears ... He lives to wipe away my tears ... He lives to calm my troubled heart ... He lives all blessings to impart ...

The chiming stops and four short strikes follow. It is a quarter past something. I turn to look at the alarm clock on the bedside table. It is a quarter past seven. The mount's last few lights begin to go dark, one after the other.

Colin may like a *palmier* and a *madeleine* with the homemade apricot jam when he comes in. A *palmier* is good with ice cream and I have some in the freezer.

-0-

I hear the growling of a motorcycle's engine.

I gave Colin a key to the front door. He will be able to let himself in. I hear the click of the front door opening and another click: he is inside now. A clattering noise drifts from downstairs followed by clinking. Colin has walked into the desk in the small front room and has knocked the tin with the pens and pencils off the desk. His footsteps come up the stairs.

"Bella?"

"Colin!"

I step out into the corridor.

"I hope I did not wake you," he says. "I collided with the desk."

"I should have left some of the lights on. Did you hurt yourself?"

"Goodness, no, but I did break the inkpot. Fortunately for me it was empty. I hope it was not valuable."

"It belonged to Goethe ..."

"Goethe?"

"Goethe."

"Oh no! You are going to tell me to leave. It was must have been ... more than valuable. Priceless."

He walks up to me, his arms stretched out as if he wants to put them around me. Comfort me for the loss of Goethe's inkpot?

I laugh.

"I'm joking, Colin. It was just an inkpot. Any old inkpot."

He is in his biker's black leather and his cheeks are red: it must have been cold on the bike riding from Avranches.

"Hello, Bella," he says. "You gave me a real fright there."

We shake hands. His are cold despite that he had worn his bikers' gloves: they now lie on top of his suitcase. Also on top of the suitcase is a wicker basket. It is wrapped in cellophane which is tied with a red ribbon.

"Would you like a cup of tea?" I ask him.

"Only if it is not going to give you work."

"It won't. I would like a cup of tea myself."

"Thank you. A cuppa will be wonderful. The tea in Paris is dreadful."

"There is a reason for that. Who needs tea when one has all that wine?"

I tell him I will see him in the kitchen.

He says he will not be a minute.

"Just want to have a quick wash down."

-0-

CHAPTER TWENTY-EIGHT

I set the tea things out in the drawing room, on a coffee table which stands between the room's two bay windows. It is cool in the room. In the days when we received guests in winter the fireplace was always lit, Fred having loaded it each morning with logs, but with me alone here in the winter, its role has become merely decorative, its red bricks cold to the touch.

I sit down on an armchair facing the coffee table.

Colin walks in. He has changed into jeans and a black polo-necked sweater. His hair is wet: he would have had a quick shower. He is holding the cellophane-wrapped basket with both hands.

"Bella, I could not resist buying you a small gift. I hope you will like it."

Hesitatingly, he holds the basket out towards me.

I get up and take the basket from him, the paper crinkling under our hands.

"How wonderful. Thank you, Colin. How kind of you."

My mother drilled it into Marius and me never to say 'you should not have' when given a gift.

"Shall I help you with the wrapping?" asks Colin.

"Please do. Yes. Thank you."

I put the basket down on another coffee table: the basket will hold fruit or chocolates or perhaps a bottle of champagne.

"Let me," says Colin.

Our hands touch. Quickly, each draws back.

The pretty red bow is a ready-tied one, an elastic band holding it in place.

"Like a bow tie," he says. "Not that I wear them. My brother does."

I take the bow from him and so too the ribbon. All along the ribbon is the name *Fauchon*.

"I know a little girl who would want these for dressing up her dolls," I say.

I lied: I want to keep the bow and the ribbon as a remembrance of this man. These will go into the box where I keep other such knick-knacks in remembrance of things past: sugar lump wrappers from when Jean-Louis and I had coffee after dinner in restaurants; pine cones and conkers from when Jean-Louis and I took autumnal walks in the Tuileries Gardens. A booklet of matches from the hotel where he and I had stayed in Rochers-de-Naye.

Colin's gift is a selection of exotic fruit: a still-life of yellow, green, orange and red fruits I have never seen before.

"May I?" Colin asks.

He takes the smallest item from the basket, a tiny, crispy, bell-shaped fruit, and carefully, as if it is fragile, places it onto the palm of my right hand.

"What is it?" I ask.

"Come," he says, "it can be sticky, so I will open it for you."

He loosens the outer part of the fruit, a husk as thin and crispy as paper, and he holds up a perfectly round yellow berry.

"Come," he says again.

Holding the fruit by the tiny stem underneath it, he brings his hand up to my mouth. Keeping my eyes down and on his hand, like a baby who has seen its mother's nipple, I open my mouth.

His fingers brush against my lips.

"Oops, sorry."

He lets go of the berry and it drops onto my tongue.

With my tongue, I roll the berry around in my mouth and, next, I bite into it. I chew slowly, my eyes on Colin's: they are anxious, waiting for my response. The taste on my tongue is not one of sweetness but acidity. Refreshing mellow acidity.

Somewhere in the night, an owl hoots.

He flicks his head towards the bay window behind us.

"A storm is on its way."

We are only a few centimetres apart: I am still holding the hand with which he had fed me the berry. Quickly, I let go of the hand.

"Delicious," I say of the berry.

I give a step away from him.

"It is a gooseberry."

"So, that's a gooseberry! My mother used to tell my brother and I about the gooseberry tree which stood in the garden of their home when they were children. She used to tell us what a little hardy tree it was. They never watered it or trimmed it and each summer it produced the sweetest berries. My father said in Germany it was called a *Stachelbeere*. The thorn berry. There were a few people in his life who were thorn berries."

"*Stachelbeere? Stachelbeere?* Good name."

"I too have ... had them in my life," I say.

"I too have had them."

"But no longer?"

He shakes his head.

"They are still there but I've come to ignore their existence."

"Lucky man. I cannot ignore my thorn berries."

"Bella, I hope my presence here ... here at Le Presbytère is not a thorn berry. Will not be a thorn berry."

His eyes are bearing a strange look. I cannot interpret it. Or can I and I do not want to acknowledge its message?

"Let's have our tea, Colin," I say.

"Sure," he says. "Let's."

-0-

There is the patter of rain on the tiles of the porch outside.

Colin is spreading apricot jam over a *madeleine*. I am glad I bought not only the *palmiers* but also *madeleines* as this is his third.

"I found Paris somewhat noisy this visit. Don't get me wrong, I adore the place, but it has become noisy," he says.

"If you are not used to noise …"

"But, oh, let me tell you about your friend," he interrupts me.

"Friend?"

"I said on the phone I met a friend of yours …"

"Oh yes. A lawyer, I think you said? A lawyer and his wife."

"Jean-Louis Gasquet. Jean-Louis and Colette Gasquet."

Colette. This name Jean-Louis could never say. Did not say, until at the end, when she had walked back into his life, and he into hers, and out of mine.

Cool night air is blowing into the room from somewhere: badly fitting windows have always been a problem here at Le Presbytère. I begin to shiver. What did Jean-Louis tell Colin? How much does Colin know?

"How did you meet?" I dare ask.

"A lawyer friend asked me along to a dinner at the Gasquets. There were eight of us. It was all rather grand."

"In an apartment in Paris?"

"No. The Gasquets' house in Fontainebleau. It was Colette's mother's house. The old lady passed away a year ago so the couple had some work done to the house, had it modernised and spruced up, and it's really beautiful. Close to the chateau it is."

"Oh."

"Anyway, when Jean-Louis heard I was staying in …

228

the village … what's its name … he said he knew it well, that he had stayed at a guest house above the village quite a few times …"

"At Le Presbytère?"

He nods.

"Do you remember him?"

I shake my head.

"Not really. Guests come and guests go."

"I think he stayed here when your mother was still alive. He didn't know she had passed away, but he did say he had heard that her daughter, Bella Wolff, had left Paris and was running the guest house."

"I can't remember … meeting him here."

"No, he said he had met you in Paris at the hospital where you had worked …"

"Chartreux. I worked at Chartreux Hospital," I say unnecessarily.

"That is it, yes. He said you were in charge of the maternity section at the hospital and his sister gave birth to her first child there. That was when he met you."

"That means there is even a smaller chance of me remembering him because babies were born there every day."

"Of course."

Shall I dare ask him what Jean-Louis had said about me? And what Colette had said about me?

"What more did he say?" I ask.

"He said you were charming. I agreed. Of course. And he said Le Presbytère is the best guest house he has ever stayed in; the reception he received was wonderful, the scenery from its windows exquisite. I agreed. Of course. His wife told me she had not met you. The name, she said, rang a bell though."

"Thank you for the compliment, Colin," I say.

Overhead a plane passes.

I have never had time for a man who kisses and then tells.

-0-

In my room I switch on only the bedside lamp. Its shade is pink and decorated with the sequined outline of the face of Marilyn Monroe. I had still bought the lamp in Paris, so it also stood on my bedside table in my Latin Quarter apartment. Jean-Louis, on first seeing it, thought it the most inelegant thing he had ever seen, and my reply was that he was the most elegant thing I have ever seen.

I loved that man. Oh God, how I loved that man.

-0-

I think of something. There are books in my library room which were gifts from Jean-Louis, and books I gave him and which he left here. We wrote silly little notes to one another in these books and as Colin said that he would like to go over the books in the library room, I need to remove all books which will reveal I did indeed know Jean-Louis and the nature of our relationship.

Like a thief, I tip-toe to the library room.

Again I switch on only a lamp, the one that stands on the desk in the room. Its light forms a pinkish circle over the desk. I know the titles of the books I will have to remove, and as quiet as I can be, I take them from the shelves and drop them into an overnight bag I have brought from the bedroom.

What memories there are in a few lines scribbled in a book.

Bean brain, here's a book which will teach you that an Einstein is not a grand piano. Stupid as you are, I love you all the same, very much and for always. Jean-Louis

-0-

CHAPTER TWENTY-NINE

One remembers beginnings. And one remembers endings. My father always said what one must remember is what had been between the two. "Beginnings become endings, Bella, if it were not so, life would be too good. Remember that."

My mother used to contradict him. She used to say there was no such thing as endings. She said each ending was a beginning of something else.

On the day of my father's funeral, getting back to Le Presbytère from 'my' rock, the mourners, having eaten and drunk their fill, and only dirty plates and empty bottles standing on the tables which Honorine and Martine had set out in the garden, I wanted to ask her whether she still believed this, but I recalled her eyes when she dropped the red rose onto my father's coffin. They told me she had come to realise an ending was just that: an end.

The ending of Jean-Louis and I began with chickenpox.

-0-

It was one of those days at Chartreux Hospital when all births had gone well. It was seven o'clock and I was off duty, but sitting in the staff room chatting to our nurses. The telephone rang: reception had transferred a call to the staff room. Nurse Bonnec took the call and passed the receiver to me.

"Darling," said the voice of Jean-Louis, "What do you

know. Both the girls have chickenpox, so I am calling to cancel our outing for this weekend."

He told me he had to lend a hand with the girls.

"Be careful, that virus is contagious," I told him.

"For God's sake, Bella, what do you expect me to do? My daughters are ill. They need me."

He and I were going to spend the weekend in Nice. We were going to drive down in the Porsche after work to return on Sunday evening.

"Jean-Louis, I will phone the hotel and cancel."

"I've done so."

"You might have checked with me. I might have gone down to Nice all the same."

"With who?"

"That," I told him, "is for me to know and for you to find out."

I had taken Monday off, so I decided to fly to London, see the sights, eat some fish and chips, have a bacon-and-egg breakfast each morning at a café in the park on Russell Square, near to the hotel where I always stayed. I went to London and I watched the squirrels play on the lawn in that park and I took a few photos and I returned to my hotel and sat at the window and told myself I did not need Jean-Louis, I did not need a Jean-Louis in my life.

On the Tuesday, back in Paris, and at the hospital, I all the same waited for a call from him, but it did not come, and I did not hear from him until it was weekend again.

He phoned.

"Darling," he said, "the girls are better."

"That's good."

It was Saturday morning and I had just come in from a solitary walk along the Seine. It was autumn, but still warm, and young boys and girls in swimwear lay on their backs, tanning, on the banks of the river.

"Bella, I will see you tonight? Around seven. Is that alright?" Jean-Louis asked.

"Alright."

"We'll go grab a bite to eat somewhere."

"Alright."

-0-

"Bella, I missed you!" said Jean-Louis.

We were sitting on a leafy terrace in a courtyard of a small but expensive restaurant on Rue Saint-Louis on the Ile Saint-Louis.

He reached across the candle-lit table and stroked my arm.

"Come on," he said, "say you missed me too."

"What are you going to order for us, Jean-Louis?" I asked.

"Oh, to hell with you woman! Be like this if you want to be like this and see if I care!"

He asked the wine waiter to bring us a bottle of *Moët et Chandon.*

"Don't say anything about it being costly," he said, turning to me.

He ordered grilled steak and French fries for us.

"I hate to wait in restaurants," he reminded me.

The steak was tender with a taste of garlic and herbs from Provence. *The Moët et Chandon* exquisite. We finished the bottle.

Leaving the restaurant, Jean-Louis put an arm around my waist.

"I did miss you too, Jean-Louis," I told him.

He drew me to him and buried his face in my hair.

"That's my girl!"

We went to sit on one of the cement benches on one of the banks of the river. In front of us was Notre Dame Cathedral, dark and silent, the sky above it decorated with stars. Not far from us sat a man, obviously homeless, his legs hanging over the edge of the bank. A breeze carried the odour of his unwashed body towards us.

"Shall we go?" I asked.

233

"No. I want to talk to you."

"You can do so while we're walking home. To my place, that is."

"No, I want to talk to you on neutral ground."

He touched my face, stroked my hair.

"What do you want to talk about, Jean-Louis?"

The homeless man got to his naked feet and hobbled off, the night's breeze sweeping his stink into our nostrils.

"Bella, this past week, and last weekend too, I stayed with the girls' mother. It was to help out with the girls. At her apartment that is."

He inhaled deeply like a smoker who had tried to stop the habit but was capitulating.

"And?"

"It went well. The visit. Surprisingly well. The girls were ... in their element ... despite the fact that they were itching like mad. They were happy to have their dad home again. Both their dad and their mom with them."

A pigeon flew over our heads, his wings fluorescently white as it caught a beam from a lamp behind us on the bank. On the river, a tourist boat sailed by, rippling the water. Some of the boat's passengers stood on the deck. They waved to us. We ignored them.

"Shall we be off?" I asked.

"Yes, let's go."

We reached the Saint Michel Métro station, there where, on our first date, we had listened to the hippies chant *Hare Krishsna Hare Krishna Krishna Krishna Hare Hare Hare Rama Hare Rama Rama Rama Hare Hare.*

"I'll take the Métro here," said Jean-Louis.

I nodded my agreement.

It was after midnight. From behind the open windows in buildings around us ceiling lights threw faint circles of blue-grey light onto the pavements.

"Come, let me hold you for a moment," said Jean-Louis.

-0-

On Sunday evening my telephone rang. I had been on duty and as I had not heard from Jean-Louis, I hoped it would be him.

"Bella, how are you?"

It was Marion.

"Can't complain, Marion. And you?"

"Can complain, but won't. How's Jean-Louis?"

"I saw him last night. He's … "

"How are the two of you?" she broke in.

"We're …"

"No problems then, dear sister-in-law?"

She had again interrupted me.

"What kind of problems do you have in mind?" I asked.

"Well, he's married."

"I know."

"He's not married to you, Bella."

"I know that too thank you, Marion."

"He has a wife."

"I've worked that out as well thank you, Marion."

"Are the two of you still on?"

"Yes."

"They always return to the wife. They wander off, but they always return to the wife. The wife and the kids. I'm warning you dear sister-in-law."

"Thank you, Marion."

"Don't say I did not warn you, Bella."

"I won't, Marion."

I asked her if there was anything else she wanted to tell me and she said, no, there was not.

-0-

Children recover from chicken pox. Charissa and Carmen just could not recover from their bout with it.

"I … in fact Col … thinks the doctor should have a

good look at them. Do some tests," said Jean-Louis on the telephone.

"Yes, do tests," I agreed.

"Bella, the girls are really in a bad way. Especially Carmen."

He was spending, he said, each free moment with the two.

I had not seen him since that Saturday night's dinner.

He phoned again. Charissa and Carmen had undergone some tests and it was found Carmen suffered from Type 1 diabetes.

"I am so sorry to hear this," I told Jean-Louis. "Poor girl to have this for the rest of her life."

"Maybe I could bring her over and you could show her how to inject. She's rather got a problem with that and her mother ... Col ... and I, are very worried about it."

"Her GP has surely shown her how to and he would not like another doctor to interfere."

"He need not know."

Three weeks passed and I did not see Jean-Louis. He phoned every evening and every evening I listened to him giving me an update on Carmen's condition.

"I'll be there again this weekend," he said on the eve of the end of the third week.

I wondered what he meant by that: had he been spending the weekends with his wife and children in her apartment. I did not dare ask him because ... I knew ... knowing that he had been, would be upsetting.

They always return to the wife, to the wife and the kids.

-0-

It was Thursday morning. My shift was to end at two in the afternoon. I was called to the staff room. There was a call for me.

"Bella ... my *belle belle* girl."

It was Jean-Louis.

He had a plan. We were going to spend the coming weekend in Rome. He was to meet a client in the Italian capital the following morning but from six in the evening he would be free. He was to fly out in a couple of hours because he wanted to meet with a colleague before he was to see the client. I was to meet him in Rome the following day.

"How does this grab you, Bella?"

He had already booked a suite in a hotel close to the Spanish Steps.

"Mr and Mrs," he said.

"Do you also want to know how that grabs me?" I asked.

"We're going," he replied. "No discussion will be tolerated."

That was Jean-Louis!

-0-

He was waiting in the arrival lounge at Fiumicino Airport. He wore a beige suit and a pink tie, and he was impossible not to see, yet he lifted himself onto his toes and waved.

"Bella! Over here!"

The beloved voice was music to my ears.

Demurely, he kissed me on my forehead. His breath revealed he had had a drink or rather a couple of drinks at his meeting.

"To hell with this formality," he said.

He wrapped his arms around me and I pressed against him for a moment. I was still holding my overnight bag and it fell to the floor.

"Hello, Jean-Louis."

"It's just good ... so good to see you, Bella. I so bloody missed you."

Rome's rush hour traffic was dense and chaotic. The driver of our taxi turned down the window on his side and, swerving around cars and dodging in and out of traffic lanes, he banged on the side of the car each time a scooter or motorcycle tried to overtake us, and blew a kiss to the rider when, on admitting defeat, the latter slowed down to allow us to speed forward.

The liveried reception clerks smiled at me when I nodded confirmation I was the *signor's* wife. They must have wondered what the *bird* looked like this businessman was going to spend a dirty weekend with. One of the clerks took my overnight bag and accompanied us in the elevator to our suite. He had looked disapprovingly at the bag on taking it from me: there were no designer logos on it.

The suite was on the sixth floor, the hotel's top floor, and its walls were the blue of the Roman sky beyond the potted palm trees on the huge terrace. The padded bedspread on the king-size bed was blue satin. On the brocaded blue upholstery of the settee and chairs in the lounge area, white winged horses galloped beside a silver lake.

Jean-Louis had been spending money: bags from Via Condotti's boutiques lay on the bed.

"Before we do anything else, this is for you," he said.

He handed me one of the bags, and I remembered what my mother had said about never saying 'you should not have'.

"Come on, Bella, open it," he urged. "I want to see your face when you see what's inside."

Inside was a *Valentino* handbag. I held it up towards the French windows to see it better as if the light from the overhead chandeliers was not sufficiently bright.

"Come on, try it," urged Jean-Louis. "Let's see what you look like."

The bag's brown and white python leather perfectly matched my beige suit, the suit which Marion thought was drab. *Bella, you are a doctor, hell! Not a waitress. You can afford to dress in a much more chic and fashionable style.*

I emptied the contents of my *Prisunic* plastic handbag

onto the bed and repacked everything into the new bag, carefully sliding in each item, watchful not to cut or tear the silk lining, the designer's logo running across it and allowing me no doubt that my lover had spent a small fortune on this gift for me.

He sat on the edge of the bed smilingly watching.

"I will thank you later," I told him.

"Can't wait," he replied.

-0-

He had ordered a pizza dinner for us. *We cannot be in Rome and not eat pizza, Bella.* A waiter, dressed all in white - even his soft shoes were white - and reminding me of Chartreux Hospital's nurses, pushed a trolley set with porcelain, silver and crystal out onto our terrace. The door bell sounded and another waiter, also all in white, pushed another trolley out to the terrace. On this trolley were a large *margherita* pizza on a black earthenware plate and a variety of green salads in a wooden bowl. The door bell sounded yet again and a third waiter, not in white but in red and black, pushed a third trolley onto the terrace. On that trolley a bottle of *Dom Perignon* rested in a silver bucket filled with crushed ice. Jean-Louis signalled to the three to leave us and yet again sly smiles were shot in my direction. *Lucky girl*, they must have thought: *he's obviously loaded.*

Jean-Louis cut two slices from the pizza and motioned for me to take one. A scent of basil rose from small leaves, forming a circle on the melted mozzarella on top of the pizza.

The cork shot from the bottle without Jean-Louis even having had to put pressure on the cork.

"I'll have that," I said of the cork.

Jean-Louis smiled.

"To keep with the sugar lump wrappers and the conkers and pine cones, Bella?"

I nodded and he rose and went to stand behind me and

239

kissed my neck, there where my hair line ended.

"You smell nice," he said. "As always. I just adore the smell of you. And ... the feel of you."

We finished our dinner and Jean-Louis rang for the waiters to clear up. They arrived within a couple of minutes as if they had stood outside in the corridor waiting.

-0-

I just adore the smell of you.

My heart filled on hearing those words.

The waiters gone, Jean-Louis went into the bedroom to change. I stayed on the terrace. I had thought of something and I was contemplating its wisdom. Did I dare? Dare do what was on my mind?

I decided to give free reign to my idea.

"Jean-Louis, I'm just popping down to the lobby. I won't be a minute. No need for you to join me. I'll be right back. I want to ask the guys at reception something. We've not had all of the champagne, so pour yourself another glass. Finish the bottle because I will bring another one up with me," I called out from the lounge area.

He called out from the bedroom that he did not like the look of the receptionists so he would certainly not want to go near them again.

Downstairs, I walked over to the bar, which I had seen when we were booking in.

The barman, tall, slim, and with a bushy moustache and eyebrows, greeted me with a broad smile. I asked for a bottle of *Moët et Chandon*. Iced, but not on ice: it would be simpler carrying just the bottle upstairs to the suite.

"Signora, *woom* number please?" asked the barman.

I did not know the number of our suite, but one of the receptionists just then walked into the bar and said it was in order for him to let me have the champagne because I was a guest of the man from Paris.

240

Off the lobby there was a corridor lined with luxury boutiques. I popped into the first one I came to which sold clothes. I noticed a beige raincoat draped over a mannequin. I told the salesgirl I wanted the raincoat: I had not even tried it on. I told her I was in the suite on the sixth floor and to charge my purchase to it.

"A bag, Signora?" she asked.

"*No grazie*," I said.

Immediately, I changed my mind.

"*Sì, grazie, per favore.*"

She wrapped the coat gently in tissue paper and put the neat parcel she had made into the bag: it bore the name of the boutique - *Molto Chic*.

I made my way past the reception desk and to the toilets: I did not even shoot a glance at the horrible receptionists.

Already a bit heady from the champagne we had with the pizza, and my courage fired up, once in the 'ladies' I stepped into the largest of the cubicles and I began to undress.

I stripped right down.

Standing in my stilettos I ripped the labels off the raincoat and washed those down the toilet. I held my breath waiting to see whether the coat fitted me. It did. I put my clothes and the bottle of champagne in the bag. I fastened the raincoat's buttons: I did not want to risk the coat falling open when I walked through reception to the elevator and me looking like a hooker on her way to a client.

I stabbed at the button for the top floor and the elevator opened almost immediately: one thing about high-class hotels was that one never needed to wait for one to come, and the elevators seemed to be wrapped in cotton wool so silent were they.

Outside the door of our suite, I listened for sounds from inside. There were none. But no. I could hear music. I knew the voice. It was Pavarotti's. I stood still. *Nessun*

241

*dorma … Nessun dorma … Tu pire, o. Principessa … nella tua
fredda stanza …. guardi le stelle … che tremano d'amore … e di
speranza …*

I have always wanted to make love with the voice of
Pavarotti in my ears.

Nobody shall sleep …nobody shall sleep …

Indeed.

I placed the bag on the floor to the left of the door and
I began to undo the raincoat's buttons, my fingers agilely
moving down from my neck to my thighs. I took the
bottle of champagne from the bag and the bag I dropped
onto the floor.

I had brought a set of the suite's keys, but, like a
chambermaid, I rang the bell.

I heard Jean-Louis' footsteps.

I held my breath. I counted: one … two… three …
The door opened. Jean-Louis stared at me with pink,
sleepy eyes. He must have returned to the terrace and had
dozed off because his face too was pink, obviously from
the sun.

What did he see in front of him?

I had let the raincoat fall open.

He continued to stare at me. Perhaps, in his state of
somewhere between being asleep and being awake, he saw
just a half-naked woman.

I loosened the coat further: it dropped to the floor.

Someone coughed behind the closed door of the suite
next door.

"Jesus … Bella!" Jean-Louis gasped.

It was a gasp filled with desire and not with
apprehension that the closed door would be flung open.

He grabbed me by a shoulder and yanked me into the
suite. At the same time he grabbed the champagne bottle
with one hand and, crouching, he retrieved the raincoat
and so too the bag from the floor. He slammed the door
behind us and almost threw me across the lounge area and
into the bedroom.

"Stand with your back to me," he murmured.

He pointed to the white and gilded wardrobe in the bedroom. I did as I was told, my naked thighs against the cold of the wardrobe's full-length central mirror. I looked in the mirror to see what he was doing behind me. He was walking to the bathroom. I heard the champagne cork pop. It hit the ceiling of the bathroom. He walked back into the bedroom. He held the open bottle with one hand and with the other, two water glasses: the flutes must have remained out on the terrace.

He was naked and he was fully aroused.

"What a very naughty girl you are walking around naked. But I like it. I love it," he said.

He gave a laugh, an almost manic laugh.

"Jean-Louis …"

"Spread your legs, darling," he said.

My head was spinning, spinning with the champagne of earlier, and with desire, but I did as he had ordered me to do.

"I'm thirsty," I said. "May I have a mouthful of the champagne, please, honey-bunch?"

"Of course, sweetheart."

He put the two glasses down on the floor and, as I bent forward to pick one up, he mouthed 'no' and pointed to the open bottle: I was watching him in the mirror. He held the bottle up above me, tilted it over, and let the champagne run slowly, almost drop by drop, over my head and my naked body.

"Lap it up," he said. "Quench your thirst."

He let the bottle fall to the floor, what champagne left in it, running over our feet, swung me round and lifted my left breast up to my mouth and stuck my hard nipple between my lips.

"Suck, Bella," he ordered.

My nipple was dry. So was my throat.

He stepped away from me.

"I want you to stay here. Don't move," he said.

He disappeared back into the bathroom and quickly I lifted the bottle to see if any champagne was still left in it. There was; a few drops. I threw my head back and let the drops fall into my mouth.

On Jean-Louis' return he was carrying the ice bucket in which the wine waiter had earlier served the champagne we had had with the pizza. The bucket was filled with water. From the steam rising from it I knew it was hot water. The floral scent of the hotel's Versace collection of complimentary bath foams clung to the flannel mitt he was holding.

"I'm going to wash you, my little baby," he murmured.

I watched him.

He dipped the mitt into the bucket and slowly he wrung it out, his hands red from the heat of the water.

Waiting, I pressed my wet and sticky back against the cold of the mirror.

Jean-Louis began washing me. He started with my neck and shoulders. Next, he washed under my armpits and under my breasts, following a centre line to my stomach and to my thighs. He rinsed the mitt and gently pushing my legs apart he proceeded to wash between them. The mitt was hot.

I threw my head back. I was completely lost in his touch and the champagne from earlier.

"Come on," he said.

My body quivered from the expectation of what he would do next.

Again, he dipped the mitt into the bucket and having again wrung it out, he handed it to me.

"Come on, sweetheart, your turn to wash your little Jean-Louis," he said.

He spread his legs and placed his manhood on the mitt.

"Wash, Bella, wash!" he ordered.

I swept the mitt up and down across his thighs, down his legs and up again to his manhood.

I was cold and I began to shiver.

He too began to shiver.

Both of us shivering, goose pimples on our arms, we held one another. Slowly, we sank to the floor and he rolled on to me and entered me gently. We were still shivering, but no longer with cold but with desire, desire for one another.

We lay on the floor for quite some time, two exhausted people, two exhausted lovers, contented, fulfilled, happy.

Later, the new raincoat again wrapped around me, I sat on the bed and watched Jean-Louis dress in jeans and T-shirt.

"Let's get another bottle of champagne," he said.

He telephoned the bar and asked for another bottle of *Moët & Chandon* to be sent up.

"And something to eat too. Crisps. Olives. Crackers. Chocolate. Figs. Do you have figs? No! Go see if you can find some."

I ran to the bathroom to shower and while I was in there the bar sent up a splendid selection of snacks.

"No need to go out for dinner," said Jean-Louis, a cracker spread with blue-black caviar in his hand.

All night we made love, Jean-Louis, a most tender lover, kissing my breasts, my feet, sucking my fingers, my toes, and holding me to him and whispering into my ears, my hair and my face that he was never going to let go of me again.

At around four in the morning I remembered Pavarotti had been singing when I came in from downstairs. I had no idea when the tape had run out.

"Pavarotti," I asked, "what happened to him?"

"I asked you whether you wanted me to replay the tape."

"Oh yes," I said. "So you did."

I had no recollection of him having done so.

-0-

In the morning, on waking, Jean-Louis told me not to wear a dress that day. I had to wear jeans.

"I take it you brought a pair of jeans?"

Over breakfast, he told me that he had hired a scooter; it was to be our transport for the day.

"Bella, this day is going to be memorable!" he said.

The scooter was turquoise. The hotel's concierge handed us two matching crash helmets the hire company had left on delivery of the scooter. He also handed us a street map for Rome.

"Speed ahead," said the concierge.

"We're speeding ahead," replied Jean-Louis.

Despite the early hour of the day, Rome's streets were already congested. Ahead of us was a sea of cars, all small, all in need of a visit to the cleaners, all ignoring the existence of such a thing as a traffic lane while scooters and mopeds, even pedestrians, dogged around, both the coming and retreating vehicles. Never having been on a two-wheeled vehicle before, despite that Marius had often asked me to go for a ride with him on his motorcycle, I gripped the back of Jean-Louis' seat tightly, concentrating on keeping my balance. The traffic was, or so it seemed to me, sweeping us along, the Tiber to our left, old stone buildings, which appeared to be holding one another up, to our right.

Going down a narrow street, we passed burly grey-haired matrons dressed in the black of mourning and selling fruit from two-wheeled barrows placed in front of alcoves through which little Romans could be seen playing oblivious apparently to half a dozen cats rummaging in discarded garbage.

I began to relax and eased my grip on Jean-Louis' seat.

A traffic cop, his stomach bulging over the white belt of his uniform, waved us forward: ahead loomed the Coliseum. A cacophony of car hooters and opera booming from car radios, made it useless for me to call out to Jean-Louis that I would like us to go round the Coliseum. Just then another traffic cop also waved us on with white-gloved hands. His white pith helmet had slipped over his forehead and he looked rather silly. Yielding to the scooter's sway, I freed one hand and signalled a salutation to the traffic cop. He blew on the whistle he was holding between his lips: his return salutation to me perhaps?

At noon, we pulled up on a square where three workmen, two standing on a columned fourth floor balcony, were holding a rope which was tied around the waist of the third who, two floors down, his feet resting in crevices, was brushing bird droppings from the top of the head of an angel chiselled into the façade.

"I'm hungry," said Jean-Louis.

We chose a *trattoria* on a narrow, cobbled side street and Jean-Louis decided we should have *cannelloni* and as always, I did not argue.

After lunch, having just had a glass of Chianti each to drink, we continued with our scooter tour of Rome.

Back at the hotel and in our suite, Jean-Louis said he had to make a telephone call to Paris.

I went into the bathroom to change into a white cocktail frock for dinner which was to be in a restaurant.

I listened to what he was saying.

"Yes, sweetie, papa knows. I am so sorry I'm not staying over this weekend, but I will see you and Carmen on Monday evening. Is that ok? Yes, give me your mom. Hello. How are things today? I'm in Rome. No, it is a business trip. I'll be back tomorrow evening so I'll come round on Monday evening. Yes, I am sure they miss me. I miss them too. Yes, certainly, I will. I'm bringing them something from Rome. Yes, I am sure. Yes, of course. Well, I will have to ring off now. Ok, put Carmen on. Hello sweetie, how are you and Charissa? Oh, Charissa is naughty eating so much ice cream. Yes, sweetie, I know, you are not allowed to eat ice cream yourself, and I am very sorry this is so, but the doctor did say when your blood sugar is down, you will be able to eat a little of it.

247

Yes, sweetie, I know. No, I will not eat any ice cream at dinner this evening. No, I'm not on holiday. I came to see a client. Yes, I am here on my own. Yes, I will bring you and Charissa to Rome. Yes, we will do so very soon. Yes, I promise. Yes, Mom can come too if you and Charissa would like that. Sweetie, I must really ring off. Ok, bye for now. I love you too, sweetheart."

-0-

We dined in a small restaurant near to our hotel. We sat at a round table for two which stood at a window behind which the Spanish Steps loomed and where tourists in jeans and sandals were buying ice cream from a Roman, dressed as a centurion. Next to the centurion another centurion was belting out *O Sole Mio*.

Ma n'atu sole ...cchiù bello, oje ne'... O sole mio sta 'nfronte a te! ... O sole ... O sole mio ... sta 'nfronte a te! ... sta 'nfronte a te! ...

Every time a coin was dropped into the metal jug at his feet, his *largamente* became a *stentato* which, once he had shot a glance at the tourist's offering and had seen it was perhaps but a few *centisimi*, again quieted down.

Jean-Louis politely asked if I would allow him to choose what we would eat. The question, in no way a surprise, I just nodded. He ordered *ossobuco* and *polenta*.

"And a bottle of *Chianti*," he told the waiter.

"Which will no doubt be holding a candle tomorrow evening," I said.

I thought he would laugh, or at least smile, but the frown across his forehead, which I had observed earlier when I had walked back into the bedroom from the bathroom, had returned.

After what was a morose couple of hours in the restaurant, despite that the maitre d' - bless his soul - had, having noticed, no doubt, that the thoughts of the male of the species were not on the food, and also not on the

248

Chianti, or on the female of the species, kept on coming to our table, each time pressing the index finger of his right hand into his right cheek, which Jean-Louis had interpreted for me as the man finding me tasty-looking, we walked back to our hotel.

-0-

"Bella, I am rather worried."

We were back in the suite, the French doors leading to the terrace, wide open, the Roman sky, starlit.

"About what Jean-Louis?" I asked.

"About *who* rather. It's Carmen. The sugar, you know. The child is really struggling with the diabetes."

What was I to say?

"Children do. Adults do too."

"I wonder if we could go to Le Presbytère next weekend and I could bring the girls along? You can then explain to Carmen how things work."

Yet again: what was I to say?

"If you think it will help."

"It is worth the try, Bella."

-0-

Reaching the suite, Jean-Louis said he needed the bathroom. I walked out onto the terrace.

I stood there thinking.

I realised that I would never be first on Jean-Louis' list of priorities. At the top would be his daughters. A close second would be the freedom his separation from his wife was allowing him. Next, his job. I knew he was a good lawyer, one of the best corporate legal minds in Paris, if not in France. I even suspected that Collette, the wife he was telling me he was no longer in love with, would rank above me on a priority scale. *Yes, Mom can come too.* Those words of his kept spinning round and round in my head.

And there was the diabetes thing and he was becoming involved with it and I was probably heading for a place where I would be no more than a 'doctor friend', someone who knew how to inject people.

"Bella, I've warmed the bed," Jean-Louis called out.

He had gone into the bedroom.

I took a deep breath, painted on a smile and sauntered inside. I had felt so very much alone out there on the terrace anyway.

He lay on the bed, naked. I undressed and lay down beside him. He rolled onto me. Purposely, yet it took all my self-control, I did not move. I just lay there, yet I wanted to cry out, *Jean-Louis! Love me! Dammit!*

"Bella," he said, "I cannot live without you. I do not want to live without you."

He rolled on to me and we held one another for quite a while before we began to make love again.

In the night, I rose from the bed, Jean-Louis lying on his stomach, fast asleep.

I went into the bathroom and I began to shower.

I looked at my face peering back at me in the mirror above the washbasin.

Were those tears I saw running over my cheeks? Tears because Jean-Louis was not wholly mine?

No, maybe it was just water from the shower ...

-0-

At four that morning I was back standing on the terrace. The stars had faded and the night was dark. Jean-Louis was asleep, his beautiful, slim body relaxed in total abandonment across the rumpled bed where he had held me and told me he could not live without me. That he would not want to live without me.

-0-

We took a taxi back to Fiumicino. While Jean-Louis stared in silence at the road ahead, the frown back across his forehead, I chatted about all and everything that came into my head. The taxi driver, obviously exasperated at this woman who would not shut up, shot me angry glances in the car's mirror below which a metal Saint Christopher medal swung in rhythm to the movement of the car.

"Bella, you won't mind if I go straight back to my apartment, do you?" asked Jean-Louis, once back in Paris.

We had already gone through customs at Orly Airport.

On the flight he had suggested we each have a gin and tonic and, yet again and as always when he decided what we would eat and drink, I had agreed.

Standing in line at the taxi rank, he kissed me on the cheek.

"Thank you, Bella. Thank you for a wonderful weekend. Sorry ... sorry if ... you know ... if my mind wandered a little ... at times."

We took separate taxis into Paris.

-0-

Le Presbytère was almost fully booked, so my mother let Charissa and Carmen have the 'Tony from Colorado' room which was free. Fred pushed another single bed in there. The only other room that was also free was the one with the rose window.

"Will it be alright if you and I go in there?" I had asked Jean-Louis on the telephone on the Friday.

"Sure. Why not? It's a lovely little room," he had replied.

My mother got Fred to push an extra single bed in there too.

Jean-Louis, Carmen, Charissa and I arrived at the guest house at eleven on Saturday morning. Because the Porsche was a two-seater, Jean-Louis hired a Volkswagen *Combi* like that of the Le Presbytère for the weekend: the girls wanted to take their bicycles along.

When we arrived, some of the guests were still having breakfast which was being served out in front of the house under the copse of trees. My mother, helping Honorine and Martine with the serving, was frying eggs and bacon on a gas plate.

"Hello girls," she greeted Jean-Louis' daughters.

Bella, what are you doing with a married man, and one who has two children, the expression on her face asked me despite the broad smile of welcome she had given the two girls. *Mother, I love the man,* was my unspoken reply.

Our overnight bags deposited in the rooms, we drove down to the mount. The girls' bikes were in the *Combi*, in case they wanted to cycle later in the day. At the mount, the tide out and the mount standing on sand, the two, dressed in jeans and sweaters like their father and I, began to jump up and down: they wanted to go to cycle on the sand.

"Maybe we can go out there, but only later, and not for the two of you to cycle on the sand. We'll go for a walk. Pick up some shells," I replied on their father's behalf.

"No," Jean-Louis overruled me. "Let's go for a walk out there. We can climb up to the abbey afterwards."

The grey, wet sand was cool under our naked feet: we were carrying our sandals and we had rolled up our jeans to our knees.

"Not nice," growled Charissa after a few steps. "The sand's all gluey."

I could have told her.

A little white and black dog found the sand to his liking and was running around yapping and soon snapping at our legs, its teenage owner not caring to restrain her pet.

"Horrible beast," complained Carmen.

"He's only playing," I said.

"Leave it, Bella," whispered Jean-Louis.

Because of the little dog Charissa and Carmen decided they would rather walk around on the mount. Immediately, we turned back the way we had come and Jean-Louis retrieved a bottle of mineral water from the *Combi* for us to wash away the sand which clung to our feet. I handed out tissues with which to dry our feet. Our sandals back on and our jeans rolled down, we walked along Grande Rue and sat down in a café: the girls were thirsty.

In the café, the four of us sat at one end of a long table. It stood behind a window which looked out to where we had just walked. The little dog was still running around; he was chasing his tail. Sylvain, the café owner and a cousin of Fred, Frascot and Gertrude came over to greet me.

"Pretty girls," he said. "Yours?"

The question was directed at Jean-Louis.

"All mine!"

He looked proud.

Both girls wanted orange juice and ice cream. Jean-Louis did not object. When I was a child, my mother would have asked me whether I thought money grew on trees and she would have allowed me one or the other, but not both. And Carmen should not have been drinking a sweet soda and eating ice cream. Jean-Louis had a beer. I said I will have some fizzy water.

"My mom hates fizzy water," stated Carmen.

She was juggling two glass ashtrays.

"You should not be having ice cream," Jean-Louis told her belatedly.

"Mom said as I was to enjoy myself this weekend, I can eat what I want."

"We all hate fizzy water," said Charissa. "My mom never buys it."

"I like fizzy water and I always have a bottle in my fridge," I replied, speaking to the wall opposite and not to the three at the table with me.

"Leave it … leave it, Bella," whispered Jean-Louis yet again.

Using the monk's zigzag technique, we ascended the steps to the abbey. Charissa and Carmen swung their arms in the air. Some other children followed suit and a few steps later so did their parents, and so did Jean-Louis, and, not wanting to be the odd one out, so did I.

"That was fun," said Jean-Louis at the top of the steps.

He was sweating: his jersey, wet, clung to his back and I wanted to lay my hands on his back and pull him towards me: he looked so masculine, so manly, so attractive. So sexually enticing.

"Daddy, Daddy," said Charissa in a sing-song voice, "we're going to race you down the steps."

"No, when we've had a look at the abbey we will walk down, and we will do so like wise people and not like baboons," I told her.

"Let the girls be, Bella," said Jean-Louis sternly and loudly. "They are just little kids."

Charissa and Carmen jumped around with glee at their father's support.

-0-

It was hot and airless in the abbey.

We sat down on a long, low, wooden bench, the sunlight from the clerestory windows behind the altar ahead of us, illuminating our faces.

On the stone altar table stood a large crucifix, also of stone. The eyes of Jesus, hanging in His very holy Glory on the Cross, were closed and a cloth covered the intimate parts of this most holy of Christian Holies. A nail with a mushroom shaped top protruded from the most holy of feet; the slim, bony right foot over the left, the nail embedded in the bridge of the foot. *The bridge of the foot is a pyramid-like collection of three bones, the cuneiform, the cuboid and the navicular bone.* Also from my anatomy text book of my first year at 'uni'. In front of the altar table stood a large basket of drooping flowers: a week or two must have gone by since they were placed in the basket.

An old couple sat down in the pew in front of us. Each

clutched a Bible and a Rosary from which hung a small metal crucifix; the crucifixes had started to rust so their owners must have had them for a long time. Drops of perspiration dripped steadily from the man's ears, and had turned the beige of his shirt the brown of a potato.

Carmen found the man's wet ears funny.

"Stop," said Jean-Louis.

He shot an annoyed glance at her.

So he can reprimand his daughters.

"Why are you not a nun?" she asked me.

"Why should I be, Carmen?"

Two nuns with what I thought were sad eyes in their pale faces just, at that moment, walked in, halted in front of the altar, and made the sign of the cross in front of the crucified Christ.

"Yes, why are you not a nun?" Charissa supported her sister.

"Why should I be, Charissa?" I repeated my question.

"You're not married and nuns aren't married either," she offered as explanation. "Our dad can't marry you because he is married to our mom."

"I ...," I began.

"Leave it Bella," Jean-Louis silenced me with a stern whisper. "Come on girls, let's go have a bite to eat," he told the two.

We descended the stairs in an orderly manner.

On Grande Rue the girls wanted to look into the souvenir shops.

"You're not going to buy rubbish," warned Jean-Louis.

They wanted to buy their mother something and from the made-in-China souvenirs on the shelves they chose a snow globe, the mount inside it.

"Is that not pretty?" cooed Jean-Louis with obvious fake delight.

The salesgirl had turned the snowball over and the fake snow was swimming around the glass globe like small fish in an aquarium.

255

"Wait, give your mom this from me," said Jean-Louis.

He put a set of a large embroidered tablecloth and twelve napkins on the counter.

"Can you wrap these nicely too?" he asked the saleslady.

Oh, those will be hell to wash and iron.

We returned to Sylvain's restaurant and we had *moules marinières* and French fries and when Carmen asked for an ice cream for dessert, Jean-Louis refused to let her have it because of the diabetes and she began to cry noisily.

Quickly, we settled the bill and left.

-0-

We drove along the coast on a winding road only locals knew of and we came to a lay-by and pulled up. Charissa and Carmen had been jumping up and down on the rear seat chanting they wanted to ride their bikes on the beach below.

I sat down on the sand and Jean-Louis walked the two, they, pushing their bikes, down to the water's edge where the sand was firmer and good for cycling. I watched the three of them: a perfect holiday snap of a father and his two daughters, fruit of his loins, as my mother referred to the little children who came with their parents for a holiday at La Presbytère. The breeze from the sea beyond which lay England and further away the American continent, rustled their hair.

The girls on their bikes and riding over the wet sand, I watched Jean-Louis walk back towards me. He had removed his sandals again and had also again rolled up his jeans to his knees. He kept on turning to look at his daughters; their excited laughter drifted towards me.

A father and his daughters.

They were not my daughters. Would never be. Therefore, what right did I have to sit there with this man and his two daughters? That was the question mulling in my head. Should his wife and the mother of those daughters not be sitting here?

Jean-Louis threw himself down on the sand beside me.

"Don't let them needle you, Bella," he said. "They are good kids."

He drew up his legs and rested his elbows on his naked knees. He wiggled his toes into the sand.

"I know, Jean-Louis," I said.

I lay back on the sand.

"Hey," said Jean-Louis, "one of us must keep an eye on the girls, so do not fall asleep, because I think I will."

-0-

It was mid-afternoon. The sun shone down on the water. Gulls, sitting on red buoys swaying on the water, began to squawk. I lifted myself up on an elbow. The gulls, half a dozen of them, were pecking at something on the surface of the water alongside the buoys. Soon, one lifted his head and had a small fish in his pointed yellow beak. He fluttered his grey wings and lifted his white body off the buoy and circled above it once, twice and a third time and, wings dipped, made a perfect landing back onto the buoy. Through a clumsy movement - perhaps - he dropped his catch onto the buoy and instantly the other gulls which appeared to have sat there sleeping, came to life, long, thin legs in waltzing movements stepping high. Amid high-pitched war cries, beaks pecked at the small fish and at each other too. Their cries became triumphant shrieks and with a wave of their wings they were airborne. After circling the buoys they flew towards the shore. The small dead fish remained lying on the buoy on which the gull had dropped it and soon a ripple in the sea swept it back into the water.

I lay down again and I closed my eyes. Jean-Louis' eyes were closed too. Charissa and Carmen's laughter was approaching.

"Bella?" asked Jean-Louis.

His eyes were still closed.

"Yes."

"You should not so go on at the girls. Just let them be. Also, I know Carmen should not be eating ice cream and such sugary things, but her blood sugar remains fairly steady with the insulin injections, so she can have a little fun this weekend. *Christ* - she is so young to have something like this hanging over her."

I said nothing. I sighed, but I remained silent.

"I've been thinking," Jean-Louis continued. "I think we ... you, in fact, should not speak to Carmen about the illness after all."

"If you think so."

"I know the purpose of coming here this weekend was for you to speak to her about it, but I think it will just make matters worse. If you know what I mean."

Certainly, I knew what he meant.

"That's fine with me," I said.

"Maybe some other time."

"Sure."

"Daddy, Daddy!" came the voices of the two.

They wanted their father to see the scallop seashell they had found.

"Are there others there?" he asked.

"Lots!" they said simultaneously.

The bicycles having been thrown down, father and daughters walked off, their feet sinking into the sand with each step and leaving distorted footprints.

I stayed sitting in the sunshine on the sand.

I sat there, the three's merry laughter in my ears, and I thought of the anxious face of a father in the moment before his child was born, as I had seen in my days at Chartreux Hospital. I thought of the love I had seen in the eyes of a father in the moment he held his newborn child in his arms for the first time; how he held the tiny finger still dirty with the blood of she who had carried the seed in her womb which he had sowed there.

What was I doing having an affair with a married man? A married man and a father?

God, how I hated myself at that moment.

-0-

We drove back to Le Presbytère. Charissa and Carmen, on their knees on the rear seat, were looking back to the mount.

"Well, what do you think of Saint Michael's Mount?" I called out to them, my voice raised over the noisy drone of the car's engine.

"It's ok," both said.

Jean-Louis took his eyes off the road and towards me and smiled.

"I'm hungry," he said.

"We'll have something nice to eat this evening, don't worry. I'm sure Gertrude is going to do one of her specials for us tonight."

"I'm not hungry!" Charissa called out, having slumped back onto the rear seat, her feet on it too.

"I want some more ice cream," stated Carmen.

She too was sitting down and her feet were on the back of my seat.

My mom had put a 'Reserved' notification on a table under the copse of trees for us.

Valentin, who some nights played the piano at the Vaybee and was another cousin of Fred, Frascot and Gertrude, was sitting at the guest house's piano which had been carried outside for the diners' entertainment. He was flipping through some sheet music deciding what to play. Honorine, in a black mini-dress and white frilly apron, her feet in silver sandals, walked up to him and bent over his shiny bald head which always had my brother and I, when we were children, giggling, because we called him 'the pomegranate' behind his back. The bald head nodded and its owner flipped back a few pages, bent forward a little, and began to play Debussy's *Feuilles Mortes*.

Fallen leaves can be picked up by the shovelful ... So can memories and regrets ... And the north wind takes them ... into the cold night of oblivion... You see, I have not forgotten ... The song you used to sing me...

Martine, dressed like Honorine, handed each of us a menu. Jean-Louis was also handed the wine menu.

This song is like us ...You used to love me and I used to love you ... And we used to live together ...You loving me, me loving you ...

"What are we going to have?" asked Jean-Louis.

But life separates lovers ...Pretty slowly, noiselessly ... And the sea erases on the sand ... the separated lovers' footprints ...

"May I suggest something this time?" I asked.

"Sure, but don't you always, Bella?"

The girls wanted French fries and ice cream: no degree of persuasion on the part of their father succeeded in changing their mind. Jean-Louis and I began with a tomato salad and our main course was *filets de merlan au gratin,* one of Gertrude's specialities and much liked by our English guests, especially when it was served with boiled potatoes. That night we also had boiled potatoes with it.

Valentin played a medley of country songs. Next, and without pausing, he played some French songs. Probably having exhausted his repertoire of French songs, he returned to the country songs, repeating those he had played before.

Jean-Louis called Honorine over and asked her to serve the man a beer.

"To give our eardrums a rest," he said to me.

Served a tankard of frothing beer and a plate of French fries, Valentin bopped his bald head in our direction. He went to sit on a folding stool some distance away, ignoring the knife and fork Honorine had handed him, preferring to eat the fries with his fingers and licking those each time he had popped a French fry onto his very red tongue.

260

Jean-Louis and I finished the bottle of *Chablis Grand Cru* Honorine had served us without us having asked for it, but just for, "Some white wine, please Honorine". When I saw the bottle, condensation on it becoming droplets, I knew it was going to cost Jean-Louis a small fortune. I planned to have a word with my mother for doing that to him.

He wiped away some of the droplets with a finger and pressed the wet finger to the tip of my nose.

"Red," I asked him, "my nose?"

"Goodness, no! Just flushed."

-0-

We sat chatting, Charissa and Carmen running around, chasing pigeons which had flown up and were pecking at the leftovers on abandoned plates which Martine and Honorine had not yet cleared away. The two girls had not eaten all of their French fries, and the pigeons, beady eyes staring at Jean-Louis and I, flew to our table and began to peck away at what the two had left. Honorine came to say that the dinner and the wine were on the house. So, my mother was not being nasty at all, but, in fact, very generous. Jean-Louis handed her a twenty franc note as a tip and handed her another to give to Valentin, sitting at a table hungrily devouring another plate of food he had been given: a grilled steak and more French fries. Again, he nodded his bald head, rivulets of perspiration running down it, in Jean-Louis' direction.

"Goodnight, Doc," said he to me on passing him.

"Goodnight, Valentin, we loved your playing tonight. Made our dinner a very pleasant experience," I told him.

"Thanks, Doc. You're always welcome, Doc."

"Nice music," Jean-Louis said to him.

"Thanks, Mr Jean-Louis," he replied.

-0-

Jean-Louis went with the girls to the 'Tony of Colorado' room to help Carmen with the insulin injection. I climbed the stairs to the 'Rose Window' room.

Quickly, I changed to a pair of unromantic pyjamas which were too warm for a hot and humid night as that one was.

I chose the bed furthest from the window. I switched off the ceiling light as well as the lamp on my bedside table. After quite a while I heard footsteps come up the stairs. I turned my back to the door.

"Bella …?"

I pretended to be fast asleep. I wonder what the time was, but could not look on my wristwatch: my mom had silenced the grandfather clock.

Jean-Louis undressed in the dark and he sighed when in his bed.

"Bella?" he called out keeping his voice down. "Are you asleep, darling?"

I did not reply.

Soon, he was snoring lightly.

I wondered whether I should wake him, but I did not want what I knew would follow. I did not know the Jean-Louis I had seen that day: Jean-Louis, the father. And I did not have sex with strangers.

-0-

In the morning, after breakfast, we piled back into the Combi. A halo of mist hung above the mount. From the chimneys of the houses of Sainte-Marie-sur-Brecque grey smoke shot into the air. The girls wanted something to eat for when we were driving back to Paris, so Jean-Louis pulled up outside the bakery. Amandine was at her usual place behind the till accepting money from customers who had gone to buy the morning's bake of croissants.

The girls wanted *pains au chocolat* and ran in to buy some, their father keeping the *Combi's* engine running.

Amandine saw me through the window and waved. I waved back.

The road to Paris, so familiar to me and having become familiar to Jean-Louis too, seemed long. The girls ate their *pains au chocolat* and stuck their chocolate-covered tongues out at children in the cars we passed. Jean-Louis and I talked about the work which lay ahead in the coming week: Chartreux Hospital had three births scheduled for each day.

"Will it be alright for me to drop you off at your place?" he asked.

We had reached Paris and we crossed the Seine on Pont Notre Dame, tourists, laden with cameras, already massing in front of Notre Dame Cathedral. Just at that moment, as if the Almighty in Heaven was heralding a welcome to the tourists, the cathedral's bells began to chime.

In front of my building, Jean-Louis descended from the car, took my overnight bag from the back and carried it for me to the building's door.

"Will it be alright if I leave it here, Bella?"

"Of course, Jean-Louis."

"I'll phone you later. Must just get the girls back to Col … their mother."

The two, having scrambled onto the front passenger seat, which I had freed, they pulled funny faces at me.

-0-

Jean-Louis came back. He did not telephone to say he was on his way: always he telephoned before coming over. My doorbell rang. Three short rings. It identified the caller as him.

"You've not turned in for the night yet?" he asked.

He wore a different sweater from the one of the weekend. This one was pink. He had a beige jacket slung over an arm. I had not yet changed into my pyjamas.

"You've not thrown my toothbrush out yet, Bella?" he asked next.

On his previous overnight stay he had told me to throw out his toothbrush because he was going to buy another.

"I forgot, Jean-Louis."

He asked whether I would like a glass of wine. He kept wine and beer at my place.

"Are you having one?" I asked.

"Need it, yes! The girls' mother ... Col ... kicked up a fuss because Carmen's blood sugar was high. She's blaming me for it."

I told him to sit down and I will bring him a glass of wine.

"I do not want to drink alone, Bella."

He never wanted to be the only one in a room to be drinking.

"I'll join you. I was thinking of having a glass before you rang my doorbell."

His hair was tousled and his face was biscuit brown from the weekend's sun.

"Did you enjoy the weekend, Jean-Louis?" I asked.

"I did, but I am afraid the girls spoiled it for you. When one is not used to children then ..."

Quite.

He followed me to the kitchen and I told him to choose a bottle of wine from my wine rack. His choice was a *Saint-Émilion*, one of his bottles, and with a jerk of his head showed me to take the glasses to the living room: he followed with the opened bottle.

In the Latin Quarter a street was never deserted and silent. That night was no different.

Jean-Louis and I stood at my open living room window. Down on the pavement, a young man was scaring girls with a small grey velvet mouse. He pressed something on the mouse when a girl approached and the mouse jumped from his hand and onto her. The girls he scared thus shrieked and jumped in the air, and patrons sitting on the terrace of a bistro, having watched and waited for the reaction, roared with laughter.

We sat down: I, on the settee, Jean-Louis in an armchair. He put his still almost full glass down on the coffee table between the settee and the armchair. He looked from the glass to me.

"Bella, the girls are going through a tough time."

"Is it because of Carmen's diabetes?" I asked.

He nodded.

"But not only."

"So, what is it, Jean-Louis? Can I help?"

"I feel responsible."

"For the diabetes?"

"For their unhappiness."

I walked to the mantelpiece where he had put the bottle of wine. My glass was empty. I filled it. Jean-Louis had returned to the open window: he stood with his back to me. Laughter, almost hysterical, was still rising from the street below. Few lights were on in the buildings across the street. I sat down on the settee.

"I feel so guilty, Bella."

He still had his back to me.

"You can't blame yourself for the diabetes," I said to his back.

"This is not about the diabetes, Bella," he said firmly and emphasised the 'not'.

He swung round, but remained at the window, leaning against the wall beside it. His glass was empty.

"What is this about?" I asked.

"It is about divorcing the girls' mother."

The patch of sky I could see through my living room window was suddenly starlit.

I wanted to laugh, dance: he was going to marry me!

"You have opted for divorce?" I asked.

"Contemplated it. Thought I should finalise the separation. I spoke to a colleague about alimony. Increasing the allowance I give the girls' mother already."

He fell silent. Walked to the mantelpiece and refilled his glass.

"Come sit," I told him.

Like a child having been ordered to do so by its mother, he sat down, again in the armchair.

"Bella, I am thinking of going back to live with the girls' mother."

Jesus! He could not even say her name, but he was going to go back to her!

"Nothing needs to change as far as you and I are concerned," he said.

He was looking down to the floor.

I said nothing. I had been struck dumb: such happiness one second and such a slap in the face the next.

"I will continue to see you," he said.

I still remained silent; still could not speak.

"It will just be that I will change my address and my telephone number."

Outside on the street, a girl shrieked in fear. It is incredible how scared a girl can be of a mouse.

"Bella, I love you. I did not plan this scenario. I want you to know that. To understand."

I was still silent.

"Bella, say something. For God's sake, say something."

I stood up to pour myself another glass of wine. *Sorrow can be alleviated by good sleep, a bath and glass of wine.* Who had said this? I had no idea.

Jean-Louis smoked, but rarely. I watched him take a crumpled packet of cigarettes and a lighter from a pocket of the beige jacket, which was hanging over the back of the armchair. Slowly, he took a cigarette from the packet, tapped it against the back of his hand. He lit it, tilting his head towards the lighter in his hand.

In the next few seconds, the acrid odour that filled my nostrils was surprisingly stimulating. Once, in my first year at 'uni' I had accepted a marijuana cigarette from a fellow student and no sooner than I had inhaled, was I drifting up to the ceiling. The world looked so beautiful from there, a luminous pink glow hung over the room down below, and I was certain I saw a fairy with long transparent wings flying about. But, was my fall from the ceiling a hard one! All of a sudden, the room was pitch-black and a horrible smell, the smell of a cadaver which I had to watch being dissected, clung to everything. Never had I touched the stuff again.

Would I yet again crash to the ground?

"Jean-Louis, are you offering me the position of First Mistress?" I asked.

The room had gone pitch-black. Yes, yet again I had crashed to the ground.

"Don't be silly, Bella," he said, crossing and uncrossing his legs.

He had looked up at me.

"So what are you offering me?" I asked. "Stolen nights? No. Full nights? Of course not. Minutes on the rear seat of your car? But no, your car has no rear seat. So what? A few minutes in an elevator? A few minutes on a service staircase? A few minutes on a park bench? Or what?"

"You are being vulgar, Bella."

He slumped back into the armchair.

"What you have just suggested to me, Jean-Louis, that is what I call vulgar!"

"Don't be like that!" he snapped.

He rose and walked back to the window. He leaned out. The only sound coming from the street was from the moving traffic: the young man must have taken his velvet mouse home, a home which was probably a small attic room.

"Bella, I will go. We can talk about this tomorrow," said Jean-Louis.

He had turned and was looking at me.

He almost ran to the armchair and grabbed his jacket. Walking to my front door, he pulled the jacket on the ground behind him. At the door he turned round.

"Bella, see you some time."

I remained sitting on the settee. The click of my front door closing, always such a soft sound, was like the detonation of a bomb in my ears.

I poured what wine was left in the bottle and in our glasses down the kitchen sink.

Wine is a false friend.

-0-

My telephone rung.

"Bella …?"

It was Jean-Louis.

"Jean-Louis. Yes?"

I wondered who he thought would be answering my phone at that time of the night? A ghost? It was after midnight.

Several days had gone by since I had last seen him.

"Bella, I've been thinking …"

"A natural process for mankind, Jean-Louis. So what makes you call me at this time of the night to make the announcement? Do you want me to phone Einstein to tell him? But no, Einstein's dead."

"Bella, don't be like that, please. Come on girl!"

He was pleading.

I said nothing.

"Bella," he tried anew, "Listen. You've not been out of my mind for a moment since …"

Since what? When he walked out of here, shooting a glance at me with the words *see you some time?*

I had told Marion about it. She was outraged.

"The son of a bitch, he ends it like that. Just like that. And after he had made you understand he was going to tie the knot with you. What a bastard!"

I told her he had never spoken to me of marriage, or he had, but not about marrying me, but about his marriage to Colette.

"All the same. What an arsehole."

Such occasions always made Marion manifest her knowledge of insults. Once, she had even called someone an arsehole in front of Father Pierre and I thought I would have to give the priest mouth-to-mouth because he hyperventilated so much.

"What is it, Jean-Louis?" I asked.

I tried to sound pleasant.

"Can we talk, Bella?"

"We're talking."

"Face to face?"

"What do you want to say?"

"I've been thinking - and please leave Einstein out of it - I want to see you, I need to talk to you. We need to talk."

I let a few seconds pass.

"No, you can't. I've just jumped from the window and this is my spirit holding the receiver."

"Please, don't be like that, Bella."

I could see his face with the eyes of my memory. He would be looking straight at me, his brown eyes asking … no pleading, for comprehension. He would scratch the tip of his nose as if his nose was itching. Normally I would have pulled that hand away and kissed the palm, the soft and warm palm.

I waited for him to continue.

"Bella, I've always liked your name. Did I ever tell you?"

"So you are phoning me to tell me you've always liked my name? Great! Will you phone me tomorrow this time and tell me you like nutmeg spread over your cauliflower?"

"I hate bloody nutmeg and you know it!" he snapped.

I said nothing.

"Bella, do please listen, will you girl? I think we ought to meet to talk. I don't want us to stop seeing each other. Bella, I love you, for God's sake. I miss you like hell. I can't stand the thought of never being with you again, of never seeing you again, of never touching you again, of never …"

"I get the message," I stopped him.

"Can I come over?"

"Now?"

"If you say I may."

"You may not."

"Come to my place tomorrow after your work."

"No."

"Shall I come to your place tomorrow evening?"

"No."

"Come on, Bella. Don't play hard to get. I love you."

"Yes, Jean-Louis, so you have said, and if I remember correctly you offered me the position as First Mistress."

"Bella, I moved back in with the girls' mother. I am trying to be a good father for the girls and this is why I moved back in with their mother. No other reason. I do not love her. I love you. I want to continue seeing you. I have to see you. I cannot live without you."

The last sentence sounded as if it had come from deep inside him. My mother would have said *men do lay it on thick* had she overheard the conversation.

"Jean-Louis, I am not prepared to be 'the other woman'," I said into the receiver.

"You won't be. The girls' mother is and will remain so."

"This is not how I understand it."

"Are you going to slam the phone down?"

"I was not planning to, but you've given me an idea …"

"No!" he cried, "do not do that. Please, listen to me. Can I come over? Not now, if you do not want me to, but tomorrow? Please? I love you, Bella. I love you."

"It is late."

"And?"

"I have to be at the hospital at five in the morning."

"And you need to sleep now, yes, Bella, I understand. So shall I come over tomorrow evening? At seven say?"

"Jean-Louis, as far as I am concerned, you and I are over. You returned to your wife. You had a choice. You chose."

"So it is really over?"

"I've said what I wanted to say."

"I am begging you, Bella."

"I have no coin, not even a centime, to drop into your paper cup, Jean-Louis."

"So, you never loved me?"

I put the receiver down. I had done so slowly, gently, as if I feared, should I slam it down, it would burst his eardrum, because with such a force would I have thrown it down.

So, you never loved me, was what he said.

I loved him. How I had loved him!

"I still say he is rat," Marion said to me.

It was forty-eight hours later and she and I met for lunch.

"I second that," said Marius.

He had joined us for an after lunch coffee.

We remained sitting in the restaurant, that of Paris's George V five-star hotel. Marion only ever wanted to go to the top and therefore, most expensive restaurants. All the other patrons had left and all but one of the waiters, a boy hardly out of his teens, had gone off duty. He probably had had no say in the matter of who would remain to tend to us.

"You must be so angry at this bastard," said Marion.

"And I won't blame you," added Marius.

"I'm not angry at him," I told them. "He loves his daughters and he wants to be with them."

"Bullshit," said Marion.

The young waiter dropped a spoon on the wooden floor.

"Apologies ...," he said.

"Bella, do be careful when you meet a man next. No married ones please. The moment you hear he's married, get up and walk away," said Marius.

My mother was more vocal.

"I never trusted him. I always thought he was going to do this. I told you he was going to leave you for another woman. I was not wrong. He left you for another woman: his wife. And Bella, you're in the wrong too. You were an adulteress. So, do not expect me to offer you a shoulder to cry on."

I told her: I don't cry.

I cried.

After each new day at Chartreux Hospital, after having put a new born child into its father's waiting arms, after having seen the love in his eyes for his child, and for the woman who had brought it into the world for him, I went home and I crawled into bed and I pulled the blanket over my head and I cried.

-0-

CHAPTER THIRTY

It is Monday.

The aroma of coffee wakes me yet again. *I am going to become used to this. To a man, this man, making me coffee in the morning.*

Quickly, I dress. I put on a pair of jeans and a red sweater. I bought the sweater in Paris still, in the city's Chinatown of the thirteen *arrondissement*. There are silver sequins across the bodice. My mother liked the sweater; Marion does not and uses a variety of adjectives when she speaks of it.

Colin is in his leather outfit: so he will be going out.

"I've made myself at home again this morning, Bella."

He was sitting at the work table when I walked in, but rose.

"How did you sleep, Colin?"

"Had a problem going off. Counted a few thousand sheep and then I did drop off. How did you sleep?"

"Like a baby."

"Are babies really masters when it comes to sleeping?"

"Like with all of us, no two babies are alike. I've come across real little horrors. I pitied the parents."

"Oh dear!"

End of this line of conversation … I hope!

"One day you must tell me about your experiences as a paediatrician, Bella."

So … no, it was not.

"Doctoring stories are boring."

Hopefully, I have ended this line of conversation.

"I'm going to walk around the mount today. Have a look around. Can I bring you anything?"

Yipee! So I did end that line of conversation!

"I'll ask you to come with me, but you probably have lots to do here," he adds.

"I … yes … I have. Sorry. Some other day perhaps?"

I pop three croissants into the oven and I set out two places on the work table.

"I watered the Peace Lily," he says. "I hope you do not mind."

He is watching me.

I mind yes, because Fred said the plant ought not be given too much water.

"I do not mind at all," I say.

"Let me do that," he says.

He points to the oven.

"Don't burn your hands," I warn. "Put on the oven gloves."

The oven door is open and he has grabbed hold of one of the piping-hot croissants.

"I have a doctor in the house," he says.

He is smiling mischievously.

"But you do not welcome any reference to you having been a doctor, do you Bella?"

His eyes are questioning me.

I start buttering one of the croissants which is now lying on the plate in front of me where he has dropped it.

"Never mind …," he mutters.

He sits down opposite me. He spreads his two croissants thickly with Gertrude's award-winning strawberry jam. Some of the jam gets onto his fingers: he licks them clean. Quite an unbecoming action, but yet one so sexual: red tongue moving with light rapid strokes over first one finger and then another.

I look away.

"You are so lucky," he says. "This is a beautiful house

and your Gertrude is a wonderful jam maker, and I do envy you."

His fingers, clean, he drops his hands onto the table.

"I'm lucky, yes."

He tells me he does not know what time he will be back from the mount and I need not prepare dinner for him.

"You are the kind of guest my parents would have adored. You've paid for meals you are not having."

I tell him about one of our English guests who, each morning, ordered a full English breakfast: fried egg, bacon, sausages, tomato, mushrooms and even baked beans. However, never did he eat the egg: not one morning did he eat the egg and each morning my parents had to throw it away. They asked him why he was ordering an egg every morning when he did not eat it. His reply was that he was entitled to an egg as he was paying for it. For the rest of his stay he insisted on a fried egg 'with no lace' on his plate and never did he eat it and each morning my parents threw it out.

"That's so uneducated," says Colin.

"In fact, he was an educated man. A newspaper editor," I tell him.

"Does he still come to stay?"

"These days, he can't make it."

"Why?"

"He's six foot under."

The grandfather clock begins to chime. Colin and I look on our watches simultaneously. It is a quarter past nine.

"I'll be off," he says.

"Have a nice day," I say.

I will spend the day walking from room to room.

No.

I will go out too.

-0-

I drive to Avranches and I go to the town's LeClerc supermarket. I do not want to buy anything; I do not need anything. I buy a bar of chocolate all the same because I am the type who does not want to leave a shop without buying something. I go to a lingerie shop. Its owner is Amandine's sister: red-head Louise.

"Like what are you looking for, Miss?" she asks.

"Like underclothes."

"Like panties? Or a bra and panty set?"

"A set. Sound's good."

I choose half a dozen bra and panty sets and Louise pulls the curtain of the fitting cubicle aside for me to step in.

"Do keep your own panty on when you try these panties on," she says.

She is in white skin-tight trousers, her buttocks jutting out, and I am sure she is not wearing a panty herself.

I buy two sets. One is black. The other is red. Jean-Louis loved red underwear.

I had told Marion this once.

"Kinky," she said. "I like a man who likes kinky."

-0-

CHAPTER THIRTY-ONE

It is going on for four o'clock and the Vaybee is almost deserted: lunch is over and the hour of the aperitif has not yet begun.

Alice sits on a high stool at the till of which she is in charge these days. She lifts a hand, which seems all red nails and shiny rings, in greeting.

"Doctor!"

She always addresses me as 'doctor' which makes me wonder what Frascot has told her about me.

He steps from the kitchen.

"What can I serve you, Miss? It's on the house."

"Just a small black coffee, please."

Rare it is that something is 'on the house' at the Vaybee. Father Pierre's meals and drinks are though.

"We're dancing tonight," Alice calls out. "We want to chase the Monday night blues."

"Great."

"Ah, you will be staying, Miss. Colin joining you?" asks Frascot.

Colin.

"I've just popped in for a coffee, Frascot."

"Colin was around earlier," he says.

"And what a dish!" comes from Alice. "Hey, hey, hey!"

"Just you shut up, woman!" snorts Frascot.

Two youths walk in and want orange juice and peanuts. Frascot says he does not sell peanuts.

"So, good, we will each have two packets. And pass the

salt too," replies one of the youths.

"I'll tell you what he will give you," says Alice. "A slap."

"I don't keep peanuts in the place and you know it, so do not come here to provoke," says Frascot to the two.

"Keep your old stinking pants on, Gran'pa," says the other youth.

He is not a bad-looking young man: dark curls fall over his face and his eyes are as black as the curls.

I am sitting at a window table. Le Square is deserted. Lights have already gone on in some of the houses behind it. It is getting darker earlier every day: soon it will be dark here already at this time of the day. Winter! I think I will go to Paris as soon as Colin leaves. Leaves?

Yes. Colin will leave, Bella girl.

Speak of the devil, or rather, think of the devil. I hear a motorcycle approaching. It is Colin. He turns his head this way and must therefore see my car: I parked it in front of the Vaybee and between two yellow lines marking a space for deliveries, but I know the space will not be needed: Frascot's deliveries are always made first thing in the morning. I also know Mayor Pares will not allow his traffic cop to give me a ticket: Le Presbytère is too big a contributor to the town hall's coffers.

Colin pulls up behind the Merc and begins to walk to the Vaybee. He is taking off his crash helmet.

"I saw your car," he greets me. "May I?"

He points to the free chair at my table.

"I went shopping in Avranches so I thought I will have a coffee before I go home."

"Glad I saw your car."

He waves to Frascot and Alice. The latter's cheeks turn a little redder than they already are with blusher.

"Who's the lady?" he asks me.

"Frascot's latest."

"Oh yes. She was at Fred's wife's party. Alice - is it? What was his wife like?"

"I never met her - they divorced when he was in his twenties - but I understand she was a very plain woman. Rather fat too."

"Any children?"

"Yes. But just one."

"That's a blessing."

"Quite."

"I've never wanted ... do not want ... children, but my brother has four. They're grown-up now of course."

"My brother also has four."

"And you, Bella?"

"I've never been married."

"You do not have a love child?"

"No."

"You give me the impression of someone who would make a wonderful mother ..."

"I am not maternal."

"I am not paternal."

"What are the names of your brother's children?"

"George, Jane, Emma ... can't remember the name of the youngest ... oh yes, it is Alfred."

"Very English."

He shrugs.

"And ... there are the garden gnomes."

"Which he sells?"

"Manufactures and sells. He names them. His newest is, if you will believe it, named Fred. The Fred range."

"I must tell Fred."

"What's this about my brother?" asks Frascot who has come to ask what Colin is drinking.

"What are you having, Bella?" asks Colin.

"Small black coffee."

"Same for me, Frascot," says Colin.

"So what were you saying about my brother?" Frascot asks again.

"Not your brother, Frascot, but mine. We were talking about my brother."

279

"You have a brother?"

"Brother, sister-in-law, nieces, nephews. Misfortune in its entirety."

Frascot shrugs and walks off to fetch Colin's coffee. I think he did not catch Colin's irony.

"You are not close to your brother, Colin?" I ask.

"We're living different lives, but no, I love my brother, especially now that our parents are deceased and it's just the two of us in the family, but as for him, he's as cold as ice."

"But he has fathered four children."

"So he has and this is the mystery of all mysteries."

He winks.

Alice brings two small cups of black coffee to our table. She never serves patrons, so it must be for Colin's benefit she does so today. We thank her; she smiles in Colin's direction and wiggles her generously-flabby bottom walking back to the till.

"You get on well with your brother, Bella?" asks Colin returning to what we were talking about before Alice's interruption.

"Very well, yes."

"Was your mother a doctor, or a nurse perhaps before retirement when she came to help your father at the guest house? I ask this because both you and your brother are doctors and when this happens usually one of the parents was and I know, from what you've already told me, it was not your father."

"My mother was a waitress. German soldiers used to go into the bistro where she worked for a drink and so my parents got talking, got talking despite the silence which fell over the place when a German walked in."

"And they fell in love?"

"Yes, and it was not to have been, and she had become a horizontal collaborator, and when the war was over the villagers shaved my mother's head and dragged her through the streets. Some spat on her. Shouted at her that she was a whore."

He nods.

"They already did that in the Great War - shave the heads of the women who had slept with German soldiers and …"

"It was not a case of 'slept with'. My mother fell in love with my father and he fell in love with her."

"Of course," he said, "do forgive me for using such an expression."

"Not to worry. There is 'falling in love with' and there is 'slept with'."

"Of course," he says again.

The coffee is hot as it always is here at the Vaybee. More patrons have walked in, some of them standing at the bar. The latter are drinking small glasses of Frascot's table wine. I hope Miss Jambenoire will not also come in for a pre-dinner drink or an aperitif. I am not usually in the Vaybee at this time on a Monday evening, so I do not know if it is her habit to do so. Father Pierre, I know, will not be walking in. He practises bination and will be saying the second mass of the day to the faithful.

"Where do your parents lie buried?" asks Colin.

We had been drinking our coffee in silence, each watching the patrons, some young, some not so young, walk in.

"Here in the local cemetery. They lie together, side by side," I tell Colin.

"It's family tradition here for all in a family to lie together, is it not?"

I nod.

"I will lie somewhere alone. But not that I want to think about that already now."

"Of course you would not, Bella."

"What about your parents, Colin?"

"My father lies in the cemetery closest to where he had lived in the last years of his life. He lived in a hotel in London's Bayswater Road. As for my mother, she lies in their cemetery in London."

"Their cemetery?"

"A Jewish cemetery."

"I see."

Four pimply youths walk in. One is pushing a shiny electric keyboard over to a corner. Another is carrying a drum. He starts to set it up beside the keyboard. The third starts to tune a shiny electric guitar. The fourth member, a girl, sets up a microphone. One of the patrons standing at the bar carries chairs over to them.

Colin looks at me and frowns.

"There's going to be music here tonight. Alice and Fred told me."

"Oh lordie!" sighs Colin just as he did at Paula's birthday party.

"We can go if you wish. I was not going to stay anyway for the music."

Darkness has fallen over the square and behind every window there is a light. Blue-grey smoke pours from some of the chimneys we can see.

A glance at my watch tells me it is half past six.

"Time passes quickly," says Colin, having seen I had checked to see the time.

"Our lives are passing, yes."

"Let us make it pass just a little slower this night. Let us stay and have a bite to eat and I may even invite you for a waltz."

He wants to know what I think of his suggestion.

"I will say that those four there," I point to the musicians, "they won't be playing any waltzes tonight."

"Not! In that case we will just listen, but what do you say about dinner?"

I tell him it will be lovely.

Why did I say that?

He calls Alice over and she's at our table within a second. No. Half a second.

"What can I do for you, *Milord*?" she asks.

"For us actually," replies Colin.

He tells her we would like something to eat and whether we could move to another table.

"Sure, sure, *Milord*," she says. "Something ... something intimate?"

"Sure, sure, Milady, something intimate," he replies.

He winks at me.

She shows us to the table beside the tall lamp with the shade of white and pink seashells where Jean-Louis and I had sat the day of our mussels lunch.

"May I allow you to choose for me?" asks Colin.

How different this man is from Jean-Louis.

"If you trust me, Colin."

"Totally."

He holds up his hand, palms to me. His lifeline is long.

Frascot makes a good *porc marengo*. I suggest it to Colin.

"Describe it to me, please?" he asks.

"It consists of cubes of pork which have been cooked in white wine for something like an hour. Added to the pork are carrots, tomatoes, onions and various herbs. It's rich and filling, so one usually has boiled potatoes with it."

"Sounds excellent."

Alice comes to get our order.

"Wine?" she asks, addressing Colin.

"Wine?" he asks me.

"A glass will do. Thanks. I'm driving."

"And I'm on my bike, so only a glass it will have to be for me, too," Colin tells Alice.

"Alice, nothing fancy, please. Just your white table variety please," I quickly tell her.

She leans over Colin to take the menu from him, but only holds a hand out to take the one I am holding from me.

"I'll bring a carafe over if you should decide to have more than just a glass. There will be four glasses in the carafe but if you do not want to drink that much, not to worry about it, Frascot will work it into something tomorrow. I mean when you leave here you will be falling straight into bed, not so, so being a little light in the head will not be a problem, not so?"

Neither Colin nor I reply.

Frascot brings the food, and Alice, the wine, and Colin fills our glasses.

"What shall we drink to?" he asks.

He has picked up his glass.

"Let us be horrible and drink to ourselves, Colin," I say. "I will drink to your dreams coming true and you can drink to …" I stop.

"… your dreams coming true, Bella."

I smile.

"Colin, I stopped dreaming some time ago."

"I too, Bella, I too have stopped dreaming some time ago," he replies.

From outside comes the patter of rain on the square.

"Winter," says Colin.

"Yes, winter. Not my favourite season. Winter in Paris is quite pleasant actually, but here it can be …"

"Lonely?" he breaks in.

"Yep."

"I understand. It's beautiful here in the village - what's its name - and up at your place, but one can't talk to a view, no matter how beautiful it is, the way one can talk to a human being, can one?"

"No. Or rather yes, the mad do."

"But you are not mad, Bella."

"I am not mad, Colin, and for this reason I agreed a moment ago that it can be lonely at Le Presbytère in winter."

"Oh Bella!"

It was a cry from deep inside of him.

Embarrassed at having revealed too much of my life to him, perhaps, I give a little laugh.

"I've just had a mouthful of wine and it has already gone to my head, so do not take notice of me please,

Colin."

He leans over the table and reaches for my hands.

"Bella, Anton Chekhov wrote: *Just as I shall lie alone in the grave, so, in essence, do I live alone.* It is true for every one of us."

Slowly, he lifts my hands to his face.

"Bella, Bella, Bella," he murmures.

He presses the palm of my right hand against his lips.

Outside, the rain has started to pelt the square.

I keep my eyes on his; I discern tenderness in them.

He eases his hold on my right hand but tightens that on my left. I watch him raise the hand to his lips as he had raised my right hand a moment earlier. He is looking at me, the tenderness still in his eyes. Quickly, he turns my hand over and presses his lips very hard against the top of my hand.

"Hey, you two!" says Alice.

She is standing beside our table; we did not - I certainly did not - see or hear her approach. She is holding a urinal pistol. A very pretty one. It is of porcelain with yellow pansies painted around it.

"For you," she says. "On the house. The *trou normand.*"

Colin looks at me.

"Bella, is this what it looks like?"

I nod.

"Certainly is."

"Wait, let me get this correct. Help me out with this. Am I supposed to … you know what … in it? Good Lord, is this the custom in France?"

He has turned red in the face.

"Yes. I mean no, you are not expected to do anything into it. We are supposed to drink from it."

"Drink what? Not what someone else has put into it?"

"*Calvados.* Drink *Calvados* from it."

"You're joking," he says. "You must be joking."

He is no longer red in the face, but has become a little grey around his mouth.

Alice is biting on her lips, trying not to laugh. Again, she leans over Colin, her low-cut black top slipping down to reveal her full breasts right to her very red nipples. The sight would have turned Jean-Louis on. Colin is not even aware of what she is showing him, offering him. He is staring at the urinal pistol.

"Doctor, you will have to explain to Colin about the *pistolet urinoir* tradition. He is … how to say it … a little worried, *non*," says Alice, straightening up.

"We call it the Norman Hole," I tell Colin. "It is offered to cleanse the palette before going on from the main course to the cheese and dessert."

"I never! A urinal pistol?"

"To be different, yes."

"Sure is that! I thought drinking an infusion after a meal was odd, but this! I wonder if the Queen comes to Normandy, will they offer it to her too?"

I laugh.

"Maybe this is why you Brits have not again tried to conquer Normandy."

He laughs.

Alice, who has returned to her chair behind the till, motions for us to drink the offered *Calvados*.

"You go first," says Colin.

He has picked up the urinal pistol and is holding it around its fat belly and swivelling its contents. Quickly, I lift the round mouth of the urinal to my lips and I tip my head back. I swallow once, and again and I begin to choke, the fiery apple brandy shooting down my throat as if a real bullet has been fired into my mouth from a real pistol.

"I … oh hell," I stutter, getting my breath back.

"My turn," says Colin, interest in his eyes.

I watch him tilt his head back and bring the urinal up to his mouth, his mouth wide open as if in a dentist's chair.

"Colin …," I begin.

I have to warn him of the potency of what he is about to drink, but the brandy is already running from the mouth of the urinal into his open mouth. He swallows, coughs, swallows again and coughs again, his eyes bulging and the brandy running down the sides of his mouth and over his leather jacket.

"Bella, what is in this thing?" he asks, getting his breath back.

I look towards Alice and she is no longer sitting down behind the till, but she is on her feet beside it and beside her is Frascot. The two are doing their best not to laugh at Colin. She is holding a hand over her mouth, and Frascot is pinching his legs together as if he needs the urinal pistol, but not to drink from, but for the real thing.

Colin too looks at the two through two red watery eyes, and as if on cue from a prompter, all four of us burst out laughing.

Our joint laughter having broken down what restraint Alice still might have had, she returns to our table, swinging her hips ever more voluptuously, and leans over the table, her face almost touching that of Colin.

"Good? *Not so*, Colin?" she asks.

Still unable to speak, he nods.

She begins to tell him the story of how Frascot began to honour the *trou normand* tradition. I have heard the story here at the Vaybee often, but for Colin's sake I fake interest.

"Frascot's parents collected old porcelain stuff and had several of these urinals. So, when he opened this place, he, then still a young buck and not averse to getting cucumbered himself, decided to introduce the *trou normand* to his patrons. Just for a laugh, you know. Must say, not all people go for the urinal thing. Women especially do not care for it. They claim drinking the brandy this way leaves a coat of slime on the tongue."

"A coat of slime?" asks Colin, his voice having returned.

Alice winks at me.

"How in heaven's name can that be?" he wants to

know, turning to me.

"Alice?" I ask.

"Well … Colin, not to say that I told you this, but if a restaurant owner buys old urinals, say from a hospital, he may not clean them thoroughly, and well … . urine residue will stick to the porcelain or plastic …whatever … interior of the urinal and the brandy will liquefy it," she explains.

Colin looks at me, disgust all over his face.

"Did you know this, Bella?"

I think he is also angry, and I rather like the dark look it brings to his eyes.

"Oh, not to worry, Colin," says Alice quickly. "I can assure you our urinals are as clean as a baby's bottle and those which have belonged to his parents have long broken."

"I hope so," says Colin.

"You need not worry about having caught anything," I tell him.

He smiles, the dark look in his eyes unfortunately gone.

"In that case, I will have another sip, because I rather liked the kick which went with it."

Duly, he raises the urinal pistol to his mouth.

"Steady, steady," Alice warns him. "You have to get up the hill on your bike."

I lean over the table and take the urinal away from him. The white of his eyes have become red.

Alice wants to know whether we want dessert and coffee. We want neither.

From outside comes a flash of lightning. It is followed with a clap of thunder. The vocalist starts to belt out a song I do not recognise … *Take good care of my heart …baby you're the first to take it … you're the only one who can break it …* She is singing with full voice, both hands clutching the microphone as if it has to hold her up, and it is suddenly very noisy in the Vaybee.

"I think we better get back up to Le Presbytère," I shout out to Colin.

"Yes," he shouts back, "let's be on our way."

We stop at the till and he shakes his head when I reach for the bill.

"No," he mouths.

Alice, all smiles, is tapping one foot to the rhythm of the music.

"Going straight to bed?" she shouts at us.

Neither Colin nor I try to shout a reply over the music.

"You are going to get soaked," I tell him, walking from the Vaybee.

"It will be fresh air. It was rather stuffy in there. And, there was the brandy."

"And, it was noisy."

"Sure was," he agrees and adds, "The singer actually did a good impersonation of Whitney Houston."

"So it was a Whitney Houston she was singing."

He nods.

"It was *Take Good Care of my Heart*. The lyrics start something like ... *Time can pass so slowly when you feel so all alone ... Then love can strike like lightning when you find your heart a home ...* Something along those lines. Very true it is. Love can strike like lightning."

The lights behind the windows of the houses on the square are casting their silvery glows onto the pools of water on the pavement. A battered *Deux Chevaux* comes bumping towards us. We jump for safety from the spray of water its wheels are throwing up.

We reach his motorcycle and my car.

"I was going to suggest I race you up to Le Presbytère, but in this rain it won't be wise," he says.

"I was going to suggest you leave the bike here and get in with me," I tell him.

He takes my hands.

"Bella, what a lovely few moments these were."

He bends forward and plants a brief kiss on my forehead. The rain is coming down in buckets, and I am sure that, drenched as I am, I am not a pretty sight. I lift myself up to my toes and I am the one to plant a kiss now. I let my lips rest for a moment on his cold and wet forehead.

"I'll risk it on the bike," he says.

"See you up on top," I reply.

-0-

He passes me on the road. He is going fast, too fast, and my first thought is to tick him off about it when we get to Le Presbytère, but, no, it is not for me to do so.

At the house, he stands at the front door waiting for me. I park the Merc beside his motorcycle.

He holds a hand out for the key. I let it dangle between my thumb and forefinger and he takes it. There is a little light on the key ring and he switches it on to be able to unlock the door.

The bland smell of damp attacks our nostrils once we are in the house. I take mental note to air the house a little, to throw open the windows on those days when the weather will permit.

Colin and I both reach for the light switch in the small front room. Our hands touch and quickly I pull back.

"Apologies," he murmurs.

His voice was deep. Filled with emotion? Or was it just because of the *Calvados*?

He starts climbing the stairs; I walk to the clock to silence it. Neither of us has switched on the drawing room light. I hear him walk into his bedroom. I do not hear the click of the door.

"Goodnight, Colin," I call out passing the door.

I looked into the room, but I could not see him. He must have gone into the bathroom.

In my room, in the dark, I stand very still beside the bed. The bed I had shared with Jean-Louis when he was here for a weekend. The bed I had not shared with another man. Oh yes, I have had sex since Jean-Louis but never here at Le Presbytère. I had too much respect for my mother and our staff to have brought men here for casual sex, and also, there was the memory of Jean-Louis which clung to this room, this bed. Casual sex was for when I went to Paris and on the holidays I took.

I go to the bathroom and undress. Naked, I splash water over my face, and, still faithful to Van Cleef & Arpels' *First* I squirt some over me, not much, but just enough to destroy the cigarette smoke from the Vaybee which may cling to me. Quickly, I clean my teeth. Next, I pull a short nightshirt over my head and let it fall over my hips; it just covers my hips.

Now what?

Standing in the doorway of my room I see Colin still has not closed his bedroom door. He also has not switched on the ceiling light in the room, only one of the bedside lamps, and it throws a pallid strip of light into the corridor.

This is a now or never moment.

I give a deep breath and I walk to the light.

Colin lies on his left side, his back to me, a book in his hands. He is wearing a white T-shirt and white y-fronts. At the door, I step out of the nightshirt I have just put on. I step over it and leave it on the floor. There is no movement from the bed. Has he not heard my approach?

I swing a leg onto the old brass bed where so many brides, here on their honeymoon, have lost their virginity, and I slip under the sheets. They smell musty like the house and confirm I must air the house. I did plan to light the fireplace in the drawing room tomorrow, but perhaps I should delay it for a couple of days.

Colin still has not moved.

Gently, I take the book from his hands. I put it down on the bedside table, making sure the pages face downwards so that he will be able to find the page where he was reading. In the bedside lamp's dim light I read the title: *Catherine the Great.* I have the book, written by Henri

Troyat, in my library room.

"Colin," I whisper. "Close your eyes."

My naked breasts are touching his face. Fumbling somewhat clumsily, I roll his white T-shirt up over his torso. For a moment I let a hand rest on the graying smattering of hair on his chest. He inhales lightly; once, twice. I pull the T-shirt over my own head, catching my hair around one of the buttons.

Colin's eyelids flutter as if he is going to open them.

"No, Colin," I say. "Eyes. Eyes. Keep them closed."

His T-shirt is far too big for me. It covers me right down to my thighs. Covered in this way I am hot, which is uncomfortable. But I love the smell of him which envelopes me.

This is the *now* moment.

I curl up close to him, my hands searching for what of him remains covered in his y-fronts. *Jean-Louis would never have worn such underpants.*

I lift my right leg over Colin's left leg, moving the rest of me up against him. In the darkness I try to see whether his manhood is erect yet. Yes, it is. I begin to stroke his thighs. He lets out a loud moan, and I, startled by such sudden vocal interjection, begin to caress his manhood. It fills my hand. He is well-endowed. I begin to roll his underpants down and as I do so his manhood lifts itself up. I move away a little from the glory of his naked flesh, and I begin to lick his stomach, just a moist brushing of my tongue. He moans loudly again.

I am the master here on this bed.

"Eyes, Colin, eyes," I say again.

He scrunches them ever tighter and I take his arms and place them between the rails of the brass headboard. As if he fears he may fall from the bed, he grabs a rail in each hand. He is holding on tightly, with all his strength; his knuckles are turning white. Working downwards, I kiss his face, his chest, the tip of his erect manhood, all the time pulling down his underpants. When he is naked, I kiss his thighs, his knees, his feet. Straightening my back a little, I take his manhood in one hand, and with a swift movement I mount him, sliding him inside me, little by little until he has disappeared totally within me. He is groaning loudly. He climaxes inside me.

He opens his eyes and searches for my face. Smilingly, his eyes sweep over my body and rest on my hard nipples protruding from under his T-shirt. He is still holding onto the headboard of the bed, but lets go of these, and, both his hands free, he sweeps them over my body. He begins to stroke my thighs. He motions with his head I must move over onto my back. I can see he is ready to enter me again. I arch my back slightly to ease his entry.

Our climax is simultaneous.

I roll off him.

Now, I feel light. Free of the weight of the loneliness of my life, free of the weight of being the daughter of a horizontal collaborator and a Nazi soldier. Free of Miss Jambenoire. Free of the memory of Jean-Louis.

"Darling," whispers Colin beside me.

"Yes, Colin?"

He shakes his head.

"Nothing. I just wanted to make sure you are beside me and I have not just had a wonderful dream."

His body glistens with sweat and I suppose so must mine.

I push my weight onto my elbows to go to the bathroom for a towel, but he grabs me.

"Where are you off to, my pretty?"

I point to the bathroom.

"No, no, no, you are not," he whispers into my face.

He swings a leg over me; he is yet again fully erect. He enters me.

"Now, you close your eyes," he murmurs.

His face is close to mine.

Obediently, I do as I am told, but I immediately open my eyes again. His eyes are smiling.

293

"Bella, I am a happy man …"

"Colin …"

He closes his mouth over mine stopping my words.

His tongue is caressing mine. He begins to suck it and next he bites it. I give a little cry of pain, pleasurable pain. He moves himself into climax, again spilling his seed inside me. Immediately, he focuses his attention on me, his hands like those of a piano virtuoso on a keyboard, over my thighs and breasts. I climax quickly and silently, my face against his.

Both of us, exhausted, we lie side by side on the bed. After a few minutes he turns out the light.

Soon, I hear his steady breathing: he is asleep.

I adjust my pillow and I look up into the blackness of the room. I see glittering stars on the ceiling where I know there are no stars.

-0-

I touch Colin's arm to wake him. His eyes manifest bewilderment.

"Sorry for waking you, but I want to say, if you do not mind I will go nap in my own bed."

I do not give him time to reply but, naked, I walk from the 'White Room'.

At the door, I pick up my nightshirt, and I turn round. Colin is lying on his back, his legs crossed. Shall I not go to my own bedroom? Shall I go back and lie down beside him again?

His eyes are closed; he opens them.

"Bella, tomorrow, or rather this morning, today, should the weather clear, I am taking you out for the day in the sidecar. All day we will ride around. And no arguing about it. And dress as if you are going skiing because it will be cold out there."

"What a wonderful idea. Thank you, and thank you for everything, Colin," I say.

I walk on to my bedroom and I close the door.

-0-

CHAPTER THIRTY-TWO

Should the rain clear. The rain has cleared. The sun is shining down on Mother Earth as I can see through my bedroom window.

Quickly, I jump out of bed.

I dress warmly, as warmly as I can. *Dress as if you are going skiing.* This is what I do. I pull woollen leggings over my panty. I put on a pair of leather trousers - *Bella, what made you buy those* asked Marion the first time she saw me in them. I pull on a thermal *Damart* long-sleeve vest, and next a corduroy long-sleeved sweater. Later, before we set off, I will add my leather jacket - Marion, surprisingly, likes it - and I will wear woollen socks under my fur-lined booties.

Sounds of someone getting out of bed and having a shower and getting dressed come from the 'White Room'. I hear footsteps going downstairs. Soon, I can smell coffee. I go down to the kitchen.

"Bella, morning."

Colin is standing at the stove. He is in his leather outfit, just like last night.

"Colin, morning."

"Did you sleep alright after ... afterwards?" he asks.

Two bowls of milky coffee stand on the work table.

"I slept wonderfully sound. And you?"

"Wonderfully sound too. Bella," he says, "I will not regret last night. I want you to know this."

I walk up to him.

"You need not say this in order to make me feel good,

or so I do not feel bad about myself."

He gives a step forward and our bodies touch.

"You were ... I loved last night, Bella. It was perfect in every way."

He encloses me in his arms and I drop my head against the cold of the leather of his jacket, each of us holding the other.

Suddenly, the smell of burning fills the room.

"The croissants!" he cries out. "I've popped some croissants into the oven."

He lets go of me so fast I almost lose my balance.

"Oops," he says. "Sorry."

I slip on a padded kitchen glove, take the croissants from the oven, pop them onto two plates and these I put on the table.

"Just in time," I say jovially.

The croissants have blackened, but just a little.

"I took a pot of Amandine's apricot jam from the cupboard," says Colin.

No apology this morning for making himself at home. I like this.

The pot stands on the table alongside the butter dish. The butter is also homemade: I buy it at a creamery in Avranches. It is the colour of a sunflower in August and it is salty and our guests adore it.

"If only I can take some of this terrific butter with me when I leave, Bella."

When I leave.

It is the second time he has mentioned leaving. Of course, he will leave. Men leave.

I ask him whether he has decided where we will go today and he says he will leave it to me to navigate for us.

-0-

I prepare a picnic lunch for us just like the ones Gertrude always prepares for our guests. In two aluminium foil

298

containers I pack two hard-boiled eggs; some sliced ham; gherkins, olives, tomatoes, small button mushrooms and two small wrapped cheeses. We will pull up somewhere and buy a *baguette,* some wrapped squares of butter, and something sweet for a dessert. I also pop paper cups, a knife, two teaspoons and a corkscrew into a basket in which I have already put a bottle of mineral water. When we stop for the *baguette* we will also pop into an off-licence and buy a bottle of wine.

"I'll get the bike and sidecar ready," Colin tells me.

He asks if he may take two cushions from the drawing room and a blanket from one of the downstairs bedrooms. I tell him of course he can; I am not sure of the wisdom of us using my beautiful and expensive drawing room cushions, but I do not want to say no to him. The picnic basket packed and standing on the work table, I go upstairs to my bedroom to finish dressing and for a last look in the mirror. I think I look like a sausage, all covered in layers of clothing as I am. One of those short, fat, sausages I so love for breakfast when I am at a London hotel.

From the window I watch Colin wipe the seat in the sidecar with a sponge from the kitchen. He leaves the cushions and the blanket on the seat, but the picnic basket he fits into the closed trunk compartment behind the seat and on which is fastened a spare wheel. I hope we will not need the spare wheel today.

"Bella!" he calls from downstairs. "Let's go, girl!"

He is holding a full-face black crash helmet, one matching his own, out to me.

"What do we do if it does not fit?" I ask.

He laughs.

"Unlike something else, these come in one size only, unless, of course, it is for a child when it is small."

The sidecar is silver-grey like the motorcycle.

"Come, I'll give you a hand, Bella."

"No," I say, "I'll get myself in and out, thank you."

He stands back and watches. A smile is quivering his lips. Quickly, I swing my right leg over the side and next my left: the sidecar is fitted to the left of the motorcycle as those in the United Kingdom are.

"Did you lock up?" he asks. "We do not want to find the house burgled on our return, do we?"

I nod.

How wonderful to have someone who is here to see to such things; how nice I need not be the one in control.

Slowly, we ride down the road towards Saint-Marie-sur-Brecque.

The morning is bright, a little windy, but we are close to the sea here, are we not?

The two cushions are on the floor of the sidecar beside my feet - I cannot get myself to put my feet on them - and I wrapped the blanket around my legs. I look neither left nor right, scared I am on this very first ride in a sidecar, for that matter, on a motorcycle. Colin, on the contrary, as I see from the corner of my eye, keeps on turning his head my way. I lift a hand to signal I am alright. I nearly have a heart attack when he lets go of the handles and too lifts a hand to signal something to me. Just keep your hands on the handlebars and your eyes on the road, I think. I take a mental note to tell him so when we will pull up later.

Before the village, Colin swings onto a narrow road going southwest. I know Saint Malo lies this way. I think he does not: so what has happened to me being the one to navigate? The sea is to our right. Sunlight is glinting on the water. We pass through a hamlet of whitewashed cottages, their shutters closed: must be holiday homes, their owners back behind their desks in Paris. A black-and-white mongrel dog, barking as if his life depends on the noise he is able to make, appears from a leafy lane. He runs beside the motorcycle. He remains beside us. At the last cottage, he jumps over the fence in front of it. He disappears from view.

Soon, we are in another village. Old men in grey

flannels, which are being held up with braces, sit at rectangle white plastic tables outside a bistro. They are drinking red wine from small glasses. Their faces are turned towards the sun. A cat lies asleep under one of the tables, legs stretched out. The day's menu is written in white chalk on a black board which advertises a beer from Belgium. For six francs patrons can have *harengs frais à la bretonne, pomme de terre en robe des champs* and a *yaourt aux fruit* - fresh herring in the style of Brittany, potatoes cooked in their jackets and a fruit yoghourt. Yes, we have left Normandy and are in Brittany.

Ahead of us is the sea: it is cobalt blue behind the village.

Colin rides on. I motion to him to turn right at the next crossroads. He nods. We pass old stone houses, logs piled up alongside them: soon the temperatures will plunge and fires will be lit in every fireplace. We cross on a wobbly plank bridge over a stream and we ride into another village. *Bienvenue à la Castille* announces a sign beside the road. The village has 208 inhabitants. This too is written on the road sign. I know La Castille is famous for its oysters. Oysters! The world's most potent aphrodisiac, as is believed.

Colin is slowing down. As another sign tells us we are on a road to the village's port. We pass small, two-storey, stone houses with grey-tile roofs. We reach a street of small shops. He pulls up at a *superette*. He takes his helmet off and I follow suit.

"I'll go in," I say. "They'll have bread too here."

I scramble from the sidecar, one leg following the other, my bottom in the air, a most unladylike posture. I glance towards Colin. He is trying hard not to laugh. I buy a bottle of *Muscadet* and a *baguette* and a packet of wrapped cubes of butter. As a last thought I add two *chocolate éclairs*.

"Let us go," says Colin. "I'm quite famished."

We continue in the direction of the port. Fishermen, carrying wet hessian sacks, obviously filled with their catch of the night, over their shoulders, come walking towards us. They wave to us. I wave back, but I am pleased to see Colin is keeping both his hands on the handlebars: the road is narrow and descending sharply to the sea.

The port is tiny. It is nothing more than a short gravel pier, a half-timbered barn at one end of it, half a dozen small boats standing on blocks of wood outside it. A couple of small fishing trawlers are moored at the other end of the pier. On them, burly men in rubber overalls are hauling in nets from the sea. Large dead fish are trapped in the nets. The men hurl the nets over the side of the trawlers and onto the decks. Beyond the trawlers, a wooden jetty stretches out to the deeper sea. On each side of it, large hessian bags, strung together in twos, sway with the movement of the sea. These are the oyster beds. Right in front of us, on the pier, are rows of wooden tables and on them trays of oysters are laid out.

Colin pulls up where several cars are parked. Some have the names of restaurants on the side: their owners have obviously come to buy oysters as a brisk trade is under way at the tables behind which men and women, like the men on the trawlers, in rubber overalls, call out to come and try an oyster.

We walk over.

Water dripping from their gloved hands, the men behind the tables are opening oysters. Colin says he wants to watch. A portly red-nosed man picks up an oyster, fits it into the palm of his gloved left hand and, holding the short-bladed oyster knife in his gloved right hand, he fits the blade in between the two valves of the oyster. He twists the knife briskly, and instantly the oyster surrenders its grip, its upper valve separating from the lower. Easing the flesh free from the lower valve, the man holds the valve out to me, the oyster half-covered in sea water. I take the valve but I hand it over to Colin. I watch him. He tilts his head back a little and allows the oyster to slide between his lips. *He must not chew. Will he know this?* He knows: he tilts his head back further, swallows once, twice, his prominent Adam's apple disappearing for a second.

"Shall we get some?" I ask.

"Sure. Let's. This is just so … so refreshing. Hell, I was thirsty without realising it," he replies.

The oyster trader will not hear of us just buying a couple each.

"A dozen each at least."

We settle for six each.

We watch the man arrange the dozen opened but reconstituted oysters, so they appear yet again closed, on a carpet of ice on a plastic platter. He reminds us to please return the platter. The woman with him, probably his wife, points to a wall alongside the sea: she tells us we can sit there to eat our purchase. Other people are already sitting there, eating oysters. We join them. Seeing they are drinking wine, Colin runs back to the motorcycle and returns with the bottle of *Muscadet*, the corkscrew and the two paper cups.

"Not too much of the yellow liquid," I say.

He covers just the bottom of the cups.

We sit, our legs dangling over the wall, and in silence we eat the oysters and drink the few mouthfuls of wine. As we see the others do, we drop the empty shells onto the pebbles which here in Brittany, as in Normandy, are called a beach.

A gull, white as snow, shrieking its delight, flies up. I know what will follow.

"Watch the gull, Colin," I say.

The gull, with a cat-like cunning, dives down and scoops up an oyster shell, but immediately drops it again.

Colin frowns.

"Look," I say, pointing.

The gull is repeating the manoeuvre. He continues doing so - picking up and dropping the shell - he is smashing it, and very soon it lies in shatters on the pebbles. Next, his wings stretched out like those of

Archangel Michael on the mount, and stepping high on his thin legs, he pecks, frantically, at the pieces for whatever nourishment has remained in them.

Finally, all nourishment enjoyed, all pleasure spent, the gull flies off.

Colin and I walk back to the tables and return the plastic tray, the smell of the sea clinging to it, to its owner. The man makes a comment we cannot hear, but the wink he gives me makes it clear what he has said.

"Where to?" Colin asks back at the motorcycle.

We agree to ride around a little more and to stop somewhere for our picnic lunch.

-0-

We leave the coast behind us.

We are cruising through green fields and apple orchards, the trees without the fruit which, because Eve had offered one to Adam and, he having accepted it, had caused the fall of humanity. *The woman you put here with me - she gave me some fruit from the tree, and I ate it,* said Adam to God, blaming Eve for the sin he had committed. *It was the serpent who deceived me, and so I ate the apple,* said Eve to God, defending herself.

We reach another village and again Colin pulls up.

"I would like to have a look at the books," he says.

We are in front of a bookshop. Carrying our crash helmets under our arms, we go in. The shop is small and in semi-darkness. An old man stands on a ladder, his back to the door. Hearing the tinkle of the door's bell, he turns round. He descends the ladder. He is wearing pince-nez glasses: these he pushes down over his nose, staring at us with watery blue eyes. I ask if we can browse and he asks if he can offer us a coffee. Politely, we decline.

The minutes tick by. I am not browsing in earnest. Colin is. He is at a shelf marked *Livres en anglais*. I want to get back on the road because, with night falling earlier these days, I want to get to Le Presbytère before dark.

"Bella, look. Shelley!"

Colin is holding a slim volume: its soft cover is torn and has yellowed.

He asks the old man how much he wants for the book.

"For you, *Monsieur*, two francs because I can see you are a poet yourself."

The old man is smiling. So is Colin. I am happy for both of them. The one having succeeding in getting rid of a book he must have thought he was stuck with; the other having found a book he thought he would never find. Perhaps also because he is pleased at being taken for a poet.

"Colin, look!" I call out.

Just inside the door is a carton full of old picture postcards.

"Do you have any postcards of Van Gogh's work?" I ask the old man.

"Only one. Van Gogh's *Sunflowers*."

"Sunflowers!" Colin and I shriek.

The old man walks over to the shelf and rummaging through the cards, he holds up two postcards, each with Van Gogh's *Sunflowers* on it.

"I can't believe this," says Colin.

"Let me buy one of the cards for you," I tell him.

"Only if you allow me to buy the other one for you," he replies.

I ask the old man what he wants for the cards and he says we can give him a franc for each. It is steep for a postcard, and an old one at that, but I dig in my purse for a franc and Colin produces a handful of coins from his jacket pocket and holds his hand out to the old man to take a franc from it. Each having paid for a card, I give the one the old man has given me to Colin and vice versa. He slips the card between the pages of the little Shelley volume and I put mine in my handbag. The old man, obviously puzzled at what we have just done, shakes his head.

The little Shelley volume was published in London in 1912.

"Before the Great War. This is such a bargain, Bella," says Colin walking back to the motorcycle.

Back on the motorcycle we drive along an avenue of trees. Ahead is a church of reddish stone. Behind it are ramparts. Two women in pleated skirts which reach halfway to their ankles, and in twinsets and flat-heeled shoes with laces, white socks tucked into them, walk along one of the ramparts. One carries a Polaroid camera. They take a picture each of the other, studying the instant pictures and nod. *Hell, am I really looking this old?* Is this what they are saying to one another?

We reach a stream and I tap Colin on his arm for him to pull up.

"Picnic time?" he asks, taking off his crash helmet.

Finding a spot where the grass is thick, we throw down the blanket and unpack our basket. I cut the *baguette* into chunks as is done in restaurants and as Gertrude does at Le Presbytère. Colin butters four chunks; two for each of us. I watch him slicing up an egg and a slice of ham. As if we are copying each other, we make sandwiches. The two eggs we have brought, sliced, we put on the ham and a generous number of tomato slices we put on top of the egg.

"I forgot the mayonnaise," I say apologetically.

"Delicious this is, even without mayonnaise," says Colin.

He fills one paper cup to the top with the *Sylvaner*, but the second cup he fills just halfway, filling it up with mineral water.

"I need to get us home, Bella."

Home.

Whenever my mother heard a guest describe the guest house as home she said it made the long hours and the hard work worthwhile.

"Bella, I want to read you a few lines from one of Percy Bysshe Shelley's poems. It is in my opinion his most beautiful, his best. It's *Love's Philosophy*," says Colin.

He takes the little book from the inside pocket of his jacket. He begins to read. *The fountains mingle with the river ... and the rivers with the ocean ... The winds of Heaven mix for ever with a sweet emotion ...* He stops reading. His eyes are closed, the little book no longer in his hands but lying on the blanket between us. He begins reciting. *Nothing in the world is single ... All things by law divine ... in one spirit meet and mingle ... Why not I with thine?* He opens his eyes. He looks up at the sky, still blue like on a summer's afternoon. *See the mountains kiss high Heaven ... and the waves clasp one another ...*

He falls silent.

"It is beautiful, Colin," I say.

"Here," he says, "the little book is for you. You can read the poem for yourself later."

I want to protest, say: *No you must keep it*, but I lean over and I take the little book from his hand. Leaning over still further, I kiss him on his forehead.

"Thank you, Colin," I say.

The *Sunflowers* postcard falls out and I pick it up and hand it to him.

"No," he says, "it is for me to thank you, Bella. To thank you for your kindness. For allowing me to stay. For everything."

-0-

It is cold in the sidecar riding home. I wrap the blanket around me up to my chin. I begin to shiver. I forget about what I had paid for the cushions and I push my feet under them. *I should have brought gloves.* Colin taps me on the knee and with a shift gesture with his hands he offers me his gloves. I shake my head.

We pull up at the village. I run into Amandine's and I

307

buy a large quiche to have when we get back to Le Presbytère.

"Look at you!" says Amandine.

"What?"

"You've been to the moon dressed like that, Miss?"

"Sure have," I reply.

In the gulley outside the shop autumn leaves are rotting.

-0-

CHAPTER THIRTY-THREE

The silence in the house is not now as threatening as it is when I have been out and returning on my own. The silence even seems welcoming. I stand in the small front room, at the desk, and if I do not know better, I will believe I can hear voices and laughter as when the house is filled with guests. However, no, the register which guests have to sign bears only the signature, a confident scrawl, of Colin Lerwick. Nationality: English. Current address: a hotel in London's Marylebone district.

"Bella, I'm going to change," the guest calls out.

He parked the motorcycle in the usual place and he has carried the basket, empty, the blanket and the two cushions indoors. The bottle of wine, still far from empty, we had dropped into a street bin in one of the villages we passed through.

"So am I, Colin, and when you've changed, you can come down for some quiche," I tell him.

I change into a pair of old jeans and a long-sleeved sweater. One of my new red panties is underneath the jeans, but I did not put on a bra.

In the kitchen, I place the quiche in the oven.

Colin walks in. He too is in a pair of jeans and a sweater.

"We are eating in here," I tell him.

From outside comes the howl of the wind.

"We got back just in time," he says.

I cut two triangles from the quiche: one triangle bigger

than the other. The larger I put on the plate in front of Colin. He covers the quiche in ketchup. Amandine and Olivier would have succumbed to a heart attack should they have witnessed this.

"I love the poem. Thank you for the thought," I tell Colin.

My hands are on the table and he puts one of his over one of mine.

"Colin," I say, "it is so good to know that you like it here at Le Presbytère."

"More than that," he says. "I love it here. I do not want to leave."

I do not tell him if he wants he can stay. Stay for tonight. Stay for tomorrow night. Stay for always.

"You go upstairs. I will clean up here," he says.

I have eaten only the one triangle of quiche but Colin cut a second triangle for him.

"You can put the rest of the quiche in the fridge," I tell him.

"Will do."

I turn at the door. He is already running hot water into the sink.

"I will see you upstairs," I say.

"Won't take me long, Bella."

The 'White Room' is dark. Walking past it, I close its door. I left the lights on in my room, but I extinguish all but the Marilyn Monroe lamp. I like the circle of pink light it throws over the bed.

I take off my jeans, but not the red panty and the sweater.

Bella, your breasts are beautiful. Divine. So perfectly round. So soft. So tender to the touch. Jean-Louis' words.

I spray Van Cleef & Arpels' *First* on my legs, on my feet and my hands, and I lift up the sweater and spray it under my arms too, and in my neck, and behind my ears.

I hear Colin's footsteps on the stairs.

"Bella?"

The footsteps pass the 'White Room'.

"I am here, Colin."

He stops at the door.

"What is this lovely scent?" he asks.

"Maybe it is me."

I am standing at the bed. Two steps and he is beside me. He is holding a white candle. Where did he find it? I do not know. It is lit, its flame quivering in the current of air being caused by his movement. He puts it down on the floor beside the bed.

"Colin, did you silence the clock?"

"Bella, forget about the clock."

Indeed.

He unzips the fly of his jeans. Slowly. He rolls the jeans over his hips, down his legs. He steps from them. *Is this a strip to turn me on?* He rips off the shirt he is still wearing and the vest underneath it. He is only in red boxer shorts, his boots and grey socks. He squats and rips off his boots and rolls the socks over his feet. I switch off the Marilyn Monroe bedside lamp. The room dark, he picks up the candle and puts it on the bedside table on the side of the bed nearest to him.

I slide under the top sheet.

Without a word, Colin slips in beside me. As silently, he pulls at my sweater and, our hands touching, I help him helping me to pull it over my head. He eases his body over mine; he is fully erect. I spread my legs to ease his entry into me. Together, gently, we move, up, down. I throw my legs over his body to perfect our union. He is kissing my face. We cling to one another, his hands on my breasts, my hands on his shoulders. His seed fills me. Seconds later, I climax. In the faint light of the candle, I search for his eyes. He is looking at me, tenderly.

"Colin, I can easily fall in love with you," I say.

He lifts his body off mine. He falls back onto the bed.

"This is not just sex for me, Bella."

He closes his eyes. After a while his breathing eases. I

think he has fallen asleep. I turn onto my side. I, too, will try to sleep.

-0-

"Bella?"

I am awake but my eyes are closed. I keep them this way.

"Darling?" he tries again.

He touches my face.

I open my eyes.

"Yes?"

"Did I wake you?"

He lifts my head with a slight pressure under my chin. Tenderly, he brushes his lips over mine.

"Did I wake you?" he asks again.

"Yes," I lie.

"I'm sorry."

His breath smells of quiche: I did not notice it earlier. I suppose, so does mine. I swing one leg off the bed to go to the bathroom to clean my teeth, but he grabs me by the arm. Quite roughly.

"I only …"

I do not finish my sentence. He is holding me by the shoulders and pressing his mouth over mine and pushing his tongue against mine. The action so sudden, so unexpected, I feel I am choking. Sensing this, he withdraws his tongue. Next, his mouth.

For a few minutes we lie in silence beside one another. He on his back; I on my side again and facing him. I am stroking his torso, my fingers playing with the hair on his chest.

Day has broken; the room is no longer dark. The candle has burnt down.

"Where did you buy the candle?" I ask.

"In a shop in Paris. I was thinking of you and I thought I will buy it."

"It is nice to know you were thinking of me when you were in Paris."

"I did so all the time. I have been ... you've been on my mind since I arrived here at the house. You are dominating my thoughts. I cannot get you out of my mind. I think ... I think I want to stay here forever. I think I am falling in love with you. I think I love you."

He stops.

"Is it such a bad thing, Colin? Falling in love with me?"

"I am ... how to say this, my darling? I am a wanderer. My home is where my typewriter is. It's how I live. I have never thought of settling. I have never wanted to settle, marry, father children ... become a father, be a father. Christ! Am I saying this all wrong?"

"It depends what you want to say?"

"I want to say, I am falling in love with you, and I do not want to leave. I want to stay here. Here with you, Bella. I have never had such thoughts. Such feelings for anyone. My mother ... she used to say I was an oddball, that I was all intellect and no emotion. She used to say she pitied the girl I was to marry because she will be starved of love. She advised me never to marry. She used to say she will pray no woman ever falls in love with me because it will be a love I will not know how to reciprocate. And now, now I am falling in love. So what now, my love?"

Is he asking me?

I do not reply because I think he should seek the answer from within himself.

I run my fingers over his face.

"Bella," he asks, "why did you not marry? Or you might have and your marriage broke up."

"No. I have never walked down the aisle."

"May I ask why you did not?"

Did Jean-Louis not ask me this same question? Do I give Colin the answer I gave him?

"It just never happened," I say.

"Never met a man you wanted to spend the rest of

your life with as they say in novels?"

"I do not read that kind of novel. But no, I have ... how shall I put it? I wanted, wanted very much to marry someone but it did not happen."

"Why did it not happen?"

"He was a married man."

"Did he not tell you this when you met him?"

"He told me."

"And?"

"And it did not matter. I still fell in love with him and I hoped he would divorce his wife and marry me."

"Should he come back, divorced this time, will you take up with him again?"

"He will not come back."

"So you are no longer in love with him?"

"To be honest with you, I do not know. If I put my mind to it, I will probably decide I am no longer in love with him, but I miss loving him. Loving. It is such a wonderful thing for me to love ... to love a man, and to know he loves me. That he cares, cares about me, that he wants me to be happy, to be safe. Forget the sex, it is not that I am talking of. I am talking of the togetherness. Of the congeniality of spirit."

He nods.

"I have never had that, Bella. I always had to be elsewhere, in some other place. I always ran. Maybe the time has come to say put."

"Maybe, Colin."

"Maybe, yes, such a time has come."

-0-

For a while longer we lie in each other's arms, my head in the hollow of his shoulder. He is playing with the nipple of my breast, the breast nearest to him. The nipple hardens under his touch. I sit up because this, I decide, is not a moment for sex. I slip from the bed. I take down the nightgown hanging behind the bedroom door. I fold it around my naked body.

Colin has turned over onto his side; he is watching me.

"My Bella," he says. "My lovely Bella."

I walk to the bathroom and in the shower I stand under the cold tap for a while.

Back in the bedroom, Colin is no longer lying on the bed. Neither is he in the bedroom.

-0-

CHAPTER THIRTY-FOUR

I am in the kitchen.

Colin and I have each had two croissants and a bowl of coffee: we were hungry.

Now, Colin has gone back to his bedroom. He told me there were a few things he needed to do this morning. I said this was alright with me. I need to go into the village for provisions, and I want to go to Salon Larissa for a shampoo and blow wave. Marion is right. A crash helmet is not kind to a woman's hair. The sea air further did its damage.

The Merc's key in my hand, I knock on the closed door of the 'White Room'. Colin does not often close the door, but he is probably writing and does not want me to disturb him. After a second knock he opens the door.

"Are you busy?" I ask.

He is working, yes. Behind him, on the bed, which he did not use last night, lie books, folders and many sheets of paper.

"Colin, I'm off to Saint-Marie-sur-Brecque. I'll be out for a while. I'll stop at the *charcuterie* and I'll get us something light for lunch. Maybe we can go out for dinner tonight. It will be my treat."

"Do you have a moment?" he asks.

"Sure."

I give a step into the room, but quickly he steps in front of me.

"I'll come down with you, Bella."

317

If I am not mistaken he said this hastily as if he did not want me in his bedroom.

"Fred may come round today," I say cheerfully to the footsteps behind me. "He always comes once a week when the guest house is closed and he did not come last week."

We go into the kitchen.

"Would you like another coffee maybe? Or a cup of tea?" I ask.

"No! I'm ok. You get along to the village."

"You wanted to say something to me?"

"I did not want you to go without me seeing you off. That's all."

"How thoughtful, Colin. Thank you."

"I'll walk you to your car."

Rain water drips from the trees in the courtyard. Overhead the sky is grey.

"It is going to rain," I say. "It is good we went for our ride yesterday because had we left it for today, we would have had to cancel it."

We descend into the parking bay. The three cars stand like sentinels in the dark. My mother's *Deux Chevaux* seems to be tilted to one side. I must really sell the car or give it away, give it to some charity to sell. *I must stop being such a sentimental.*

Colin holds a hand out for me for the car key.

"The door's not locked. No need to lock it as no one can get in here," I tell him.

"Don't be so certain of that," he says. "A determined thief can get in anywhere."

This man actually cares about my safety.

"Good, I will lock the car from now on."

"Bella," he says. "It is so good to be here, here with you. I can tell you I have not ever been as happy as these days here with you. You are a super human being."

He leans forward and pulls me against him.

"Colin …,"

His lips stop my words. His kiss is tender. Tender but

long. The weight of his body pressing me against the car. Slowly he lets go of me.

"Now, off with you," he says, "or I may change my mind."

Change his mind about what?

I get into the car and I turn the key in the ignition. At the entrance to the parking-bay I lean out the window and look back. Colin is standing in the doorway. He raises his right hand, his fingers together, his thumb tugged against the hollow of his hand, his forearm straight and horizontal to the floor, and with the tip of his forefinger he touches the outer edge of his right eyebrow.

He is saluting me again.

-0-

Larissa has gone back to being blonde. She has several yellow curls hanging over her heavily made-up face. Jonny too has yellow hair now. The colour is an improvement to the green of before. So is the 1920s cinema idol style of a heavily-oiled short back and sides.

As Larissa is in tight white pants and tight white sweater, while Jonny is in tight black pants and tight black sweater, the two look like a Hollywood dancing duo.

The salon is crowded, a woman sitting at every lilac heart-shaped mirror and one sitting on each of the chairs at the wash basins and on the chairs under the dryers. It makes me happy to see because Larissa, being so busy, she will not have time for chatting to me this morning. Neither will Jonny. *They might just ask about my winter guest.*

"Not any of your fancy conditioning stuff, please, Larissa," I say.

"Doctor Wolff is in a hurry," comes from Jonny.

He is busy applying dye to the hair of one of the village's elderly female inhabitants.

One, two, three and my hair is washed, the collar of my T-shirt wet and soap in my eyes, and I too am sitting in front of one of the lilac heart-shaped mirrors. I close my eyes when Larissa begins to wrap strands of my hair around a round brush to which other women's hair cling, in order, as she says, to make me look "even more beautiful than you are, Miss."

Looking as I always look, my hair though much less unruly than when I walked in, I pay Larissa and discreetly drop a five-franc coin into Jonny's palm as a tip.

Back in my car, I drive to Avranches. There, at the *LeClerc* supermarket, I buy quite a few things. Not that I need any of it, but I want to give Colin a treat. I will also definitely telephone Gertrude to ask her to come up one evening to cook us one of her specialities.

Both arms on my watch pointing to twelve, my shopping done, I am back on the road to Le Presbytère. There is little traffic because it has started to rain, rain heavily. It also means, I cannot drive as fast as I wish. I am eager to get back to the house.

In Sainte-Marie-sur-Brecque I see Fred going into the Vaybee. I make a U-turn. I will go and tell him that should he see Gertrude to ask her to give me a ring about coming up to the house one evening to cook a meal.

"No lunch for me, Frascot," I say walking in.

I saw him glance over the already crowded Vaybee to see where he can seat me.

Alice is behind the till. She waves to me as if we are the closest of friends. Reaching her, she confirms this: she throws both her arms around me and hugs me, a perfumed cheek brushing against one of my perfumeless ones.

"Where's the hulk, Doctor?" she asks.

To me a hulk is green and ugly as I've seen in a television series.

I join Fred at the bar. To please Frascot I say I will have a glass of orange juice.

"Sounds a good idea," says Fred.

He assures me he will give Gertrude my message.

I drink the juice while listening to a joke one of the

patrons is telling. I laugh because everyone is laughing, although I fail to see the joke. It is something about an elephant and a mouse walking into a bar.

Driving up to Le Presbytère I turn the window on my side of the car down. I ignore the fact it is raining into the car and onto my left arm. Soon, my arm is wet and so too the hair I have just had done. I keep the window open.

A cat shoots across the house's driveway. He is chasing a pigeon which, fortunately, has the sense to flap its wings to fly higher and out of the cat's reach. The cat dives under some vegetation.

Colin's motorcycle is not parked under the copse of trees.

He must have gone out.

I park the car in the parking-bay and I start carrying my purchases to the kitchen. What needs to be frozen, I put into the freezer. The rest I set out on the work table. First, I will go upstairs to rescue what can be rescued of my blow wave and then I will come to pack the stuff away.

I shoot up the stairs. Colin has left the door of the 'White Room' open: a strip of light falls from the room into the corridor. This is the first time he has left the door open when he has gone out. I reach the doorway. I look into the room. His typewriter is not on the writing table. There is nothing on the writing table. I step into the room. His bags, transistor radio, his tape recorder and his tapes, some of it having stood on the writing table, the rest on the two bedside tables, are gone. I look into the bathroom. I cannot see his shaving things on the shelf above the washbasin. I walk into the bathroom; the toilet seat is down and the extra toilet rolls which are usually in the cupboard under the washbasin are on the seat. I walk back into the bedroom. I open the wardrobe. It is empty but for coat hangers.

Has he moved into my bedroom? He must have. How wonderful.

I run to my bedroom. I look into the room from the

doorway. I do not see his things. I walk through the bedroom. His things are not in my bedroom.

He has gone. Dear God, he has gone. He has left. Left Le Presbytère. Left me.

I return to the kitchen. I sit down at the work table. I look towards the Peace Lily. A piece of paper has been pasted to the terracotta pot with sticky tape. I do not have to get up to see what the piece of paper is. I know what it is. I remain sitting at the table. I stare at the piece of paper. The chime of the grandfather clock brings me to my senses. I walk to the Peace Lily. Holding the piece of paper, folded double, I sit down at the work table again. I open the piece of paper, flattening it against the surface of the table.

Bella … I will never forget these days here with you. Now - I have to go. I will never forget you. Colin.

My telephone begins to ring. I listen to the message being left on the answerphone. It is Gertrude's voice. Fred has given her my message and she is asking when I would like her to come up to the house to cook a meal for Mr Colin. *What about a vegetable soup followed by grilled fresh ham and a cheese soufflé, Miss?* She wants me to call her back.

-0-

CHAPTER THIRTY-FIVE

It is two in the afternoon.

I see dust and dirt everywhere in Le Presbytère.

If I start to clean immediately by five or six the house will be clean. I will be free then. I will be able to drive off with the certainty no one will find a dirty house when they come in here.

But where to start?

I have poured myself a cognac and here I sit in the drawing room on the armchair where I sat on the night of Colin's return from Paris and he walked into the room holding the cellophane-wrapped basket. *Bella, I could not resist buying you a small gift. I hope you will like it.*

Liked it?

I liked you, Colin. I can even say I allowed myself to fall for you, fall in love with you. Just as I had fallen in love with Jean-Louis.

I am talking out loud to myself. My parents once had a guest from Argentina who talked to herself. She walked through the house speaking to herself. "If only she will speak in English we will know what she's on about and we will be able to calm her," said one of our English guests. One day, in one of her calmer moments, the woman told my mother in broken English how she had lost both her sons and also her husband, her father, two uncles and two nephews during Argentina's military rule. "They should have killed me too," she said. I wondered why she did not do so herself. Being that lonely, that miserable, her future a black hole, why did she continue to live, to torture herself with this thing known as life.

It is raining. Raining buckets as our English guests always say. In the distance the mount has vanished in mist. There are though still cars on the causeway driving towards it.

I start cleaning. I start in the drawing room. I dip a cloth into a large bucket filled with wax which Gertrude makes. It smells of lavender because she adds lavender oil to the beeswax and paraffin and what-not she mixes together. Honorine and Martine sing when they wax the furniture - it annoys some of our guests - but I wax the furniture in silence. Standing on a chair to reach the niche above the bay window, I see dust has gathered in the holes forming the crucifix. I wax the niche too. Stepping from the chair I cannot stop myself looking towards the copse of trees where Colin had parked his motorcycle and where, now, there is nothing but fallen and rotting leaves.

The two downstairs bedrooms are tidy. Only the mirrors in the rooms and in the en-suite bathrooms are a little grey and need cleaning. I close the heavy chintz curtains throwing the rooms into darkness. I close each bedroom's door. I wonder where Tony of Colorado will holiday next summer.

The house's marble floors I will not attempt to clean. They are not dirty anyway.

Upstairs, I need to clean only the two bedrooms which have been used since Honorine and Martine's cleaning. At the door of the 'White Room' I hesitate at the door. Inhaling deeply I walk in. There is no dust on the furniture. Did Colin dust before he left? Nonetheless, I try writing my name on the surface of the writing table: I cannot. So he did dust. He must have worked fast because he also had to pack his belongings and carry all downstairs to the motorcycle. In the bathroom, I sit down on the side of the bath. I can smell mint. Am I imaging it? Is Colin's smell filling my nostrils because I so much want him to be here? No. I can definitely smell mint. I take the toilet rolls from the toilet and lift the seat and in the water lie three small sachets of mint-scented bath oils. One sachet has been opened and is empty. Having discarded the sachets, he had not flushed the toilet. I take the sachets from the water and wrap them in toilet paper. I will throw them away. I pull the sheets off the bed. Again, the scent of mint fills my nostrils. Having folded the sheets neatly, I put them on top of the bed. I sit down beside them. Immediately, I jump up, glance across the room and walk, almost run, from it. I leave the door ajar.

Frantically, I dust in the library room. Darkness has fallen, and I am running out of time, time to do what I must do. Do before it is another day.

On the desk lies the small volume of Shelley's poems Colin gave me. I sit down at the desk. I need to read the poem he read to me. *The fountains mingle with the river* ... I hear his voice. It is as if he is here in the library room with me, standing here at the desk. I hold my hands over my ears: I do not want to listen.

With a red pen I draw a circle around the last lines. *And the sunlight clasps the earth ... and the moonbeams kiss the sea ... what is all this sweet work worth ... if thou kiss not me?*

I leave the little book on the desk, open as it is at this poem.

The postcard of Van Gogh's *Sunflowers* has fallen from the book. It lies on the floor. I pick it up and I put it on the desk beside the little book.

-0-

A storm is raging. Rain drops, like hail, grate against the window panes. I take a long draw of breath and I pick up my car keys. The telephone starts ringing. The answerphone is on, so I let the ringing continue.

In the courtyard, the overhanging branches sway in the wind. A streak of lightning falls on the bench where Colin and I sat on the day of his arrival. *Maybe I should not have allowed him to stay.*

I walk on to the parking bay.

I do not look back at the house.

I did not close the back door. The front door I did close, but lock it I did not.

The clock I had silenced.

-0-

I swing the Mercedes from Le Presbytère's driveway onto the road to the coast.

-0-

Back in the house the tape of the answerphone is turning.

"*Bella … hello … this is Jean-Louis. You will … you may remember me. With all my heart I hope you do.*

"*Bella, listen, I've left Colette.*

"*I only returned to her because of the girls and now they are grown-up and they no longer need me. Carmen is pregnant.*

"*I stopped loving Colette a long time ago. When I went back to her I did not again become her lover.*

"*Bella, I never forgot you.*

"*Bella, I never left you. In my heart I never left you.*

"*I am calling to say I will be in Normandy this weekend. I am coming to see you. I have to see you. I will come to the house.*

"*Bella, I missed you.*

"*Bella, kiddo, I never stopped loving you.*"

-0-

EPILOGUE

Both the drawing room and the kitchen of Le Presbytère are packed with people. Captain Contepomi, a head taller than the others in the house, is clutching a notebook into which he scribbles whatever those he talks to are saying.

Gertrude, Honorine and Martine sit on the sofa in the drawing room. Never have they allowed themselves the audacity to sit down anywhere in the house but in the kitchen. Fred too is in the drawing room. He stands underneath the niche. He is not looking up at the crucifix formed by the holes, but he may all the same be seeking comfort from knowing it is there above his head. He is crying, crying bitterly. The handkerchief he is clutching and with which he dabs at his eyes and his runny nose is wet. Every now and then he shakes his head: he appears to be unable to believe what is going on at the house.

A car, a Maserati, comes driving up the driveway. The man behind the wheel - he is the only one in the car - frowns seeing police vehicles parked in front of the house.

"Fred?" he asks, walking into the drawing room. "What is going on here? Why are the police here?"

"Mr ... Mr Jean-Louis ...," mutters Fred.

"Come on, man, what is going on here? Tell me! Where is Bella?"

Gertrude jumps to her feet and rushes over to Jean-Louis.

"Mr Jean-Louis, Miss Bella is gone."

She too is now crying.

327

"Gone? What do you mean gone? Gone where? Has there been a robbery here? Has Bella been hurt?"

Captain Contepomi walks up.

"You are who, *Monsieur*?" he asks.

"It's Mr Jean-Louis, a friend of Miss Bella," explains Gertrude.

"*Monsieur*, when did you last see Doctor Wolff?" asks the captain.

"What is that to you, Captain?" replies Jean-Louis.

He has become angry.

"Mr Jean-Louis, Miss Bella has killed herself."

It was Fred who said this.

"No, no, no!" cries Gertrude. "We must not say this. We do not know she did. We must hope."

Jean-Louis, white in his face, steps back to lean against the wall behind him.

"Captain, what is going on here?" he asks.

"Come, sit down," says the captain.

The two men walk over to a corner of the room and sit down on two upright chairs.

"I regret to have to inform you, *Monsieur*, that we have found Doctor Wolff's vehicle abandoned beside the shore, the key in the ignition, but the doctor is missing. We believe she went into the water deliberately to end her life," says the captain.

"It can't be. Why would she have done that?" asks Jean-Louis.

"Maybe you can tell us, *Monsieur*."

"I have not seen the doctor for quite a long time. A few years."

"So I understand, yes. You left a message for her …"

"On her answerphone, yes."

A young gendarme walks up, whispers something to the captain who gets up immediately.

"We will speak again, *Monsieur*, but for the moment I will offer you my condolences. So sad. So sad. And she was making money here. The place was thriving. A

328

goldmine, if you ask me."

Jean-Louis remains sitting on the chair. After a few minutes Fred, no longer crying, but his face wet with tears, walks up to him.

"Mr Jean-Louis," he says, "why are you here?"

He sits down on the chair from which the gendarme captain has just risen.

"I want to speak to Miss Bella. I need to say something to her which I should have said a long time ago, Fred."

"Mr Jean-Louis, Miss Bella is dead. She killed herself. Went into the water. There where she went into the water that is where she used to go with a boy from her class to sunbathe on the rocks. His name is Baudelaire Brodard and he lives in Paris. His father was ... but no, it is not a time to speak of that now. Beau - we all called him that because he was such a handsome kid - used to tease her because she couldn't swim. Never learnt, you know."

"Fred, why would Bella have killed herself?"

"I can't tell you that, Mr Jean-Louis, but there was Colin ..."

"Colin who?" Jean-Louis breaks in.

"Colin Lerwick. He was the last guest here."

"And?"

"Just that. He was the last guest here at Le Presbytère."

"Colin Lerwick? You said Colin Lerwick?"

"Yes. He was Miss Bella's last guest."

"Colin Lerwick! But I know him!"

The End

SONGS AND POETRY

<u>Chapter 6:</u> - *I know that my redeemer liveth* ... from George Friderik Handel's 'Messiah' written in 1741.

<u>Chapter 7:</u> - *Pray that your loneliness* ... (Dag Hammerskjöld, Swedish diplomat, second United Nations Secretary-General, and Nobel Peach Prize Laureate;
- *Here's to you* from the song 'Ballad of Sacco and Vanzetti', released in 1971, lyrics written by and sung by Joan Baez, music by Ennio Morricone;
- *In restless dreams* ... from 'The Sounds of Silence', released in 1964 and a new version in 1965, sung by Simon and Garfunkel, lyrics and music written by Paul Simon.

<u>Chapter 9:</u> - *Non, Je ne regrette rien* ... from the song of which the music was written by Charles Dumont, the lyrics by Michel Vaucaire and first sung by Edith Piaf in 1960
<u>Chapter 22:</u> - *My my at Waterloo* ... from 'Waterloo', the music and lyrics by Benny Anderson, Björn Ulvaeus & Stig Anderson and performed by Abba for the first time in 1974.

<u>Chapter 23:</u> - *Hello! Is it me* ... from 'Hello!' written and sung by Lionel Richie for the first time in 1984;
- *It's now or never* ...from 'It's Now or Never', the lyrics written by Wally Gold & Aaron Schroeder and based on 'O Sole Mio' by Eduardo di Capua and performed by Elvis Presley for the first time in 1960;
- *Out of the night that covers me* ... from the poem 'Invictus' by William Ernest Henley (1849-1903).

<u>Chapter 24:</u> - *It swept it swept on all the earth* ... from the poem 'Winter Night' by Boris Leonidovich Pasternak (1890-1960) written in 1946.

Chapter 26: - *Say me, say you* …from 'Say Me Say You' lyrics and music by Lionel Richie and sung by him for the first time in 1985.

Chapter 27: - *Petit Papa Noël* … from 'Petit Papa Noël' written by Raymond Vincy & Henri Martinet and first sung by Tino Rossi (1907-1983) in 1946.

Chapter 29: - *Nessun dorma, nessun dorma* … from the aria of the final act of Giacomo Puccini's opera 'Turandot';
- *Ma n'atu sole* … from 'O Sole Mio', lyrics written by Giovani Capurro and music by Eduardo di Capua in 1898
- *Fallen leaves can be picked up* … from 'Feuilles Mortes', the lyrics written by Jacques Prévert (1900-1977) and the music by Joseph Kosma (1905-1969) in 1945 and performed by Yves Montand (1921-1991) in 1946.

Chapter 31: - *Take good care of my heart* … from 'Take Good Care of my Heart', music by Stephen Hartley Dorff and Peter James McCann, lyrics by Whitney Houston (1963-2012) and first performed as a duet with her and Jermaine Jackson in 1985.

Chapter 32: - *The fountains mingle with the river* … from the poem 'Love's Philosophy' by Percy Bysshe Shelley's (1792-1822) written in 1820.

ALSO BY MARILYN Z. TOMLINS

DIE IN PARIS

A spring night in Paris. The most beautiful city in the world is dark and silent. Uncertainty devils the air. As does normality: war time normality. The Nazis' Swastika flutters from the Eiffel Tower. The Parisians are huddled indoors.

Suddenly the night's stillness is shattered by sirens and excited voices. For days foul smoke has been pouring from the chimney of an uninhabited house close to the Avenue des Champs-Elysées. Police and firefighters are racing to the house to break down the bolted door. They make a spine-chilling discovery. The remains of countless human beings are being incinerated in a furnace in the basement. In a pit in an outhouse quicklime consumes still more bodies.

Neighbors say they hear banging, pleading, sobbing and cries for help come from inside the house deep at night. They say a shabbily-dressed man on a green bicycle pulling a cart behind him comes to the house, always at dawn, or dusk.

The house belongs to Dr Marcel Petiot – a good-looking, charming, caring, family physician who lives elsewhere in the city with his wife and teenage son.

Is he the shabbily-dressed man on the green bicycle?

If so, what has he to say about the bodies?

Marilyn Z. Tomlins has crafted an enthralling and suspenseful page-turner about one of history's most fascinating and notorious serial killers. This grisly World War Two era thriller will have you teetering on a slippery edge from beginning to end.

Don Fulsom, veteran UPI and VOA White House correspondent, Washington, D.C. reporter, author of the bestseller Nixon's Darkest Secrets: The Inside Story of America's Most Troubled President, and a professor of government at American University in Washington.

With style, Marilyn Z. Tomlins' Die in Paris, tells the incredible story of France's most prolific murderer. Readers will discover a truly psychotic serial killer.

J. Patrick O'Connor, author of the bestsellers The Framing of Mumia Abu-Jamal and of Scapegoat: The Chino Hills Murder and the Framing of Kevin Cooper, and the creator and editor of www.crimemagazine.com

"Die in Paris" will give you new insights into the horrors of Occupied France.

If you have a smartphone, you can scan the barcode below to buy Die in Paris:

Or go to:

http://www.amazon.com/dp/B00BCRUKXW

ABOUT THE AUTHOR

Marilyn lives and writes in Paris. She writes whatever takes her fancy: spoof news, book reviews, posts for her blog, gossip about showbiz stars, short stories, books, poetry. She also reports on crime.

She was born in British Colonial Africa and is a British national.

Eight years ago she became interested in the Second World War French serial killer, Dr Marcel Petiot and she researched him for two years. Over the next two tears she wrote DIE IN PARIS and, then, for the following two, rewrote it and then edited the rewrites.

CONTACT DETAILS

Visit Marilyn's website:
www.marilynztomlins.com

Follow Marilyn on Twitter:
www.twitter.com/MarilynZTomlins

Like or join Marilyn on Facebook:
www.facebook.com/marilyn.tomlins

Cover designed by: Raven Crest Books
Photographer: Paula Rae Gibson
Model: Allison Willow

Published by: Raven Crest Books
www.ravencrestbooks.com

Follow us on Twitter:
www.twitter.com/lyons_dave

Like us on Facebook:
www.facebook.com/RavenCrestBooksClub